my butterflies

butterflies
book one

B. Evans

Cover by Miblart
Illustrations by @akumabrushes and B. Evans
Blurb and author bio written with Cate Hogan

First edition 2024

- ISBN 979-8-9902910-1-0 (Paperback)
- ISBN 979-8-9902910-2-7 (Hardcover)
- ISBN 979-8-9902910-0-3 (Ebook)

Published by Platinum Rose Publishing
authorbevans.com

author's note

The characters in this series have experienced, and will experience, life-altering events that some readers may want to be aware of. If you'd like to know more about this, please check out my website:
https://authorbevans.com/butterflies/

one

TESSA

JOLTED BACK TO CONSCIOUSNESS, I sat up in an unfamiliar bed and struggled to remember where I was.

My phone was on the nightstand, and my book bag and laptop were on the desk at the foot of the bed. Unclenching my fists, I felt the familiar fuzziness of my favorite blanket.

That's right, I reminded myself. *This is my room until graduation.*

As I slowly exhaled a calming breath, a breeze from the open window cooled my heated skin. The moving air felt good against my sweat-slicked body.

Throwing off the covers, I hopped down from my bed. Since my room faced nothing but a dense line of trees, I didn't bother closing the shade before I stripped out of my dampened clothes. The best thing after a bad dream was a run to clear my head.

Gorgeous weather, fresh air, and music blaring in my ears were what I needed to rid myself of the memories, or at least push them aside for a while. After donning a blue sports bra, cropped gray leggings, running shoes, and earbuds, I set off.

Forty minutes and thirty-seven seconds later, I turned the corner back onto my street. After double-checking my watch, I smiled when I saw the time I'd made. As I got closer to the small rental house that I'd be calling home for my last year of university, I slowed to a jog then walked.

As I came upon my next-door neighbor, an athletic guy from years of playing soccer, he kicked a soccer ball my way, calling out, "Tessaaaa!"

"Hey, Chuck," I greeted as I stopped the ball with my foot. After kicking it up in the air for a few bobbling tricks, I shot it over to the guy who was with him, figuring they'd been playing together. It went right by him without even an attempted kick.

"Oh, I don't play," the tall guy said.

Feeling a little foolish for assuming, I said, "Oh..." At least my cheeks were likely already red from running. "Sorry!" I called to Chuck as he ran after the ball.

Looking back at Chuck's friend, I locked eyes with him and froze. *Oh. My. God.* For a couple of long seconds, we held each other's gazes as my brain stopped functioning.

His piercing eyes looked away first when Chuck dribbled up to us.

Kicking the ball up and balancing it on his forehead, Chuck commented, "When you and I were hanging out by the gym in high school, he was hanging out in the music wing."

"Weren't you hanging out in the music wing too?" asked the man, who also had quite the physique.

Letting the ball drop to the ground, Chuck conceded, "Good point. Oh, speaking of music, Tess, what're you doing tomorrow night?"

"Uh..." He wasn't about to ask me out on a date right in front of his hot-as-hell friend, was he? Throwing a nervous glance at the other guy, I noted he didn't seem at all surprised. *Ugh.*

Chuck had seemed nice enough for the month I'd known him, and although not bad looking, with his bleached-blond hair with blue spiky tips and light-brown eyes, he wasn't my type. Especially since I could look him straight in the eye barefoot. I liked guys who were taller than my above-average stature, a guy who I could wear heels with and he'd still be taller than me. A guy who was smokin' hot, like his friend here.

"You should come to Smythie's tomorrow night. My band's playing. We play every Friday night." Chuck pointed to his still nameless friend. "He's in the band too."

Drop-dead gorgeous guy is in a band? Yes, please.

Going for nonchalance, I shrugged. "Oh, yeah, sure." Wincing, I asked, "But, uh, what's Smythie's?"

The two men exchanged a disbelieving glance, causing my cheeks to prick.

"You don't know what Smythie's is?"

Hot guy rolled his deep, ocean-blue eyes. "Not everyone goes to Smythie's, Chuck." Turning to me, smokin' hot explained, "It's a bar that turns into a nightclub Friday and Saturday nights. Eighteen to enter, since most college kids aren't twenty-one yet. It's about a fifteen-minute walk from here if you cut across campus." Sticking out his hand, he introduced himself, "I'm Jax, by the way."

I reached out and took his hand as Chuck said, "Oh, whoops. Sorry, I'm so used to Jax knowing everyone already. This is my best friend, Jax. Jax, this is Tess."

Grateful that Chuck had remembered his manners, I had a moment to regain myself after being stunned into silence by the spark I felt when Jax's skin came into contact with mine. Had he felt it too?

Even though Chuck had already given it to him, I told Jax my name, "Tess." I hoped I hadn't sounded as breathless to them as I did to myself. *Maybe they'll think it's from the run,* I thought to comfort myself. *The run! Arg!* Remembering I was all sweaty and gross, I made a hasty exit, pulling my hand away as soon as it was polite to do so. "Nice meeting you, Jax. Uh, yeah, I'll try to make it out tomorrow night. Maybe I'll see you guys there."

I waved before turning and heading for my house.

After entering and shutting the front door, I leaned back against it, and slid down with my hands covering my open mouth. Chuck's friend... He was... *Phew.* I had no words. Besides being tall with those defined muscles and the most beautiful eyes I'd ever seen, he wore a fitting black tee and tight black jeans. With small hoops in each ear, he definitely looked the part of a rock star, even if it was a local band. His styled sandy-brown locks reminded me of just-had-sex hair. It looked soft, and I wanted to run my fingers through it.

A spontaneous but not unwelcome image flashed in my mind of

my hands tangled in his hair, holding his head between... "Oh Jesus," I said out loud between huffing breaths. *Holy cow, I'm panting.*

For the first time in too long, I felt a tingle where I'd imagined Jax's head. After so many years, a guy had finally caught my attention and awoken me.

chapter
two

JAXON

I WATCHED Chuck's new neighbor until she disappeared into the house next door. Pivoting to my best friend, I asked, "She lives next to you?"

"Yeah, her and that girl, Tina Reynolds. I think you know her." Chuck stopped playing with his ball and wiggled his eyebrows. "She's pretty hot, huh?"

Pretty hot? She's a fucking goddess! Ash-blonde hair in a high ponytail ripe for grabbing, twisting around my fist and pulling, and a perfect body accentuated by her tight workout clothes, topped off with a belly-button ring that might as well have been a cherry on top of a sundae. "Uh, yeah," I agreed with Chuck, even though I knew I probably shouldn't.

Following him through his front door, I tried to sound causal. "You said something to her about the gym?"

"She's on the women's soccer team."

"She's a freshman?" I asked in disbelief. A voice in the back of my head screamed, *No fucking way that woman is a freshman!* But, thanks to the bar, I thought I knew pretty much everyone. And I sure as hell would've remembered a face like hers.

Chuck's expression made me feel like I said something dumb. "Nooooo... Does she look like she just graduated high school?"

Definitely not.

The look on my face must've conveyed my confusion because he elaborated, "She's a senior."

I let out an incredulous laugh. "A senior, seriously?" I'd never seen her once in the last three years, and this wasn't a large campus.

"Yeah, she's a transfer."

"From where?" Why was I asking so many questions?

We made it to Chuck's kitchen, where he dug around in his fridge. Pulling out a bottle of water, he said, "I don't know. I only met her over the summer when the guys and girls' soccer teams had joint practices. She mentioned she and her friend were trying to find a place together to rent. The house next door was available, so they took it."

Chuck's mom and stepdad owned most of the houses on this street, which was conveniently located next to campus. Renting to multiple college kids per house was more lucrative than to an individual family.

"So she's living next to you?" I asked.

Chuck looked at me like I'd lost my ability for deduction. "Yeah, dude, that's what I said. And you saw her go into the house next door." He tilted his head. "What's with the interrogation?"

That's a great question. I have no idea, I lied to myself. Blowing out a breath, I shrugged. "It's rare I come across a new face that isn't a freshman. I don't remember seeing her around at all. It's unusual for someone to transfer for just senior year. Weird."

"Yeah, I guess."

Based on her reaction when he'd asked her if she was free tomorrow night, it didn't appear like Chuck actually had anything going on with her, but I didn't ask since he was already getting suspicious of all my questions. One reason I liked Chuck was because he read me better than most, but given the way he was looking at me in that moment, I kind of wished he was a bit more illiterate when it came to me being an open book.

Changing the subject, I asked, "What time are the other guys getting here?"

He gestured toward the backyard. "Ashton's here already. Ryan can't make it because of work, and Randy will probably be here soon. I gotta take a leak. I'll meet you out there."

I nodded and pushed the back door open. Walking across a patch of asphalt between the house and detached garage, I glanced at the house to my right. Mentally scolding myself, I looked forward again at our makeshift studio and forced myself to forget about the blonde beauty within that house's walls.

chapter
three

TESSA

AS I STEPPED onto the cold tile floor, I wrapped myself in a towel. Hearing the front door, I called out, "Tina?"

I rolled my eyes at myself. *As if it'd be anyone else.*

"Yeah," my bestie yelled back, "I got food!"

"Awesome! I'll be right out."

After drying off, I slipped on a pair of black leggings and a blue tank then headed for the kitchen. The statuesque beauty with a dark pixie cut was leaning against the counter in our cramped kitchen, munching on some buffalo chicken pizza.

I grabbed a slice of the gooey deliciousness. "Hey, you just get back from Jamar's?" I asked, referring to her boyfriend of the last three years.

While I took a bite, she responded, "Yup. You had practice?"

I swallowed. "Yeah, short practice earlier, so I went for a run. No practice tomorrow or Saturday for move-in weekend."

After finishing off my slice of surprisingly spicy pizza, I turned to get a glass out of the cabinet and spotted Chuck's friend, Jax, exiting the garage behind his house. I only saw him for a moment before he quickly disappeared inside the house, but it was enough to make my heart skip a beat. Forgetting my need for a drink, I stayed focused on the back door, waiting to see if he'd reemerge.

"Earth to Tessa Givens!" I jumped and spun at the sound of Tina's loud voice.

Like a child caught doing something naughty, I sputtered, "Huh? What? Sorry!"

On her toes, trying to peek out the window over my shoulder, she asked, "What are you looking at over there?"

"Oh, nothing. I thought I saw something, but it was nothing. What were you saying?"

"I asked what you were looking at."

I nodded as I finally reached into the cabinet for a glass. We ate and drank in silence for a few minutes, Tina distracted by her phone while I gathered my courage.

Although I knew I was about to dive headfirst into a rabbit hole, I asked, "So, have you heard of Smythie's?"

Tina snorted. "Who hasn't? Everyone on campus knows Smythie's." She cocked an eyebrow at me. "Well, almost everyone. Why are you asking about Smythie's all the sudden? I must've asked you a hundred times last year to go with me, but you never did."

"Oh, it was that place?" I did have some vague recollection of her asking me to go somewhere, but she'd given up after I kept saying no.

Trying to come across as indifferent, I reached over for another slice of pizza. "That Chuck guy is in a band, and they play there on Fridays. He invited me out."

Tina's mouth dropped open mid-chew.

Throwing a bunched-up napkin at her, I squeaked, "Eww, Tina! I don't wanna see your food!"

She stuck her tongue out, and we cracked up. Thankfully, she didn't choke.

"Sorry." After swallowing, she asked, "Did Chuck ask you on a date or something?"

Waving frantically, I shook my head. "No, nothing like that! Nice guy and all, but not my type."

Tina smirked. "I don't know about that. Maybe you'll change your mind after you see the band. He's the bass player but also the backup vocalist. He's pretty good. I know you have a weakness for guys who can sing."

I pretended to be shocked, but Tina knew me well. When we were kids, the only celebrities I'd daydreamed about were the boy-band types. Growing up, although I couldn't sing, I joined the chorus until high school year, for the boys. By then, I only had eyes for—

I took a cleansing breath before continuing. Bracing myself and avoiding eye contact, I mentioned, "I did come across a guy... He was pretty good-looking."

Nothing. No response. Not until I heard a thud. Looking over, I noted the thud must've been Tina's pizza hitting the floor. She'd actually dropped it, her hand still in midair. Bending over, I picked it up and chucked it into the trash can.

In a whisper, she asked, "You met a guy? Who? Did you exchange numbers?" Her voice was full of surprised excitement with a touch of hope.

Shaking my head vigorously, I said, "No, we didn't exchange numbers or anything!" Chewing on my lower lip, I debated with how much I should reveal. Deciding I needed to give her a little more, I admitted, "He's supposed to be at Smythie's tomorrow night."

Tina looked away, her lips twisting. I was staring at her so intensely, trying to figure out what she was thinking, that I jumped when her eyes snapped back to mine and narrowed.

"Does he have a name?"

Not wanting to tell her yet—after all, I'd feel like a fool if I admitted to liking a guy who might've been a jerk or something—I quipped, "Obviously."

"What? You aren't going to tell me who it is? I know a lot of people 'round here, especially if they hang out at Smythie's. I might be able to tell you more about him if you told me his name."

I tapped my lip in fake contemplation. "I only met him for a minute. I don't think I caught his name," I lied.

She didn't buy it. Crossing her arms, she asked, "What does he look like?"

I looked away, trying to fight the smile that wanted to form as I imagined his appearance. "Hot. Really, really hot. And tall. From the looks of it, he works out but wasn't overly built or anything."

"You know what they say—beauty's in the eye of the beholder. So your description doesn't help me at all."

I shrugged then took a drink, not wanting to tell her anything else. Thankfully, she dropped it. Tina knew I would tell her when I was ready. After all, admitting I liked a guy after so long was a big step. She wasn't going to rush me.

After finishing her third slice, she looked at me with a glint in her eyes.

Almost afraid to ask, I did anyway, "What?"

Smirking mischievously, she instructed me, "Get your purse, girl. We're going shopping."

"Why?" I whined. I hated shopping.

Tina put her hands on her hips and gave me a look that said, "You aren't getting out of this." What she actually said was, "Because I've seen your closet, and you have nothing to wear, especially if you're trying to impress a guy. I'll find you something that will bring the man, whoever he is, to his knees."

chapter
four

TESSA

AROUND NINE-THIRTY FRIDAY NIGHT, Tina and I were at the bar, waiting for our drinks. Disappointed, I scanned the vast space for the guy who'd caught my eye the day before.

Leaning in so Tina could hear me over the booming music, I asked, "I thought you said this was the place to be on Friday nights? There's hardly anyone here."

Before she could respond, the bartender, a woman in her late twenties or so with turquoise hair, lots of piercings, and tattoos from the neck down, delivered our drinks.

Tina handed her a credit card. "Keep the tab open."

After nodding, the bartender walked away. Tina handed me my drink. Clinking our glasses, she toasted, "To the start of our final year of school!"

Tentatively, I took a sip of my cocktail. The sweet drink was perfect. A place like this, I figured it'd be terrible or have no alcohol in it, but this was dangerously good. I'd have to pace myself.

I smiled at Tina. "Let me know how much I owe you. I'll give you the money tomorrow."

"Girl, no way!" Tina shouted. "This is the first time I've been able to drag your ass out since you finally decided to join me on the West Coast. Besides, it's Jamar's treat tonight." Tina winked.

"Speaking of, is he coming? Haven't seen him since May."

Tina nodded as she sucked on her straw. "He'll be here soon."

Going back to the question she hadn't answered, I asked again, "Is it normal for this place to be dead? Will it fill up later?"

"It gets really busy during the school year. But since campus move-in doesn't actually start until tomorrow, there aren't many students around yet. Trust me, next week it'll definitely be packed, especially since it's the first weekend back. I think tonight is kind of like a practice run for the band. They don't perform during the summer, so I think this is probably their first show in a couple of months. If something goes wrong or there are any kinks to work out, better it happens when there isn't much of a crowd, right?"

"Makes sense." I took a sip. "Hmm."

"What?"

"You seem to know a lot about the band."

Tina shrugged. "I've been watching them for a couple of years now. I know three of the guys and have even had a couple of classes with the singer over the years. We've chatted, and he's told me about the band."

Averting my eyes, I looked down at my drink. *So she may very well know Jax.*

I jumped when Tina exclaimed, "My boo!"

Turning, I caught the tail end of Tina hurling herself into Jamar's open arms. They immediately locked lips as if they hadn't seen each other in a month, not a day. Pretending I wasn't third-wheeling it, I took the opportunity to get a better look at my surroundings since I'd been too preoccupied with trying to get a glimpse of Jax before.

Smythie's was an old converted firehouse. The gray metal bar counter ran along the right wall from the entrance. With my back leaning against it, a stage equipped with instruments and microphones was to my right, opposite the entrance. The front wall, on my left, still had the old firehouse garage doors, but I doubted they opened anymore.

A DJ booth occupied the back corner, left of the stage. There was a hallway with a neon sign indicating the bathrooms between the booth and stage. A large dance floor was in the center of the room. Flashing, moving, and changing lights hung from the ceiling. Hulking speakers were dispersed throughout the spacious area. It was dark, but not so much that it was impossible to see across the space.

When I'd stepped into the bar, I'd noticed a roped-off spiral metal staircase near the front with a bouncer standing guard. Tina explained it led to a loft area that was no longer available for use. It was visible from the dance floor, but not my current vantage point, as it was located above the bar. An old brass fireman's pole was next to the spiral stairs, although a railing surrounding it prevented patrons from trying out their skills at pole dancing, or so I assumed.

After Tina had showed me the bathrooms earlier, I'd noticed a second staircase in the back corner, opposite the DJ booth. Like the front stairs, it was roped off with a bouncer in front of it.

I could see why the vibe would be appealing to college students. The pulsing music was meant to get people out on the dance floor. Although there weren't any dancers at the moment, if the bar got as crowded as Tina claimed, I had no doubt there'd be a swarm of partying college kids gyrating around the floor in the coming weeks.

My preoccupation was interrupted by Jamar. "Hey, Tess."

Smiling at him, I lifted my glass. "Hey! Nice to see you. Thanks for the drink."

Jamar had the friendliest smile I'd ever seen, and he blessed me with it then. "You're welcome! What number are we on, ladies?"

Tina threw her glass back and finished her drink in two gulps, then declared, "I'm ready for my second!"

Jamar laughed and waved the bartender over. Noticing my barely touched drink, Tina frowned.

Holding up a finger, I started drinking. After finishing half my cocktail, I took a break to say, "My max is two tonight, so don't rush me too much."

Tina smirked as if to say, "Yeah, sure."

While Jamar ordered the next round, I headed to the restrooms. The hallway that led to them seemed never-ending, and the further I walked, the quieter the music got.

As I was rinsing the soap off my hands, the club music faded out. Pulling open the bathroom door, the band started. I recognized their first song immediately. It was a song about a desperate love and a relationship filled with issues, yet they would never give up on it.

The singer had an amazing voice with the perfect edge a rock singer needed. Without having even set my eyes on him, I could feel the emotion in his voice from the lyrics he sang. The power of it reverberated through my body and pierced right into my soul. Impatient to see who could sing in a way that affected me so much, I hurried my pace.

Stepping into the main room, Tina spotted me and waved furiously from the middle of a crowd that seemed to have appeared out of nowhere. I glanced up at the stage but as the singer's back was to me, I couldn't see who it was. As I squeezed between moving bodies, I felt eyes on me. Reflexively, I turned my head in the direction I felt them from. My step faltered as my eyes locked with the singer's, the same magnetic eyes that had caught my attention a day ago.

Jax is the singer? Oh my God, Jax is the singer!

He was looking right at me, but after a second he released me from his gaze as his eyes wandered around the crowd. Turning away, I continued through the crowd until I reached Tina and Jamar. When I arrived, Tina handed me my second cocktail. I took it, and she clinked our glasses again. After taking a sip, she turned her attention back to the stage and began moving to the beat, which was a little surprising. Tina was more into R&B than rock. She and I had a lot of things in common, but music was not one of them. Still, she was enjoying the show.

Swallowing a gulp of the pale pinkish liquid, I faced the stage. Gazing up, I caught Jax's eyes moving away from my direction. *Had he been looking at me again?*

My heart fluttered at the thought. Something bubbled to the surface that I hadn't allowed to happen in years: excitement over a guy. And of course, Jax was the singer. Did I really expect anything less from myself? It was like I had a sixth sense for my type.

Throughout the band's first set, my eyes met the sexy singer's multiple times. At first, I looked away shyly. It'd been forever since I'd had eyes for someone, and my cheeks heated at the thought that maybe this guy had noticed me too. Why else would he be making so much eye contact?

Grateful for the cold drink in my hand, I continued sipping at it as my body loosened and swayed. Then I sang along to the music, familiar with nearly all the songs the band played.

Thanks to the liquid courage I consumed, I stopped looking away from the intense eyes up on stage. When my glass was empty, I decided one more drink wouldn't hurt. After all, tonight was about having fun. I got Tina and Jamar's orders before heading to the bar. On the way, my eyes met another woman's. She looked away quickly, and in my tipsy state I thought, *She shouldn't look so sour. She's too pretty for resting bitch face.*

As expeditiously as I could, I returned to Jamar and Tina with drinks in hand. Feeling more relaxed with each passing minute, I got swept up in the band. More specifically, the singer.

Jax took control of the mood in the room with his performance. He was mesmerizing to watch. Although the crowd was apparently small, it didn't effect the band at all. Their energy was unreal. Jax sang with incredible passion, like the lyrics were his own words and he meant every single one that left his lips. *His lips... What I want those lips to do to me...*

Regardless of my attraction, his performance would've still captivated me. As the band wrapped up their first set, with the help of the alcohol coursing through my veins, I made a plan. I'd see if an interaction with Chuck could turn into an interaction with Jax, so I thought of something related to soccer as an excuse to talk to him.

As the crowd dispersed, the club music started up again. Over it, I told Tina, "I'll be right back."

She raised her brows in a question, but I ignored it. Taking a deep breath, I took a step toward the stage. But what I saw stopped me. My lungs deflated in a whoosh as my stomach sank. Jax had jumped down from the stage and right into the arms of that pretty girl with the miserable scowl.

The petite redhead slung her arms around his neck and pulled his mouth down to hers, kissing him passionately.

Dammit!

chapter
five

TESSA

A KNOCKING sound roused me from my alcohol-induced slumber. At first, I didn't know if it was the banging inside my head or knuckles against wood.

"Tess?" Tina called out from beyond the closed door.

A real knock...ugh!

Allowing myself a brief pity party, I tried ignoring her, but Tina being Tina would not let me off the hook, which was one thing I loved about her. If your friends didn't give you shit for messing up, who would?

Fed up with my lack of a response, she announced, "I'm coming in!"

I groaned.

When she got to my bed, she asked, "You okay, girl?"

"No. Go away," I grumbled.

She snickered. "Drink a little too much last night?"

That's an understatement. My only audible response was another groan.

"Whatever happened to sticking with two drinks?" she teased.

I kept mum, especially since I couldn't recall how many drinks I'd ended up having.

Poking me, she said, "Come on. Go shower and I'll buy you brunch."

Brunch? "What time is it?"

"Eleven."

"Seriously?" It was very unlike me to sleep in. But then again it wasn't like me to drink to excess either. And it sure as hell wasn't like me to embarrass myself by ogling some guy.

Forcing my body to move, I rolled out of bed. After blinking a few times, my eyes focused, and I trudged toward the bathroom.

Following a step behind, Tina assumed, "So that guy never showed up at the bar, huh?"

Muttering, I said, "No, he was there, but his tongue was occupied inside some petite redhead's mouth."

Several seconds passed without a response, so I looked over my shoulder. Tina's mouth was slightly open and eyes wide. Finally, she whispered, "Oh my God...it's Jax?"

I didn't answer, as there was no need to.

Tina's features transformed into concern. "Sorry, Tess, but Jax has a girlfriend. They've been together for a couple of years. I'm pretty sure they even live together."

After seeing Jax and his girlfriend's game of tongue twister, I didn't think it was possible to be more disappointed, but I was wrong. Knowing they were a serious item squashed all hope for me. If she had been a fling, maybe I would've had a chance, but having a live-in girlfriend meant I was shit out of luck.

As I turned on the shower and waited for it to get hot, I guessed, "So you saw them making out too?"

"No, but him and Brooke, his girlfriend, are kind of known for—how should I put this?—their public displays of affection." Lowering her voice as if there was someone else around who might hear, she said, "There's even rumors they've had sex at the bar...more than once."

I snapped my mouth shut after realizing it was hanging open. Digesting the gossip, although shocking, there was a part of me, a deeply buried part, that thought that was kind of hot. Not them in particular, but to have such a passionate relationship that you couldn't keep your hands off each other? A twinge of jealousy toward that Brooke girl needled me.

Testing the shower spray, I tried to brush it off. "It's not like I really liked him or anything. I thought he was hot, but I know nothing about him, so it doesn't matter."

"Really?" I could hear the amusement in her voice. She knew he was my type. Tall, hot, nice body, rock band boy, and a singer.

"Um hmm." I hoped she'd let it go.

Thankfully, she did and left me to shower in peace.

WE SLID into our cracked-pleather booth at a diner near campus, and Tina called to someone behind me, "Hey, Ashton! How's it going?"

Twisting around, I looked over my shoulder to see who Tina was talking to, and came face-to-face with *him*. Jax was sitting directly behind me. Only the seat back separated us. Knowing I couldn't like him anymore, I forced my gaze away and focused on the person sitting across from him. It was one of the guitarists from the night before. He was somewhere between Chuck and Jax's height and quite good-looking, with deep-set dark-chocolate eyes, a huge smile, closely cropped hair, and bulging muscles. Jax and his friend appeared to be by themselves, no redhead or other band members in sight.

The guy named Ashton smiled. "Hey, Tina. All good, all good. How 'bout you?"

I looked back at Tina while she answered, "Same here. Hi, Jax. Great show last night, guys. You all set for next week?"

Even with my back turned to him, I recognized Jax's voice when he responded, "Thanks. Yeah, we're good to go." Not wanting to come across as rude, I turned back while he spoke. Our eyes met again briefly before he looked past me at Tina. "More people there last night than we expected."

"It seemed like a small crowd came in right when you guys were about to start. That must've been nice. Oh, sorry! This is my best friend and roommate, Tess. Jax and Ashton are the singer and one of the guitarists from the band."

I could've kissed Tina for pretending she didn't know I'd already met Jax. Since I had no chance with him, I didn't want him knowing I had spoken about him to Tina at all.

Giving a little wave, I greeted them, "Hey."

Jax gave me the sexiest half-smile I'd ever seen. "Nice to see you again, Tess." To Tina, he said, "Chuck actually introduced us on Thursday."

Giving me a wide smile, Ashton said, "Nice to meet you."

"You too," I muttered, even though my throat was still dry from Jax's panty-dropping smile.

While Tina and Ashton had a side conversation, Jax asked me, "Did you like the show last night?"

Feigning ignorance but unable to keep eye contact, I asked, "Oh, you saw me there?"

When I glanced back at him, his brows were slightly raised while a glint shone in his eyes, and a corner of his mouth was tugging up. He knew that I knew he had, but Jax played along. "Yeah, I noticed when you entered with Tina and were around during our set. When I'm on stage, the bar keeps the lights up enough so I can usually see at least most of the crowd. More fun that way."

My heart skipped. I tried sucking in some air as I searched my mind for something casual to talk about with a stranger, but neither my lungs nor my brain were working very well. Thankfully, the delivery of Jax and Ashton's food ended our conversations.

Cheerfully, I said, "Enjoy your meal!"

When I turned back to Tina, she eyed me suspiciously. Had she noticed how my chest was rising and falling quicker than normal? Had he?

Ignoring her, I picked up my menu, trying to appear calm. For my sake, I truly hoped that I wouldn't cross paths with Jax much over the next few months, so I could forget about him and the way he made me feel as soon as possible.

chapter
six

TESSA

TUESDAY MORNING, the first day of the fall semester, came quickly after long, hard soccer practices on Sunday and Monday. Our first game was soon. I was excited to be out on the field again after a years-long hiatus, but I had to get through the first week of school.

Unfortunately, my very first class started at eight in the morning. If that wasn't bad enough, it was the one class I was dreading and had put off until my senior year even though I needed to pass it in order to graduate. I would've preferred to push it off until my last semester, but if I failed on my first try, I needed the extra semester to try again. I wasn't a dummy, but I was terrible at math.

In an attempt to improve my mood, after a quick shower I made more of an effort with my outfit than I usually did for class. Instead of my normal lounge pants and hoodie, I put on my favorite tight red jeans and a sleeveless black shirt. I even dabbed on a small amount of eye makeup and tinted lip balm.

Making more of an effort had absolutely nothing to do with the potential of running into a local rock band singer. I'd never run into him last year, so I doubted I'd see him anywhere other than the bar this year. And maybe I'd catch a glimpse of him if he was at Chuck's.

Yet, in some cruel twist of fate, a few minutes before eight, Jax was looking me square in the eye. The first thing I saw when I stepped inside my classroom was his gorgeous face. *Am I in the right classroom?* There was no way we actually had a class together, was there?

"Excuse me," an impatient voice said behind me.

Stepping out of the way, I muttered an apology. Ignoring my heated cheeks, I scanned the classroom but didn't see anyone I knew, which wasn't surprising because I didn't know many people thanks to my antisocial nature.

Jax motioned to the empty seat next to him. Looking behind me, I checked to make sure he meant for me to join him. After confirming no one else was by me, I caught Jax trying to hide a smile. Was he laughing at me?

My feet automatically carried me over. Could he tell how bewildered I was at that moment?

After I sat down, he greeted me, "Morning."

"Good morning," I squeaked then cleared my throat. Geez, I needed to get a grip. I avoided eye contact and took out a notebook from my bag to act like I was busy.

"How's it going?"

I shrugged. "Meh, it's the first day and my first class is not only obscenely early—it's also statistics." I made a disgusted face.

Jax chuckled. "Not a fan of math, huh?"

I grimaced. "No. Who is?"

He laughed again. The sound was warm and easygoing. It made my stomach flip, and I had to look away.

Tapping my fingers against the tabletop, I stared at the clock, wondering when the professor was going to show up. After a minute, I peeked over at my desk mate. Unlike the way I felt, he looked calm, cool, and collected as he occupied himself with his phone.

Unable to stand the silence, I blurted, "I'm surprised you had an empty seat next to you." I mentally spanked myself. What the hell was wrong with me? Apparently, my lack of a social life over the last few years had dampened my ability to socialize without sounding like an idiot.

Jax stopped looking at his phone and stared at me for a moment before asking, "Why do you say that?"

Trying to cover myself, I shrugged, "Oh, uh, Tina said your band was super popular around campus, so I figured you'd know a lot of people and…" I wondered if I sounded as stupid to him as I did to myself.

Jax looked around the classroom. "No, I don't know anyone else here. I think there's a lot of freshmen in this class." He lowered his voice. "I doubt any of them have even heard of my band. They probably haven't even heard about Smythie's yet."

I nodded then realized something. "That reminds me…"

"What?"

"What's the name of your band?"

"The Last Word," he said, the corner of his mouth lifting slightly.

I twisted my lips. *Hmm…* "Does that have a special meaning?"

Jax made a noise that almost sounded like a laugh. "Something like that." Rubbing his lower lip, he observed, "You never did answer my question the other day."

I furrowed my brows. "What question?"

"If you enjoyed the show Friday night."

"Oh! Yes, I did. You guys are great, and you play a lot of the music I like."

Jax perked up. "Really?"

I nodded as the professor came rushing through the door, putting an end to our conversation.

The round man stood in front of the class. "Good morning, students. I'm Professor Stanley. I know it's early, but it will be early every Tuesday and Thursday for the next sixteen weeks. So wake up and pay attention! Open your books to page five, and let's begin."

An unguarded breath of frustration escaped between my lips. A movement to the right caught my attention. Glancing at Jax, he raised an eyebrow. In my notebook, I jotted down large enough for him to see.

I HATE math!

He looked down then quickly away, covering his mouth. While he successfully kept silent, I saw the laughter in his eyes.

· · ·

AFTER ENDURING ninety minutes of torture, the teacher finally dismissed the class. Frustrated, I shoved my textbook and notebook into my bag then hurried out of the classroom, forgetting to say goodbye to Jax.

Oh, well, I thought, *it's not like we're friends or anything.*

But about halfway down the hallway, I realized I didn't need to feel bad about not saying goodbye, since Jax was keeping pace with me.

Neither of us said anything until we stepped into the warm, bright campus courtyard when he observed, "You weren't kidding about not liking math, huh?"

Looking down, I asked, "That obvious?"

"You seemed..." He thought for a moment. "...frustrated during class."

Was he paying attention to me, or was it impossible to miss? If it was the former, I hadn't noticed. I was too busy trying, in vain, to understand what the heck the professor was trying to teach us.

"If you don't like it that much, why'd you take this class?" Jax asked.

I blew out a breath. "I have to in order to graduate."

"I see. You know, statistics can be kind of fun."

I stopped and stared at him like he'd told me he was a million-year-old alien from three galaxies away and had come to dissect me. Or, in other words, like he was completely insane, and I was horrified and disgusted by what he'd said.

After shaking my head to clear it, I started walking again while thinking out loud, "The student center has tutors. I guess I'll be visiting there this semester...often."

Jax stopped walking, so I turned to face him. Rubbing the back of his head, he offered, "I could help you if you need it. I'm actually pretty good at math."

"Really? You'd help me?"

He shrugged a shoulder. "Yeah, why not? I used to be a student tutor, but I don't feel like doing it this year. But I'll help you since I know you and we have class together. When are you free during the week?"

"Umm..." My eyes scanned our surroundings, as if my school and soccer schedules would magically appear. "I should be free most Wednesday nights. I don't have any classes then, and soccer practice usually ends around five. I can't remember if we have any Wednesday night games. If we do, it's not many."

"Wednesdays work. I actually go to the library every Wednesday at six-thirty to do school work."

"Really?" I hesitated. "Oh...no. If that's your study time, I don't want to interfere with it."

"It's fine. My classes are all easy this semester."

"Except for this one."

He cleared his throat and rubbed his lips, trying again, and failing, to hide his smile.

Since he felt so confident in his math skills, I agreed, "Okay, thanks."

"Let me get your number in case something comes up."

After Jax and I exchanged our cell phone numbers, I looked up and froze. We'd been joined by a third party. A smiling redhead, who was staring daggers at me with her hazel eyes, clung to Jax's arm.

He turned and placed a kiss on the top of her head. "Hey, Rook."

Rook?

I swallowed the lump in my throat and put on my best cheerful face. "Hi, you're Brooke, right?"

Jax's head snapped back to me, probably because he knew he'd never mentioned her to me, yet I knew who she was.

Meanwhile, with a big-ass fake smile, Brooke said, "Yes. Hi."

Although she hadn't asked, I gave her my name anyway. "I'm Tess. Nice to meet you."

"You too," she said, her monotone tone making it clear she didn't mean it in the slightest. Geez, she looked like a wild animal staking her claim. "Hey, weren't you at Smythie's the other night? I think I saw you there."

"Uh, yeah. It was actually my first time there."

"Oh? So you're a freshman? How cute," she cooed. "Who would've thought a freshman would know about Smythie's already? Are you local?"

I glanced at Jax, who looked a little confused. "Uh, no and no. Not a freshman. Not local. But never went before."

"Bet you're regretting that, right?"

Scrunching my brows, I asked, "What do you mean?"

"I saw you watching the band. They're great, right? You seemed to really like one of the band members. I saw you eyeing the stage." She leaned in conspiratorially. "Is it Chuck? He's single. Want me to introduce you?"

Realizing my mouth was open, I shut it.

Jax came to my rescue. "She knows Chuck. She lives in one of his parents' rentals."

"Oh my God! That's so convenient!" She sounded downright jolly but fake as hell.

Holding my hands up in front of me, I said, "It's not like that. I like live rock music."

"O-oh," she squeaked. "Bet you're glad your found Smythie's then?"

"Uh, yeah."

Thankfully, Jax ended this awkward-as-hell conversation. "Don't you have class?" he asked Brooke. "Come on, I'll walk you there."

Brooke beamed at him. "Okay! Thanks, Jaxy!"

Jaxy? Ew!

Turning back to me, Jax said, "See ya around."

I waved. "See ya."

I watched Jax and Brooke stride off. She slung her arms around his waist, hugging him as they walked. They really were an attractive couple. She was almost as good looking as him, but unlike Jax, I suspected Brooke's beauty wasn't all natural. Her red hair, which framed her heavily made-up face, was too red. Her dark, lipstick-covered lips looked awfully plump. And her boobs... Well, they looked bigger than mine, which I thought were perfectly proportional to the rest of my body, and I was maybe five inches taller than her. Brooke was also super skinny.

As I wondered if she had sounded as fake to Jax as she had to me, Brooke looked back over her shoulder and sneered at me. I almost laughed because it was like something out of a movie. I had suspected she was subtly warning me off, but that look confirmed it. She must've known or at least suspected that the one I'd been watching on stage was Jax. *But it's not like I continued to ogle him after I saw you guys making out!*[1] I silently defended myself to her.

"Wow. That was a death glare if I'd ever seen one."

chapter
seven

TESSA

STARTLED, I spun toward the voice of the person who'd apparently witnessed Brooke trying to kill me with her eyes. A tallish man with a dark-blond crew cut and dressed like he'd been on the golf course in kakis and a pale blue pull-over collared shirt, stood to my right. He was still looking toward the couple who'd departed a moment before.

"Whatever you did, I wouldn't worry about it. I've known her most of my life, and she can be kind of a bitch. She's also quite possessive of Jax."

"I didn't do anything," I argued, even though I had no idea why I was talking to this guy I'd never met.

Maybe having a sixth sense, he faced me and stuck out his hand. "Hi, I'm Eli."

I took his hand automatically. "Tess."

"You're a friend of Tina's, right? I saw you two hanging out at Smythie's the other night."

"Yeah, you know her?"

"A bit." Eli glanced at his phone. "I gotta get to class." He looked back up at me. "It was nice meeting you, Tess. Maybe we'll see each other around."

I gave a slight wave. "Maybe."

I GLARED at my dinner while Tina was damn near choking on hers. "Oh, girl! She was definitely telling you to back off," Tina said as she wiped tears from her eyes.

Jamar arrived as I grumbled, "Ha ha."

"Good evening, ladies." Jamar leaned over and gave Tina a kiss on the cheek. "What's so funny?"

I was too busy stabbing a piece of penne pasta with my fork to answer. It had been a long day, and I was exhausted. First, it had started way too early with a class I didn't comprehend at all, then soccer kicked my ass. It didn't help that I'd been distracted during practice, over-analyzing my behavior Friday night and how it had led up to my interaction with Jax's girlfriend.

Tina finally caught her breath and answered, "Tess was telling me about her day."

"And?" He sounded hesitant, like he wasn't sure he should be asking.

"Brooke was staking her claim while pretending to be nice."

"What does that mean?"

Tina gave him a thankfully brief version of what I'd told her. Dropping her voice conspiratorially, she added, "But at least there was one bright spot in her day."

"Huh?" I didn't remember anything particularly positive happening.

Cupping her mouth like she was telling Jamar a secret, Tina whispered loudly, "Tess met Eli."

A thoughtful look crossed his face. "Brooke's ex Eli?"

My hand paused on the way to my mouth, a forkful of pasta midair, my mouth hanging open. *The girl dressed like she stepped out of an advertisement for a punk-rock clothing line was the ex of the preppy guy I met earlier?* Talk about opposites. But if they were exes, that might explain why he'd called her a bitch. Bitter feelings and all.

"Yup," Tina confirmed then raised her eyebrows at me. "Catching flies, Tess?"

I stuck my tongue out before shoving my fork in my mouth.

Jamar smirked. "Were you trying to flirt with Jax or something?"

I answered before Tina could've mentioned we exchanged

numbers, "No! We were talking about math! And there is nothing sexy about math!"

Tina's body shook as she held in her laughter.

Jamar pursed his lips. To Tina, he said, "Eli... Isn't he the guy who—"

"Wait!" she interrupted. "We gotta go! We're going to be late for our reservations!" Grabbing her boyfriend's hand, Tina dragged Jamar not only out of the kitchen but out the front door.

Dumbfounded, I stood in the kitchen for several seconds. *They had reservations? Really?* Not only had she been eating dinner with me, but Tina was wearing sweatpants and an old t-shirt. What kind of restaurant did you need reservations for when you could show up dressed like that?

Obviously, she'd cut him off for a reason, and enough had been said for a ball of suspicion to knot in my gut. I hoped I was wrong, but knowing Tina, I seriously doubted I was.

chapter
eight

JAXON

THURSDAY MORNING, Chuck and I ran into each other on our way to our respective classes. We were discussing the set list for the next night when a giggle nearby stopped me mid sentence. Like a reflex, I looked in the direction the cute sound had come from. Tess was staring at her phone as she headed our way.

Noticing where my attention had gone, Chuck called out, "Hey, Tess!"

When she looked up, she was smiling, but... Did her smile fade when she saw me? No, that'd be crazy. She had no reason to be wary of me.

Still, her approach was tentative. "Hey, guys."

"Morning," I said but only got a brief glance from her.

"You coming to Smythie's tomorrow night?" Chuck asked, "There'll be more people this week, and then you'll really get to see us in action." He had hope written all over his face, and for some inexplicable reason, that bothered me. Pushing it aside, I waited for her response.

Tess's eyes flickered over to mine for a split second. "Oh, uh... I'm not sure. I have practice tomorrow, and then we're going to be watching your game."

"Yeah, exactly, we have our first match tomorrow," Chuck said, referring to the men's soccer team, "but I'll be heading to the bar as soon as we're done."

Tess looked down. "I'll think about it, I guess."

I didn't like how she was acting. What? She didn't want to go? Didn't she say the other day she'd liked the performance, the songs and rock music?

Wait, why the hell would I even care if she liked us or came to the bar?

Chuck crossed his arms over his chest and tapped his lip with a finger, trying to act casual. "So, Tess, a friend of mine was wondering if you are available."

My eyes bulged. *What the hell?*

"Available for what?" Tess asked.

Was she playing coy, or did she really not understand?

"You know, like single? Do you have a boyfriend? Or girlfriend or whatever?"

A glimmer of understanding shined in her eyes, but instead of answering, she asked her own question. "Are you friends with a guy named Eli?"

There was a moment of silence as my jaw hit the ground. I could imagine Chuck's shocked face, although I didn't see it, as I was staring at Tess. In unison, Chuck and I both blurted out, "Eli?"

Thankfully, since Chuck said the name at the same time I did, I didn't think she caught the distinction in our tones. Chuck's exclamation conveyed surprise, while mine was of disgusted disbelief.

Her cheeks turned pink as she looked around, probably wondering if anyone had heard. Considering the amount of students meandering about, some must've. However, I wasn't worried about that. *Fucking Eli! Are you shitting me?*

Disheartened, Chuck responded, "No...not really. He comes to Smythie's a lot, but we don't really know each other."

Frantically waving her hands in front of herself, Tess sputtered, "O-oh, never mind! Forget what I said!" Checking her smartwatch, she noted, "Class is about to start."

I looked at my phone to confirm the time. "She's right. We gotta go."

Chuck waved glumly. "See ya."

As Tess and I hurried to class, I glanced at her a couple of times. She kept her eyes forward, never looking my way. After we were seated with our books out, she continued to ignore me and fixed her gaze on the dry-erase board at the front of the classroom. Was she intentionally avoiding me? Had I offended her? I didn't remember doing or saying anything that could have been offensive.

Breaking the silence between us, I asked, "How are you today?"

Barely glancing over, she said, "I'm fine, thanks. You?"

Definitely avoiding me. Looking away myself, I answered, "Same old, same old."

She exhaled, and I twisted to face her. A small smile played on her lips as she spoke, "You know, I don't know you, so I have no idea what that means. I don't know if that's a good thing or a bad thing."

I couldn't help but stare at her for a moment. No one had ever asked me what I meant by that before. Sure, she didn't ask directly, but it was implied.

I shook my head, then whispered, "Maybe I'll tell you sometime."

That got your attention. Tess stared into my eyes for several seconds, like she was trying to see right into my head. Her gaze was so intense that she may have very well been able to see inside. I wanted to look away but couldn't. She had captured me and locked me in with her blue-green irises.

I didn't know how long our soul searching would have continued if it hadn't been for someone in the back of the class asking, "Hey, how long do we have to wait for the professor before we can leave?"

Released from what I was sure were a pair of keen eyes, I glanced at my phone. It was seven minutes past eight.

Another person called back, "I'd give it fifteen minutes."

Facing forward again, Tess tapped her fingers on the table.

Back to my original mission of trying to figure out why she was avoiding me, I asked, "Did you have a game last night?"

"No?" It sounded like a question.

"Practice run late?"

She made a face that read as if to say, "Why are you asking me this?" Verbally, she responded, "No."

"Oh…" I paused, waiting for her to look at me again. When she did, I said, "I thought I'd see you at the library last night, but you never showed up." Her mouth opened then closed, so I pressed, "You seemed like you were going to need help, so I thought you'd stop by."

Tess looked away and cleared her throat as she readjusted herself in her seat. Her cheeks were a little pink again. *Damn, she's cute when she blushes.*

In an attempt to be nonchalant, she shrugged with an excuse, "Since we're only one class in, I thought I'd try to see if I could do it myself first."

What the hell? I couldn't understand it. Why had her demeanor changed from two days ago? Even from last Thursday when we'd first met?

Professor Stanley stormed into the room waving his arms like some fucking cartoon character. "Students, I apologize! There was extra traffic this morning. But don't worry, we'll stay a few minutes late to make up for the lost time." He ignored the chorus of groans reverberating throughout the classroom. "Alright, put everything away. Time for a pop quiz."

After throwing my notebook and textbook under the table, I glanced at Tess while readjusting my seat. Gone was her blush, replaced by a death pallor. Leaning over, I whispered, "I'll be at the library every Wednesday night from six-thirty to eight-thirty. It's an open invitation."

Her eyes shone with genuine gratitude as she mouthed, "Thank you."

AFTER WE TOOK our twenty-question pop quiz, the professor instructed us to switch papers with the person next to us. As Tess handed me her paper, she grumbled, "What is this, grade school?"

I chucked quietly, but Tess wasn't laughing. Looking down at her paper, I understood why. She hadn't finished, and the few she had done were wrong.

After Professor Stanley finished going over the answers, he announced he wouldn't be collecting this quiz and the results wouldn't count. He wanted to make sure we were all taking the class seriously and vowed the next one would count toward our grade.

Tess signed in relief, until we moved on to the day's lesson. If a person hadn't picked up the stuff from the first class, they were screwed. By the time nine-forty rolled around, she looked damn near haggard.

AS WE ENTERED THE COURTYARD, Tess vented, "That wasn't a pop quiz! That was a damned pop test! Who gives that kind of thing during the second class? Shouldn't he at least give the students a chance to ask some questions about the homework or something before springing that on us!"

Shit, she could be fiery. It was cute as fuck...not that I cared. Looking away to hide my smile, I agreed, "Yeah, that was pretty brutal."

Tess cackled forcefully. "Says the guy who got a perfect freakin' score!"

I shrugged. "I told you that I'm good at math. Anyway, are you busy Saturday?"

Tess stopped walking and almost looked afraid. "Why?"

"You won't be able to do today's homework unless you understand Tuesday's lesson. And you won't understand next week's stuff unless you understand today's lesson. So I'm not sure waiting until next Wednesday is a good idea."

Taking a deep breath, Tess looked off into the distance. Why was she so hesitant to accept my offer of help when she'd been ready enough Tuesday? And why the fuck did I give a shit? Whether or not she passed and graduated had nothing to do with me, yet I wanted to help her.

"Are you sure your girlfriend won't have a problem with us studying together?"

Ah... I finally understood.

"No, why would she?" I answered, as carefree as possible. In actuality, there was a strong possibility Brooke would throw a hissy fit, but that was nothing new. It was a daily occurrence lately. What was one more? Besides, it wasn't like I used to fuck Tess, unlike Brooke, who was still friends with some of her exes, like that fucker Eli. And it wasn't like I'd ever given her a reason not to trust me. What could happen in a library besides studying anyway?

Tess bit her lip, and for some strange reason I felt the need to look away. It was a good thing my hands were already in my pockets—less obvious when making adjustments as I shifted my weight.

After a few seconds, she said, "We actually have our first game on Saturday. I'll probably be pretty tired afterward. Are you free Sunday?"

"Sunday works. How about one at the library?"

"Yeah, one sounds good." Finally looking at me, she gave me a small smile. "Thanks, I really appreciate it."

"It's really no problem. See you tomorrow night at Smythie's." Turning, I left before she could respond or resist the implication she'd be at Smythie's.

chapter
nine

TESSA

LIKE DÉJÀ VU, I found myself in the same place at the same time doing the same thing as last Friday night. Tina and I waited as the same bartender prepared our same cocktails. However, tonight, I was definitely sticking to just one since I had a game in the morning.

A clatter behind us let us know our drinks had arrived. Picking mine up, I clinked glasses with Tina. After taking a sip of my beverage of choice, I yelled over the booming music, "Jamar coming?"

Tina shook her head. "No, he's traveling for work. I won't see him until next weekend."

"That sucks."

"Yeah, tell me about it," she said with an eye roll. "Oh, Eli!" Tina's annoyance turned cheerful way too quickly. "Fancy seeing you here."

The guy I'd met the other day was now standing in front of us.

He smiled. "Evening, ladies. You're a sight for sore eyes."

I nearly groaned at the cheesy line but caught myself and looked down at my drink instead.

Tina grabbed Eli's arm and pulled him right in between us. "I heard you two met the other day."

Eli smiled at me, perhaps pleased I'd mentioned him to my friend. "Hi, Tess." Turning back to Tina, he said, "We did."

By the mischievous grin on Tina's face, it was clear Tina liked the idea of me and Eli. My gut had been right about what Jamar had almost let slip the other day. It was strange though. I hadn't been interested in dating for years, and although she'd offered to introduce me to guys here and there, I always declined. Maybe Tina had decided to stop offering and moved on to straight up doing? What she did't know yet was that I actually was interested in dating again. Unfortunately for me, the first guy to pique my interest wasn't someone I had a chance with.

Looking back and forth between us, Eli asked, "Can I buy you two your next round?"

I shook my head. Pointing to my drink, I shouted over the music, "I'm sticking with one tonight. But thanks for offering."

"Next time then," he promised with a smile. He had a friendly smile with good, clean teeth.

"Sure," I answered automatically before what I'd agreed to sunk in. Embarrassed by my inadvertent consent for him to buy me a drink some time, I averted my eyes, pretending to find something interesting out on the dance floor. Since I wasn't talking, Tina took over the conversation. The two of them discussed what they'd done over the summer, but I couldn't hear much over the music, not that I cared. I already knew Tina had spent her summer doing an internship at a prestigious PR firm, and since I didn't know Eli, I didn't care what he did.

As I sipped my cocktail, my eyes wandered around the bar, wondering if I could make out anyone I recognized through the color changing lights. I waved at a couple of my soccer teammates on the dance floor. They smiled and waved back. Seeing them made me feel better about being out the night before a game. Eventually, my gaze made its way over to the stage area.

Instantly, I wished I'd kept my eyes focused on the crowd of moving bodies. Next to the stage, Brooke had her back up against the wall, and Jax was leaning over her. Her hands were on his waist, and from my vantage point it appeared either he was talking into her ear or kissing her neck. Either way, it was an intimate moment I didn't want burned into my brain.

Turning, I put my back to them, facing Eli and Tina. They were still engaged in their conversation, so I looked down the length of the bar.

My eyes met a guy's. I didn't think I knew him, but since he smirked and didn't look away, I took an extra second to think back through my memory. *Perhaps I had a class with him junior year.* If I did, I couldn't remember.

I looked away, getting the impression he'd been looking at me before I saw him, and the fact that he'd stared so purposely made me squirm.

"Tessa! You made it!" Chuck bellowed next to me. I turned and gave him a wave. Chuck leaned over to be heard over the music. "You look great tonight!"

"Oh, thanks," I replied, thankful that the dark and colorful lighting hid my fiery cheeks. I took another sip of my drink, as I didn't know what else to say.

"You plan on staying after our second set?"

I shook my head then leaned close to his ear. "Game tomorrow, remember?"

"Oh, right." Chuck looked a little sheepish. "Since the guys have to be there too, guess I won't be getting much sleep until tomorrow afternoon."

"Congratulations on the win today."

He smiled proudly. "Thanks! Good luck tomorrow."

"Thanks. I'm leaving after the first set to get some sleep."

Chuck frowned and gave me sad eyes. I giggled at the same time as the music faded and the flashing club lights stopped. The ceiling lights came on dimly, enough so everyone could see each other.

Jax's voice came through the speakers, "Care to join us on stage, Chuck?" The crowd roared in laughter as we turned to see Jax, Ashton, the drummer, and other guitarist already set up on the stage, waiting for their bassist.

Nervously, I scanned the bar, my fears confirmed. All eyes were on Chuck and I. Had they seen us close together in what might've looked like an intimate moment? *Ugh!*

"Ticktock, Chucky," Jax teased.

Chuck loudly whispered, "Whoops." He then flipped Jax the bird and ran to the stage, calling out, "Enjoy the show." The crowd laughed again.

Checking the time, I noted they were running a few minutes late, so Jax's stunt seemed acceptable, although I wished it hadn't involved me. The lights went down again and I looked back up at the stage. Chuck was setting up, so I let my eyes wander over to the singer. Our eyes met. Tearing my gaze away from his, I looked down into my half-empty glass. Not only could Jax see me even way over by the bar, he'd been looking right at me, even with Chuck on the stage. Why? Was he trying to see if I was interested in his friend? Like if I had watched him as he ran up on stage? I hoped not.

Before I could analyze it any further, Tina jeered, "Look at you, getting poor Chuck in trouble."

One glance at Eli revealed he hadn't found it as amusing as everyone else. I shrugged. "He was talking to me. I wasn't holding him up."

Tina grabbed my hand and dragged me toward the middle of the crowd gathered in front of the stage. "Let's get a better view."

Squeezing through the mass of bodies, we found a spot a little way back but still in the center. Tina placed me between her and Eli. Was he planning on sticking with us all night? I didn't have time to think anything more of it as the band started, drawing my full attention.

Chuck's prediction had been right. This week was way better than the previous Friday. Electricity pulsed through the bar, charging the air. The crowd loved the band, and Jax loved playing with the crowd. They fed off each other. He was a performer through and through. The way he could control the room was the closest thing to real magic I'd ever seen. Jax was absolutely captivating to watch, and I couldn't tear my eyes away from him.

That was until I got a weird feeling. It felt like someone was watching me. I scanned the guys on stage, but none of them were looking at me. Turning to Tina then Eli, I saw they were both focused on the performance. I even glanced in Brooke's direction, but she wasn't paying me any attention. Discreetly looking over my shoulders, I noticed nothing. My eyes hadn't locked with anyone's. Still, I couldn't shake the feeling. I tried ignoring it and getting back into the music, but I couldn't. The set was almost over anyway.

I pointed to the bar and yelled, "Water!"

Tina nodded, and we squeezed our way back to the bar with Eli in tow. The latest song ended while we waited for water. Instead of another one starting, Jax announced, "We're gonna do something a little different tonight. A very special lady is going to join me for the next song. Brooke, where are ya?"

Eli rolled his eyes, and Tina groaned, "Oh God, not again."

Clueless, I asked, "What?"

Eli explained, "They do this every year, although usually it's later in the semester. They met their freshman year—"

"Here at karaoke night," Tina interjected.

Eli went on, "They're gonna sing a song they sing every year."

Tina piped in, "Honestly, it was cute the first time they did it, but now it's kind of cringe."

The music started, and my attention went back to the stage. The song was surprising, more pop-rock than the stuff the band normally played. As I watched them, I couldn't deny that they had great chemistry as they sang together. Not only could Brooke sing nearly as well as Jax, she was quite the performer too.

For the first time in my life, I felt inferior to another woman. Maybe it was because I had only ever had one boyfriend, and we'd both been each other's worlds. I'd never had to compare myself to another girl, as there had never been any competition, not that there was one now. Although I knew I not only shouldn't compare myself to her, didn't need to, I couldn't help it. And at that moment, she was miles ahead of me. Gorgeous, talented singer, big boobs, pretty ivory skin, glossy hair, and lips so perfect, I was even more convinced than the other day she got fillers. Not to mention she had a killer wardrobe, not that we dressed alike.

To top it off, her boyfriend was the most attractive man I'd ever seen, and she lived with him and got to see him every day, probably naked, and could do him whenever she wanted. A guy who was not only hot but nice and smart and could sing.

I rolled my eyes at myself.

Even if Jax was single, I doubted I was his type. I was tallish, fit but not toothpick thin, had a relatively simple wardrobe, was low maintenance with imperfect nails, and rarely wore makeup. Brooke and I were near opposites as far as I could see, so the chances I had with him, regardless of his relationship status, seemed nil.

Turning my attention to Eli, I observed him more carefully. He was quite handsome. If Tina was trying to set me up with him, he was a good one. Although I preferred guys who were taller, he was taller than me in my low heels, so it was fine. If a bit preppy, he dressed nicely and carried himself well. I didn't really like the fact that he was Brooke's ex, but everyone had a history.

Finally, the duet ended. The crowd roared, so apparently at least a chunk of them didn't mind the annual performance or had never seen it before. The corner of Jax's mouth lifted into a panty-dropping smile, and damn... Butterflies started fluttering in my belly at the sight of it.

Bringing the mic up to his mouth, he said, "Hey, Brooke, I think they want more."

The butterflies died.

"Oh? What'd you have in mind?" she purred at him.

Eli groaned.

Ditto, Eli. Ditto.

"Why don't you stay up here for the next one?" Jax suggested salaciously.

The song was about a couple who couldn't get enough of each other and went at it day and night until they couldn't walk anymore. My eyes would never unsee what went on up on that stage. While Jax stayed professional, Brooke shook her ass like her life depended on it. If I was into girls, I probably would've enjoyed it. Admittedly, she could dance. Add that to the list of things she had going for her.

Not wanting to see anymore, I turned to Eli and Tina. "I'm gonna head out."

Eli was surprised. "You're leaving?"

I nodded. "Yeah, I have a game tomorrow morning."

"Game?"

"I'm on the soccer team."

"Oh, what time is your game? Is it a home game?"

"Yeah, it's a home game. Starts at nine."

Eli nodded.

Tina jumped in, "I'm going to stay longer. Eli, do you think you could walk Tess home?"

Agreeing immediately, he said, "Of course!"

Don't get too excited there, buddy.

Leaning into Tina's ear, I questioned, "You sure this guy's trustworthy?"

Tina nodded enthusiastically. "Not that you'd need to, but you are more than capable of defending yourself. Especially to a skinny-ass guy like that," she said as she subtly pointed at Eli. "He's a good guy though, so you don't have to worry."

"Alright." I shrugged. "I'll let him walk me home. See you tomorrow."

Tina smiled widely. "Good night!"

Much to my surprise, I enjoyed the walk. Eli was easy to talk to. Although I barely knew him, my intuition told me Tina was right. He was a good guy. He had a warm smile and laughed easily. We even had a few things in common. We liked the same types of shows, true crime and sitcoms. Both of us grew up in small towns, though on opposite sides of the country. In high school, we'd both ran spring track. Over-all, the fifteen-minute walk was pleasant.

When we arrived at my house, we said good night, and he waited until I was in the house before walking away, like a gentleman. As I brushed my teeth, I decided I'd be interested in a gentleman.

WITH SECONDS LEFT on the game clock, I intercepted the soccer ball from the opposing team as one opponent tried passing it to another. Sprinting down the field, I dribbled the ball while careful to keep possession. Making it look like I was going to kick left, I shot right as the goalie went the wrong way, giving me the opening I needed to score the winning goal. The referee's whistle blew, signaling the end of the game.

I leaned over, resting my hands on my knees, panting, smelling sweat, grass, and dirt as my teammates ran toward me. As we celebrated winning our first game of the season with high-fives, I heard my name in the cheers coming from the spectators in the bleachers.

Completely focused on the game, I hadn't noticed the crowd in the stands. Spotting Tina among the attendees was easy since she was the loudest, but the people with her left me flabbergasted. Sure, Eli was on one side of my best friend, but that wasn't too surprising. However, on her other side was a cheering Jax, and next to him was Brooke, seated and engrossed in her phone. *What in the world?*

chapter
ten

JAXON

ATTENDING Tess's soccer game was unplanned, but that wasn't to say I was unhappy I got to watch her play. Other than a couple of Chuck's home games, I hadn't been to any sports matches for our university. Brooke had needed to drop off her costume for alterations for an upcoming play she was in, and when we were headed back toward the parking lot, we passed the soccer field.

Even from a distance, I immediately recognized the girl with the blonde ponytail flapping around as she ran up and down the field. Distracted trying to get glimpses of the game, I hadn't noticed Eli approaching. When our paths crossed, Brooke said, "I gotta talk to Eli about something."

Not that either saw, but I rolled my eyes even as I followed along like an obedient dog as Brooke walked with Eli toward the field. When we got to the stands, I saw Chuck sitting with the men's soccer team, but he was focused on the game and barely gave me a wave. We ended up in the stands as Eli and Brooke continued to discuss some charity event both their parents were going to. Thankfully, Brooke had a play that weekend and couldn't drag me to it.

With no end in sight for Brooke's conversation with Eli, I sat down next to Tina in the stands. Turning to me, she asked, "What are all of you doing here?"

I shrugged. "I don't know. Brooke wanted to talk to Eli." I swallowed the bitter taste in my mouth. "I guess Eli was coming to see Tess."

"Ah, so you and Brooke aren't sticking around?"

"Probably not," I responded, although I wasn't in any rush to leave.

I knew little about soccer but quickly got invested. Time flew as I watched Tess sprint back and forth. She was fast, very fast. Faster than any of the other players on either team. Not only that, but in my novice opinion, she was the best player out there. Tess's focus and intensity impressed me. Sometimes when I was on stage, I let the music take over and became oblivious to everything else. It appeared to be the same for Tess and soccer.

Along with Eli and Tina, I cheered when Tess scored two of their three goals. A part of me wanted her to hear me and look our way, but she didn't until after the final whistle, when Tess heard Tina whistle through her fingers and shout her name. Her jubilant expression from their win changed to pure surprise when she spotted us. Recovering quickly, she went back to celebrating with her teammates.

As the spectators disbursed, Brooke whined, "Okay, Jaxy, the game is over. Can we leave now?"

What? I wasn't the one who led us here, nor did I ask to stay. Although I was happy we did. Torn, I weighed the risk of Brooke's wrath versus appearing rude by not staying to congratulate Tess now that she knew we'd seen her game. It was probably better to avoid another argument with Brooke. Lately, all she and I did was argue, and I was exhausted. Besides, I didn't owe Tess anything. I could congratulate her tomorrow. Holding out my hand, I said, "Yeah, let's go."

LIKE WE'D PLANNED, I met Tess at the library on Sunday afternoon. Unlike our plan, Brooke tagged along. She insisted on coming even though she denied having any issue with me helping Tess. Brooke claimed she had some stuff to look up at the library and promised she wouldn't bother us or interfere. Reluctantly, I agreed.

Not that it bothered me that my girlfriend would be around, but I hoped Tess wouldn't be uncomfortable.

As Brooke and I approached Tess, her expression changed from surprise to neutral so quickly that I almost missed it. Thankfully, she didn't appear annoyed, embarrassed, or angry.

Arriving at the table she was seated at, Tess brightly greeted both of us. "Hi! Thanks for lending me Jax's brains, Brooke."

Brooke slapped on her fake smile. "Yeah, no problem. Don't mind me, I have some stuff to look up, so I figured I might as well hitch a ride with my man. Pretend I'm not even here." She sounded sweet, but I knew better. Tess might've missed it, but I didn't miss Brooke's claim on me.

"Yeah, no problem," Tess said graciously.

As I sat next to my classmate, Brooke set her bag on a chair across from me then wandered off. Tess already had her notebook, textbook, and pop quiz ready to go.

As I pulled out my own books, I whispered, "Sorry, she insisted on coming. I hope her being here doesn't make you uncomfortable or anything."

Tess forced a smile and waved like it was nothing. "I don't care." Looking back down at her textbook, she swallowed hard, confirming she definitely cared.

A few minutes after we started, Brooke came back with a few magazines, some of which were the same as the ones on our coffee table at home. She put her earbuds in and kept her promise to not bother us.

But then Tess said, "Oh my God! I totally get it now! That makes so much sense. Ugh, I'm such a dunce when it comes to anything related to math."

Brooke snorted before catching herself and tried to cover it up with a cough. I glared at her, but she pretended not to notice. Apparently Brooke had been listening the entire time, only pretending to listen to her headphones. Tess caught it too but said nothing.

Continuing like she hadn't heard, she said, "Thank you so much for your help! You don't know how much I appreciate this. I was starting to think I'd never graduate because of this class. Do you need this class to graduate too?"

I looked away. "Uh, no, this is an elective for me."

Horrified, Tess asked, "What? Are you serious? Why?"

Shrugging, I admitted, "I'm minoring in math."

Tess's jaw almost hit the table. "Have you gotten your head checked out?"

Brooke didn't bother trying to hide her laughter that time.

Without looking up from the fashion magazine she was skimming, she commented, "That's what I said. How anyone could like math is beyond me."

Tess laughed, but it wasn't her usual giggle. It sounded nervous, which wasn't a surprise considering Brooke's presence. Closing her books, she said, "I think I can handle the rest of the homework from here. Again, thank you so much."

Brooke threw the magazine on the table and jumped up. Ignoring her, I responded to Tess, "It's really no problem." I grabbed my books and put them in my bag before I stood. "See you Tuesday."

Tess gave a small wave. "Yup. See you then. Bye, Brooke."

Brooke smiled, sort of, and wiggled her fingers at her.

Pointing to the pile of magazines, I asked my girlfriend, "You going to put those back?"

She scoffed as if it was beneath her. "They pay people to do that."

Although I loved her and could never leave her, sometimes Brooke could be a real snob. Incredulous and disgusted, I stared at her, telling her to go put them away with my eyes.

Rolling hers, Brooke huffed. Spotting a young guy with a name tag walking by, she slapped on a smile bright enough to stun a person. She practically purred at the library employee, "Excuse me, I can leave books and magazines on the tables when I'm done with them, right? I mean, I don't want to accidentally put them back in the wrong place."

"Oh, uh, uh..." The pimple-faced kid, who must've been a fresh-man, was having trouble speaking. Eventually he squeaked out, "Oh, sure. No problem."

Brooke beamed at him again. "Thanks!"

Turning to me, she cocked a carefully plucked eyebrow at me.

I took a deep breath, trying to eradicate my annoyance. Looking back at Tess, I said goodbye again then turned and headed for the exit. Brooke caught up and grabbed my arm, clinging to it. I glanced down at her in time to catch the tail end of her last dig at Tess.

chapter
eleven

TESSA

AS JAX and Brooke headed toward the exit, the latter glanced over her shoulder and gave me a sneer that I interpreted as, "Nice try, bitch. He's mine. Back off!"

Staring blankly at the tabletop, I went over the last hour and a half in my head. Had I done or said anything that would've given the impression that I was trying to steal Jax? That I even liked him? I didn't think so, especially since I wasn't trying to steal him. All we did today was talk about statistics for Pete's sake! I'd done nothing wrong!

Or perhaps it had nothing to do with me. I might've imagined it, but there seemed to be some serious tension between those two. And not the sexual kind.

AS SOON AS I sat down next to Jax Tuesday morning, he said, "Morning. I forgot to say congrats on your game."

I smiled. "Hey, thanks. How'd you end up there anyway?"

"Oh, well..." Jax explained how it happened. To say I was surprised that Brooke and Eli were still friendly, especially after he called her a bitch, would be an understatement. It was almost as surprising as him and Brooke staying for the entire game.

Jax put his elbow on the table and chin in his hand. "So, I was wondering, is Tess a nickname? Like for Theresa or..."

"Tessa."

"What's your last name?"

"Givens."

"Do you have a middle name?"

Why was he asking me so many questions about my name? Not that it mattered. "Yes, May."

Jax looked away, rubbing his lower lip. Almost like he was talking to himself, he repeated, "Tessa May Givens."

Hearing my full name on his lips woke the butterflies within me and sent my pulse racing. Trying to calm myself, I took a couple of deep but quiet breaths. When I was sure I wouldn't sound breathless, I asked, "What about you? What's your full name?"

Smiling at me, he stated, "Jaxon Marcus Smith. Jaxon with an X. You can call me Jax or Jaxon."

Looking away, brows furrowed, I thought there was something about his name...but I couldn't put my finger on it. When my eyes wandered back to his, he was observing me curiously. Quickly, I said, "Same. You can call me either."

"What? You want me to call you Jax or Jaxon?" he teased.

Covering my heating face with my hands, I muttered, "You know what I mean. Tess or Tessa."

He laughed as I peeked at him through my fingers. The professor walked in, and the class quieted. Right before Professor Stanley started speaking, Jax leaned in and whispered, "Okay, Tessa."

My body stiffened, save for a sharp inhale, at the sound of him whispering my full first name. It was the sexiest thing I'd ever heard in my life, and he hadn't even been trying. It was electricity, jolting my heart back to life.

Pretending I hadn't reacted both physically and mentally, I tried to relax and reminded myself to breathe. Determined to forget about what happened, I focused on the professor and his teachings, never looking at Jax. Not even when I felt his eyes on me.

Was I just some foolish girl to him? Could he tell I was reeling? Did he know it was because of him? And did he even care that he affected me so much?

twelve

TESSA

PULLING OPEN THE LIBRARY DOOR, I glanced at my phone for the directions Jax had texted me. Apparently, he didn't like the spot I'd chosen on Sunday. At a specified bookshelf, I turned and walked down the aisle. By the time I reached the table where he was sitting, I was sure there was no one else anywhere near us.

"Hi, Jax," I said.

He looked up from a textbook and smiled. "Hey, Tessa. Glad you were able to find me back here. I was prepared to go find you if needed."

Again, my heart skipped a beat when he said my name. "Your directions were spot on and easy to follow, so no issues." I sat down next to him and looked around, inhaling the smell of old books. "I didn't even know this part of the library existed."

"Few people do. That's why I like it. It's quiet, and since there's rarely anybody back here, we shouldn't disturb anyone."

Pulling out my books, I asked, "Why didn't we sit back here on Sunday then?"

He looked away, and his teeth sunk into his bottom lip. "Actually... this is my secret spot. Brooke doesn't know about it."

But you're sharing it with me, someone you hardly know?

As if I understood why he wouldn't tell his own girlfriend about it, even though I didn't, I replied, "Well, I'll be sure to keep your secret. Shall we get to it?"

Jax walked me through the last lesson and tomorrow's, so I'd be able to get through the homework over the weekend. He really did know numbers and was incredibly patient as I struggled to grasp the formulas. When I thought I got it, Jax watched as I completed the homework.

Finally done, I put my pencil down and stretched. Glancing at the time, I said a little too loudly, "Oh my God! It's already after nine!" Spinning to Jax, I apologized, "I'm so sorry! I didn't mean to keep you so late!"

"It's okay," he reassured me. "Understanding this foundational stuff is important, otherwise you'll be lost later on."

"Thanks to you, I might actually graduate! I've been putting this class off for the last three years."

Jax rested his elbow on the table with his chin in his hand, facing me. "You're a senior, right?"

"Mm hmm."

"Can I ask why you transferred here for senior year?"

I suddenly felt foolish for not doing much last year. No one knew me, even with the small size of our student body, and it was one hundred percent my fault. I was the one who stuck to myself. "I transferred here last year," I admitted quietly.

"You did?"

Watching my hands spin my water bottle around on the tabletop, I nodded.

Several seconds of silence passed, so I looked at him. His brows were scrunched, and his eyes were moving around the room, maybe searching his brain for some kind of memory of me from last year. I doubted he would find one.

Looking back at me, he asked, "Did you play soccer last year too?" The way he'd said it made it clear he couldn't understand how he hadn't known me until now. From what I'd gathered, he knew pretty much everyone, and everyone knew him because of the band, except for maybe the freshman who had yet to discover Smythie's.

Unable to keep eye contact and not wanting to reveal too much, I explained, "No, there wasn't a spot for me last year. Actually, I almost didn't make it this year either, but during summer training, someone got hurt, so they called and asked me to come and try out to see if I was still any good. So I didn't start with the team until the beginning of August, which is pretty late."

"Their loss for not taking you last year. I don't know much about soccer, but it looked like you were the best one out there."

I quietly thanked him before taking a few sips of my water, hoping to cool my cheeks. Glancing at Jax, I bit my lip.

"What?" He sounded genuinely interested in whatever I was thinking about.

Taking a second to gather some courage to share a bit more, I inhaled deeply through my nose. Big mistake, well, maybe. My stomach flipped as the delicious scent of a man's body wash or soap or shampoo or something filled my nostrils. I'd faintly smelled the scent before around him, but since there'd always been others around, I never realized it was him. Releasing the breath through my lips, I wondered if he heard how unsteady it was.

After swallowing, I threw out a theory I had. "They might've been mad at me."

His forehead crinkled. "Mad? Why?"

Tina was the only person other than the school and my parents who knew, but Jax was easy to talk to. "I actually had a full athletic scholarship for soccer when I was a freshman, but I pulled out at the last minute, right before I was supposed to fly out here and start training with the team."

Surprised with a touch of concern, he asked, "Why? Did you get hurt?"

Not in the way you're thinking. "Not exactly."

For several seconds, he observed me. When I didn't say anything else, he quietly concluded, "So you really didn't know about Smythie's, huh?"

"Tina had tried to get me to go with her a few times last year, but..." What could I say? *I've been antisocial since my senior year of high school. I threw myself into seclusion for the last few years. I haven't allowed myself to have fun because I don't deserve to.* I didn't want to lie, but giving him the truth was out of the question.

Deep down, I knew my self-induced punishment was unnecessary, but I still couldn't stop the guilt I felt every day I was on this Earth. Also, I sure as hell wouldn't admit that the only reason I'd decided to go to the bar at all was because of him. It'd be inappropriate and totally not like me to reveal how he had affected me so much that I'd broken out of my personal prison to see him again. Jax would never know how grateful I was to him for giving me the final push I needed to start my escape, because now that I was free, I didn't want to go back.

Nearly four years is long enough, right?

I'd been numb for so long, but thanks to him, my mind, body, and soul were jounced back to reality and life, ready to feel again. Nothing could be worse than what had happened, right? As disappointed as I had been when I'd discovered Jax wasn't single, there were other guys out there, and I missed being loved and lusted after. I missed being the center of someone's universe. And I missed having those feelings for someone too.

It had been silent for too long since I'd trailed off. Maybe thinking he'd asked too many questions, Jax apologized. "I'm sorry. I wasn't trying to pry. You don't have to explain."

Taking the opening to change the subject, I said, "You're a senior too, right?"

"Yeah, been here since freshman year. I grew up in SoCal, about an hour north of here."

I thought back to our conversation on Sunday. "You said your minor's math, what're you majoring in? Music?"

"Nah." Jax shrugged. "I love music, but it's a hobby. I feel like if music became my job, it wouldn't be fun anymore. Chuck's majoring in music. He can play any instrument you give him. He wants to be a music teacher. The thought of Chuck being addressed by a bunch of kids as Mr. Aguilar cracks me up."

I giggled at the way he said it then asked, "Isn't the bar work?"

His mouth twisted. "Technically...but it's not a career. I don't have to sing in a band, it's for fun. And it feels more like a bonus that Smythie's pays the bills."

"Oh," I laughed, wishing I could get paid doing a hobby. "So, your major?"

"Oh, right. Political science," he said. "I want to be a lawyer. So I'll head off to law school next year."

I wasn't expecting that. *Good Lord!* Jax was the hottest nerdy band boy I'd ever met. Smart? Check. Nice? Check. Tall? Check. Hot? Check. And as a bonus, a singer? Check. Also, I'd gotten a few glimpses of his sense of humor in the little time I'd spent with him, and it seemed like he had a good one. *I hope you know how lucky you are, Brooke!* I screamed in my head.

"Do you know what law school you'll be going to?"

He shook his head. "No, too early. I'm still applying."

I nodded as I tried processing how this guy could be real. What was wrong with him? No one was perfect, so what were his flaws?

Interrupting my musings, he observed, "Looks like you're contemplating life."

Ha! That's one way of putting it. Still half-lost in my thoughts, I responded, "I'm trying to wrap my head around you."

"Uh...what?"

Realizing what I'd said, I mentally kicked myself as I tried to think on my feet. Tripping over my words, I blurted out the first thing that came to mind, "I mean, math and poli-sci usually don't go together. And you're a really talented singer that I'm sure could make a career out of it. That's all I meant." *Well, not really.*

"Oh, I'm doing the math stuff to bring up my GPA." He sounded so nonchalant about math. "I mean, I am taking a freshman statistics class as an elective."

I rolled my eyes dramatically. Then, again without thinking, I asked, "Your GPA? What is it? Do you need a higher one for law school?" My hands flew to my mouth. "Wait! Never mind! Don't answer that! Sorry! None of my business."

"Three-point-nine. It would have been a four-point-oh, but I had some...things going on freshman year."

My jaw might've as well been on the table. *What the hell?* I couldn't keep it in, "So what the hell is wrong with you then?"

He squirmed in his seat. "Wh-What?"

Sighing into my hands, I rested my elbows on the table and buried my head. *God!* Why was he so easy for me to talk to? What else would I embarrass myself with next?

"Sorry." My voice was muffled since I was still hiding from him. "I meant, what's your flaw?"

"My flaw?" he asked, unsure.

My cheeks were already flaming, so I figured I may as well keep on going. Popping my head up to look at him, I explained, "Oh, come on. You're smart, talented, and good-looking. Next you'll tell me you're rich, want four kids, two dogs, and a cat. Oh, and that you can cook."

Jax pressed his lips closed, but he failed to hold in his laughter. He'd been smart to hide us in the back of the library, because we were definitely not respecting the library volume rules. Holding his stomach, it took him a minute to rein himself in.

Then, the punk ticked off on his fingers while he said, "Funny, charming, nice car, great in bed..." He winked after that last one, and I knew my face was the color of a tomato. "I'm kidding... Well, kinda." He leaned in and whispered, "I'm just going by what I've heard."

Groaning, I flopped my head back into my arms and wished I could start the conversation over. The sound of his laughter didn't help, but it sounded nice. After peeking over at him, I joined in and giggled a little.

Finally, he regained his composure. His face sobered as he stared off into space, absently rubbing his wrist. The mood around us dipped tangibly. When he spoke, his focus remained somewhere far away. "I'm far from perfect, Tessa. Everyone has things they're good at and things they struggle with."

Pulling up his sleeve, he showed me his wrist and a black bracelet with an engraved circle of arrows. Eyebrows scrunched, I stared, racking my brain for anything familiar about it. Nothing came to mind other than I had noticed him wearing a bracelet when he was on stage. I assumed it was part of the rock-star aesthetic, but apparently it was more than that.

When I looked up, he pursed his lips, and his intense stare made it difficult for me to speak. "Uh… umm…"

"I'm showing you my flaw," he explained somberly, but that wasn't an explanation. Before I could ask for some more clarity, his phone vibrated against the wooden table. Checking my phone, I saw another forty-five minutes had passed.

Picking up the phone, he answered, "Hey."

Jax pulled the phone away from his ear, and I jumped as I heard the shrill female voice scream at him, "Jaxon! Where the hell are you? Aren't you done yet? What the fuck is taking so long? What time are you going to be home?"

What the hell?

"We're finished. I'm leaving in a minute," he responded flatly. Alarmed, I watched as Jax transformed in front of me. His eyes became vacant and glazed over as he stared straight ahead. He didn't even seem surprised by Brooke railing into him. Did she always talk to him like that?

The volume of the screeching lowered as Jax's finger pressed a button on the side of the phone. Even with the adjustment, I could still hear the nearly incoherent banshee.

"You better! And you better not be fucking around either! I was sick of waiting for you, so I ate without you. Why did you make me wait and not say anything? You know what, you can find your own goddamned dinner!"

The hollering stopped, and Jax put the phone down.

Feeling guilty for getting him in trouble, I said, "I'm so sorry I kept you for so long." Standing, I gathered my stuff. "Again, thank you so much for helping me."

"Don't worry about it. And you didn't keep me. I'm sometimes here until closing anyway. I'm glad I can help. See you tomorrow." Although not as emotionless as when he was talking to Brooke, he still sounded rather desolate.

"See ya tomorrow. Goodnight." I hurried away, trying to wrap my head around what I'd heard and seen. A pit formed in my gut for my new friend, who I hoped had nothing more serious going on.

chapter
thirteen

JAXON

FUCK! This wasn't good.

Okay, I found her attractive, but so what? Other women had caught my attention over the last couple of years, but it was never anything more than acknowledging an attractive woman. But this felt inexplicably different. I hardly knew her, but every time I learned more about Tess, the more I liked her as a person.

A warning sounded from my subconscious, *Be careful.* I mentally rolled my eyes at it.

As soon as Tess turned the corner out of sight, I pushed thoughts of her aside and picked up my phone. Hitting Brooke's name, I waited for her to answer.

After three rings, she did. "What!"

Seething through clenched teeth, I demanded, "Get that shit out of the apartment right now, or I'm not coming home."

"I don't know what you're talking about." She sounded indignant.

"I know you're high right now! I'm not a fucking idiot. What was it? Your go-to nose candy? Get it out!"

There was a long pause before she responded, "I used it all, so you don't have to worry. And it wasn't even that much."

"I don't have to worry? Are you fucking kidding me?"

"It's fine, Jax. Besides, I'm not the one with the problem here."

I felt like throwing my phone, or maybe a bookshelf, at a wall. "If I find any of that shit in the apartment, I am leaving and not coming back. Got it, Brooke?"

"Yeah, yeah, whatever. Hurry up and get your ass home already. I'm horny and want to fuck." The line went dead. She loved hanging up on me.

I huffed as I gathered up my school stuff. If she thought I was going to go touch her while she was blitzed, she'd be disappointed.

WHEN I ARRIVED HOME, Brooke was lazily sprawled out on the couch, watching TV. Walking straight to the coffee table, I spotted remnants of Brooke's favorite white substance next to her fancy-ass chessboard. I pointed at it. "You missed some."

To her credit, she jumped up immediately, grabbed a cleaning wipe, and got rid of it. Not to her credit, she muttered, "What are you going to do, lick the table or something?"

I counted to three...then five...then ten, inhaling and exhaling slowly.

Brooke threw out the contaminated wipe and asked, "So?"

What now? "So what?" I responded tiredly.

"Did your little friend, the dunce, show up?" Brooke mocked.

I sighed. "She's not a dunce. And yes."

Brooke held up her hands. "Her word, not mine." She gestured to the chessboard. "Anyway, your move." Brooke was an avid chess player, and we had a constant game going.

Fed up with her figurative games and ignoring her literal one, I asked, "Is there a problem? I thought we had an understanding that we'd stay out of who the other person was friends with? I mean, that's why you're still friends with a bunch of guys you've messed around with, including your BFF Eli."

The fucker wasn't really her BFF, but I hated that they were still friends, sort of.

Brooke glared at me. "It isn't a bunch, and I never said you couldn't be friends with her, Jaxy."

God, I hate that nickname! Besides sounding like she was whining when she said it, she only used it when she was annoyed at me.

Sneering, she added, "And since you only recently met Tess, I hope you're not implying you've messed around with her and now want to be friends with her."

I let out an exaggerated breath, my head rolling along with my eyes.

Brooke walked up to me and put her hands on my abdomen. Slowly, she moved them around my sides and encircled me in her arms as she cooed, "I'm going to take a shower. I'd love some help washing myself."

Bored, I looked at the darkness out the window. "No, thanks."

"Excuse me?"

"You're high—"

"Hardly. That was like hours ago," she interrupted. "Besides, whose fault do you think it is that I needed a little something?"

Recoiling, I exclaimed, "What?"

Brooke closed the gap between us again. "My man was basically on a study date with some other chick. I was anxious and needed a little something,"

What the fuck? "Look, if you have a problem with me helping her, then say so. Otherwise...stop." Flustered, I couldn't even come up with a decent retort.

She waved a hand in the air dismissively. "It's whatever, Jax, I know you like tutoring people or whatever. Do whatever the fuck you want." Grabbing my dick through my jeans, she moved her hand up and down. Of course, my body started reacting. "Come on, rock star, I know you want to join me in the shower and fuck my brains out." Standing on her toes, she released my semi and wrapped her arms around my neck to pull me down closer to her. Into my ear, she purred, "You know I'll clean you up too. Lick you clean." Her tongue slid along the edge of my ear.

"Can't. I still have work to do." I'd never been so happy to have homework in my life.

Becoming more demanding, Brooke yanked on my shirt. "Finish it later and come fuck me! Now!"

Standing up straight, I pulled myself free of her and headed to the kitchen. "I'm tired."

Brooke called after me, "Fine, whatever. Suit yourself, Jaxy."

That goddamn nickname again! *Whatever.* I had work to do since I'd spent my normal study time with Tess. I'd have to finish my other work some other time or get to the library earlier if I was going to use my time helping Tess, which I'd continue to do since I'd given Brooke a chance to tell me to stop, but she hadn't, so she must not have cared that much.

Sitting on the cold, hard wooden chair at the kitchen table, I pulled out my books and laptop, determined to put both Brooke and Tess out of my mind. Tess shouldn't have even been there to begin with.

AFTER READING the same paragraph five times and not knowing what it said, I sat back in a huff. Looking at the glowing green numbers on the oven clock, I thought it was likely Simon was still awake. I noted the living room lights were off. Listening, I heard nothing, so I figured Brooke was in the bedroom's bathroom shower or had gone to sleep.

Picking up my phone, I went into my call log and hit the fourth name from the top. Simon answered after the second ring. "You're calling late, Jaxon. Everything okay?"

Drained, I muttered, "Brooke was high when I got home."

chapter
fourteen

TESSA

FOR THE FIRST time since school started, I got to class before Jax. When he arrived, his appearance shocked me. Dark circles I'd never seen before hung under hooded eyes. His hair looked more bedhead than sexy-messy, and he was wearing sweats, not his usual tight jeans and t-shirt.

As he slowly took his books out of his bag, I asked softly, "You okay?"

The corners of his mouth lifted a little, but I couldn't tell if he was trying to fake smile or really smile but couldn't. "I'm okay. Didn't get much sleep last night."

"That's what I meant."

Jax studied me with his somber eyes for a long moment, maybe trying to figure out why I cared. Eventually, the corners of his mouth lifted higher. "I'll be fine. Thanks."

Although doubtful, I nodded.

"Hey," he sat up, perhaps trying to prove he really was okay, "I meant to ask how you liked the show on Friday. I thought you liked it since you were dancing and seemed to know all the words to all the songs. But then you left after the first set."

How many times did you look at me to know I knew ALL the words to ALL the songs?

"Oh… I left because I had the soccer game Saturday morning. I didn't want to be out too late. And I told you that you guys play a lot of songs I like. It's like you stole my playlist or something. Rock is my favorite genre, and I love how you play stuff from the last twenty years or so, not only recent stuff."

As we discussed a topic we both liked, Jax's body became less rigid, and the tension in his face faded. "I grew up listening to some of those older songs. My brother—he was a bit older than me—played in a band too. I loved watching them practice. It motivated me to keep working and develop into a better musician. So you liked the show then?"

My response was delayed as I processed what he'd said. Jax said his brother "was" older than him. Unsure if I should comment about it or not, I ultimately kept the chipper mood. "Yeah, for the most part."

Jax's head snapped over to me. Chagrined, he questioned, "For the most part?"

Oh, shoot! Although true, that last part had slipped out. Seeing Brooke up on stage singing and dancing like a ho was something I wished I'd missed. Recovering quickly, I waved it off, "Oh, just an expression."

He faced forward. "Do you have a game Saturday?"

"An away game, yes."

"Will you make it out to Smythie's tomorrow?"

Why all the questions? Why would he even be curious about my comings and goings?

"I think I'll be able to stop by and see the first set. The away game isn't that far, so we're leaving early Saturday morning. If an away game is further away, we have to leave the night before so I'll miss those Fridays. What do you guys do when Chuck has a conflict with soccer?"

Jax shrugged. "What can we do? Ashton switches to bass and backup vocals, so it really doesn't matter much. This year, there's only one conflict. The season ends in October, right?"

"Yeah, our school really isn't that competitive. Bigger schools go into November, some even December, but we're not there. The school is trying to be more competitive, which is why they started giving out athletic scholarships, but as of right now our season ends at the end of October."

We remained quiet for a moment. Jax's demeanor had distracted me. Sure, he'd said he was tired, but I suspected there was more to it. He seemed melancholy, but not knowing him that well, I could've been wrong. I was itching to ask him again but doubted he'd say anything other than his excuse of being tired.

Discussing the bar reminded me of something I was curious about, so this seemed like a good opening to ease into it. "Does the owner care if there are four guys instead of five on stage when Chuck's absent?"

"No, he understands."

So the owner is a man. "Is the owner ever at the bar?"

"Yeah, he's usually there two or three times a week, but the management is good, so he doesn't need to be there that much."

"Oh, interesting…" I paused before digging deeper, "I heard a rumor that only the employees know who the owner is."

"That's kind of true. Only some of the employees know. He likes to keep a low profile."

"That's what Tina said."

For the first time since we started speaking, Jax didn't respond right away. It was only a beat slower, but I noticed. "What else did Tina say?"

"Only that. No one other than the employees know who the owner is and that he keeps a low profile. She didn't even know the person was a man."

"Why do you think the owner is a man?"

"Because you said 'he' a couple of times."

Jax chuckled. "Or maybe that's a figure of speech." His brow cocked and the corner of his mouth lifted.

"Why does he, she, or they," I emphasized, "want to keep a low profile?"

Professor Stanley scurried into the room, late again, and started rushing us into work, like it was always our fault he was late. Jax leaned over and whispered, "If you ever meet the owner, maybe you could ask."

With that, the class from hell started.

"WAKEY, WAKEY!" Tina sang, rousing me from my late afternoon nap.

I groaned into the couch cushion, "Ugh...so tired."

"I know, girl, but if you don't get up now, you won't be able to sleep tonight. Why are you so tired anyway?"

Rolling onto my back, I explained, "My first class on Tuesdays and Thursdays starts at eight. Then I have another class then practice all afternoon. Practice seriously kicked my butt today. I'll probably be sore tomorrow."

"Why'd you take a class so early? And senior year too!"

"When I joined the team, they had to adjust my schedule, and this class didn't have any other times available that worked with my soccer schedule, so unless I wanted to risk it and put it off to my last semester, I was stuck."

"I'm still torn about how I feel about you playing this year. I think it's great you're playing again, but they wouldn't give you back even a partial scholarship, yet they practically begged you to join the team a month before the season started!"

I sighed. "It's my fault I lost the scholarship, Tee. They only have so much in funds. When I gave it up, they had to give it to someone else. I'm just glad I got to play one more season."

Briefly, my mind wandered, asking questions that could never be answered. *What if I had been here freshman year? Would I have met Jax first? Would I have been at the bar every Friday, ogling Jax on stage? Would I have liked him back then, like I do now? Would I have had a chance with him before Brooke? Would he be my live-in boyfriend and not Brooke's?*

"If you don't mind, then I guess I don't either." Tina's phone beeped, and after a second I heard her typing a reply. "Man oh man, I love him so damn much!"

"What'd Jamar do this time?"

"He got us reservations to a new restaurant a couple of towns over! I've been dying to go there. Unfortunately, the reservations for the restaurant are booked out a bit. But I've heard it's worth the wait!"

"You two are too cute together. It makes me want to vomit," I said dryly.

Tina scoffed playfully as a decorative pillow flew my way. "You're just jealous!"

"Yeah, sure. Whatever you say," I said, laughing, but honestly it was true. I missed and wanted the highs and even the lows of a relationship. Because one thing I'd learned over the course of the last few years was that you could learn and grow from the lows. And I was ready to find someone I could grow with.

chapter
fifteen

TESSA

THE BARTENDER HAD HANDED Tina and me our drinks right when Tina's phone lit up. After checking, she shouted over the EDM playing through the speakers, "It's Jamar. I gotta get this."

Taking a sip of my cocktail, I gave a thumbs up. She handed me her cup then headed for the exit. Turning to face the bar, I put our drinks down in front of me. Mindlessly, I stirred mine, letting my thoughts wander like they had so often over the last couple of weeks.

I wondered if Eli was going to crash our girls' night again. Bummed I could only see the first set again, I wondered what songs the band was going to play while I was there. Although it had nothing to do with me, I wondered where Jax was at the moment. I glared at my drink, disgusted as the image of Jax and Brooke making out flashed through my mind, then disgusted at myself for thinking about an unavailable man so much.

"What'd that drink ever do to you? Tastes that bad?" I jumped at the voice in my ear. Jax made an oops face and mouthed, "Sorry."

Laughing it off, I shouted, "No, nothing, the drink is fine. I was thinking...about something unpleasant."

His eyebrows rose, asking me for more information, but I ignored the silent question. Seeing as I wasn't indulging him, Jax called to the bartender, "Hey, Cory, couple of bottles of water, please?"

Automatically, I looked over to the bartender who usually worked this end of the bar on Friday nights, the one who usually made my drinks. *Ah, so that's her name*, I thought as I watched her nod but hold up a finger to Jax, indicating she needed a minute.

Not feeling talkative, I went back to stirring my drink.

"Hey, Tess, are you—" Stopping himself, Jax shook his head then asked something different, "What're you drinking?"

"My usual," I said over a particularly bassy song.

Jax gave me one of his signature smiles, the lopsided one. "You know, I don't know you—that well—so I have no idea what that is."

Despite my dismal mood, I giggled at Jax basically repeating what I'd said to him not long after we'd met. It could've been the lights, but I saw his eyes shimmering as he smiled back at me.

Answering his question, I said, "Cosmo on the rocks with a splash of pineapple juice."

Jax's lips twisted as his eyes scanned the ceiling. "Isn't that a bay breeze or something?"

I corrected him, "No, I need the lime, orange liquor, not juice, and only a splash of pineapple. It's different."

Jax looked like he was chuckling, but I couldn't hear it over the noise. Leaning in, he commented, "Interesting."

I held up my cup. "Wanna try?"

He shook his head. "No, thanks. I don't drink much."

"Really?" I squeaked. *And to think you work in a bar.*

He nodded but didn't provide any explanation.

Even with the loud atmosphere, standing close together in silence felt awkward, so I said, "Where's Brooke?"

He turned to face the dance floor, his back leaning against the bar. "She's around...somewhere."

Scrutinizing him, I inquired, "You still...tired?"

His eyes snapped to mine, alarmed, or surprised at a minimum. We held eye contact for several seconds and in my head, we had a silent conversation.

Jax: You saw right through that one, huh?
Me: Yep.
Jax: How?

Me: I have a pretty good BS detector. And you look miserable.

Jax looked away and laughed without humor. "Yeah...tired."

Cory arrived and passed two bottles over to Jax. He thanked her then turned to me. "Hope you enjoy the show. And good luck at your game tomorrow."

Smiling, I waved. "Thanks."

I watched longer than I probably should have as he headed toward the stage. Pursing my lips, I stood on my toes, looking over the crowd for Tina. She had been gone for a while.

After a few seconds, I heard her. "Looking for someone?"

Turning toward her voice, I found a pensive-looking Tina only a couple of feet away, leaning against the bar, arms crossed. She didn't say anything, so I lifted my shoulders and mouthed, "What?"

Instead of answering, she walked over, picked up her drink from the bar, and took a sip. Before taking another, she warned, "Be careful, Tess."

Feeling defensive, I shot back, "What's that supposed to mean?"

She didn't look at me but stood close enough that she didn't have to shout. "You know what I mean. I know you like him, but he's in a long-term relationship with someone else. And I realize he's the first guy you've shown any interest in since Sammy, but he's off limits, girl."

Letting out a breath of frustration, I spun away, facing the dance floor.

Next to my ear, she continued, "I know it sucks. I want you to be happy, and if he wasn't taken, I'd tell you to go for it, but he is taken. Getting close to him seems like a bad idea. I don't want you to get hurt, and you would be the one hurt."

I ground my teeth but held my tongue because Tina was one-thousand-percent right. Sighing, I released the tension in my jaw. Spotting Eli heading our way, I threw the rest of my drink back and vowed to push Jax out of my thoughts. After putting my empty cup back on the bar, I said to Tina, "He's only my friend. Don't worry."

I sauntered off, intercepting Eli. Fueled by liquid courage, I asked, "Wanna dance?"

Pleasantly surprised, Eli nodded. Grabbing my hand, he led me to the middle of the dance floor. As I moved in Eli's arms, guilt pricked. Was I using him to get over my crush on Jax? But he seemed like a decent guy, and I promised myself I'd give him a chance if he was interested.

We only danced to a song and a half before the music faded for the band to start. Instead of following the crowd to the front of the stage, Eli and I returned to Tina, who was still leaning against the bar where I'd left her. The band started, but I kept my back to the stage, determined not to watch.

"Want a drink?" Eli offered.

Smiling, I shook my head. "No, thanks. I have to be up early tomorrow for a game, so I already had my one for the night."

He nodded. "Want to watch the band?"

Before I could answer him, a shriek of excitement pierced the air. Glancing in its direction, I caught sight of Tina as she jumped into Jamar's arms. He must've gotten back from his business trip early and come to surprise her. Immediately, they became lost in each other as they put on some serious PDA. Despite their hardly appropriate behavior, I smiled. It was nice seeing my best friend so in love. I could only hope that one day I'd feel the same and have a man who was crazy for me too.

Always conscious of drawing attention and always trying to avoid it, I glanced around to see if the commotion had caught anyone's notice. Jax was looking at them as he sang. Maybe I stared too long, because his eyes shifted to mine and lingered longer than I would've expected them to. Once released from his gaze, I turned my back to the band once again.

Tina was no longer clinging to her man but was speaking into his ear. When I turned my attention back to Eli, his expression changed quickly into a smile. But I had still seen it. He had been watching me. *For how long?* Had he seen Jax and I exchange glances?

I couldn't wonder about it for too long, however, because Tina announced, "We're headed out."

Startled, I sputtered in disbelief, "You're leaving... Where are you going?"

Tina cocked a brow. "I haven't seen my boyfriend in almost two weeks. Where do you think I'm going?"

My mouth gaped.

She waved her fingers then left arm in arm with Jamar, leaving me with Eli. Couldn't she have waited? I'd planned on leaving in less than forty-five minutes for crying out loud! As I pivoted toward Eli, I glanced up at the stage and caught Jax quickly look away. Was he still watching us? Why?

Eli broke into my musings. "Looks like it's us two now."

I laughed to myself. *Of course it is. Thanks so much, Tina.* To Eli, I shrugged nervously, "Looks like it."

He must have sensed my apprehension, because he declared, "Don't worry! I don't bite...much." I burst out laughing, my hesitation melting away. He was so good natured that I couldn't help but like him as a person. It was yet to be seen if I could see him as a person special to me.

Once again, taking a peek over at that stage, I thought I saw Jax's eye move away from Eli and I. *He was scanning the crowd*, I told myself, *totally not interested in what I'm up to.* Jax surveyed the audience a lot while performing.

Unable to stop myself, I sighed.

"You okay?" Eli inquired.

I rubbed at an eye until I remembered I'd put on makeup. "Actually, I'm kind of tired. I think I'm going to head back home."

Eli grew concerned. "Can I walk you back? I'd feel much better if you'd let me. I'd offer to drive you, but I took a ride-share here."

Smiling, I said, "Thank you, yes, I'd appreciate it."

He grinned. I didn't pull away when he grabbed my hand and led us toward the exit. As we headed out, I tried to ignore it, but the feeling of the eyes burning a hole into the back of my head was overwhelming. For the particularly angry and high-energy song the band was playing, strobe lights flashed around the bar, lighting up the room for milliseconds at a time. With one foot out the door, I took one last look behind me. As if in slow motion, an effect from the flickering lights, I made eye contact with the man who actually made my heart flutter.

Thankfully, there were no uncomfortable silences between Eli and

I as he walked me home. He kept the conversation flowing with casual topics. When we arrived in front of my house, Eli asked me the question I figured was coming.

"Do you have plans tomorrow night? If not, I'd like to take you out. On a date. If you're available."

Had he purposely given me an out? I could've easily said I had plans, but I wasn't going to. Although this wasn't unexpected, a shy smile formed on my lips. It'd been years since I'd been on a date. To my relief, I didn't sound as nervous as I felt.

"I have an away game tomorrow, but I'll be back and ready to go in the evening."

Eli smiled widely, like I'd made his night. "How about I pick you up at eight? That way, you'll have some downtime. I imagine you get tired after running around a field all morning."

His consideration touched me. Nodding enthusiastically, I said, "Yes. That sounds great."

Before leaving, Eli leaned in, brushing a kiss on my cheek. I waved goodbye and headed into my house, smiling. Okay, maybe he didn't give me butterflies or make my heart race or send tingles throughout my body, but I'd only ever had one prior relationship, so what would I know?

Eli was a nice guy, and those kinds of feelings and sensations would develop over time, right? Feelings that grew into love were what was important. Chemistry could and would develop. Passion was gradual, right?

chapter
sixteen

TESSA

AFTER SHOWERING and styling my hair with some curls framing my lightly made-up face, I donned a blue-green cocktail dress that brought out the color of my eyes. It was form-fitting and flattering, showing a touch of cleavage with its square neckline. Since Eli was taller than me, I slid on my favorite nude high heels to finish off my date-night ensemble.

As I stepped out of the bathroom, Tina whistled at me. "Girl, Eli is going to die when he sees you. You look stunning."

Happy my efforts had paid off, I beamed at her. "Thanks!" Then deadpan, I added, "But I hope he doesn't die. I don't feel like hiding a dead body tonight."

Tina rolled her eyes but laughed. As we stepped into the living room, the doorbell rang.

Tina clapped and squealed. "He's here!" Scurrying toward the front door, she chimed, "I'll get it!"

A few seconds later, Eli entered the living room, followed by Tina. His step faltered when he saw me. I looked away as I felt a blush rise on my cheeks at his reaction. Dressed in slacks and a dinner jacket, he looked quite handsome. Still a little preppy but good looking. Unfortunately, it wasn't butterfly-inducing.

Give it time! I chastised myself.

Eli smiled widely. "You look gorgeous, Tess."

"Thank you," I said softly. *Oh, right, I'm supposed to be trying with him.* "You look great too."

He smiled again. Tina piped in, "Alright, you two, have fun!" Then she practically shoved us out the door.

When we stepped outside, I saw a slick blue sports car at the curb. It was low to the ground, very sleek…and looked very, very expensive. I stopped and pointed. "Is that your car?"

"Yeah," he admitted a bit sheepishly.

"And it's not like your dad's car or a rental or something?"

Eli laughed, "No, it's mine, but my parents bought it for me when I graduated from high school."

I nodded. *So Eli's rich.* As we approached the car, Eli took a couple of faster steps so he could open the door for me. Thanking him, I climbed in and sank into the luxuriously soft leather. While buckling, I noticed the car was clean, with a pleasant, comforting smell.

He got in, fastened his seatbelt, then smiled at me. "Ready to go?"

"Ready," I answered, even though I wasn't sure that was true. My hands were clammy, and my stomach knotted as my heart pounded, but not from excitement. As my first date as an adult and the first one with somebody I didn't really know, I had no clue what I was supposed to do! What if the conversation fell flat? What if there were awkward pauses? Was there a certain etiquette that I should follow? *Oh my God! I was so sweaty!* Had I remembered to put on deodorant?

The panic inside my brain probably would've continued if Eli hadn't taken charge. With natural ease, he kept the conversation going as he drove us to the restaurant, and eventually I forgot all about my nervousness.

After being shown to our table, I looked around, taking in the romantic ambiance. Candles provided additional lighting to the clothed tables in the dimly lit room. Hushed conversations were a low murmur, barely audible over quiet jazz emulating from discreetly placed speakers. "This is a really nice place."

Keeping his eyes on me, Eli agreed, "Yeah, it is. And the food is excellent. It's worth the drive."

I hope so, since it took us forty-five minutes to get here!

"I bet you take all your dates here," I teased.

For the first time since I'd met him, Eli's face fell. His expression reminded me of a deer in the headlights.

I laughed. "I'm kidding, Eli. I don't care if you have. It's not like I think you've never been on a date before."

He laughed nervously while looking relieved. The server came to take our drink orders, so that was the end of that conversation.

While we waited for our food, Eli made an unexpected confession. "I've actually wanted to ask you out since last year, but I never got the opportunity."

With bulging eyes, I squeaked, "What?"

Adorably, Eli had a little trouble meeting my eyes while he explained, "Yeah, I saw you around campus sometimes."

"Are you sure it was me?"

"Yeah, definitely you. You're hard to miss. And you're harder to forget." Eli's face turned a little pink. I was glad I wasn't the only one blushing at that moment. Sheepishly, he said, "Wow, that sounded kind of cheesy, didn't it?"

I giggled. I'd noticed that during our brief acquaintance, he easily made me laugh. *Sweet, but still no butterflies.*

"Anyway," he went on, "I saw you around campus but never anywhere else. Like never at Smythie's or the cafeteria or campus stores. I felt weird walking up to you randomly on campus so—"

"But isn't that what you ended up doing?" I ribbed.

He laughed. "Yes, but that's because I swore to myself that if I saw you this year, I was going to talk to you." He gave me a sly grin. "If I had known you were friends with Tina, I would've asked her to introduce us sooner."

It was my turn to no longer be able to meet his eye.

"Tina said you didn't go out much last year. Why is that?" he asked, with genuine interest.

"Oh, I guess I'm a bit of a homebody," I lied, not about to go into details on a first date.

"I'm glad you decided to show your pretty face out and about more." As soon as that left his lips, he looked horrified. "Oh God! Why do I sound so cheesy tonight?"

I chuckled. His laugh was more self-deprecating. Rubbing the back of his neck, he said, "I guess you have that effect on me." He slapped his forehead. "Jesus Christ, I did it again." Folding his hands in front of him, he advised, "I'm going to stop talking now."

His self-effacing behavior was cracking me up. Tears squeezed out of my eyes as I held my hands over my mouth, desperately trying not to disturb the other diners with my laughter. It took a good minute to regain my ability to speak. Thankfully, Eli was humble enough to laugh at himself too.

Deciding I should take the pressure off him, I asked, "Are you a senior?"

His lips twisted in thought. "You could call me a super senior." Seeing my scrunched forehead, he explained, "I'm in my fifth year. I'm doing a five-year accelerated accounting and CPA program."

Wow, another good-looking nerd. Unfortunately, still no heart flutters with this one, but I was positive they'd come with time.

"I heard from Tina that you're a senior. What's your major?" Eli inquired.

I smiled to myself, anticipating his reaction. "Criminal justice. I want to be a cop."

I giggled at his surprised expression.

After a few seconds, Eli cleared his throat. "Really? I didn't expect that." Maybe thinking he'd offended me, he joked, "Baby, you can cuff me whenever you want." Water almost came out of my nose as he winked. Holding up a finger, he assured me, "That one was on purpose."

After catching our breaths from our laughing fits, Eli looked thoughtful.

"What?" I asked.

"I'm surprised. You seem pretty shy."

I almost snorted. "I'm not really shy, quiet maybe."

"Hmm."

Our meals arrived, but our conversation didn't end. We discussed a variety of topics while we ate, subjects that I imagined were typical for first dates. Eventually, our discussion moved on to our families, which I supposed was natural. He was the youngest of four with two older brothers and one older sister. His parents were still married, and they'd provided a fantastic childhood.

"Do you have any siblings?" Eli asked in ignorant bliss.

I knew it was coming, but I still wished it wouldn't. The question I dreaded and one reason I had a hard time getting to know new people. I didn't want to explain. It was an innocent question, and I tried not to blame the people who asked since they didn't know. They had no idea the pain they were causing. But there it was, ringing in my ears.

I looked away. "No."

Eli noticed the shift in my demeanor, and a look of concern crossed his face.

Cheerfully, I changed the subject, "Hey, want to get dessert? I saw some that looked good being delivered to other tables."

Straight-faced, Eli said, "But I thought you were dessert?"

That time, water did come out of my nose. After Eli helped me clean up, he said mischievously, "You do realize I'm going to try to say as many cheesy lines as possible from now on, right?"

Giggling, I gave him a condition. "As long as you bring some wine with that cheese."

Eli pressed his lips together and held up a finger while he composed himself. When he could open his mouth without laughing, he noted, "They have a lovely cheese plate on the dessert menu. Shall we get it?"

We giggled throughout our remaining time at the restaurant, and it felt good. When we first got into his car to head back toward campus, I had been a little worried about questions he might ask on the way, but thankfully he stuck with surface-level topics, like favorite vacations, flavors, pets, and music. When he learned rock was my jam, he teased me for staying home and missing an entire year of listening to rock songs every Friday night at Smythie's.

As soon as we turned onto my street, I saw Jax's SUV parked in front of Chuck's. *God! Why is that man everywhere?* While I was enjoying my time with Eli, I had almost forgotten about him—almost. Last year, I'd never come across Jax. Now I couldn't get away from him! That wouldn't have been an issue if I didn't like him, but I did, so it was driving me a little bonkers.

Eli parked in front of my house then came around to open the passenger door for me. Holding out his hand, I took it as he helped me out. I thanked him for dinner and let him know I had a great time as he walked me to the front door, because it was true. When we reached the front door, Eli gave me another kiss on the cheek.

After he pulled away, I told him, "I told you I'm not shy."

Confusion crossed his face right before I kissed him. His surprise immediately turned into enthusiasm. Putting his hands on my hips, he gently pulled me closer. Eli was a decent kisser. I hadn't kissed anyone in years and hadn't realized until that moment how much I'd missed kissing. It was nice. But kissing Eli, that was all it was. My pulse stayed steady. There were no flutters in my chest. No heat coursed through my veins.

Begging my body to react, I kept kissing him, but it didn't. It was just nice. Guiltily, I compared it to evaluating a hat in the store. *Nice hat, I think I'll try it.*

But I wasn't about to give up, still convinced passion and butter-flies and all that would develop over time. The one actual relationship I'd had was during my moody, angsty, hormonal teenage years. There were fireworks, but in hindsight I didn't think our explosive relation-ship was a particularly healthy one. So for all I knew, relationships that started off with fiery passion, lust and crazy chemistry turned volatile, and relationships that built up gradually were more likely to succeed.

More determined than ever to give Eli a real chance, I ignored the guy standing on the steps of the next house over, watching us.

chapter
seventeen

JAXON

STEPPING out Chuck's front door, I saw Eli's car at the curb in front of Tess's house. Instinctively, I looked at her front door and instantly regretted it. Tess was on her front steps with Eli...kissing. No, kissing was too tame for what they were doing since it looked like they were playing a game of who could lick the other person's tonsils first. *Come on, Tess, you can do better than fucking Eli!*

Shaking my head, I headed to my car, not interested in seeing... that. After turning over the engine, I checked my mirrors to pull out but caught them in my rearview, still making out. A strange and uncomfortable feeling developed in my gut. It got worse as I drove back home. I hated seeing Tess with Eli, but wasn't sure why. I huffed in frustration.

Why the fuck should I care?

Maybe it bothered me because Tess was my friend, and Eli was an ex of Brooke's, kind of. Although he was a year older than her, Eli and Brooke had grown up together. Early in their teenage years, they'd had a short-lived thing. From what I knew about him, Eli wasn't a bad guy, but I didn't like Tess playing tonsil hockey with him, or playing with him at all.

I sighed. *Tess...* She looked gorgeous. A halo from the porch light surrounded her head, like she was a deity. *A fucking goddess!* Even with the distance between her front steps and Chuck's, I could tell she'd taken the time to style her hair for their date. She'd probably taken extra care with her makeup too, not that she needed any. In fact, she was so naturally beautiful that I thought she looked better without it. If she had something covering her face, how would I see when she blushed? Pink-tinted skin looked good on her, and I'd bet a full-body flush on her would be—I gripped the steering wheel, trying to get my thoughts under control.

It didn't work. My eyes, of their own volition, had canvassed her body, and I knew her dress was on another level. *God, that fucking dress!* It was short, hugged her curves, and damn near made my tight jeans very uncomfortable. *Dammit!* I couldn't get the sight of her perfectly shaped backside out of my head.

Fucking great! I was going to walk into the apartment with a boner. At least Brooke could take care of that for me. She knew how to satisfy me. I smiled at the thought. Yeah, Brooke and I might've had our issues, but she could be very affectionate and giving, especially in bed.

STARING AT THE CEILING, I still couldn't get Tess out of my head.

Why am I still thinking about her? Dumb question. I knew what the pit in my stomach was. But it didn't make sense! Why the hell would I be jealous of fucking Eli? For a fraction of a second, a reason flashed through my brain. *No!* It couldn't be that. It was only because I didn't like Eli. *That's it, nothing else.*

Closing my eyes, I focused on Brooke and what she was doing. The feel of her wet mouth and tongue... An image of Tess's tongue tangoing with that guy's broke into my mind. *Fuuuuck!*

"Umm, Jax?" I looked down at my girlfriend. She was holding my half-hard dick. She gave a pointed glance at it then looked back at me. "What the hell?"

My head flopped back onto the pillow as I rubbed my eyes. "Sorry, I guess I'm tired." *Tired...there's that word again.*

"Seriously? You're only twenty-one. Aren't you a little young to be having this issue? Is there something wrong with you? Do you need medicine or something? I can buy you some medicine if you need it. Is this why you've barely touched me the last few weeks?"

And down the rest went, completely deflated with zero chance of going back up. I got up from the bed. "I'm going to shower."

"Hey!" Brooke yelled as she jumped off the bed directly into my path. "Are you seriously going to go jerk off in the shower instead of fucking me?"

Rubbing my forehead, I answered honestly, "No, I'm not. I'm tired. I want to shower and then go to sleep. You can sit in the bathroom and watch me if you don't believe me."

I pushed past her and ignored it when she shouted, "Some man you are!"

Thankfully, she never came into the bathroom. I hadn't really wanted her in there, but I really didn't want another argument to escalate. I was so tired of the constant fighting.

Staying under the hot stream for longer than my normal showers, I hoped Brooke would be asleep when I got out.

SHE WASN'T SLEEPING. Although she was lying in bed with her eyes closed, she was on her back, and she rarely slept on her back. Still, I pretended not to notice, getting into bed as gently as possible. Not wanting to face her or have her come over to cuddle, I rolled onto my side with my back to her.

Her voice broke the dark silence of the room. "Sorry, Jax. I'm just frustrated."

I knew the reason but asked anyway, "Why are you frustrated?"

"You've barely touched me in weeks. I was so excited when you came home all horny. Do you know when the last time we had sex was?"

"No." That was a lie. It'd been nearly a month, which for us may as well have been forever ago. It was the day I'd met Tess, an hour or so before actually. Brooke and I had gotten into another huge fight about God only knew what, then we had a quick, anger-filled romp. Instead of feeling satisfied afterward, I'd felt...weary. Maybe the fact that I had little desire for my girlfriend should've clued me in, but any time something started bubbling to the surface, I pushed it down.

"Neither do I," Brooke whined. "That's the problem!"

Not interested in another argument, I stayed quiet, even catching myself before I sighed too loudly. Several seconds of nothingness passed before Brooke huffed. The bed moved, and without looking I knew she had become a mirror of my position.

We were in trouble. Things had been bad for months, but I didn't know how to fix it. It was so exhausting to even try, since it felt one-sided. But the thought of leaving had never been a consideration, because if it weren't for my Rook, I'd be rotting away with the others.

A SMILING Tess sat down and pulled out her notebook and textbook. "Good morning, Jax!"

Wonder what's got you so fucking cheerful. I hoped it wasn't because of that fucker. It'd been three days since I'd seen her and Eli playing tongue twister, and the memory still gutted me.

Glancing at the clock, I noted she was earlier than normal. "Morning, Tessa." I tried to smile back.

Had her face frozen for a split second before she beamed at me?

"You and Eli, huh?" Clamping my mouth shut, I wished I could take back the question as soon as it left my mouth.

Suddenly occupied with examining her notebook, she shrugged. "I heard he's a nice guy, and he asked me out, so why not?"

Why not? Why not! I'll tell you why not! But I didn't and wouldn't. Her personal life had nothing to do with me.

Tess hesitated. "I heard he's actually an ex of Brooke's."

I snorted. "Hardly."

Her facial features bunched as she tried figuring out what I meant.

I rolled my eyes. "Their parents are friends. Brooke and Eli grew up together. They went to the same private boarding high school and screwed around a bit. From what Brooke told me, you couldn't even call it puppy love." I tried sounding as nonchalant as possible, but I hated Eli. He'd taken my girlfriend's virginity like it was no big deal, so he'd always be a complete douche in my mind. And now he was trying to fuck Tess! I couldn't explain it, but I really hated that thought. *Fucking horny bastard!*

I squirmed in my chair as my conscience reminded me that I was no better than him when it came to sleeping around, more than likely worse. Or at least that was how I used to be.

Tess's keen eyes were inspecting me. Feeling bitter and uncaring about anything at that moment, I stared right back. Blushing, she looked away and busied herself with her cell phone. When I realized I was grinding my teeth, I forced myself to relax and wiggled my jaw. At the rate I'd been grinding my teeth of late, my jaw would start locking up. Maybe she'd noticed my tension. I got the impression Tess was more observant than most.

Absently playing with my pencil, I noted, "You left the bar early on Friday."

I felt Tess's stillness before she went back to fooling with her phone. "Oh, you noticed?"

Of course I did. And you know it. You literally looked at me when you were leaving.

I decided to play along. "Yeah, I happened to notice when you were leaving. I'm always keeping on eye the crowd when I'm on stage. I like to know what's going on around the bar."

"Ah."

"So…" I hesitated, still not sure why I gave a shit. "Was everything okay? I thought you were going to stay for the first set."

She shrugged. "I was tired." A second or two passed, then she said under her breath, "Actually tired." It was confirmation that she knew that when I said I was tired, I wasn't talking about a lack of sleep. *As I thought, observant.*

chapter
eighteen

TESSA

THE FIRST MONTH of school was over in a blink. Between classes and school work, soccer practice and games, spending time with Eli and studying with Jax, there was more than enough to keep me busy. I'd missed one Wednesday session with Jax and one Friday night at Smythie's because of soccer. Eli and I had gone on several more dates, but we spent most of our time together at my house with Tina as a third wheel.

Honestly, it was too fun being around other people. Since our first date, Eli and I had an ongoing competition of who could say the cheesiest thing. We'd say our cringey lines in front of others like we seriously meant every word and watch their reactions, doubling over in stitches at some of them. Tina eventually caught on and would roll her eyes before joining in on our laughter.

However, it'd be a lie if I said I wasn't purposely avoiding being alone with him as much as possible. Sure, we'd had some intense make-out sessions with some light petting, and it was clear he'd go as far as I'd let him, but I wasn't there yet. The heart palpitations and urgent, needy desire to be with him weren't there. So I'd wait, sure undeniable and desperate lust would come eventually.

There was another reason I avoided being alone with him. If it was only the two of us, there'd be more opportunities for Eli to ask the questions I was desperate to avoid. He probably wasn't trying to pry, but it felt like he was. Occasionally, I had to dance my way around answering some of his questions, like, besides soccer, what else did I do for fun when I was growing up, and what was it like growing up as an only child? Things I wasn't ready to talk about with him.

With Jax, it was never like that. When he and I spoke before class and on Wednesdays, the conversations flowed naturally. If anything, I was too open with him. Thankfully, we hadn't gotten into anything too deep, so it never felt like Jax was being intrusive. After a month of knowing both of them, it felt like I knew Jax better than the guy I was dating, and that he knew me better than Eli. Sure, Eli cracked me up often, but Jax not only made me laugh, he was so easy to talk to. Humor was important in a relationship, but you had to be able to talk effortlessly too, right?

Jax knew more about my relationship with Tina than Eli. When I told him about it, how she and I had grown up together and had been inseparable since kindergarten, he told me it was the same with him and his other best friend, Ashton, except he'd met Ashton in preschool. During our conversations, I realized Jax and I had more in common than I had with Eli.

While Eli and I liked the same types of movies and TV shows, Jax and I shared a variety of interests. We liked true crime documentary series, the same cuisine, and travel. We both hated snow and loved summers, beaches, and boardwalks where we could play arcade games. And of course there was music. Eli liked live music, but he wasn't specifically a fan of rock or metal. Jax not only loved rock and metal but was a singer in a rock band. I loved the music Jax loved.

His devotion to being in a band was a lot more than I had thought. I assumed he only learned the songs and sang. But there was more to it. Chuck's garage, which was insulated to not disturb the neighbors, served as not only their place to practice but also a recording studio. The band recorded their own backtracks with instruments they couldn't play while on stage. The DJ from Smythie's, Donald Jones, nicknamed D.J.—yes, D.J. the DJ—helped the band with recording. He was basically a sixth band member in charge of playing the backtracks and making sure they kept time with the band. When Jax told me about the band's rehearsals, I wanted to ask him if I could come watch sometime since I was right next door, but I thought that'd be too presumptuous, so I kept mum.

One time when Jax and I had been talking, there would've been a perfect segue into asking about family, but as I held my breath, waiting for the inevitable question, he moved on, passing right over the chance to ask the dreaded question. He not only did not ask about my family, he never mentioned his either, except for that one time he'd mentioned his older brother. There was something about his avoidance of the topic that felt familiar, but I hoped I was imagining it.

PUTTING my completed statistics homework into my book bag, I felt proud. I was finally starting to get it, and I'd flown through the assignment this week with minimal help from Jax. When I turned to say goodnight to him, he was leaning on his elbow, which was perched on the table, watching me, his pointer finger rubbing his lower lip. Not that I minded, but Jax didn't normally stare like that.

Glancing around, I asked, "What?"

Slowly, he asked, "Remember how I said I watch the crowd when I'm on stage?"

"Yeah."

"I do that because I want to gauge the crowd's reactions. Do they like the songs we play? Do they know the songs and are singing along? Are they enjoying the show as a whole? What's the atmosphere like around the bar? Do we need to change our performance up or learn new songs? Stuff like that." He hesitated. "I think you know this, but I see you a lot. You dance and sing along a lot."

Chuckling, I confirmed, "Yeah, I do. I know pretty much all the songs I've heard you guys play."

"What's your favorite?"

I bit my lip. "Hmm. Favorite song that I've heard you guys play, or my favorite song in general?"

"Both."

For my favorite song they'd played, I named a song about toxic relationships where the singer both loves and hates someone at the same time. As far as my all-time favorite song, I gave him the band, then the song's name, "Stardust."

"I know that one."

"You do? Isn't the beat so catchy? Turn up the bass and it hits you in the chest. I love when I can feel the music!" Hopeful, I asked, "Have you guys played it before?"

He looked away. "No, we haven't."

Shrugging like it didn't matter, I hoped he didn't hear the disappointment in my voice. "Oh."

Jax turned back toward me, eyeing me curiously. He remarked, "I'm kind of surprised. Isn't that song a little...vulgar?"

"That's one way of interpreting it, but I think it's kind of romantic," I said dreamily. "The singer can see how in love the other person is through their eyes, and in the singer's eyes, the person is perfect. But that's the great thing about music, isn't it?"

"What is?" he asked, a smile on his lips.

"That songs can mean different things to different people." I looked away, seeing the metaphorical forest, not just the trees. "One person can relate a specific song to their own situation in life, while another hears the same song but differently and relates it to their life, which could be completely different than the first person's life. Yet the artist who actually wrote the lyrics could've had an entirely different meaning!"

Hearing the excitement in my voice, I paused to bring it down a notch. "Speaking of song lyrics, what a great way to send a message, huh?" I laughed to myself. "It's like texting. Sometimes it's easier to say something through a text or in a song than face-to-face. If I had any skill for it, I'd be a songwriter, but I have zero musical prowess."

Jax appeared content in listening to my blabbering, so I went on, "I one-hundred percent believe that with well-written lyrics and music, a person can truly express themselves. Music lets you feel emotions you aren't actually experiencing at that moment. Angry music can make you feel anger even if you aren't. With sad music, you can feel the sorrow even though you yourself have nothing to be sorrowful about. Happy music can make you feel good even if you are anything but. And so on."

My eyes wandered around the room while my mind went to a faraway place, getting lost in the memories of how music had helped me cope over the last few years.

Blinking, I came back to the present. Wondering if I had sounded stupid or maybe completely insane, I chewed on my lower lip and peered over at Jax. I didn't know what I'd been expecting, but what I saw was certainly not it. Turning my body toward him, I got a better look.

It may have been the reflection from the lamp in the center of the table, but there was something in Jax's eyes I'd never seen. It reminded me of moonlight shimmering on the surface of the ocean at night. The sight was breathtakingly beautiful.

The air stilled, and time seemed to stop as we searched each other's eyes, trying to take a peek into the other's soul.

My phone vibrated on the table, and I jumped, breaking our eye contact. After checking the text that popped up, I looked back at Jax. He hadn't moved, but his eyes were back to normal, dim, like a dark cloud blocking out the moonlight.

Breaking the silence, I asked, "So what are the other band members' names? I know you and Chuck. I've met Ashton. Who's the drummer and other guitarist?"

"Ryan is the drummer. He's a long-time friend of Chuck's. Honestly, I don't know him that well. He's not even a student here but plays with us on Friday nights. He's got a full-time job as a mechanic. The guitarist is Randy. He's a family friend of Ryan's. He's a few years older than the rest of us with a wife and kid. He's a biology teacher."

"Really?" The guy had long hair and looked like a complete metal head. His arms were covered in tattoos, but I guess he could hide them at work if needed, or maybe the administration at his school didn't care.

Jax chuckled and nodded.

"How long have you known Chuck?"

"We met freshman year at the bar. When he found out I was making a band, he tried out. We've gotten pretty close over the last couple of years."

"When you and Chuck sing screaming lyrics, doesn't that hurt your voices? Do you ever lose it?"

The corners of Jax's mouth lifted as his eyes started shimmering again, his face transforming in front of me. He still hadn't moved from his position of leaning on the table and resting his head on his closed hand. "You're curious tonight."

I adverted my eyes. "Oh, sorry. I wasn't trying to—"

"I didn't say I had a problem with it," he interjected. "You usually don't ask so many questions, that's all."

I looked down, having crossed some line by asking so many non-school related questions. "I'm sorry. I'll stop."

"Yes, I've lost my voice before, but depending on what kind of screaming we need to do or how much of it, Chuck and I sometimes use voice distorters to prevent our voices from getting strained. There's a technique to screaming-singing, if that's what you want to call it, but I don't do it that often. Singing rock for ninety minutes alone, even with a break in the middle, can strain my voice if I'm not careful. Although, if I'm really into the music, I might forget or purposely skip the distorter."

I kept my eyes down. After a beat of silence, he reassured me, "I really don't mind answering your questions, Tessa, especially if it's about the band. Don't worry about it."

Like a reflex, my head snapped over to him at the sound of my name on his lips. I hoped I looked calm on the outside, because on the inside, every time he said "Tessa," my blood sang as it raced through my veins. After a few seconds, I forcefully tore away from his gaze and dug into my bag, looking for nothing in particular.

"You didn't rent that house next to Chuck's last year, right?" Jax asked.

"Right," I said as I continued to search for God only knew what in my bag. "I was in the dorms last year, and Tina had another roommate somewhere else."

"Ah, that might explain it."

"Hmm? Explain what?" I asked as I casually pulled out some lip balm and swiped it over my lips.

"The dorms are all the way on the other side of campus. I rarely go over there. I would've remembered if I'd seen you before."

I snorted. "Yeah, sure."

"I don't forget pretty faces."

Searching in my bag again, I let my hair fall in front of my face to hide my flaming cheeks. I tried to take a deep, calming, quiet inhale, but it felt like I couldn't fill my lungs.

"Sorry! I... I meant—" He stopped and took a breath. I peeked at him through my dangling hair. He'd sat up straight. "I'm a guy. I notice pretty girls."

Giving up on trying to find something else to distract me, I put my bag back down and turned to him, hoping my cheeks had cooled enough not to be noticeable.

A mischievous smile formed on his lips as he tapped his chin in fake contemplation. "Wait a second, we never went over your qualities."

Confused, I asked, "Huh? What qualities?"

"You ticked off a list of my attributes," he teased. "What about you? One of them is that you're beautiful."

I rolled my eyes. "You said pretty. And thank you." I was proud of myself for sounding so cool about getting such a compliment from the guy who'd created a butterfly conservatory in my soul.

"I meant to say beautiful."

Oh, God... It was like my stomach was doing an infinite loop of flips in time with the flutters in my chest. He'd said it so seriously that there was no doubt he wasn't teasing. I reached for my water bottle and took a large gulp, thankful it was still cold.

Jax counted off on his fingers. "You're an outstanding soccer player, I think."

I glanced at him briefly with a small smile before mumbling, "Thanks."

"Let's see. What else..."

"We don't have to do this," I practically gasped between swallows of water.

He ignored my protest. "Oh, yeah, you want to be a cop." A corner of his mouth went up, his eyes danced, and his voice changed like he was genuinely impressed. "That's pretty badass, Tess."

I chuckled despite myself. Resisting the temptation to brag a little, I could have mentioned that I was a very good shot with a handgun.

Jax continued, "You're smart—"

I rolled my eyes. "Says the freakin' genius who does math for fun," I spit the word math out like it was dirty.

Jax, still with that sexy-as-hell half smile on his face, said, "Even if math isn't your strong suit, that doesn't mean you're not smart. I can tell you are from our conversations over the last few weeks." He paused. "That reminds me. Why were you so hesitant to accept my help? After our first class, you seemed relieved when I said I could help you, but then you didn't come to the library and seemed reluctant the second day of class."

Trying to buy more time before I responded, I cleared my throat then sipped more water. I wasn't sure what I should tell him. Should I tell him I was afraid to make an enemy out of his girlfriend? That, although she hadn't said anything directly, she'd made it clear the day we met she wanted me to stay away from him? Or that even now I was still a little nervous about it since she'd given me more than a few death glares over the last few weeks?

"You're taking too long to answer," he pointed out. "That means you don't want to tell me. So now I really want to know."

I took a deep breath. Avoiding eye contact, I mumbled, "I guess I was a bit concerned about what others might think."

"What? Who?" he asked like that was the silliest notion ever. "We have a class together and we're doing schoolwork in a library."

I swallowed again before answering. Staring at my hands, I whispered, "Brooke. I was worried about Brooke."

He took a moment to think. "But when we first discussed it, even though you hadn't met her yet, you knew who she was," he reasoned, likely remembering how I knew her name even though he'd never mentioned her. "So what changed?" Was there a tinge of suspicion in his voice?

Not sure what to say, I avoided his gaze as I inhaled deeply, one of those deep breaths where your whole upper body moved.

"Did she say something to you?" Jax quietly asked.

"Not exactly. I've only ever spoken to her twice, and you were there both times. I guess you can call it women's intuition. She doesn't want me hanging around you, even if it's to study." I shrugged. "Honestly, I can't blame her. I'd probably be possessive of my boyfriend too."

Jax looked away as he gnawed on his lip. He remained quiet for several seconds. "Don't worry about her. I've talked to her about it, and she says she's fine with it. Brooke is...kind of protective of me."

Ha! Is that what you call it?

Since his girlfriend had entered our conversation, I suddenly felt the urgent need to get out of there. I wished Jax a hurried goodnight and left.

chapter
nineteen

JAXON

NOT WANTING to wake Brooke if she was sleeping, I turned the key in the lock and opened the front door as quietly as possible. Unfortunately, she was there to greet me with fire in her eyes, ready to pounce. I hadn't even taken my shoes off before the interrogation started.

"It's nearly midnight! Where were you? Did your simple little friend need extra help today or something? Have you been with her this whole time? What the hell were you two doing?"

Setting my bag down, I kept my voice neutral, "She's not stupid. And we finished about the same time we always do." It wasn't a lie. We had finished the same time we always did, but then we stayed another hour chatting. But I still hadn't come home right away.

Brooke jumped up from where she was perched on the couch and, in a decibel short of a scream, exclaimed, "Then where were you?"

Kicking off my shoes, I told her the truth, "I was with Ashton. We got dinner at the diner."

"Why didn't you tell me?"

"I did, right before I left."

"No, you didn't," she said haughtily.

Then I guess you weren't paying attention. Wasn't the first time, nor would it be the last. Sometimes it felt like I was talking to a wall.

Her demeanor changed. "I'm sorry for yelling, Jaxy. I was worried."

Then you should have called or texted, I shouted in my head.

Brooke walked over and started drawing circles on my abdomen. In her babyish tone, she admonished, "You could've at least sent me a text letting me know when you were going to be home." Wrapping her arms around my waist, she leaned closer and whispered, "I've been waiting for you." Standing on her toes, she puckered up.

Walking out of her embrace, I went to the couch and plopped down.

Turning to face me, Brooke stomped. "What's your problem?"

Stomping, Brooke? Are you five? "That's what I'd like to ask you," I muttered as I inspected the chessboard on the coffee table.

"Excuse me?"

I let out a heavy sigh and leaned back into the couch, not in the mood to play her metaphorical or literal games. Rubbing my forehead, I asked, "Did you say something to Tess? About us studying together?"

Brooke made a disgusted face at Tess's name. "No, I haven't spoken to her in weeks. And you were there."

I exhaled loudly.

"What?" she asked with an attitude.

"Somehow, Tess got the impression you have an issue with her and I studying together." Brooke gave me a look of disbelief, but I didn't give her a chance to whine again. "It must've been from all the dirty looks you've been giving her over the last few weeks."

"What? Did she tell you I've been giving her dirty looks? That's a bunch of bullshit."

"No, she didn't tell me. But it's clear she thinks you have an issue with me helping her. So where do you think she got that impression from?"

"How the fuck should I know?"

"I've seen the looks, Brooke. The first time you met her, the library, and all the times at the bar."

Laughing, Brooke said, "You're seeing things. I've barely looked at her at all, let alone given her a dirty look. And I don't give a shit if you study together. I know you like tutoring people so you can put it in your law school applications. Besides, you're mine."

"I'm not a possession," I said, bored. I didn't correct her assumption that helping Tess would count as something I could include in law school applications. When I'd tutored in the past at the student center, where it was official, sure. But casual studying together didn't count.

Brooke rolled her eyes. "God! You know what I mean." Her eyes narrowed. "But this makes me wonder. What put these thoughts in your head? Could it be that maybe you're thinking something you shouldn't be? You know, like having a guilty mind about something?"

"What? No, I've seen the looks."

"Whatever, Jax," she huffed. "You're imagining things, but believe whatever you want."

I had seen dirty looks directed at Tess, right? There must've been at least that first one after they met, because otherwise how would Tess's mind change about studying together so rapidly? Or had I imagined it, and Tess only changed her mind when she met Brooke? Maybe she wasn't sure if I had a girlfriend but heard I might. But who would've told her I might've had a girlfriend when Brooke and I had been together for years? I didn't want to believe my girl was lying to me, but something did happen that affected Tess's decision. Also, I had twenty-twenty vision. I seriously doubted my eyes were lying. *Dammit!* None of it was making sense!

Brooke sauntered over then bent down in front of me, giving me a clear shot of her boobs through the loose neckline of my t-shirt she was wearing. She wasn't wearing a bra. Peering at me with her horny eyes, she purred, "Since that's out of the way, how about you come to bed with me?" Wrapping her arms around my neck, she crawled into my lap. "As I said, I've been waiting for you. I'm a bit riled up and need you to help me relax."

I let her kiss me. It had been a while, and maybe I had been neglecting her, so no wonder she was mad when I got home. And maybe she hadn't been sneering at Tess. After all, she denied it, and Tess never told me she saw the looks. She called it women's intuition. Maybe Tess assumed Brooke would have a problem with it, like she admitted she probably would have. *Hmm...* was Tess the possessive girlfriend type? Even if she was, I couldn't imagine she'd be like Brooke.

A moan from Brooke as she ground into my erection through my pants pulled me back to her. Scoping up my cute little redhead, I carried her to bed, giving her the attention she was craving.

"HEY, GUYS," I greeted my bandmates like I wasn't a half hour late. "Have you had a chance to look at the new song?"

"Thanks for joining us...for the rehearsal you requested on a freakin' Sunday morning!" Chuck said sarcastically.

"Uhhh... sorry. Brooke needed my help with something."

Chucked walked away muttering, "Yeah, sure, help coming, you mean."

I ignored him, especially since that was definitely not it. We had fought again, because what the fuck else was new? This time, it was about moving to New York City after graduation. My response was equivalent to, "Fuck that." Needless to say, that hadn't gone down well.

Pushing the last hour of headache-inducing aggravation aside, I asked, "So, the new song, what do you think?"

They all liked it and had even learned all their parts already.

Stepping up to my mic, I said, "Great, let's try it."

Before Ryan could count off, Ashton asked, "Where'd you get the idea for this song?"

I shrugged. "A friend."

Ashton, who knew me too well, pressed, "Which friend?"

"Uh..." I cleared my throat. "Tess."

Ryan, who rarely spoke much, piped in, "Oh God, you gonna talk about her again? If I didn't know better, I'd think she was your girl-friend, not Brooke."

I felt the color drain from my face. Was that true? Did I really talk about Tess that much? Trying to play dumb, I said, "I don't know what you're talking about. We've played songs for our friends before so..."

None of them responded. They all stared but with differing expres-sions. Ryan looked bored, Randy rolled his eyes, Ashton was annoyed, and Chuck appeared smug. I held out my hands as if to say, "What?"

Chuck was the first to speak. "Why do you think I gave up on Tess so easily?"

I looked around the makeshift studio like it'd give me a clue. "Because she's dating Eli?"

Chuck snorted. "Nah, dude. Bros before hos."

Having no idea what to make of that, I kept my mouth shut. Thankfully, Randy got us back on track. "Can we play now? I gotta go grade some tests."

I took my mic off the stand as Chuck slung his bass strap over his shoulder. Ashton, who'd already been holding his guitar, walked over. In a low voice only I could hear, he asked, "Jax, seriously, what's going on with Tess? People are talking."

They are? Who? Talking about what? Was that the reason Brooke was so aggravated lately? I'd have to be more careful. I responded to Ashton with the truth, "She's my friend. That's it. And it's not like Brooke doesn't know what's going on. Brooke's told me more than once she doesn't give a shit, so why should you or anyone else?" The last part came out harsher than I intended, but I used up all my giving a fuck's for the day already.

Ashton didn't look convinced but dropped it and walked back over to his place. Counting off, Ryan banged his drumsticks together, then the notes of "Stardust" filled the garage.

chapter
twenty

TESSA

FOR ONLY THE SECOND TIME, I was able to stay for both of the band's sets. Due to the size of the crowd, Eli, Tina, Jamar and I were near the back, unable to get any closer to the stage. Since I hadn't been able to see the second set since my first visit to Smythie's, I had no idea how much the place filled up later into the night.

A couple of minutes earlier, the club music had faded, triggering the mass of bodies to migrate from the dance floor and bar to the stage. Normally there wasn't much of a lag between the music fading and the band starting, but nothing was happening yet. The four of us were conversing when I glanced toward the stage to see what the holdup was.

All five band members were in place, but Jax had his hands up, shielding his eyes from the lights. I was surprised since he'd mentioned that he could usually see most of the crowd, but while scanning the room, there was something or someone he couldn't see. Other spectators noticed the delay, and some even started looking around too, not that they knew what he was searching for. After several more seconds, Jax made a hand gesture. The lights adjusted, making the large room slightly lighter, and Jax looked around again. Our eyes met for a moment before he signaled again, and the lights faded back to their normal band-on-stage setting.

Lifting his mic to his lips, Jax said, "Hey, Ryan, do me a favor and turn up your bass drum mic. Chuck, turn your bass up too. I want everyone here to feel this next song reverberating in their chests."

As the first drumstick hit, a memory flashed in my brain. Jax and I were in the library the week before. I'd made a similar comment to him. A heavy drum and guitar started, and the atmosphere in the bar changed in just a couple of notes. There was a tangible charge in the room as the heavy beats shook the floor. I gaped at the stage, wondering if I was actually hearing correctly or if my ears were playing tricks on me.

Jax was watching me. He winked. The half-smile on his face and laughter in his eyes told me he enjoyed my reaction. When I recovered from the surprise, nothing could've stopped the face-splitting smile hurting my cheeks. I was so happy—no, I was euphoric! So much so that I thought I might cry. The band was playing "Stardust!"A song they'd never played before. And they were playing it for me. No, Jax was singing it for me! He must've had them learn it in the week and a half since he'd asked me.

More excited than I'd been in ages, I threw my hands in the air, dancing to the beat and singing at the top of my lungs. Jax smiled as he sang, his eyes never wandering too far away from mine.

Maybe I should've seen it coming, but I hadn't. The day before in class, he'd been curious if I was planning on coming to the bar. When I confirmed I was not only coming but was going to be able to stay for both sets, he gave me two neon-pink wristbands for tonight. One for me, and one for Tina. The wristbands were given to anyone twenty-one and over after they paid the cover charge. If you already had the correct color band, you got in for free. To avoid people trying to game the system, the color changed randomly every week.

I hadn't commented on the fact that he'd specifically said the second wristband was for Tina, not Eli, but I did laugh to myself. The two didn't seem to like each other.

When the song ended, I turned and grabbed Eli's arm, completely giddy. "That was my favorite song! Wasn't that awesome?"

He nodded and raised his voice as the band started their next song. "Yeah, that was a good one."

I pointed at my mouth. "I need water. You want anything?"

"No. Want me to come?"

I shook my head. "Be right back."

Making my way through the throng of bodies, I felt someone grab my ass. Turning, I expected to see Eli, but he hadn't followed me and was still where I left him, out of reach. His focus wasn't even on me. Was he glaring at the stage? Not sure what to make of it, I turned my attention to the people standing close enough to touch me. No one was looking at me, and I didn't know any of these people, so it wasn't like it was a teammate playing a joke. *Perhaps it was an accident?* Brushing it off, I continued to the bar.

Considering the band was on stage, the bartenders were surprisingly busy, so I had to wait to ask Cory for some water. As I did, I wondered if my over-exuberance at the band playing the song clued Eli in as to how happy Jax had made me? But how would Eli even know Jax had the band learn that song specifically for me? I doubted anyone had told him. But why was Eli glaring up at the stage, or more likely Jax, like that? Was it possible Eli was seeing the thing I was so desperately trying to hide from everyone?

As I mulled it over, the heat of a body invaded my personal space, but I ignored it. After all, tonight's crowd was the largest I'd seen. Stale cigarettes and beer invaded my nostrils as the person next to me asked, "What're you drinking, and can I buy you another one?"

Trying to sound cheerful even as my stomach churned, I said, "No, thanks. My boyfriend already bought me plenty, and I'm done drinking for the night." *Thank goodness for Eli!* He wasn't exactly my boyfriend, but close enough. If I hadn't been dating anyone, I might not have been able to brush the guy off so easily.

Leaning in more than necessary, the person who didn't seem to grasp the concept of personal space said, "Well, come find me when you lose that wimp."

Glancing over my shoulder, I watched the guy get lost in the crowd. He seemed vaguely familiar, but after wracking my brain, I came up empty. With only seeing the back of him, and with the bar's lighting, I couldn't place him. Regardless, even if available, it would've been a hard pass.

Turning my attention back to the stage, I watched the man who, if available, I'd never refuse. As his gaze once again locked with mine, I wondered if he would've given me a chance had he been single.

chapter
twenty-one

JAXON

THE PING of my phone stirred me out of my trance-like state. I'd been in the middle of eating a bowl of cereal when my mind wandered to the night before. Although it attracted the notice of some, I didn't regret giving the signal for the crew to change the lighting so I could find Tess. Seeing her reaction made my night. I wished I'd asked about her favorite song sooner, because her happiness was contagious and intoxicating. It had me smiling for the rest of the night, which made singing the sad and angry songs a bit off, but I didn't give a shit. Nor did I give a shit that Eli looked pissed.

Maybe you should try harder to make her happy, Eli, because it sure doesn't look like you're getting the job done.

I grinned at being the one who made Tess's eyes sparkle last night, not him. She'd given me her full beaming smile that was so rare, not him. Her jubilation as she sang and danced was because of me.

Shifting my weight, my lower half started stirring at the memory of Tess's body moving to the music. Her perfectly sized breasts bounced with her perfect body in the tight-cropped tank top and tiny skirt that accentuated the shape of her perfect ass. I hadn't been able to keep my eyes off her, not when she was on the dance floor, nor when I'd been on stage.

It was wrong, but I couldn't control my thoughts as my imagination took over, picturing what her body looked like under that sexy-as-fuck outfit she'd been wearing. Her everyday clothes were on the conservative side, but she liked running in sports bras and leggings. And the outfits she'd been wearing to the bar had gradually morphed from something for dinner with the parents to more like a temptress capable of seducing anyone she wanted.

What would it feel like with her in my arms, grinding to the heavy beats of the club? Would she let me hold her tightly or keep me at a slight distance like she did with Eli? I'd bet our bodies would fit together nicely both on and off the dance floor...

I stared at my soggy cereal in horror. *What the fuck?* Where did my mind just go? Yeah, Tess was hot as hell, but I could not be thinking about my friend in that way, especially since I had a girlfriend. I must've been thinking with the wrong head, like my dick was protesting about its lack of use over the last few weeks. It'd been what? Twice? Three times at the most? Had I ever had this little sex since I lost my virginity? I didn't think so...but it was so hard to fuck Brooke when we were constantly arguing.

Angry sex got old when it was the only kind you had.

Looking down into my bowl of mush, I wondered how long I'd been daydreaming about my beautiful blue-green-eyed friend. Shaking my head, I tried ridding my mind of the intrusive thoughts.

After dumping the cereal soup, I picked up my phone. Like I hadn't admonished myself a moment before, I smiled when I saw Tessa's name on the screen.

TESS

OMG Jax! Last night was so awesome! Thank you so much!! I loved it so so so much!!

JAX

I'm glad you liked it. It was a fun song, and the crowd seemed to agree. They got pretty into it.

TESS

You seriously made my night! And you never even dropped a hint. I was totally shocked!

JAX

That was the goal.

TESS

Mission accomplished!

Feel free to play that song whenever you feel like it. It'd be a shame to go through the trouble of learning it to only play it once ;-P

JAX

LOL noted

TESS

Have a great weekend! See you Tuesday.

My closed-mouth smile transformed into a wide, toothy one. Tess sounded downright giddy, a rare side of her few people got to witness I suspected.

"What are you smiling at!" Jumping, I nearly dropped my phone at Brooke's accusatory tone.

Tiredly, I looked over at her glaring but still gorgeous face. "A guy joke from Ashton. I don't think you'd appreciate it." Well, that was true about an hour ago.

Disgusted, Brooke sneered, "What? He sending you tit pics or something?"

Rubbing my head, I laughed in disbelief. "No, Brooke. Why would I want to see other girls' boobs when I have yours?" *Your big, fake, unnaturally hard boobs that I'm not actually a fan of.* They were too big for her slight frame. *I wonder what Tessa's feel like? I'd bet every cent I had that hers were real—shit! Not again, you asshole!*

"Then why do you have a boner right now?" Brooke taunted.

Fuck! I was hoping she wouldn't have noticed, but since I was only wearing a pair of old gray sweatpants, it was hard to miss. While not being fully truthful, my response wasn't a lie either, "Gee, I don't know? Maybe because I'm a horny twenty-one-year-old guy?" *Who hasn't been getting much action lately.* Not that I wanted, nor expected, to fuck Brooke at that moment.

I vaguely registered Brooke's voice in the background, but another unwelcome and inappropriate thought overshadowed it in my brain.

"Jaxon!" An object went flying past my head and hit the wall behind me. "Are you even listening to me?" Brooke screamed.

I jumped again. Why was I so jumpy lately? *Probably because of your indecent fantasies, dude,* my conscience thought snarkily.

Wait, had Brooke thrown something at me? I looked down and saw a book on the floor that wasn't there before. Turning, I saw a mark on the wall.

Dumbfounded, I gaped at my enraged girlfriend.

"What?" she bit.

My voice was one notch above a whisper. "Did you just throw a book at me?"

Rolling her eyes, she scoffed, "Please, I wasn't actually aiming for you. You were just completely spaced out and ignoring me."

"And that makes it okay to throw something at another person? Whatever happened to waving your hand in front of their face?"

She shrugged like she couldn't care less, then continued to glower at me.

"What, Brooke?" I asked through my teeth. "I'm not in the mood to play games right now."

"I need to get to my appointment for my portfolio pictures, remember?"

I searched the kitchen, trying to remember if she had actually told me about it. Even if she had, what did it have to do with me? "Okay…"

Stomping her foot, she said, "I need you to take me!"

Stomping again?

Opening the calendar app on my phone, I checked my schedule for today. It was blank other than a reminder for a paper I had to write. "Why do I need to take you? And, no, I don't think you told me about it. I have a report to write, which I'd been planning all week to work on today. If I'd known about your appointment, I would've worked on it yesterday."

Her expression morphed into something that reminded me of an evil schemer. "Well, I did tell you. You either forgot or weren't paying attention. Probably the latter, based on your recent behavior. Anyway,

I need you to take me because I don't want to get all stressed out driving somewhere I've never been to before, right before I get my close-ups." Her face changed again, this time to contempt. "If you need more time to work on your paper, perhaps you shouldn't waste your Wednesdays helping that—" She stopped, probably because of my narrowed eyes. "Perhaps you're spending too much time helping Tess, and it's affecting your own school work. Maybe you should skip your Wednesday session this week to make sure your paper gets done."

Running my finger back and forth across my lower lip, I pretended to contemplate what she'd said. "You're right… I don't want you going to some strange place alone, so I'll drive you to your appointment. But my paper is due Monday, so I guess I'll have to work on it later and tomorrow."

"But we're going to my parents' house tomorrow!"

Did she really not think I didn't know what she was doing? I stared her down. "What a shame. Guess I'll have to skip it."

Stalking out of the kitchen before she could argue more, I headed to the bedroom.

As I got dressed, I wondered, *Was it worth it, Brooke? Now I get to skip going to your parents' tomorrow, and you can drive the entire two hours there and two hours back yourself.*

Fuck, I was tired.

chapter
twenty-two

TESSA

BLOWING OUT A BREATH, I unplugged the curling iron from the wall and reflected. *Another Saturday night, and another date with Eli. And probably another night of turning him down.*

As I put on some pale-pink lip gloss, Tina entered the bathroom and whistled. "Mmm, girl, you look gorgeous!"

Meeting her eyes in the mirror's reflection, I tried to smile. "Thanks."

Her face dropped. "What's wrong?"

I sighed. "I feel like Eli's moving a little fast." Looking away, I added, "He's even starting to throw love around."

Tina's dark eyes grew wide as her mouth popped open.

Holding up my hands, I quickly explained, "He hasn't actually told me he loves me, but he says stuff like, 'I love being with you' or 'I love your sense of humor' or 'I love watching you play soccer.' That sort of thing."

"Awe," Tina cooed. "Sounds like he really likes you. I don't know if him telling you all that is moving too fast. Everyone's different, and every relationship is different. I mean, look at Jamar and I. We've basically been inseparable since we met. I slept with him after meeting him at the bar, before he'd even taken me out on a date. It's like that with some people, but if you aren't there yet, don't worry about it. If he cares about you, he'll wait for you."

"YOU WANT to head back to my place?" Eli suggested a few hours later as we walked together.

Ugh, not again... Although not unexpected, I groaned internally at Eli's obvious desire to get laid. It's not that I didn't want to have sex—it'd been freakin' years—but I was still waiting for those damned butterflies to show up around him, or for him to at least get my blood pumping. It'd been a month, but still there was no desire for him, not even after some heavy petting.

The first sleepover invite came at the end of our third date. Apparently Eli was a three-date rule kind of guy. Me? I didn't care about time, only sparks. And there weren't any when it came to him. It wasn't for the lack of trying either on both our parts. I willed my body to react to his lips and touch, but it didn't. Meanwhile, Eli was a gentleman and had taken me on some very romantic dates.

This evening it'd been a cute and delicious Italian restaurant located in a nice downtown area a couple of towns over. A couple of blocks away from the eatery was a small park with a walking path lit by strings of lights hung from the tree branches above, which was where we were currently strolling hand in hand.

Not even bothering to look at my watch, I commented, "It's getting late..."

Eli shrugged. "Then stay over."

Looking away, I took in a shaky breath before exhaling it slowly.

He went on, "You know I don't have a roommate. I get so lonely sometimes."

Trying to play along, even though I wasn't really in the mood to, I quipped, "Is that the best you can do tonight?"

"Oh, come on. I've had a few good ones. Can't bat a thousand all the time."

Chuckling, I agreed, "True."

Eli gently grabbed my arm to stop me then turned our bodies so we faced each other. "Tess, I really do want you to stay with me tonight. Based on your reluctance, I'm assuming you're not interested in doing anything other than sleeping, which is fine with me. I'm not the kind of guy who's going to push you."

Looking off into the dark distance behind him, I quietly tried to excuse my hesitation, "I'm sorry. We haven't known each other that long...and you're the first guy I've dated in years. You're the first guy I've dated as an adult. I..."

Eli brushed a blowing curl behind my ear and took a step closer. Lowering his voice, he tried reassuring me, "You don't have to explain yourself, and you don't have to be sorry. Do I want to be intimate with you? Of course. I like you and you're gorgeous, but what fun would it be if you weren't into it or stressed out?"

Biting my lip, I considered our situation. Was this normal? I didn't know. I lacked experience. The only time I'd been in a relationship was when I was a hormonal, horny teenager, and the guy was someone I'd crushed on for as far back as I could remember. Did I like sex? Hell yes, and I missed having it. But I would not do it with just anyone.

A pesky voice in the back of my mind whispered, *If it was Jax, you would've already slept with him.*

Yes. Yes, I would have. I was ready to hook up with him the moment I saw him, but he was the first guy to give me butterflies in years, the second ever. My body reacted to him of its own accord, and I had no control over it. He'd never even touched me, and I was ready for him. Nothing would have had to be forced with Jax. With Eli, I felt exhausted from trying so hard to muster even a fraction of what I felt toward Jax.

"Tess." Eli pulled me back as he stroked my cheek. "I'd love to cuddle up with you tonight, but if you don't want to, it's fine. Yeah, it's true that we haven't known each other long, but I can't help my feelings, and I'm crazy about you. Whoever said you had to know someone for a certain amount of time before you could fall for them?"

Who indeed? I thought as Jax's panty-dropping smiling face took center stage in my mind.

Continuing, Eli professed, "When I'm with you, it feels like my heart is in a race for yours, and I'm okay with waiting until yours catches up."

My eyes prickled. I wasn't sure if he was trying to be cheesy or not, but seeing the genuineness in his eyes, I knew even if he was, that didn't take away the fact that he meant what he'd said. *I gotta give this guy more of a chance! He's so freakin' sweet!*

Decided, I took Eli's hand in both of mine. "Eli, that was one of the cheesiest things anyone has ever said to me, but it was also one of the sweetest. And so we're clear, I really do like your kind of cheese."

He chuckled.

"Okay," I said, a small smile turning up the corners of my mouth, "I'll cuddle with you tonight."

ABOUT NINE OR so hours later, I had hit the lobby button in the elevator, on my way out of Eli's apartment building, when I heard another apartment door close. Not wanting to be rude, I held the button, keeping the elevator doors open so the person wouldn't have to wait for it to come back up. It wasn't like I'd know the person, so who cared if they saw me in my date-night clothes early on a Sunday?

"Yeah, I'm leaving now. Be there soon," the voice said. The familiar male voice...

I froze. *What? It can't be... Can it?*

It was too late to move my finger to the close doors button, and the guy stepped into the elevator. Distracted by his phone, he gave a cursory glance to say a quick thanks before doing a double-take.

For the first time in my life, I regretted having manners. *What a wrong time to be a nice person?* I thought as I looked into Jax's startled blue eyes.

chapter
twenty-three

JAXON

THE ANGRY PING of the elevator telling me to get the fuck out of the way so the doors could closed jarred me out of my stupefied state.

Stepping in completely, I wasn't sure where to look, but knew it should definitely not be at Tess in her body-hugging dark-red mini dress, sky-fucking-high black heels that accentuated her long legs, mussed hair, and slightly smudged makeup, so I turned and faced the closed metal doors and fixed my eyes on a tiny dent in one of them.

Accepting it would be the longest elevator ride of my life if we stayed silent, I forced myself to greet my friend, who suddenly felt like a stranger. "Hey, morning. Thanks for holding the elevator."

I peeked at her through the corner of my eye. She was looking everywhere but at me. "Sure, no problem."

"Leaving Eli's?" I regretted it as soon as that left my mouth. I really didn't want the image of her fucking that fucker in my head! Tess's face went from pink to fire-engine red.

In a whisper, she confirmed, "Yeah." After a second, she asked a decibel louder, "Why're you here?" It wasn't accusatory, merely a question.

Surprised Eli hadn't mentioned it at some point, I responded, "I live here."

She finally looked at me, mouth gaping. Forgetting her embarrassment for a moment, she gestured with her hands, indicating the opulent building we were in. "You live here?"

I shrugged. "Yeah, it's Brooke's apartment."

Tess's face paled. Looking away, her brows furrowed together as if she was trying to figure something out. Her mouth pressed into a hard line. *Is she clenching her jaw?*

After the longest few seconds of my life, the elevator doors opened to the lobby. Almost running, I got the hell out of there while muttering, "See you Tuesday."

From the second I'd seen it was her in that elevator, my chest had felt heavy, making it impossible to breathe. I hoped once I got outside in the fresh air that I'd be able to catch my breath, but it didn't help. As the day went on, nothing helped. It felt like I was suffocating and going to die a long and painful death, and I didn't know why...not that I would admit anyway.

chapter
twenty-four

TESSA

SITTING in the back of the ride-share on the way home, I replayed the last couple of minutes of my life in my head. Jax had run out of the elevator so fast I nearly took a whiff of myself to see if I smelled. The only thing that stopped me from actually doing it was sheer exhaustion. I hadn't slept at all, too tense to relax. It was weird sleeping in a bed with a guy.

Here and there over the years, I'd slept in the same bed with friends and teammates, but they were all female. Maybe Eli had felt my tension, because he had stayed on his side of the bed all night. But instead of making me feel better, it made me question why I was even there. Eli said he wanted to cuddle, yet we hadn't.

Whatever. It didn't matter. I wasn't planning on doing that again anytime soon, if at all. Especially since I now knew Jax lived not only in the same freakin' building but on the same freakin' floor! It was a luxury high-rise about a ten-minute drive from campus. I'd heard it was a popular place for well-off college students, but I had no clue Brooke had that kind of money, although her enhanced appearance should've clued me in.

During the elevator ride from hell, a disturbing thought rattled around in my head, making my stomach churn. Was Jax with Brooke because of her, or her family's, money? I didn't want to think so, but how well did I actually know him? Was that the kind of guy he was?

Looking out the car window, I noticed an SUV similar to Jax's parked on the side of the street. It was a luxury brand. Perhaps the vehicle he drove was actually Brooke's? Or maybe Jax's family was well-off too? I hoped it was the latter. Not that I cared about wealth or had any presumption about having a chance with him, but it would crush me to learn he was the type to stick around for money.

After being dropped off in front of my house, I trudged inside straight through to my room. Not caring I was still in my dress from the night before, I plopped down face first onto my bed. I sensed Tina before I heard her.

"Well, well, well. Is Ms. Givens doing the walk of shame? Was it good?"

Mumbling into my pillow, I said, "We didn't have sex, just made out for a bit." I turned over. "Eventually we went to sleep, but I didn't sleep at all. I wasn't comfortable there. Not that he did anything wrong, but I'm not feeling it no matter how hard I try. And this morning, on the way out, I ran into Jax. God! It was so embarrassing!"

Confused, Tina asked, "Uh...why? So you ran into Jax when you were leaving your boyfriend's. Who cares? Jax must know Eli lives there."

"Boyfriend is a strong word."

"What? Eli isn't your boyfriend?" Tina's voice was full of disbelief.

"We haven't talked about it."

"Maybe not, but I'm pretty sure he considers you his girlfriend."

"That's besides the point." Gesturing to my outfit, I continued to bitch, "I can't believe I ran into Jax looking like this!"

"Like I said, who cares? You're a grown woman and can do whatever and whoever you damn well please."

Sitting up, I tried to make Tina understand. "It was so awkward! It felt like we were barely acquaintances instead of friends."

Tina chewed on her lower lip with her forehead scrunched.

Feeling defeated, I flopped back down and changed the subject, sort of, "That building...holy cow."

"Yeah, Eli's family are one-percenters. And Brooke's a trust-fund baby."

Although not convinced I wanted to know, I was dying to get Tina's opinion on it. "Do you think Jax is with Brooke because of her money?"

"Girl, I have no idea. But if he is, then that'll at least help you get over your little crush on him."

It's not a crush, Tina, I cried in my head.

She left me alone to sleep. I stripped off my dress, hoping being more comfortable would help me fall asleep. However, although exhausted, I remained awake in bed for a long time, torturing myself. My sleep-deprived mind convinced myself that Jax was indeed with Brooke because of her money. And that left me so, so disappointed.

chapter
twenty-five

JAXON

AS I WALKED toward the front door, I called over to Brooke, who was watching TV on the couch, "See ya later."

"Where are you going?" she yelled back, sounding a bit shrill.

Confused, I took a few steps backward. "The library. It's Wednesday."

Brooke jumped off the couch. "Do you have to study with her every week?"

Maybe it shouldn't have, but her attitude threw me. "I always go to the library Wednesday nights, regardless of if Tess is there or not." I didn't add that she was always there unless there was a conflict with soccer, which was rare.

"But she's going to be there tonight, right?"

Where was this attitude coming from? Didn't Brooke tell me more than once she didn't care if I helped Tess? "I think so. She didn't say she wasn't going to be there."

"Don't you think," Brooke mocked, "if she hasn't learned it by now that she won't ever get it? She's wasting your time at this point."

What the fuck? My girlfriend was not daft. "Seriously? Every class there's a new lesson. And it's not an easy class for most people."

Flipping her hair, Brooke argued, "Look, maybe you don't have to spend so much time with her anymore."

Geez, she made it sound like we were hanging out for fun when all we were doing was math.

Twirling her hair and trying to be cute, she said, "How about you stay here with me tonight? I mean, missing one study session won't make her fail, right?"

My eyes rolled into the back of my head. "No."

Brooke scoffed then whined. "Why not?" She was bordering on tantrum mode.

Rubbing my forehead, I asked, "What has gotten into you? I thought you didn't care if I helped her."

With her hands balled into fists, Brooke's face turned into nearly the same color as her red hair. After a second, she exploded, "You! You have gotten into me lately!" She crossed her arms and gritted her teeth. "Actually, that's not right. You haven't gotten into me lately! Maybe that's because you've been getting it somewhere else!"

For the second time in only a couple of minutes, my jaw dropped. "Have I ever given you a reason not to trust me? Why would you think I'd cheat on you?"

"Because you act like you don't even care about me anymore. You're always putting everyone else before me. And we hardly ever have sex anymore! What guy your age doesn't want to fuck his willing and able girlfriend unless he's using his juice up somewhere else?"

Have I been putting other people before her? I didn't think so. Dumbfounded, I stammered, "Tha-that's not true."

"Arrrrrgh! You don't get it!"

"Brooke—"

"You don't give a shit about me anymore! You never do anything for me!" She screamed as she struck the chessboard off the coffee table, sending it and the pieces everywhere.

Rubbing my throbbing temples, I quietly asked, "Is this about New York?"

"It's about everything!"

Letting out a breath in frustration, I thought back. I guess I had been distant lately, but it had been to avoid the constant fighting. And hell, even I could understand her being frustrated by the lack of sex over the last few months, since our average used to be at least once a day. Even I was frustrated, but being yelled at all the time was not a turn-on. Maybe it was my fault, this distance between us. Lately, we hadn't spent much time together. I guessed I wasn't doing my part to make sure she was happy. With that realization, I started to feel guilty and took out my phone, intending to let Tess kno—

Bang! Before I could react, my phone hit the wall, barely missing the mounted TV, before falling to pieces on the floor.

What the hell?

I stood motionless, my hand in the air like I was still holding the phone. For several seconds, my eyes traveled back and forth between the dent in the wall and my broken phone on the floor.

Slowly turning to my out-of-control girlfriend, I whispered, "What the fuck? Why would you—"

"I was talking to you, but you decided it was a good time to check your phone!" Hissing, she said, "Let me guess. You got a message from Tess."

Stupefied, I explained, "I was going to tell her I wasn't coming, since you said you wanted me to stay."

It was Brooke's turn to look surprised. "Oh... uh..." At least she had the decency to look guilty. "Sorry."

Sorry? Sorry! I glowered, "Sorry doesn't cut it, Brooke!"

With some effort, I unclenched my balled up fists after realizing that my bitten-off nails were digging into my palms.

"Wait! Where are you going?" Brooke cried as I headed to the door.

"Away from you and your fits," I seethed.

"I'm not throwing a fit! I'm trying to talk to you!" Surely she must've heard how unconvincing she sounded.

Opening the door, I said, "I need to cool off for a while. I'm really fucking pissed."

I let the door slam behind me. A few steps down the hall, I heard something bang and shatter up against our closed door. Absently, I wondered what she'd broken that time.

ALTHOUGH RUNNING late thanks to Brooke's antics, I wasn't in the mindset to see Tess yet, so when I arrived in the library parking lot, I stayed in my car with the windows rolled down, letting the unusually chilly night's air cool me down while I kept an eye on the door to see if Tess would leave since I hadn't showed or texted.

Calming down was hard. All I could do was think about mine and Brooke's issues. Things were bad. Terrible actually. I didn't fuck her because all she did was piss me off. I didn't spend time with her because all she did was yell at me. Every day she'd pick a fight about something else. Today it was Tess, but it wasn't like she was the actual problem.

Things had been going downhill for a while. But what was with the accusations? Brooke had plenty of guy friends, including exes or guys she'd hooked up with in the past, but I never said shit about any of them, because I trusted her. Had I done something to make her distrust me? I didn't think I had. I'd always been loyal to her. But her behavior had been so bad for months that I knew it wouldn't even help if I did stop studying with Tess.

Searching my memory, I tried remembering a time when Brooke hadn't been such a brat. Either it was so long ago that I couldn't remember, or she'd always been like this but I'd only noticed when I'd become the one on the receiving end of her wrath. But when did that start? Maybe when I had officially moved in with her and brought over all my stuff.

Glancing at the dashboard's clock, I noted it was already seven-fifteen. I needed to get in there. Sitting out in the car and trying to figure anything out with my head in its current state was pointless. Making Tess wait wasn't fair.

SITTING in our usual secluded spot, Tess had her brows furrowed in concentration as she looked back and forth between the textbook and her notebook. I paused—it was the first time I had been able to get a really good look at her. At the bar, she usually kept her eyes on me while I was on stage, so I couldn't really observe her much there, not to mention the distance and lighting made it hard to get a good look. In class, and even here at the library, she knew when I was looking at her, so I had to be careful about it to avoid giving her the wrong impression.

Eventually, unsure how much time had passed, I stopped staring and shuffled over.

After I sat, Tess turned and smiled. "Hey! I was wondering how long you were going to stand there."

Fuck! She knew I was standing there, watching her. *Screw it, I'm not even going to try to make an excuse.* I was too tired to.

"Sorry I'm late," I muttered. "I would've texted you, but my phone broke."

With an encouraging smile, she said, "Oh, that's okay! I don't have any claims on you, so it's fine if you ever can't make it." Handing me her notebook, she pointed to her homework answers with her pencil. "I think I did these right."

I stared at the page absently, not seeing anything that was written on it.

"Jax?" Tess questioned softly.

I jumped.

"Sorry!" she winced. "Is there something wrong with what I did? You've been staring at that page for a while." She had genuine concern in her eyes. She was so genuine. And caring. And nice. I couldn't imagine her acting like Brooke. "You seem upset. Are you okay?"

Swallowing against the tightness in my throat, I looked away and dropped the notebook on the table. After taking a deep breath, I admitted, "No, I'm not."

chapter
twenty-six

TESSA

ONCE JAX CONFIRMED what I had suspected, it was like the floodgates opened. "Brooke and I had another fight," he vented. "All we ever do lately is fight! She's being such a bi—"

Jax stopped and glanced at me, maybe wondering how I'd react to him calling his own girlfriend a bitch.

I shrugged. "I don't care if you call her a bitch."

Jax turned away from me. His jaw clenched before he continued through his teeth, "Every. Single. Fucking. Day. It's something new we fight about. Anything and everything sets her off. I feel like I'm going to lose my fucking mind." He turned and met my eyes, an angry blaze in his that I was glad wasn't directed at me. "You know why my phone broke? It's because she threw it against the wall!"

I felt my eyes widen. *Geez.* I might've been inexperienced when it came to what a mature adult relationship was supposed to be like, but I was pretty sure it didn't include throwing and breaking each other's things.

Jax leaned forward, resting his elbows on the table and dropped his head into his hands.

"I can't figure out if she's alway been like this or if something's changed. Maybe I didn't notice it until we moved in together, or maybe she's changed since then. I don't know. Or maybe we can't live together. Maybe we aren't as compatible as I thought." He sat back and let out an audible breath. "But that doesn't make sense either, because before I moved my stuff over to her apartment, we were together all the time anyway."

He'd lost steam. His voice had become less harsh until it was quiet and exhausted.

"I'm sorry you're going through that." And I meant it. He was hurting, and I didn't want that for him. The next logical line would have been to say I hoped they'd work it out, but that would have been a lie.

Jax sat up in his chair and started taking his books out of his bag. "Thanks for letting me vent."

"Sure. You can vent to me whenever you need or want to. We're friends, and that's what friends do."

Jax gave me a small smile. "Thanks."

I took in a slow breath through my nose, debating if I should break my own rule about never bringing family up first. Acknowledging that my stupid rule was insignificant compared to Jax's situation, I asked, "Have you talked to your family about it?"

The subtle smile playing on his lips disappeared before he looked away. After a few seconds of silence, he said, "No...I can't talk to my family."

None of them?

With a heavy sigh, Jax focused back on our school books. Holding up the notebook with my completed homework problems, he said, "These are all right. Nice."

ALTHOUGH WE STARTED LATE, we finished early.

Jax stood. "I can give you a ride home. I'm going to Chuck's anyway."

I was suddenly full of disappointment. "Oh... Actually, Eli's picking me up, so I'll wait for him." *Dammit! Of all the days Eli decided to pick me up, it had to be today!*

It was the first time Jax had ever offered me a ride. I almost wanted to cry. A sour look crossed his face. Afraid he might've been annoyed I gave away the location of his secret hiding spot, I added, "When he gets here, I'll meet him outside by the entrance."

Jax sat back down. "I'll wait with you."

"You don't have to."

Shrugging, Jax said, "Chuck's not expecting me early anyway."

I nodded, but I wasn't sure he saw. Focused on the table, Jax remained silent, like he was debating something. Sounding reluctant, he offered, "I can drop you off at Eli's if you want."

Hell no! "No, thanks. We're going out to get dinner, and you're going to Chuck's, so it would be a waste of a trip." All true, but the real reason was that I didn't want to go to Eli's apartment. What if he got the wrong idea, like I went there to hook up or something? "So, uh, that apartment building you all live in is really nice. You said it's Brooke's apartment?"

"Uh huh. Her dad rents it for her. I moved in there at the beginning of last spring semester." There was a slight pause as Jax glanced at me. "I still pay my share of the bills."

What the hell? Why are you telling me that? That's none of my business! A little defensive, I said, "I—I didn't ask."

"I know, but a lot of people assume I'm with Brooke because of her money. That couldn't be further from the truth. I don't give a shit about that and never take anything from her that I can't give back or return in some way. When we go out, I've never let her pay once. I only agreed to move in with her when she relented and let me pay my half of the bills."

Wow. His own defensiveness surprised me, but still I was relieved. He'd squashed the fear I had a few days before. I gave him a half smile. "I never doubted you were a gentleman." *Well, almost.*

Jax let out a small chuckle. It was nice seeing him smile and hearing his laugh, even if only a little.

After more seconds passed in silence, curiosity got the better of me. "How long have you and Brooke been together?"

"We met early on during freshman year. Started...hanging out immediately. Eventually we became exclusive, but I couldn't put an exact date on it. We never talked about it. At first, she said she didn't want a commitment and said she was too young to settle down or whatever and was seeing other people. I didn't care because—" Jax stopped and threw an uncertain glance my way. When I said nothing, he went on, looking down at the table, "Being a singer in the local band... I never had an issue finding someone who wanted to hang out." Internally, I rolled my eyes at Jax's euphemism for hooking up. "I guess we lost interest in other people."

"How'd you meet?" I was clueless as to why I was torturing myself with these questions about their relationship. Maybe I was a secret masochist.

"Smythie's. It was called Smokey's back then." Jax turned to me, amused. "They have karaoke every Wednesday night. I actually choose Wednesdays for my library nights on purpose. Otherwise everyone wants me to go. I used to go a lot years ago, but it was too much strain on my voice because everyone made me sing so much."

"I love karaoke, although I'm not a very good singer."

Jax laughed. "I wouldn't mind seeing that actually."

"You'd have to liquor me up first. I'd definitely need to be tipsy before singing in public."

Jax, still smirking, went on, "Ashton said there was a girl he liked who was planning on going, so I went with him as his wingman. Brooke was on stage singing a duet, but she didn't have a guy singing the male part, so I jumped on stage and started singing with her."

Ugh... "That was the song you guys did together a few weeks ago, right?"

"Yeah. We do that every year because Brooke wants to. It's kind of old now, and most of the crowd's sick of it, but sometimes I have a very hard time saying no to her. This was the last year anyway, so what the hell?" Jax took a breath. "I'd seen her around campus a few times and was thinking of trying to talk to her, so even if we hadn't met at karaoke, I think we still would have ended up together."

Hmm... So maybe even if I had come here freshman year, nothing would've happened with Jax and me anyway. But then again, I'd been a hermit crab hiding in my shell until a few weeks ago, very different from the person I was now, so I might not have even met him back then either.

Begrudgingly, I admitted, "She's a talented singer."

"Yeah, she better be, since she's a triple threat."

"A what?"

"Singing, dancing, and acting. A triple threat. She's a performing arts major." Jax's demeanor turned dreary. "She wants us to move to New York City after graduation. She wants to try her luck and skills in the theater scene, but I want to stay in California. I like visiting New York but don't want to live there. I told her we can move to L.A., but she wants to do theater. I've pointed out there are theaters in California, but that's not what she wants." Jax paused for a few seconds. "It's one of the things we've been fighting about lately."

Although I had been the one to bring it up, I didn't want to talk about Brooke anymore, so I noted, "You're a phenomenal singer, Jax. You have quite the vocal range and can change your voice to match the song you're singing. Like during rougher songs, your voice sounds gruffer. Or you can sing sweetly during those few slower songs you guys play. You're very talented. And when you perform, you really bring the songs to life."

Jax ducked his head, trying to hide his smile. "Thanks. I actually did some drama and musicals in high school, so that helps with the performance." Pausing, Jax rubbed his finger over his bottom lip. "What're your plans after graduation? Are you planning on staying in California or... Wait, where are you from?"

"I'm from a smallish town in upstate New York, but—" My phone cut me off, vibrating on the table. Checking it, I announced, "Eli's here."

Jax stood. "I'll walk out with you."

WHEN JAX and I stepped out of the library's front doors, Eli grabbed my hand and pulled me in so he could plant a kiss on my cheek. "Hey, cupcake. I meant to ask you, are you a magician by chance? Because you make everyone else disappear."

I giggled even though I thought that might've been a creative dig at Jax. Keeping up our shtick, I batted my eyelashes at Eli and said, "You know, because of you, I laugh a little harder, cry a little less, and smile a lot more."

I peeked over to see Jax's reaction and nearly burst out laughing.

He looked shocked, repulsed, and confused with a bit of "are you guys completely insane" all mixed up into one priceless expression.

Eli continued, "So, I'm in the mood for pizza... A pizza you."

I gave him my best gooey, mushy love face, like he was the best damn thing in the world. He returned the look, and we stayed like that for as long as we could. I slipped first, doubling over in laughter, followed quickly by Eli. We laughed so hard at Jax's face that we had to wipe tears away. Holding my stomach, I struggled to regain my breath. Likely from our laughing fit, Jax's face had changed to complete and utter dumbfounded confusion.

I winked at him as we walked away. "Bye, Jax. See you tomorrow."

As we headed for Eli's car, he threw his arm around me. "Night, Jax," he said over his shoulder.

Jax was still standing where we'd left him when Eli pulled out of the parking lot. I could guess what he was thinking. "What the hell was that?"

twenty-seven

JAXON

BROOKE STRODE into the living room on a mission and stopped in front of me. Disturbing my study of the lyrics for a new song we were trying to do the next night, she bent over and took an earbud out of my ear. "I need to talk to you about something."

Irritated but trying to hide it, I asked, "What's up?"

Determined, she stood up straight. "It's about New York."

Goddammit! Again? This is the third time this week! No longer bothering to hide my annoyance, I put my earbuds away and asked, "What?"

"I've gone through all the pros and cons, both yours and mine, and I know New York is where I need to be. We have to go to New York after graduation."

Slumping into the couch, I put my head back, closed my eyes, and counted to five. When I was done, I kept my eyes closed and didn't move, save for my lips. "There are no guarantees out there. All our friends and your parents are here. We don't even know anyone in New York."

"We can make new friends! And there are some elite law schools over there."

In a low, controlled voice, I summarized, "So you expect me to pack up my entire life to go all the way across the country for your dreams and career, and I get no say in this? Is that it?"

"You're making it sound like this is a terrible idea, but it's the best for me. You want to be a lawyer and can do that anywhere."

I let out a frustrated sigh.

"Come on, don't you think you're being a little bit selfish here?" she whined.

Snapping my head up, I looked over in disbelief. "I'm being selfish?"

"You say things like pack up your whole life, but it's not like you have any family or anything keeping you here."

I froze as the color drained from my face, only to come back red hot.

Stumbling backward, Brooke sputtered, "Uh, I... Umm, I didn't mean—"

Venom coated my every syllable. "I can't believe you said that." Slowly, I stood, grabbing my school and laptop bags, new phone, keys, and wallet off the coffee table. Halfway to the door, I turned around. Through gritted teeth, I declared, "I'm done."

Full-blown panic took over her. "What? What do you mean?"

"I'm done with you," I said, trying to control my voice. "We're over. Tomorrow, when you're in class, I'm packing my shit and leaving."

Storming out the front door, I left Brooke crying and yelling behind me, not caring if the entire building heard the door slam.

chapter
twenty-eight

TESSA

EXHAUSTED, I turned the corner inside the women's locker room after soccer practice, dreading my walk home. A couple of my team-mates were chatting animatedly. I didn't mean to eavesdrop, but they weren't quiet, and their conversation piqued my interest.

"Yeah, at the bass player's house. That guy Chuck."

"But they're outside? Why?"

"Not sure, but I'm going to shower and change as fast as I can. I wanna try to catch at least some of it. I think they've been at it for a while already. It's like a bonus show!"

Chuck's house? Show? Quickly, I gathered my things and headed for the exit.

One of the girls called out, "Everything okay, Tess?"

I waved and smiled. "Yeah, I'm good. I still have some energy, so I'm going to run home."

With the possibility that what I thought might be happening was actually happening, I got a burst of adrenaline.

Hitting the sidewalk outside the locker room, I sprinted toward my house. Not only did I not have time to put my earbuds in, I needed to keep my ears open for rock music from a different source. I didn't have to wait long. As I got closer, the music changed from distant noise to distinct rock band practice. Instruments would start, stop, then start up again. However, one sound was missing. Jax's voice.

Feeling like I might die, I finally arrived at my house. Wanting to avoid the crowd gathered in Chuck's driveway, I ran inside. I dropped my bags and kicked off my cleats right inside the front door then grabbed a bottle of water out of the fridge on my way out the back door.

For the first time since I'd moved in, I stepped out into my backyard onto the soft grass. There was no place to sit, not even a patio, so I leaned against the house, facing the band, as I caught my breath from my run home. The band members, along with Smythie's DJ, had positioned themselves right outside the open garage door in Chuck's backyard. Chuck, Ashton, Randy, and Ryan were in their usual stage positions while Jax was over by D.J., looking at a tablet. D.J. had a table set up with what I assumed was mixing or recording equipment. Beside it was a double keyboard.

Taking a few steps, I peered around the back corner of my house and noted that the crowd was being held back by Chuck's closed chain-linked fence, which separated the front yard from the backyard halfway down the driveway. People lined the entire length. I'd never noticed before, but the fence connected to our rental house as well. A good thing too, otherwise I was positive we'd have unwelcome guests trampling our backyard.

Since the band wasn't playing at that moment, I walked over to a group of students near the end of the fence, careful not to get too close since I hadn't yet showered, and asked what was going on.

One overly excited girl explained, "They usually practice inside the garage, but the AC is broken. They said they want to play a new song tomorrow night but have to finish recording the backtrack for it or they won't be able to play it. Apparently, the DJ from Smythie's helps them with that. They've been recording different instruments and stuff all week, but they still have more to do. The song sounds familiar, but they haven't played it through yet, so we're not sure what song it is. It sounds like a dance song. So maybe it's like a collab or something."

"Ah, I see," I replied. "Thanks for the info."

"Sure!"

It was a collaboration between a metal band and an EDM artist. Now that the girl had suggested it, I knew what song it was. While running home, I'd recognized some of the sections I'd heard. As excited as I was to hear the band play another one of my favorites, I was also surprised. I'd never heard them play this kind of song. Perhaps they were trying something new.

The theme of the song was not new. It was about an unhappy relationship where it was easier to ignore the problems and suffer than to part ways. It was a recurring theme in the songs the band played, something I'd picked up on over the last few weeks. Sometimes, with Jax-the-rock-band-singer, there was more than met the eye.

It took several shows of observing, but from what I gathered about what was going on in Jax's personal life, I was convinced that the songs the band played had a lot to do with how Jax was feeling. When he sang certain songs or specific lyrics, his entire demeanor changed. There was more passion. He got a look in his eyes that provided glimpses into what was going on inside him. He'd spit the lyrics out, like he was directing them at someone.

It wasn't all the songs the band performed, as they played a variety, but lately the songs about toxic relationships, unhappy endings, or being stuck in a miserable situation were the songs that really transformed Jax, like he was singing from his heart. Without even seeing him sing it yet, I knew this was going to be one of those songs.

After a few more minutes, the band members looked like they were getting ready to do something. Although Jax was not yet behind his microphone, front and center, Chuck, Ryan, Randy, Ashton, and the DJ were all in place. I admired how professional and focused they all were, yet was a little disappointed Jax hadn't looked my way at all, so he didn't even know I was there watching. Since I was back behind my house and not part of the crowd, he definitely would've seen me had he looked my way.

Jax walked over to a music stand in front of the double keyboards and placed the tablet on it. Then he sat down behind them. I gawked.

He can play the piano too? Dammit! How could this man get any sexier than he already was? *Hello, Jaxon Smith! I might die of a butterfly attack over here, but you go ahead and stay over there, completely oblivious to what you do to me, and keep looking delicious!*

My internal monologue was interrupted when Chuck spoke into

his microphone. "Alright, guys and gals, we let you stand there and watch us, so you all better show up at Smythie's tomorrow night. Now, we're gonna play the song through twice—hopefully only twice. The first time is to record some parts that it'd be too much of a pain in the ass for Jax to try to do tomorrow without messing up other parts of the song, so don't do anything stupid to fuck up the recording. Well, don't distract him at least, since he'll be the only one recording. What he plays goes directly to the recording so it's not like you have to be quiet or anything, but don't distract him. Got it? Good. Thanks, enjoy. I better see you tomorrow night!"

Observing Jax's setup more carefully, I noted he had multiple tablets on multiple stands, along with a microphone. Besides keyboard pedals, it looked like there were some other pedals on the ground too. No wonder they wanted to record a backtrack. With so much equipment around him, I assumed he wouldn't be singing while recording at all. I assumed wrong.

A soft guitar started, followed by Jax playing. My heart started doing funny things as I watched. It ached for him because I knew what this song meant. It longed for him because seeing him play was too much. My entire body hummed with desire for him. And then he started singing.

Convinced I was going to pass out from the physical effect he had on me, I leaned against the back of the house again. Fixated on the beautiful man with the beautiful voice and talented fingers, I couldn't look away even if I tried. Thankfully, from my position, only the band members and D.J. would've been able to see me, so I didn't have to worry about any nosy spectators noticing. But D.J. and the guys were all focused on what they were doing, and none looked my way. Or maybe Chuck, Ashton, Randy, Ryan, or D.J. had, but I didn't notice.

If someone could only hear Jax singing, they'd assume he was doing a normal practice at the mic, not playing the keyboard and pressing buttons and stepping on peddles and swiping tablet screens and switching back and forth between keyboards, which were set to give off different sounds. Sure, he occasionally stopped singing for a few words here and there while he concentrated, or he messed up the lyrics he was still learning, but what his hands were doing didn't affect the passion in his voice, even when they flew across the keys during complex sections.

Seeing Jax lost in the music was a sight to behold. His free foot stomped to the beat as his body moved with the rhythm, never missing a note. Or not that I could tell anyway. *Damn... he's amazing.* Without question, I was wholly in awe of this man, completely enthralled by his performance.

The song ended, and Jax appeared a little breathless. I was breathless myself for entirely different reasons. Sweat dripped from the edges of his hair, and his skin shimmered in the late afternoon sun. While D.J. listened on his headphones, Jax stayed at the piano and downed a bottle of water. After several minutes, what I imagined was probably the length of the song, D.J. gave a thumbs up. Jax smiled, the tension visibly leaving his shoulders knowing he didn't have to do it again.

The band members waited patiently while Jax finished his second bottle of water. Once his water break was over, he stepped up to the microphone in his normal spot, ready for a full run-through of the song. I had expected his usual stage performance where he connected with the audience, but that wasn't what we got.

Jax seemed oblivious to the onlookers, including me. During the first half of the song, his attention was on his phone, which I assumed was him looking at the lyrics. Midway through, he put it away in his back pocket and went full-on Jaxon Smith, rock band singer.

He continued to ignore the spectators, even closing his eyes. Yet he sang with such tangible intensity that I felt every word pierce me, shaking my soul to its core. He was the one exerting himself, but I was the one with the racing heart and panting breath. About the same time he'd put his phone away, I wished I hadn't left mine in the house. I should've been recording this, but if I left to retrieve it, I'd miss some of this impromptu performance. So I stayed put, watching, completely taken in by him, as always.

At the end of the song, Jax's voice echoed in the air for a moment until the crowd burst into cheers so suddenly and loudly that I jumped. Being out of sight and completely enraptured by the sexy singer, I'd forgotten they were there.

At last, Jax acknowledged the large group on the other side of the fence. Smiling, he brought his microphone to his lips, and in a slightly strained voice, said, "As Chuck said, you all better be at Smythie's tomorrow night."

People from the crowd called out they would while others cheered again.

D.J. shouted, "Hey, Jax, your voice gonna be alright for tomorrow?"

Concerned, Chuck asked, "What do you mean?"

D.J. shook his head. "I had to keep turning his mic down because he was singing so loudly."

Chuck and Ashton exchanged a glance before looking back at Jax expectantly. *Do they have the same suspicion I do about Jax's song choices?*

Jax forced a smile and waved like it was nothing. "Yeah, I'm fine. Don't worry about it."

Neither the band members nor D.J. looked convinced, but none of them said anything else. Instead, they started to put away their gear. Without Jax ever glancing my way, I headed inside to shower. I'd tell him next time I saw him how good he was.

Since I had nothing to do for the rest of the night, I took my time to wash, dry, then straighten my hair. When I was done, I headed to the kitchen to find some dinner but stopped dead after entering the living room.

I wasn't alone.

chapter
twenty-nine

TESSA

JAX WAS SITTING on the couch, staring off into space. When he noticed me, he jumped to his feet. "Sorry, I hope I didn't scare you! Tina let me in before she left and said I could wait here while you were in the shower. I hope that was okay."

Checking my phone for the first time in hours, I saw that Tina had sent me a text letting me know Jax was there. I must not have heard the message notification while blow-drying my hair. His own hair was a bit damp, and he'd changed, so I assumed he'd showered at Chuck's before coming over.

Responding, I reassured him, "No, you didn't scare me. And it's fine. I don't mind, but I am a bit surprised. It's Thursday, right?" I'd been at the library with him last night and class with him this morning.

Jax chuckled. "Yeah, still Thursday." His voice was still a little off, so D.J. may have been right to be concerned about him pushing his voice too hard.

I waved at the couch, motioning for him to sit back down. "Have a seat."

He did. I sat down next to him but stayed far enough away we wouldn't touch. Bringing my legs up on the couch, I leaned back against the armrest and faced him. Since he had come to me, I assumed he had something to say, so I sat quietly and waited.

Jax leaned forward, elbows resting on his legs, his eyes fixated on his hands folded in front of him. He seemed *tired*.

"How are you?" I asked after several moments of silence.

He turned his head to look at me. A long moment later, he answered, "Tired."

I knew it!

He looked away again. "You know what I mean when I say that, don't you." It was more of a statement than a question. More to himself, he said, "You seem to see right through me."

Still, I responded, "I have an idea of what you mean by it, yeah." I paused, unsure if I should ask, but did anyway. "Is it that bad?"

Instead of answering, he asked, "Do you remember what you told me at the library one night about songs being a good way to send a message without being so direct?"

"Yeah."

Again, there was another long pause. "What'd you think of the song, the new one?"

My eyebrows shot up, and my surprised silence must've lasted too long, because he glanced at me. "Oh...uh, umm. You saw me watching you guys?"

Shaking his head, Jax laughed to himself. He rubbed his temples and quietly admitted, "I think I rarely don't notice you."

My breath caught, and after a beat I forced myself to breathe evenly, although it wasn't easy since my heart thought I was at a full-on sprint.

With his hands over his face, Jax explained, "It felt good to sing outside. I wasn't confined by walls and could sing as loudly as I wanted. If I didn't need my voice for tomorrow night, I wouldn't have bothered with my voice distorter at all."

Not that he was looking, but if he was, he probably would've seen bewilderment on my face.

Jax laughed to himself again. "Maybe I won't use it tomorrow. Because then I can't..."

Finding my voice, I repeated my question, "How bad is it?"

Jax looked at me. He opened his mouth to say something but either couldn't or stopped himself. He looked away and swallowed.

"Sorry," I said gently, "you don't have to answer that."

Still not looking at me, he said, "No, that's one reason I'm here. Ashton always takes Brooke's side, and Chuck can't stand Brooke. There really isn't anyone I can or want to talk to about it."

"I hate to say it, but I'm not exactly neutral either."

He nodded. "I know." Pausing, his eyes searched the room. "You don't sugarcoat things, but you aren't malicious either." He took a deep breath. " You know, if it wasn't Brooke, I would've left already."

"Why? Why's she so special?" The pain and sadness radiating off of him seeped into my voice. Or maybe it was from my own emotions?

Jax looked at me with glistening eyes. "She saved my life."

What? How? Was she even capable of that? To me, she only seemed like a mean person, to put it nicely.

Taking in my surprised expression, Jax muttered, "Wow...you really don't know, do you? I thought everyone knew."

Knew what? Whatever it was, I didn't like the sound of it. And when he looked back at me, I didn't like the torment in his eyes either. After a sigh of resignation, Jax took off his long-sleeve t-shirt. Holding out the wrist with his bracelet, he asked, "I guess you never figured out what this is."

He had realized I didn't know what the significance of the black band with the circle of arrows was, yet he hadn't explained it.

Unable to meet my eyes, he held out both arms to me, wrists and forearms facing up. "Look around my elbows."

I did. All the air left my lungs in a whoosh. Dozens of tiny scars. Needle scars. I finally understood what it was. *A sobriety bracelet!* Vaguely, I recalled seeing a recovery symbol like it.

My mouth opened, but I was speechless. Jax quickly put his long-sleeve shirt back on, maybe ashamed or afraid I'd keep staring at his arms.

Whispering, I asked, "How long have you been sober?"

Without hesitation, he responded, "One thousand, twenty-eight days."

Nowhere near good enough to do the math in my head, I took an educated guess, "Freshman year?" One night in the library, Jax had said he went through "some stuff" his freshman year.

"Yup."

"How long...did you use for?"

"Not long. It started as I imagine it does for a lot of others. For fun. First, it was cocaine at parties. I mean, I sometimes smoked pot in high school, but not much. I never tried anything harder until I went to a party with Brooke and her friends. There was a pile of white powder on the table, and everyone partook. After that, I experimented with anything and everything, but I wouldn't say I was addicted yet. It was only to party. I knew I wanted to be a lawyer, so I knew how important school was." He took in a shaky breath. "But one day—" Jax's voice cracked. With his forehead resting in his hands, a tear created a wet trail down his cheek. Reaching onto a table behind the couch, I grabbed a tissue and handed it to him.

He took it. "Thanks."

"I'll be right back." I hurried to the kitchen and grabbed two water bottles from the fridge. Back in the living room, I handed him one as I sat back in the corner of the couch.

He thanked me and took a couple of sips. After he collected himself, he faced me. "Last night, I realized you still didn't know. I had assumed someone would've told you. Anyone who was around freshman year knows about it."

"About what?"

"My family."

"You said you couldn't talk to them about what's been going on with Brooke."

"What I meant was that I can't talk to them. At all. My mom, dad, and older brother James...they're all dead."

Gasping, my hands flew to my mouth as Jax's face became blurry.

"About three years ago, my parents and brother died in a car accident." His voice had become disconnected.

My vision cleared as the tears spilled down my face. Jax looked around, found the box of tissues behind him, and this time handed one to me.

Absently taking the tissue, I whispered, "Oh my God." I was half shocked, half in disbelief. "I'm so sorry."

Jax continued, "So you can probably guess what happened next. I turned to drugs, but not for partying. I needed them to cope." He paused, probably reliving what happened in his head. "Before that, I never knew that emotional pain could cause physical pain. The pain was debilitating, and the drugs numbed it and helped me forget for a little while. They helped me function because school and work don't stop even when you can barely move. Even showing up to classes high, I somehow passed all of them. I went on stage high, and from what I've heard, some performances were better than others. I don't really remember much of that time though.

"After the funerals, I'm not sure if I would've made it back to class or the bar at all if it wasn't for Brooke. Once, she tried dragging me to the shower, said she could smell me from outside, but she's small and not very strong. Eventually, she gave up and called Ashton and Chuck. They showed up and dragged me in there for her. She cut off my clothes, stating they were ruined anyway, washed me while I sat on the shower floor, dried me, and dressed me. Then told me that if I didn't want to stay in the bathroom, I'd have to move myself.

"All I wanted to do was stay in bed and forget. Or maybe die. Deep down, I knew I didn't actually want to die, but living was so fucking painful. I needed the pain to go away. My clothes became baggy because I lost a lot of weight. Brooke tried to get me to eat, but I hardly ate anything. At first, she hadn't realized that one of the reasons I was hardly able to take care of myself was because I was fucked up on drugs. She thought it was a very deep depression. When she started suggesting I get help and maybe check into a mental health facility, I eased up on the drugs enough to function and smoked pot so I would eat more. Because if I got help, I wouldn't have been able to get the drugs my body desperately needed at that point. I'd heard about withdrawal and didn't want any part of it. Besides, I didn't want to stop because I was afraid the pain would come back.

"Brooke had me stay with her pretty much all the time. I guess you could say that's when we became official. We weren't exclusive until after they died. Anyway, Brooke found my stash and realized how bad my use had gotten. And in a short amount of time too. My family died in October, almost exactly three years ago." Jax's voice broke, and he cleared his throat. When that didn't work, he took a few swallows of water. "My birthday is December twenty-second. So it was my birthday and the holidays. And I didn't have any family...at all. Both of my parents were only children, so no aunts, uncles, or cousins. My grandparents were all long dead. My dad's best friend is like an uncle to me, but we weren't close back then. Brooke and I had only known each other for a couple of months, and I didn't even realize she'd stopped seeing other guys. Ashton's parents treated me like a son, but it's not the same, you know? I felt so alone."

Jax took another break to drink more and take a few deep breaths. "When Brooke found all those drugs, she was petrified I was going to overdose. So, she got NARCAN. A lot of it. They were in every room of her apartment, in her car, in her purse and school bag. Apparently she'd put some in my backpack and car too, but I didn't even know they were there."

At the mention of the opioid antagonist, my heart sank. I knew where this was going.

Staring off into space, seeing the memories in his head and not what was in front of him, Jax continued. "It was my nineteenth birthday. School had let out for winter break, so I thought I could go a little harder. But it felt like the drugs weren't working that day, so I didn't stop..."

He stayed silent for so long that I wasn't sure he was going to continue, but eventually he did. "To this day, I honestly cannot tell you if I was trying to overdose or not. I don't think I was, but things from back then are murky. Some things I remember too well, like the pain and grief, but other things I don't have any memory of at all.

"Brooke found me. She used the NARCAN then called nine-one-one. She actually used two of them, and the paramedics used another. If she had been a few minutes later, I wouldn't be here today." Jax turned and locked eyes with me. "So when I say Brooke saved my life, it's not a metaphor. Without her, I would be dead, relapsed, or maybe even in prison."

I broke away from his gaze, not liking what I saw. It was like his eyes were pleading for me to understand why he refused to leave her.

"I went straight from the hospital," Jax went on, "to an intensive inpatient rehab center that Brooke paid for out of her trust against her parent's wishes. I had a month before the spring semester started. That month was hell—physically, I mean.

"Besides saving my life, Brooke made sure I didn't completely screw up my GPA freshman year, preventing me from messing up my chances at a good law school. Since I wasn't going to be able to leave and go to class yet, Brooke registered me for all online classes. Mostly general education stuff. She came to the rehab facility every evening and on the weekends with a laptop. She sat while I did my school work. Sometimes she brought her own work, sometimes she brought something else to amuse herself with, and sometimes she would take a nap. As if I wasn't feeling guilty enough, the first time she fell asleep there, I realized how much she was doing for me. She had no time to rest. The rehab place wasn't close to school, but she still came every single day."

As I listened, I'd never been so conflicted about a human before. It seemed like there was a decent person buried somewhere deep inside her, but why was she acting like a giant bitch now?

"I was released after a couple of months," he continued. "A week or two after spring break, I was able to sing at the bar again. I only got off my antidepressants early this year." Jax took a deep breath then turned back to face me, again his eyes looking like they were pleading with me to understand. "So that's why I can't leave her. I owe her my life."

A selfish thought bounced around in my brain. *Is this Jax's way of telling me that I don't have any chance with him?* But I didn't really think so, because I didn't think he had any idea that I wanted anything other than friendship with him.

I swallowed as I wiped tears away. "I'm glad Brooke was there to save you." My voice was raspy from crying. "I'm also very proud that you've stayed sober. I don't know what it's like, but I understand it must be difficult. Thank you for telling me."

He nodded and looked away.

But I wasn't done yet. "However, just because she saved your life does not mean you owe her yours. What's the point of being saved if you're going to be miserable?" Jax's mouth opened, maybe to protest, but I held up my hand. "Please let me finish. She may have saved your life, but isn't she the reason you got into drugs to begin with? Maybe she felt she owed you."

Jaxon's whole body reacted. His mouth opened and eyes widened as he sat back a little like I'd shoved him. Opening and closing his mouth multiple times, he tried to say something but couldn't.

Now that I had given him some food for thought, I turned to what I knew was the more painful topic. "I'm sorry about your family. I couldn't imagine losing my entire family all at once, but..." I sighed, and he gave me a curious look. "I have a better understanding than you might think." His curiosity changed to concern. Before he had a chance to ask, I put an ending to that idea for now. "But this conversation isn't about me. I want to hear about what happened to your family, if you're willing to tell me."

"A fucking drunk driver happened," Jax spat out. "The three of them were in my brother's new-to-him sports car. It was old enough not to be very safe." Jax shook his head. "And it could barely hold more than two adults. Anyway, they were on their way here to see me. I was living with Ashton off campus at the time. After getting a text from my mom that they were only a few minutes away, I went outside to wait. While I was out there, I heard a lot of sirens and emergency vehicles. I figured they must've gotten caught in traffic since whatever was happening sounded bad. It was a nice day, so I stayed outside to wait. When Ashton saw I was still out there waiting, he joined me.

"I tried calling and texting them, but they didn't answer. I started to get a bad feeling but pushed it aside. Because stuff like that only happens on TV, right? Never to you or your family. You're never the statistic, right?" Jax let out an ironic, unamused laugh. "Eventually, a patrol car showed up. As soon as I saw it, I knew something had happened. When they asked for me, my knees almost buckled, because cops only come in person when there's a death, right? I'd seen enough TV shows to know that much."

Jax swallowed several times before he could speak again. Then he tried washing the lump in his throat away with more water. Tears streamed down his face. In a voice that pained me to hear, he went on, "My brother died at the scene, and my father died on the way to the hospital. My mother was alive and coherent enough to give them my name and contact information. She died in surgery before I got to the hospital." Nearly sobbing, Jax croaked out, "And that son of a bitch who killed them only had a broken leg and bruises." Jax needed a full minute to collect himself. "At least he's in prison now...I guess."

My hands were clamped over my mouth again. Hot tears burned my face. I wanted to burst out crying but was afraid if I didn't hold in the sobs, I'd set him off again. I managed to say, "I'm so, so sorry. That's terrible. It's no wonder you wanted to forget."

Changing my position on the couch, I leaned forward toward him. "Listen to me, Jax. You are not alone. You have some great friends, and it's clear they love you very much. Please, don't ever feel like you're alone. Regardless of if you're in a relationship or not, you are not alone."

I wasn't sure if I should have said that last line, me subtly telling him that he shouldn't be afraid to end things with Brooke, but as he said, I didn't sugarcoat things.

Jax looked at me and held my gaze. I couldn't tell what he was thinking, but his eyes filled with tears until one then the other spilled over onto his cheeks.

chapter
thirty

JAXON

I COULDN'T LOOK AWAY as Tess implored me to understand that I wasn't alone in the world. But my focus was on one particular thing she had said. She told me my friends loved me. And she and I were friends. So did that mean Tess loved me as a friend? Even after what I'd told her today? She'd accused me of being perfect, but now that she knew I was far from it, had her feelings toward me stayed the same?

Looking into her eyes, I got the confirmation I needed. My past hadn't negatively affected the way she felt. Anyone who looked at another person like the way Tess was looking at me was unquestionably someone who felt a deep love for the other person.

A stirring inside of me snapped me out of my trance. I looked away and cleared my throat. Hoping I hadn't ruined her mood for the night, I said, "Thanks for listening."

"Of course," she said through a sympathetic smile. "I told you I'm here anytime you want or need to talk."

I gave her a smile back but then remembered something she'd said a few minutes before, and my smile faded. "You said you knew a bit about how I felt. Is there anything you want to talk about?"

She sighed. "Not right now. Thanks though."

I nodded. Maybe that was better. How much misery did we really want to share in one night? I let out a breath, not sure what to do now. Being alone at that moment did not sound appealing, but I sure as hell wasn't going back home. Chuck had company. Ashton had plans too. Tess still had a melancholy demeanor. Maybe telling her that all in one go was too much? I felt a little bad even if she was willing to listen to my sob story. Luckily, I got an idea.

"Do you have plans for tonight?"

Surprised, she shrugged. "No, not at all. I was going to watch TV."

"Would you like to go somewhere with me? I'll feed you dinner too."

Tess's eyes lit up as she beamed at me. "Okay!" Her transformation was so sudden and absolute that it was like we hadn't been talking about some of the heaviest shit possible for the last hour or so.

Are you that excited to hang out with me? "Uhhh...you don't even know where I want to go," I noted slowly.

Tess jumped to her feet. "Doesn't matter! I'm pretty adventurous."

I smirked. "Why am I not surprised?"

After shrugging, she ran off to another room, calling over her shoulder, "I'm going to get my shoes. I'll be right back!"

FEELING THOROUGHLY DEFEATED, with my hands in my pockets and shoulders slumped, I stepped out of the arcade into the salty breeze and onto the wooden planks of the pier. Tess was giddy and practically skipping next to me. She had thoroughly kicked my ass.

"I told you I was good at arcade games," she said in a singsong, playful tone.

She had told me, but that good? Seriously? She had won every single game we played! I was both impressed and crestfallen.

"How'd you get so good, anyway?" I muttered, playing up my dejection a bit.

Tess giggled—a sound so sweet it made my heart skip. Every time I heard it, warmth spread from my heart through my entire body. It made me happy to hear the small, beautiful sound of happiness.

Answering my question, she explained, "I used to hang out with my brother and his best friend a lot. We were like the three musketeers. As competitive as I am, I was not about to let a couple of stinky boys beat me."

At that, I laughed. She looked pleased I was no longer moping.

"Wait, you have a brother?" Looking around but not seeing anything, I searched my memory for some clue about him. Not finding any, I said, "I thought you were an only child for some reason. Is he older or younger?"

Tess took in an audibly shaky breath. Her face tensed, and it took a moment for her to answer. When she did, she sounded tormented. "He was older...by two minutes."

Holy fuck... My heart sank into my stomach at her use of past tense. Maybe I should've said something more profound, but I could only think of one thing. "Sorry."

She gave me a tepid smile with glistening eyes.

Desperate to get our happy, fun mood back on track, I asked, "Do you like rides?" I pointed down the pier. "They have a bunch down there."

Her smile expanded, and she nodded. By the time we had gotten to the end of the pier with the rides, genuine excitement had returned, like the last minute of our conversation hadn't happened. Tess stopped walking and looked up. I followed her gaze...to my worst nightmare, kind of.

At the very end of the pier, there was a gigantic Ferris wheel, the biggest one on Earth by the looks of it. It was lit up with neon lights against the dark backdrop of the night sky and ocean behind it. My heart started pounding as my insides formed into tight knots. Fearful, I glanced at Tess. She was eyeing it excitedly. I winced when she turned to me. She was about to ask exactly what I hoped she wouldn't.

Observing my face, her excitement transformed into curiosity. "You look a little pale. You okay?"

I nodded. "Yeah," I muttered. "I'm good." Looking around for a distraction, I spotted the carousel. "Wanna go on that one?"

A smile I didn't like crept onto her lips. *Fuck!* How was she this perceptive?

Tess slowly shook her head. "No, Jax, I want to go on that one." She pointed up to the massive wheel of death. I looked around, freaking out, but her voice made me look at her again.

"Jaxon Smith, are you afraid of heights?"

I swallowed hard. "Uh—" I was about to deny it but couldn't get the words out fast enough.

"Everyone has fears, and that's okay. One thing I've learned over the last few years is that you can't let them stop you from living your life." Her eyes never wavered from mine. "I never would've gone to Smythie's that first night if I let fear stop me. And I definitely wouldn't be here with you now."

Did she have a fear of getting close to people? I wasn't sure. Or maybe she'd been talking about multiple fears like crowds or... I stopped at the thought of Brooke. Shaking my head, I sighed heavily. "Alright, but you're not allowed to make fun of me."

She nearly blinded me with her toothy smile as she jumped up and down, clapping like an excited kid. When she stopped, she leaned in conspiratorially. "I promise nothing."

Then she bolted, literally running off to the ticket booth. I caught up and tried to pay for the tickets, or at least my own, but she wouldn't allow it since she was the one dragging me on that unsteady-looking circular piece of metal.

Standing in line, the temptation to run in the opposite direction was overwhelming. As our basket or car or whatever the fuck it was called approached, I eyed the exit, wondering if it was too late to escape. Ultimately, I decided against it. Tess made me want to face my fear. Or that was what I told myself. The reason I got into the swinging metal box that literally had mine and Tess's lives in its grasp for the next several minutes was definitely not because I didn't want to miss one second of my time with her tonight...right?

When the door slammed and locked us into the cage that was only keeping us alive by some probably rusty rod, I regretted my life's decisions. Then I saw Tess's face light up at the view of the pier below us. I gasped. *Below us! When the fuck did we get so fucking high?*

I might've started to hyperventilate, but Tess pulled my attention away from the situation outside the car. "It's okay, Jax. You're okay. Focus on me, and don't look outside."

My heart rate slowed as I stared at her. Instead of enjoying the lit-up pier, she held my eyes. My heart started pounding again, but not from nerves or fear. I wanted to kiss her.

I'd like to think that my relationship status, which was ambiguous at that moment regardless of what I'd said to Brooke, was what stopped me from reaching over and doing it, but if I were honest, it likely had more to do with the fear of making the car move more.

Gripping my seat with both hands, I looked down at the metal floor in shame. Even though I felt guilty as hell, I couldn't stop myself from wondering how Tess would've reacted. Would she have allowed it, or would she have pushed me away? It took several tries before I could swallow away the tightness in my throat.

Catching a movement with my peripheral vision, I glanced up at Tess. She was hugging herself, her hands rubbing her bare arms. We'd left her house so quickly that I hadn't even thought to tell her to bring a sweatshirt or jacket. I pulled my hoodie over my head and handed it to her.

Surprised, she asked, "Are you sure?"

"Yeah, I'm starting to sweat anyway," I lied. "You know, from the nerves."

She thanked me and put it on. *Damn, she looks cute in my hoodie.* Tess stilled. Then I could've sworn she took a whiff. *Shit!* Did I smell? I'd showered and changed at Chuck's right before I went to her house.

Tess caught me looking at her. My face may have been a bit horrified.

"Oh, it's nice and warm," she explained while refusing to meet my eyes.

As the never-ending ride continued, Tess gazed out the side of the car. It was the second night in a row I could observe her. She had a dreamy expression with a slight smile gracing her lips. Occasionally, she took deep breaths through her nose. *Good, if she's breathing through her nose, then my sweatshirt must not smell bad.* She looked happy, and I wondered what had put that look on her face.

Suddenly, she faced me, startling me. "You really don't like heights, huh?"

Looking at her like she was nuts, I shook my head. I may have been crazy for liking math, but she was crazy for liking this thing they called a ride.

"I'm sorry you can't enjoy the view, because I'm really enjoying it right now," she said, her eyes never leaving mine.

It was hard to breathe, and I struggled to inhale. I wasn't worried about her seeing it, since I was sure she'd assume it was because of my fear of heights. But what actually made me breathless was that she'd said she liked the view "right now" while looking at me. Wrong or not, I hoped she was talking about me.

As my chest rose and fell with rapid, shallow breaths, Tess grew concerned. "Are you okay? Try to slow down your breathing."

Unlike what she assumed, the reason I was starting to hyperventilate was because at that moment, I acknowledged that I liked Tess. Really liked her. Way more than a person who lived with someone else should like another person. And that had me freaking out. Sure, I had wanted to kiss her a few minutes before, but you could kiss someone you like less.

Needing a distraction, I asked, "Since you are one of the few people who know my fear, isn't it only fair I know yours?"

Looking a little sad, Tess peered down at the pier. "I suppose that would be fair."

I waited, but when she didn't say anything, I asked, "You aren't going to tell me?"

She pursed her lips and looked at me through the corner of her eye. "I'm trying to decide which one."

"You have more than one?"

"Who doesn't?"

She had a point. "You don't have to tell me if you don't want to."

"I'm afraid of getting hurt."

I held her gaze for a few seconds, trying to see into her through her eyes. "You're not talking about a sports injury, right?"

"I want to be loved the same way I love. I don't want to love a person more than they love me. I want our love to be equal." She swallowed. "If he won't love me the way I love him, that's the kind of pain I fear."

She must've had experience with that, otherwise why would Tess have such a fear?

Staring at the floor again, I wondered how Eli felt about her. How did she feel about him? Something told me his feelings for her were stronger. Was that because Tess was holding back, afraid he'd hurt her in the way she feared? A thought needled me in the back of my mind. What if she already loved a person who couldn't love her back, or not in the way she wanted?

Deciding the conversation had gotten too dismal, I changed the subject. "Can I ask you a question?"

Tess shrugged. "Sure."

"What the fuck is wrong with you and Eli?" I pressed my lips together, trying not to laugh.

She didn't hold back and doubled over, holding her stomach. Unable to resist, I joined in. Her laugh was infectious. All of them. From the little giggles to the ones that made your belly ache. "We have a running joke...about who can say the cheesiest thing. And we enjoy seeing people's faces when they think we're being serious. Your face— oh my God." She used my sweatshirt sleeve to wipe her eyes. My fingers twitched, wanting to wipe her tears away myself.

"He calls you 'cupcake,'" I commented incredulously.

She giggled. I wasn't sure if I had made her giggle or a memory of Eli had. The thought that it could be him annoyed me. "It's from another cheesy line. He said I was the sweetest thing he's ever—" Her eyes widened as she clamped her mouth shut. *Was she about to say 'tasted?'* My stomach turned. I hated that. Really fucking hated that. But was it because it was cringy or because I hated that Eli had tasted her and I—

I rubbed my eyes, trying to get my mind back on the right track.

"Anyway," Tess shrugged, "I think the nickname is kind of cute." She grinned. "Your face yesterday was priceless. I wish I'd taken a picture of it."

That gave me an idea. Rubbing my lip, I asked, "You know, I don't think Ashton would believe that you actually got me on this death trap. Maybe we should take a picture as proof."

Her face brightened. "Yeah, sure!" She pulled out her phone and held it up as she leaned over with the pier lights behind her. "Lean in and meet me halfway. The car shouldn't move that much."

I did and tried my best to smile for the camera. Tess clicked the button on the side of her phone, and a selfie flashed on her screen. Sitting upright again, she tapped on her phone. "I'll send it to you."

A second later, my phone vibrated. Opening our text chat, I saw our smiling faces. Clicking on the picture, I made it bigger and stared. God...she was radiant. Her eyes sparkled, and her smile was brighter than the whole damned pier in the background.

Since it was a live photo, I held the screen and watched our movements before and after the picture was taken. Then I did it again. And a third time.

I wasn't imagining it, was I? Right before she took the picture, while I was smiling at the camera, she'd looked at me. It wasn't the fact that she looked at me that had my pulse quickening, but how she looked at me.

I swallowed hard. This wasn't good. I was headed down a slippery slope, and instead of ice cleats that would've prevented me from slipping, I wanted a damned sled.

chapter
thirty-one

JAXON

"I'LL PUT that right in for you!"

The waitress walked away, leaving Tessa and I to ourselves. We were in a corner booth, secluded from the few patrons in the restaurant. Clearly, the hostess thought we were on a date and had given us what was probably the best date table in the restaurant.

It was late, and although Tess said we didn't have to stop, I'd promised her dinner, so I insisted. I meant to feed her at the pier, but we were having so much fun that we forgot to eat. Her stomach reminded me while we sat at a red light during one of the few moments of silence between us. Thankfully, I was familiar with the area and knew about this late-night sushi place.

"So what're your plans for Thanksgiving?" I asked, trying to sound casual, but there was more to the question than friendly chit-chat.

Tessa smiled widely, excitement dancing in her eyes. My heart skipped a beat. "My parents are coming here! They're flying in on Thursday and will be here for the long weekend. Then they're driving up the coast the following week for vacation. What about you?"

Looking down at my folded hands on the table, my answer sounded downright dismal compared to hers. "Probably going to Brooke's parents," I said quietly. "That's what we usually do." *Brooke, Brooke, Brooke... What am I going to do about Brooke?* Technically, I'd said we were over, but since I'd calmed down, I knew it was unlikely that I'd actually leave her. Everyone has said dumb shit at some point, and after everything she'd done and said in the last few months, commenting about my lack of family was rather tame.

At the thought of family, a strange feeling developed in my chest, but it wasn't the usual pain from missing mine. Was it jealousy of Tess, not only that she still had her parents but that they were close? I peeked up at her, maybe trying to seek clarity. She was typing quickly with her two thumbs on her phone screen, so she didn't notice me observing her.

For what felt like the billionth time tonight, her beauty took my breath away. Although gorgeous, her personality was amazing. She was nice but not naïve. While honest, she wasn't mean. She loved to laugh. Even though she'd spoken of fears earlier, I thought she might have been the bravest person I knew—she wanted to be a cop for Christ's sake! She was one of the most caring people I'd ever met. While competitive, she was a good sport. She had a killer body thanks to her athleticism. And it felt like she understood me better than anyone ever had before. Including Brooke.

Sometimes it seemed like we were on the same wavelength, like what she'd said about song lyrics sending a message when you're unable to say something directly. It'd been years, and Brooke still hadn't picked up on that, yet I'd only known Tessa for a couple of months. She was truly incredible. If our situations were different, if we'd both been single, I would've asked her out on a date.

I froze. Then had to remind myself to breathe. It wasn't pain, nor jealousy. The fluttering in my chest, although unfamiliar since I hadn't felt it in years, wasn't even a bad thing. Or at least not in most cases.

"Earth to Jaxon Smith!" Tess pulled me out of my head.

"Sorry! I was…" Not knowing what to say, I stared blankly. I sure as hell couldn't tell her what had been going on inside my head. "Chuck's Halloween party is next weekend, Saturday night. You should come. His parties are usually pretty epic. They go late, but no one complains since his family owns most of the street, and he invites everyone. The party spills out into the front and back yards, so it doesn't really get too crowded inside."

"Hmm…that's the day of my last soccer game. It's an away game, but I'm sure I'll be back in plenty of time." Her brows scrunched together. "But I don't have a costume."

I shrugged. "Who cares? You don't have to wear one."

"What are you going as?"

"I don't know. Probably a rock star."

Tess's cocktail almost came out her nose. "Guess you won't have much trouble finding an outfit then."

"Nope." I chuckled. "Seriously, I'm going to wear my normal clothes and let Brooke paint my face however she wants."

"What's she going as?"

I thought for a moment. "Actually, I have no idea." I didn't add that it was probably going to be something tight and skimpy, like the last couple of years. There was a slight lift of Tess's brows, but she didn't comment on my lack of interest. Reluctantly, I asked, "You think Eli will come?"

She shook her head. "No, he's doing some stuff with his nieces and nephews."

Can't say I'm sorry he won't be there! Fucking prick. Changing topics, I noted, "You never did answer my question."

"What question?"

"Did you like the new song?"

Tess took a visible breath and looked away. She seemed uncomfortable. Maybe that was why she'd never answered the first time I asked. As I was starting to regret asking her again, she responded, "Jax, it was amazing. You were amazing. You're so talented. I had no clue you could play the piano. Honestly, I was awestruck."

Air escaped in a rush through my lips. I had not expected that kind of response. Looking down at my water, my cheeks felt a little heated. *Did Tessa just make me blush?* I took a sip of water, then a deep breath. "My mom was a music teacher."

"Your mom's skills have blessed us all," Tess said, teasing me. "Can you play any other instruments?"

"Not really. I used to play the piano and sing with my mom all the time. Sometimes with my brother too. But he was ten years older than me."

Tess looked surprised.

I elaborated, "My parents were teen parents. Luckily, my grandparents were all very supportive of them. They helped my parents out so they could finish high school then get their degrees. Once they settled down, they had me. I don't know how they did it. Chuck's got a baby half-sister, and I've seen how much work babies can be. I want kids someday, but not anytime soon. I couldn't imagine being a father at my age, let alone as a teen." I grimaced for emphasis. Tess chuckled at my expression. I shook my head. With a bit of irony, I said, "It feels like that's the only thing Brooke and I agree on, no kids anytime soon."

Tess looked away, her smile fading until our sushi rolls were delivered.

THE REST OF THE NIGHT, dinner and the drive back toward campus, was filled with fun and light-hearted topics. We laughed, poked fun at one another, and played games like name that tune, in which I was the only one humming and she was the only one guessing. As we got close to campus, we stopped at a red light. I glanced over and met her eyes. They were sparkling in the dark. Had she really enjoyed her time with me that much?

A few minutes later, as Tess climbed out of my car, I realized that, except for the fact that tonight wasn't a date, it would have been the best one I'd ever been on, and I wasn't even getting laid at the end of it. Admiring my friend as she walked to her door, I had an epiphany. Did I even want to fix things with Brooke?

chapter
thirty-two

TESSA

IT WAS past one in the morning when I dragged myself into my room. The day had been exhausting both mentally and physically, but totally worth it. My outing with Jax had become my all-time favorite night up to that point. If being friends with him felt that good...my heart fluttered imagining what an actual date with him would be like. Would he have kissed me at the end of it? Or would he have come in and stayed the night?

Groaning, I kicked off my shoes. Why the heck couldn't I get over my hardcore crush on him? While ripping open my pajama drawer, Tina knocked on my open door frame.

"Oh, hey," I said as I continued digging around in my drawer, "I thought you were staying with Jamar tonight."

Tina ignored my greeting. "What the hell are you doing?"

I stopped and looked over at her. Assuming she wasn't asking about my hunt for my favorite PJs, I asked, "What do you mean?"

"I saw Jax drop you off. Do you have any idea what time it is? And why are you wearing his clothes?"

I looked down. I'd forgotten to give him back his hoodie.

"Did you hook up with him?" Tina whispered fearfully.

Shock was not an adequate enough description for how I felt at that second. "What? No! Why would you think that?"

"Why else would you be wearing his sweatshirt after getting home in the middle of the night?"

"I was cold." Still flabbergasted, I asked, "You know we weren't here, so where in the world would we have even had sex? Brooke's?"

"He's got a car. And there are these things called hotels."

My blood started to boil. "Are you serious? He's got a girlfriend. We're friends. Regardless of if I like him or not, we can be friends."

"You need to be careful. Otherwise, someone is going to get hurt."

"What? Why? Who?"

"Either you or Brooke. Either Jax doesn't return your feelings or Brooke gets cheated on. But there's one common denominator. Jax isn't the one who gets hurt."

Furious, I snapped, "It's just a stupid crush! I'll get over it!"

Tina looked doubtful. "Keep telling yourself that." She left without another word, closing the door behind her.

I was left reeling, probably because deep down I knew Tina was one-hundred-percent correct. And I'd been fooling myself.

chapter
thirty-three

JAXON

SINCE IT WAS SO LATE, or early, I unlocked and opened Brooke's apartment door as quietly as possible. Not wanting to wake her, I headed to the spare bathroom, which given how often Brooke took over the master bath, had a full set of my toiletries. I'd crash on the couch given how our last conversation had ended.

Unfortunately, the moonlit living room wasn't empty when I returned. Sighing, I headed to the couch, resigning myself to the oncoming onslaught I was positive Brooke was about to unleash.

However, when she spoke, her voice was quiet and raspy. "I'm so sorry, Jax. That was a really insensitive thing to say. Please forgive me. I'll never say anything like that ever again, I swear. I was just trying to make a point. I'm sorry."

With my vision adjusted to the dim lighting, I got a better look at her face. It was red and blotchy with swollen eyes, making me feel so guilty that it hurt. While I'd been off having the time of my life with another girl, Brooke had been here, crying her eyes out. Still, I didn't regret my time with Tess. It wasn't like I'd done anything wrong. Sure, there'd been a few inappropriate thoughts, but that was all they were.

Exhausted, I let out an audible sigh and leaned back into the couch. I didn't know what I should do or say.

After several seconds of me not speaking, with tears streaming down her face, Brooke said, "I was so worried about you. I knew you had rehearsal, but it got so late, and you never came back. I contacted everyone I could think of, but no one knew where you were. I was so scared that I made you so angry that something had happened...or maybe you did something," she added, insinuating I might've relapsed.

Shit...Even if I was mad at her, she didn't deserve to have to worry like that. But I wasn't going to let her off easy either. I was still pissed. "I thought we broke up. Where I am isn't your business."

Although I didn't think it would've been possible, Brooke's expression became more pained. "I thought you said that out of anger. Are you really breaking up with me?"

Another glance at her face, and I knew I was one word away from shattering her heart. I took in a shaky breath. Could I...Should I end it right now? Sure, it'd hurt both of us, but with time we'd get over it, right?

Rubbing my forehead, I said, "Come here, Brooke." After she sat down next to me, I said, "Look, I'll tell you where I was, then I'll let you decide what you want to do."

"Umm, okay." Brooke's tone rang with uncertainty.

"If you yell at me, the conversation is over, and so are we. You aren't going to like what I say, and we can talk about it, but we won't resolve anything by constantly yelling at each other." That last part was generous, since I rarely yelled at anyone, including her.

I took a deep breath, wondering how this was going to play out. "I was with Tess." No reaction. "After practicing with the guys, I went to her house and told her about my family and addiction. I explained how you saved my life when I OD'd. I told her about the rehab and how you stuck by me when I needed you the most. By the end of the conversation, we were both feeling pretty down, so we went and played arcade games and rode rides at a pier near where I grew up."

Figuring Brooke would be hurt enough by what I was telling her, I left out the part about the Ferris wheel. She'd never been able to get me on anything like that, so telling her I'd gone on one with someone else seemed cruel. Plus, for some inexplicable reason, riding it with Tess felt special, and I didn't want to ruin the memory with Brooke dragging me there to go on with her.

"On the way back, we stopped for sushi. I dropped her off, and now I'm here."

Brooke looked down at her hands and whispered, "Did you sleep with her?"

"No. She's my friend."

Still speaking softly, she pointed out, "People hook up with their friends. You broke up with me. So in your mind, you were single again, right?"

"Do you really think our relationship means so little to me, Rook?"

She didn't answer.

"I am not happy right now, but I am trying to get through whatever it is we're going through because you are the most important person in my life. I don't know what's happening to us, but if we don't fix it, and fix it soon, I don't know how much longer we can do this. If this," I said, gesturing between the two of us, "wasn't important to me, I would've left already."

Brooke's crying turned from silent to audible. Afraid this would be one of the few times I'd have to say everything I needed to get out, I continued even though I knew I was hurting her.

"I don't know how much more I can take. I'm close to my limit. Do you understand what I'm saying? I want to fix this if we can, but it feels like we're close to the point of no return."

She nodded. "I'll try to be more understanding. You've always been that way with me." Brooke gave me a teary smile. "I'll stop hounding you about your friendship with her too. I was worried, but since you didn't hook up with her today when maybe you had the chance, I know you guys really are just good friends."

Locking eyes with her, I said, "If I wanted to, and if she wanted to, we would have had the chance. We were in her house alone for close to two hours. As soon as we were done talking about my fucked-up life, we left and hung out in public. But we could have easily stayed there if that was going to happen. Which it wasn't."

Brooke nodded, relief relaxing the stress lines on her face. Standing, she asked, "Are you coming to bed?"

"Yeah, but I'm going to get some water first."

She nodded again then headed to the bedroom. Lingering on the couch a while, I tried figuring out if I had been honest with my girlfriend. And if I was even being honest with myself.

chapter
thirty-four

TESSA

IT WAS in between the band's two sets, and the bar was hopping. Although I was probably going to pay for it during my soccer game in the morning, I was determined to see Jax play that new song they were practicing Thursday and record it. I theorized they were going to play it at the end of the second set, and all I could do was think, *At least my soccer game is a home game.* Unfortunately, my plan was for naught.

Tina, Jamar, Eli, and I were on the edge of the dance floor, opposite the wall with the bar. Eli spoke into my ear, "I'm going to get another beer. Want anything?"

Giving him a polite smile, I shook my head.

When he turned to ask Tina and Jamar if they wanted anything, she whispered into Jamar's ear, then Jamar volunteered, "I'll come with you."

As soon as they were out of sight, Tina walked closer to me, glaring. Not having any idea where the hostility was coming from, I was about to ask when she snapped, "I'm going to ask you this one more time, and I swear to God, if you aren't honest with me, I will never speak to you again...for a month!"

"What?" I squeaked.

Hissing close to my ear, she enunciated each word, "Did. You. Have. Sex. With. Jax?"

Startled, I stepped back, holding up my hands, "No! I told you nothing happened!"

To match my step back, she stepped forward, probably trying to keep our conversation private from the people around us. "Then why was he acting like that?"

I tried to speak, but nothing came out when I opened my mouth. So I shook my head instead.

Tina rolled her eyes. "Oh, come on. Don't try telling me you haven't noticed."

Although I was pretty sure I knew exactly what she was taking about, I tried to come across as clueless and shrugged with another head shake.

"Jax has been going back and forth between looking at you and looking at Brooke the entire night! It's so obvious that I wouldn't be surprised if everyone in the whole goddamn bar noticed!"

I feigned ignorance. "He was scanning the crowd like he always does." Brooke and I had been on opposite sides of the vast room, so it seemed like a logical explanation, but unfortunately I sounded as unconvinced as I felt. After all, that's what it looked like to me too.

"Are you lying to me?"

"We didn't do anything! We're friends! That's it!"

"Ha! Friends my ass!"

"What's that supposed to mean?"

"It's clear he likes you too, Tess! As more than a friend! Something changed. He's looking at you differently tonight."

My mouth opened in a gasp. Was that true? No, it couldn't be... Could it? The possibility had crossed my mind a few times, but I'd chalked it up to wishful thinking. After all, he was still with Brooke.

Without meaning to, I turned my head and searched the bar for him. He was next to the stage with Chuck. Our eyes locked for two long seconds before I forced myself to turn away.

Tina continued to badger me, but I hardly heard her since my heart was pounding in my ears. She was right. There was something new there.

chapter
thirty-five

JAXON

"OOO LA LA. CAT FIGHT!" Chuck said, sounding too pleased.

Glancing up from my tablet, I asked, "What are you talking about?"

With a mischievous grin, he said, "Tess and Tina look like they're about to throw down."

Spinning around, I searched in the direction Chuck was looking. I watched them for several seconds. Sure, Tess and Tina were obviously arguing, but I wouldn't say they were close to throwing punches. Still, I used it as an excuse.

"Shit, I can't have any fights breaking out. I'll be right back."

They had drawn a few curious eyes, but with the thundering music, most of the bar was oblivious to the confrontation. I couldn't hear anything until Eli and Jamar had returned, and Tess turned to Eli. "Eli, let's go! I'm ready to go home!"

Although clearly surprised, he agreed, "Oh! Sure, want to go to my place?"

By the look on her face, I thought Tess was going to deck him. *I could probably let her get away with throwing one punch*, I conceded, especially since I also felt like hitting him.

She didn't, choosing to yell instead, "No! I want to go to my home! And if you don't stop pressuring me to fuck you, I assure you it'll never happen!"

What?

Tess turned on her heels and stormed away. But before she did, our eyes locked. The rage burning in her eyes extinguished into shock. She knew I'd heard. *They haven't had sex yet!* Why did that make me so fucking happy?

Eli didn't notice me. "See you guys later, I guess," he said before following Tess.

Jamar turned to Tina. "What happened?"

Tina crossed her arms. Lifting her chin in defiance, she spat, "Can I help you with something, Jax?"

Woah, is she mad at me? "Uh, you guys okay?" I asked apprehensively.

Tina scoffed...at me. Stepping closer so only I could hear her, she hissed, "Know your place, Jax, and stop screwing with other people's feelings!"

I jerked back like she'd slapped me. Then, like Tess had less than a minute before, she turned on her heels and marched away, her boyfriend trailing behind her.

What'd I do?

"What was that about?" said Brooke, who was standing next to me. How long had she been there? "Did they get into a fight?"

Hesitantly, I answered, "I guess? I'm not really sure."

"Oh. Want to dance since we're here?" she asked, gesturing to the dance floor.

I had no excuse not to dance with my girlfriend, so I took her into my arms, and we started moving to the beat. Brooke gyrated into me, but with my thoughts so preoccupied, my body didn't react. *What did she mean, "screwing with other people's feelings?" And why is she mad at me?* By the time I took the stage for a second time that night, all I knew was that it was about Tess.

MORE INSIGHT ARRIVED after one a.m. I hadn't been able to get Tess out of my mind since Thursday night. Wait, who was I kidding? I hadn't been able to stop thinking about her from the moment I'd first seen her on Chuck's front lawn. She was always there, if not at the forefront, in the back of it. The more time I spent with her, the more she was at the center of my thoughts. And lately my thoughts had started wandering to places they shouldn't.

But I was worried about her. She was my friend and looked pretty upset earlier. Maybe it was a bad idea, especially since she had a soccer game in the morning, but I picked up my cell phone to send her a text, figuring she was sleeping anyway.

JAX

You OK? You looked upset when you left the bar.

A few seconds later, I almost jumped when my phone vibrated in my hand.

TESS

I am upset, but I'll be fine. Tina and I hardly ever fight, but it does happen.

JAX

Want to talk about it?

There was a slight delay before she responded.

TESS

Thanks, but I'm not sure I should talk to you about it.

Me specifically? My mind ran through a million possibilities in a split second.

TESS

Because we were fighting about you.

I almost dropped my phone. Tess's comment about texting popped into my head, "Texting: sometimes it's easier to say something through a text than face-to-face." Or something like that.

JAX

Why?

TESS

How honest do you want me to be?

JAX

I'd rather you always be completely honest with me.

TESS

She thinks there's something going on between us. To be more precise, she thinks we hooked up Thursday night.

My stomach flipped as I took a shaky breath.

JAX

Why does she think that?

TESS

Because we hung out and I came home in the wee hours, wearing your hoodie.

Which I still need to return to you, sorry!

JAX

I don't get it, so what? Brooke knows. It's not like she was the one arguing with you.

TESS

You told Brooke?

JAX

I tell Brooke everything.

Almost.

JAX

Didn't you tell Eli?

TESS

No.

I guess it makes sense for you to tell Brooke though. You two have been together for years. Eli and I are NOT serious.

But it's nice that Brooke doesn't care if we hang out.

JAX

I wouldn't go that far. She does care, and she's not exactly thrilled about it. But she's accepted it, and we try not to meddle in each other's friendships.

Any other reason Tina thinks there's something going on?

TESS

Should there be?

What does that mean? I was stunned by her response. No, she definitely didn't sugarcoat things.

JAX

That's a pretty big assumption to think there's something going on between two people who are in relationships with other people.

Especially since we've only hung out once outside of doing schoolwork…

TESS

Exactly what I thought! That's basically what I told her.

Anyway, I guess there isn't really any other reason.

I really need to sleep now. Good night!

Even though I'd said I wanted her to be completely honest with me, I got the distinct feeling she wasn't.

chapter
thirty-six

TESSA

I WAS STARING at my leftovers slowly spinning in the microwave when Tina got home. I expected her to ignore me, but she came into the kitchen and sat down at the island. After pulling out some school-work, she started working on it, or pretended to anyway.

About two minutes into eating my dinner, she finally spoke. "Next weekend is Chuck's Halloween party."

"Yup, I'm going," I said between blowing a forkful of pasta.

Tina muttered under her breath, "Gee, I wonder why…"

I swallowed the bite I'd taken. "You're really pissing me off, Tee. Weren't you the one who begged me to go last year?"

Tina sighed. "I'm worried. You've finally come out of your self-induced mental prison, and I'm relieved. Now that you're getting back to being the fun and happy Tess I grew up with, I don't want you to get hurt and go back to that dark place you've been in for so long."

I wanted to but couldn't explain to her that Jax was the reason I'd started having a life again. The moment our eyes met that first time, it was like my entire being—heart, mind, and soul—came alive. But telling her that would only make it worse.

Instead, I mumbled, "There's no comparison to what happened in the past to whatever's happening now. This is a stupid crush and I'll get over it."

"From everything I know about Jax, he's a good guy. But even good guys slip." She gave me a pointed stare down. "And good girls. Even though Brooke's known for being a snooty brat, Jax has always been loyal to her. They've been through a lot together. I don't see him leaving her."

"I don't expect him to! Nothing's going to happen! We're friends."

"I don't know, Tess. I see how the two of you look at each other. The more I see you guys near each other, even across the bar, the more I'm convinced he sees you as more than a friend. I think others are seeing it too. Anyone paying attention, that is. If something does happen between you two, you'll be the one who ends up hurt and alone."

More upset than mad, I looked away, praying the tears I felt wouldn't fall. "I'm not over here hoping something will happen. I don't expect anything to, nor do I want to get caught up in some love triangle. But I can't control my feelings for him. I'm trying to fight it, trust me, I am. But..." I choked as treacherous tears rolled down my cheeks.

Tina got up, came around the kitchen island, and hugged me. "I know. As long as you don't get your hopes up, you'll be okay, and eventually your feelings for him will pass."

AS MY TEAMMATES waved to people in the bleachers, I focused on getting my head in the game. It wasn't like there was anyone in the stands to watch me. I had asked Tina if she could come, but she said she didn't think she could make it since she had plans with Jamar and the game was two hours away from campus. A fleeting thought whispered in my head that, had I made more of an effort my first year in California, perhaps I would've had some supporters here to cheer me on for the last time I ever planned on stepping onto the field.

Trying not to let it bother me, I listened to the heavy beats blaring in my ears, getting my adrenaline pumping for the next, and last, ninety minutes of gameplay. As my favorite song played, an unwelcome thought ran through my head. *I wish I had a recording of Jax singing.*

It had been an uneventful week since Tina and I had our fight and subsequent reconciliation. Still, I had skipped Smythie's last night and used this game as an excuse. The team had to leave campus very early in order to make sure we arrived with enough time to change, stretch, and warm up. In reality, I didn't want to be under Tina's scrutiny again. I was sure I'd have to deal with it at the Halloween party later.

When it was time, I removed my earbuds and headed to my position on the field. As I waited for the whistle, I heard my name coming from the crowd in a familiar male voice. My head snapped over to the bleachers. I gaped at a group of spectators, then wanted to cry. I hadn't been hearing things. My dad, who was standing next to my mom, was cheering me on.

They flew all the way here to see my last game?

If that wasn't shocking enough, on the other side of my mom was Tina, and next to her was Jamar. In front of them, Chuck was sitting next to Jax, who was sitting next to Brooke, who was sitting next to Ashton. Eli wasn't there, but I'd known he wouldn't be since he'd left for his parent's house after his last Friday class.

When the group saw me looking, they all jumped up cheering, yelling my name, and whistling. I lifted a hand in a half-wave, stunned by my personal cheerleading squad. *Brooke too? Seriously?* I was tempted to look up to see if there were any pigs in the sky.

The whistle blew, and reflexively I was off. Digging my feet into the grass, I forgot all about anything other than where the ball was until the final whistle.

chapter
thirty-seven

JAXON

TESS WAS SITTING on one of her team's sideline benches with her back to the stands. She had her earbuds in and looked focused, at least from my vantage point. She hadn't once turned to look at the crowd since Ashton, Brooke, and I had arrived.

Twisting around, I asked Tina, "Did she see you guys before we got here?"

Tina shook her head. "No. Tess is super focused before games and blocks everything else out. She's got her own pregame routine. Honestly, she might not even notice us until the end."

Smirking, I turned back around, not missing Brooke rolling her eyes, which I ignored. I was shocked she'd joined us. Tina had asked me a few weeks ago if I could attend the game, since it was Tess's last game and she didn't have many people to cheer her on. I'd agreed immediately and told Brooke about it. She hadn't said anything one way or the other, but a few days ago she'd asked if she could tag along.

Of course, I had no reason to deny her, but it had taken me a second to answer. When Ashton found out we were going, he wanted to join too. It was a relief that the people I was closest to had started accepting my friendship with Tess.

Glancing around to see if there was anyone from school I recognized, I spotted an older couple walking in our direction. Seeing the woman's face, I did a double take. It was like I was seeing Tess thirty or so years into the future.

"Mrs. Givens! Mr. Givens! Over here!" Tina yelled from behind us.

They looked in our direction, smiled and waved. Tess was a spitting image of her mom, only younger. As the couple climbed up the metal bleachers to join our group, I couldn't help but note that Tess was going to age very gracefully.

Tina was jubilant as she hugged first Tess's mom then her dad. After asking them about their flight here, she introduced everyone.

After my introduction, her mom, with irises the same blue-green as Tess's, eyed me curiously. I actually squirmed, not that anyone would've thought anything of it considering we were all sitting on hard, cold metal. However, Mrs. Givens simply said, "Nice to meet you."

I suspected she'd heard my name before. *Did Tess tell her mom about me?*

With introductions complete, Tina asked the couple, "When's your flight back?"

"Oh, later today actually." Mrs. Givens sounded disappointed then laughed. If my eyes had been closed, I would've thought Tess was sitting behind me. "Maybe we're a little crazy to fly twelve hours round trip for a soccer game, but what could we do? We didn't want to miss her last game. I mean, she's been playing since she could walk."

"I can tell," Chuck chimed in. "She's awesome! It's like the ball is an extension of herself."

Ashton asked, "Twelve hours? You guys on the East Coast?"

"We live in upstate New York," Mr. Givens replied.

"Wow, that's great you were able to make it out. Tess is lucky to have supportive parents."

I couldn't have agreed more. No wonder Tess was such a great person. Look at the people who'd raised her! She must've grown up in a very loving and nurturing household.

Drawing our focus back to the field, Chuck advised, "They're about to start."

Tess stood, removed her earbuds, and jogged out to the middle of the field. Her dad yelled her name, whistled, then clapped. Tess's head snapped over in our direction. Tina and Jamar, followed by the rest of us, jumped up and cheered for her. Brooke even stood and clapped, although less enthusiastically. The look on Tess's face had our group howling, even Brooke snickered. She lifted her hand in a wave, but then the whistle blew, and she immediately transformed from a surprised girl to a competitive athlete.

I'd been looking forward to the game ever since Tina asked if I wanted to go. It was my turn to watch Tess on her stage. Although I'd seen part of that one game earlier in the season, I was sorry I hadn't seen more. Tess told me once that I was mesmerizing to watch. Well, so was she. She ran round the field like a cheetah, aggressive in taking and keeping the ball from her opponents. Once the morning haze cleared away, her skin glowed and shimmered in the sun. I'd never considered sweat sexy before, but holy fuck...I swore Tess got more beautiful every time I saw her, which was a high bar from the start.

I got more caught up in the game than I thought possible, but that wasn't to say I kept my eyes on the ball the whole time. Thankfully, Tess had possession of the ball a lot, so for the most part it appeared my focus was on the ball, not the girl. She scored the three goals her team got.

I asked Chuck, "Is it me, or is Tess doing all the work out there for her team?"

"It's not you. She pretty much is." He sounded annoyed for her. "Almost all their starters got hurt, so mostly everyone out there is a backup. Technically, Tess is a backup too."

"Bet the team regrets that," I muttered, wondering if I would've met her last year had she been on the team.

Chuck whistled. "She's always really good, but today she's on fire. I guess she wants to make her last game count."

Unfortunately, Tess couldn't win the game alone, and her team lost three to four. It wasn't like she could play offense, defense, and goalie at the same time. Despite the loss, her demeanor was cheerful, happy with her own play, I guessed. She even smiled as she shook hands with the other team before heading to the sideline.

Calling out over the fence, Tess asked, "What are you all doing here? You're all crazy! Mom, Dad, did you seriously fly all the way out here for this?" She was damn near giddy, and her happiness was contagious.

Tina called back, "We couldn't let you play your last game without a proper sendoff, could we?"

"Did you arrange this, Tee?"

"What wouldn't I do for my bestie?"

Tess mouthed, "Thank you." Then she hugged her parents over the fence, as they had gotten down from the bleachers by then. Slowly, the others started down, but Brooke didn't move, so I stayed with her.

Watching Tess talk and laugh with her parents, she said, "She's lucky. I can't even get my parents to come to one of my plays, and they only live a couple of hours away, not a couple thousand miles."

I put my hand on her leg and rubbed it comfortingly, because there were no words that could. Brooke's parents were giant assholes.

"I wonder if Tess would come to one of my plays," Brooke pondered out loud.

"Of course she would. You came here for her," I said.

Brooke turned and narrowed her eyes in disgust. "I didn't come here for her, Jaxon. I came here for you. She's your friend, not mine. But I told you I would try harder, so I am." She stood. "But she's not my friend," she reiterated for emphasis before taking a step down.

Stopping and looking over her shoulder at me, she sneered, "Oh, and please don't bring her to one of my plays. I don't want her there, and I have plenty of friends who'll support me. I don't need a fake one, nor do I need to ask my friends to come see me."

The happiness I felt emanating from Tess vanished. Brooke wasn't being nice and she sure as hell wasn't "trying" like she claimed. She'd come here to antagonize Tess, I was sure of it. She'd stood up and cheered when we all did so Tess would see her. Suddenly very tired, I was dreading the two-hour drive back.

By the time I descended from the bleachers, Tess had already started heading back to a building I assumed held the locker rooms. Her parents were going to meet her by the bus after she showered and changed, say their goodbyes, and catch their flight back. I didn't get to say anything to her. Not even a quick greeting, encouragement, or a farewell. Disappointed, I watched as she walked away. Glancing over her shoulder, she caught me watching. I held up a hand. She smiled and waved back.

Sighing, I turned toward the parking lot to catch up with Ashton and Brooke. We had to get to Chuck's to help set up for the Halloween party. His parties were always big and unforgettable.

chapter
thirty-eight

JAXON

"HOLY SHIT."

At Chuck's appreciative explicative, I looked up from my phone. He was biting his fist. Not bothering to look at who he was drooling over, I asked, "Find your sleeping companion for the night?"

Chuck looked at me like I was crazy. "What? No. I don't want you to beat me to death."

"What? Why would I—"

Leaning in, he whispered, "Tess, dude."

Looking toward the front door, I spotted Tina then the blonde bombshell next to her. I almost dropped my drink. *Holy fuuuuuck...*

Chuck grumbled beside me, "Damn, I kinda wish I was Eli right now. He's a dumbass for missing her in that."

Shit. I kinda wished I was Eli too...for about half a split second, before remembering it was fucking Eli. I kicked that thought right out of my brain. I knew I was gawking at the sexy pirate named Tess, but Jesus Christ, I couldn't stop myself. She had on a tight one-piece bodysuit in typical black, white, and red pirate pattern, fishnets, and boots that came up to the middle of her thighs. A bandana was over her long, straight hair.

I'd never realized how long her hair was, as she usually had it styled or tied up. My subconscious wandered without permission, noting that the pale locks were long enough to cover her breasts. I'd seen Tess in shorts and a sports bras before, so it wasn't hard to imagine her only wearing those thigh-high boots with her hair down covering her chest. *Fuck!*

Forcefully dragging my mind out of the gutter, I took in the rest of her outfit. A pirate jacket and fake sword completed her ensemble.

Ashton elbowed me. "You're gawking. Better not let Brooke see you staring like that. Don't feel being an accessory after the fact when she murders you and needs help burying your body."

Bringing my cup up to my lips, I took a swallow of my ice water, hoping it'd cool me down. If it didn't, I might've had to do something I really didn't want to, like fuck Brooke in the bathroom. *Seriously, what the fuck is wrong with you?* I berated myself. I hadn't struggled this much to keep myself from getting hard since middle school.

I tried averting my eyes but kept glancing at Tess as she moved toward the table with alcohol, greeting people along the way. Knowing I had to stop looking at her, I turned my back and faced Chuck, who was still eyeing her. He was right. I did want to beat his ass.

"Chuck, you really going to stand there and fantasize about her all night?" I said, trying to hide my annoyance, although he probably noticed it anyway.

He rolled his eyes. "Relax, dude. I can appreciate a beautiful woman, especially one looking sexy as hell. Don't be mad because you have to be a good boyfriend," he mocked.

Feeling obligated, I defended my girlfriend. "Hey, Brooke looks hot in that tiny little dress." For good measure, I added, "I'll probably fuck her in it later."

I had no intention of actually doing that, still pissed about her motive for going to Tess's game. But Chuck would never know. Sure, he and Ashton knew things were tense between Brooke and me lately, but they didn't know the half of it. If they had, Chuck would've hounded me again to leave her, and Ashton would've made me feel worse than I already did.

Eyeing Brooke in her sparkly red mini dress adorned with a tail and horns that sat atop her head, a look of disgust crossed Chuck's features. "Her costume is...appropriate. Matches her personality perfectly." Looking at me, he wondered, "Are you sure that's a costume?"

I almost decked him. She was still my girlfriend after all, but Ashton interjected, "Shut up, Chuck, otherwise I'll be helping Jax with your body instead."

Chuck rolled his eyes and walked away. As the host, he probably shouldn't have been standing around and checking out girls all night anyway. He was good at keeping everyone in line, so nothing got out of hand. At his mom's direction, he'd also hired discreet security to help keep an eye on things.

Time passed and my eyes unwillingly betrayed me as they kept searching for the pirate goddess. While I might've scolded Chuck for fantasizing about her, I was just as guilty, if not more, since he was single and I wasn't. As I watched her get another drink at the makeshift bar, I chuckled to myself. *Eli, you dumb prick. You missed your girlfriend dressed like a sexy goddess to go trick-or-treating with your nieces and nephews?* I loved family, hoped to have a big one some day, and appreciated families that were close, but Chuck was right. He was definitely missing out. Whatever, his loss. Couldn't say I was sorry for him.

As I subtly watched Tess sip her drink, I was glad I didn't drink much, because if I had, it might've been a bit more obvious that I was looking at her more often than I should've been. Like when she dropped her phone and bent to pick it up. All I could do was imagine fucking her bent over a table in those thigh-high boots. If I had been single, I would have done everything in my power to do just that. But then again, if I had been single, I was positive I would've already brought her home, if she would've been up for it.

Fuck! I needed to stop imagining that kind of thing. I had a girlfriend, and I was in public wearing tight jeans!

Speaking of Brooke, I scanned the room and found her. She was with her friends, and they all seemed to be having a little too much fun. *Dammit, Brooke!* I suspected they didn't only have alcohol in their systems. Not about to go over there myself and find out for sure, I walked over to Ashton and told him my suspicions. He'd make sure I wouldn't be tempted to go over there, not that I thought I would be.

· · ·

A WHILE LATER, Tess joined Ashton and I. With her signature beaming smile, she said, "Thank you so much for coming to my game today! I was so shocked to see everyone there. I really, really appreciate it. Next time we hang out at the bar, I'll buy you guys a round...or something." She glanced at me.

Ashton smiled at her. "No problem. I'm a huge fan of soccer, and Chuck hasn't shut up about how good you are."

"Really? Chuck talks about me playing soccer?" she asked with pink cheeks.

"Yeah, and after watching you today, I completely agree." Ashton took a swig of his beer before asking, "Jax told me you want to be a cop. Why's that?"

She shrugged but had a subtle grin on her face. "I want to help people and catch the bad guys."

Every time Tess opened her mouth, I was more and more intrigued by her. She was special, and whoever she ended up with would be one lucky guy. I hoped it wouldn't be Eli.

"Oh, heeeeeeeya, Tess!" Brooke nearly crooned as she popped up next to me.

Tess smiled. "Hi, Brooke. Thanks for coming to my game today. That was really nice of you."

Intoxicated, Brooke smiled, although it looked more like a grimace. "I know. So sorry that you lost your last game. Really sucks to go out like that, huh?"

I gaped in horror at her. *What the fuck, Brooke? This is you trying? You may have fooled me before, but now you're not even trying to pretend to be nice!*

I glanced at Tess, about to apologize, when she responded, "Oh, that's alright. I've won a lot more than I've lost in the last seventeen years or so, so it's not a big deal. I didn't think I was going to play again, so anything I got to do this year was a bonus."

Classy. Add that to Tess's list of attributes. Looking down at Brooke, I glared. She looked unhappy, and after a second or two she mumbled, "Whatever." Then she stumbled away, worse off than I thought.

Unable to meet Tess's eye, I whispered, "Sorry."

I went after Brooke. It took me a few minutes, but I eventually found her outside, raiding a bowl of candy. To avoid the potential of making a scene, I didn't engage but kept an eye on her. Unfortunately, a couple of freshman girls who reeked of alcohol came over and started making things really awkward. After surrounding me—one of them even put her hands on my stomach—they made it clear they'd be up for some fun if I wanted.

"Uh...I have a girlfriend," I said, feeling a little panicked as I took a step back and watched said girlfriend stalk off.

"Oh, we don't care. She can join us if she wants."

Hastily, I said, "No thanks." I headed off to find Brooke again.

Eventually, I found her dancing on a table back inside. While trying to get her to come down so she wouldn't break her neck, Tina grabbed my arm in a panic.

"Have you seen Tess? I can't find her! I thought maybe she was at home, but she's not there. I've looked all over!"

Out of patience with my girlfriend, I grabbed Brooke's waist, removed her from the table, then held her next to me. Turning to Tina, I said, "Last time I saw her, she was talking to Ashton."

Tina bolted over to him. I followed, dragging Brooke over with me as she put up a weak fight while stumbling and giggling. When I got to Tina and Ashton, he told her, "We were talking, but then she seemed sort of out of it. I asked if she was okay. She said she wasn't feeling well and needed to use the bathroom. Then she headed off that way." Ashton pointed in the direction of Chuck's bathroom, which was in the opposite direction of the front door.

Brooke's laughing fit continued with a few snorts. "What a wimp. Can't even hold her liquor." *Definitely high.*

Tina ran toward the bathroom. Guiding Brooke into Ashton's arms, I asked, "Watch her, please?" Not waiting for an answer, I followed after her. The bathroom was dark and unoccupied. With fear in her eyes, Tina faced me.

"Go check your house again. Maybe you missed each other," I suggested.

She nodded and sprinted toward the back door. I was about to go find Chuck when he came around the corner. Something caught my eye, and I turned. A flickering was coming from under his spare room's door.

I put my hand on his chest to stop him and pointed. "Is there supposed to be anyone in there?"

"No," he said, pissed that someone had broken into the locked room that had a sign barring entry.

I tried the knob. Unsurprisingly, it was locked.

Chuck banged on the door. "Hey! Stop fucking around! You're not allowed in there!"

The only answer was some crashing noises. My gut told me we needed to get in there. "Open it, Chuck," I demanded.

Chuck grimaced. "But what if they're naked or something?"

With panic bubbling up, I yelled, "Open the fucking door!"

Confused, he slowly, too slowly, felt above the top of the door frame while calling out, "We're coming in!"

There were more noises. Not liking Chuck's slow movements, I knocked his hand away, grabbed the small tool he kept stashed on top of the frame, and jammed it into the lock, twisting until the lock gave way. I pushed, but the door wouldn't open.

"That asshole blocked the door!" Chuck huffed.

"Sorry, Chuck," I said right before shoving the door open with all my weight, likely breaking things along the way. Scanning the dark room, I saw nothing except junk and an open window.

"They escaped out the window? What douches," Chuck muttered.

Continuing to search the room, I shoved boxes and other shit out of the way. Then I found her unconscious on the floor, half-dressed.

"What the fuck?" Chuck shouted, "Tess!"

Crouching down beside her, I ripped off my shirt to cover her as I yelled, "Go get Tina!" Looking over my shoulder, I noticed a small crowd had gathered outside the door, probably hearing the commotion. "Get those assholes out of here!"

As Chuck yelled at the group to go away, a security guard arrived. After giving a brief explanation, Chuck instructed him to get Tina and shut the party down but also to see if anyone saw who went out the window. Meanwhile, I called Tess's name as I gently shook her. She was breathing, and there weren't any obvious injuries. She must've been in a drug-induced slumber, having passed out from whatever toxin had been slipped to her.

Groaning, Tess tried rolling over, but fearing she would be exposed again, I restrained her. She resisted for a moment then gave up. I considered putting the shirt on her, but I'd have to sit her up, exposing her again, and I couldn't do that. I'd already seen more of her than I should've and felt like shit for it, even if I was trying to help.

Ashton called from behind me, "What happened? Is she okay?"

"I don't know," I said, answering both his questions. My voice sounded rough, like I might cry. Swallowing back the tears, I asked, "Where's Brooke?"

"With Maisie," he answered, referring to Brooke's best friend.

"Can she bring Brooke home?"

Tina came flying into the room before he could answer. Stopping, she took in the scene. Tess unconscious on the floor, my shirt covering her, cut-off pieces of her costume strewn about. Kneeling down beside me, she asked what happened. After giving her a summary, she asked us to leave so she could take a closer look at Tess in private.

As we stood outside the door, Ashton asked, "Do you think she was—"

"I don't think so," I interrupted him, because if he had actually said the word, I would've lost it. Rubbing my forehead, I explained, "She wasn't completely..." I swallowed against the tightness in my throat. "She wasn't completely undressed." My voice cracked.

Chuck arrived and gave us an update. "No one saw anything. That window faces the side with nothing but a bunch of trees. It's dark, and no one was over on that side of the house. When we asked if people saw who Tess was with, most people didn't even know who she was. So no one saw anything." Looking between us, Chuck asked, "Shouldn't we call the police?"

Before I could give my opinion, Tina opened the door. "Tell me again exactly what happened and what you saw. You need to be as specific as possible."

We told her.

She sighed. Wiping a tear away, she said, "Okay look, I think you guys stopped anything too bad from happening. The bottom of her costume intact so…" Almost to herself, added, "Thank God she wasn't wearing a skirt or dress…"

We stood in silence as her implication sunk in.

"We should call the police," I suggested.

Tina shook her head. "No. I know Tess better than anyone. She won't want to call the police if nothing happened."

"But something did happen!" I argued.

Chuck asked, "But doesn't she want to be a cop? Doesn't she trust them?"

"I need to talk to her about it first. I can take her to get checked out or whatever she wants to do in the morning," Tina said.

Ashton, Chuck, and I all objected, but none of us had any right to have a say, and Tina held firm. Turning to me, she asked, "Can you help me bring her home?"

Although unhappy about not calling emergency services, I agreed. What else could I do? Chuck ran to my car and grabbed the shirt I had worn that morning to the soccer game. Tina had put my t-shirt on her. I bent down and scooped Tess up into my arms. She was a lot lighter than I expected. Sure, she was skinny, but she was taller than the average woman and toned with muscles.

Trying to avoid as many eyes as possible, I carried her out the back. Walking to her house, I realized tonight was the first time I had come into physical contact with Tess since we shook hands the day we met. First, trying to shake her awake, now carrying her. I hated it. It wasn't that I hated touching her, but rather the fact that she wasn't aware of it.

In the weeks I'd known her, she'd always been so careful not to touch me. Was I violating her myself right now? I was helping her, but she wasn't aware and had never said I could touch her. If she was okay with it, maybe I'd give her a hug the next time I saw her.

After we stepped into her and Tina's house through the back door, Tina pointed down the hall to Tess's room. As I walked past Tina, Tess's hand glided up my chest, and I nearly froze. Not wanting to draw any attention to it, I forced myself to keep walking, determined to put her down and get out of there as quickly as possible. But Tess had other plans.

She made a noise like she was enjoying running her hand up and down my chest. Then she nuzzled into it, and my breathing faltered as sweat broke out on my forehead. Did she have any idea what she was doing? Did she even know it was me that was holding her?

"Mmm...you smell so good," she purred. "I love the way you smell."

That did stop me. "Tess?"

"Mm hmm?"

I swallowed. "Go back to sleep, okay?" Holy shit, I sounded like a teen boy whose voice was changing. Cracking and unsteady. Good thing she was out of it, or she might've caught on that my breathing had grown ragged and my heart was pounding against my ribcage.

Only a few steps away from her bed, she wrapped her arms around my neck and hugged me, burying her face in my neck. "Why? When will I ever get to do this again?"

Do what? Wait, did she know it was me?

Finally, I'd reached her bed. Bending over it, I placed her down as gently as possible. But she didn't let go and mumbled something I didn't understand.

"Go to sleep," I whispered.

She sighed but let go of my neck. Before I could walk away. She grabbed my hand. "I have a secret, Jax."

Holy shit... she knew it was me.

A nervous laugh escaped. "If it's a secret, you shouldn't tell me."

"I wish I could. It's about you, you know. Maybe I can tell you one day." Her speech was slow, a little slurred and almost dreamy.

I had a feeling I knew what the secret was. "Maybe. Goodnight, Tessa."

Looking at me with hooded eyes, she reached up and cupped my cheek. There was a real possibility I was about to go insane. Gently, I took her hand away, but she placed it back on my cheek, her thumb stroking back and forth against my night stubble. "You have pretty eyes. They're my favorite."

I couldn't stop my smile. She wasn't going to remember any of this, was she? "Thank you. You have pretty eyes too."

She smiled sadly. "Thanks."

In her uninhibited state of mind, she couldn't hide it. I wouldn't lie to myself anymore. Tess liked me as more than a friend. She'd tried to hide it, and that was one of the things I admired about her. Over the years, there had been plenty of girls who'd made it no secret they were interested, regardless of if I had a girlfriend or not, like the group of girls earlier. But Tess wasn't trying to interfere with my relationship. She pretended all she felt was friendship and was even dating another guy. Although not the biggest fan of Brooke, she accepted I was with her.

The more I got to know her, the more I liked her. Actually, if there was one thing tonight's events had done, it was that it made me realize I loved Tess. As a person and friend. I wouldn't allow myself to consider anything beyond that. But I would go on pretending I didn't know how she felt, because she wasn't choosing to do or say any of this. It was the drug, and she probably wouldn't even remember. I hoped she didn't because maybe it would be less traumatizing.

Seeing if she would be okay with what I wanted to do, I whispered, "I'm going to kiss you on your forehead, if that's okay?"

She closed her eyes and sighed, a contented smile on her lips. "I really want you to kiss me."

Leaning down, I kissed the center of her forehead, knowing full well that it wasn't the type of kiss she wanted. After standing up, I caught a movement out of the corner of my eye. Tina was standing in the doorway. I looked at Tess once more before walking away. She was out.

As I approached, Tina stopped me. "What'd she say?"

Avoiding her eyes, I lied, "Mostly a bunch of gibberish."

Tina narrowed her eyes. "Really?"

I took in a shaky breath then shook my head.

"What'd she say?"

Unable to look at her, I admitted, "Nothing I didn't already suspect."

"What are you going to do about it?"

I shrugged. "What can I do? Go on like normal, like I don't know, I guess."

Tina glared. "Do not hurt her. You understand?"

"Why would I hurt her? I care about her."

"In what way?"

Feeling a little lost, my eyes pricked. After swallowing the lump in my throat, I said, "I haven't figured that out yet." Was I actually telling Tess's best friend this?

"You should probably tell her when you do figure it out. That way, maybe she'll be able to move on."

I stared at her. "Why do you assume that's what I want?"

"Because you have a girlfriend," Tina hissed. "I would expect that if for some reason you didn't want to be with her anymore, you would've left her, right? So why would you want a girl who doesn't have a chance not to get over it?"

Still not sure why I was having this conversation with her, I said, "Right. Anyway, goodnight. Let me know if you need anything. I need to go find Brooke."

*Brooke...*What was I going to do with her? I was fucking pissed. She'd said she was going to stop the drugs! I didn't care about her drinking, but this was too much. She lived with a recovering addict, for fuck's sake! What was she doing?

With a sigh, I set off to find my girlfriend.

chapter
thirty-nine

JAXON

WHILE I LOOKED around for the intoxicated redhead, Ashton informed me that Maisie had put Brooke in a ride-share back to our apartment. Relieved, I headed home after promising Chuck I'd be back in the morning to help him clean up.

As soon as I shut our apartment's front door, ice-cold water soaked the front of my shirt. Jumping back, I exclaimed, "Ahh!"

"What were you doing with her?" Brooke screamed at me while waving an empty glass around.

Not understanding what she was going on about this time, I couldn't answer right away.

"Huh? What? What were you doing, fucking her?" The cup went flying, shattering against the door behind me, as Brooke ranted on.

"What are you doing?" I knew what she was doing, but why she was throwing a drink and cup at me and saying stupid shit? I had no idea.

"What do you think I'm doing, asshole?"

Trying to remain calm, I kept my tone even. "Calm down. And stop screaming."

"No! You don't get to tell me what to do! Not when you're fucking some whore behind my back! Is that it? Is that why you won't fuck me anymore, because you're getting it somewhere else?"

"Can we go into the living room, or do you really want to talk right next to the front door?"

Standing on her toes, trying to get in my face despite our height difference, she yelled, "You're an actual piece of shit! You know that? I've done nothing to deserve this!"

Huffing, I said, "Fine, I guess we're having the conversation right here. I helped Tina bring Tess home. We found her passed out in Chuck's spare room. We think she was drugged."

Stomping away a couple of steps before turning back around, she shrieked, "Why is that your problem? She's not your problem! You should have been with me! I'm your girlfriend! Me! Or did you drug her yourself so you could fuck her?"

What? I put my hands on my throbbing head and rubbed my palms into my temples. "I'm not cheating on you, and I don't want to have this conversation right now. You're drunk and high. I don't wanna deal with you when you're like this and saying some fucked-up shit."

Brooke stomped back over to me. Poking my chest, she said, "Too bad for you. You live in my apartment, and I can kick you out with one word, so you better watch yourself! And right now, I don't want you here! You're disgusting! How could you think about coming home and sleeping in my bed after cheating on me?"

I'd never seen her this belligerent before. The incomprehension of the situation began boiling my blood. "Move your hand, Brooke," I whispered through my teeth.

"Make me."

After taking a step to the side, I tried passing her, but Brooke matched my movement. "Excuse me, did I say you could be here in my apartment? I think not. I think I told you to leave." Raising her voice, she yelled, "You don't get to be here unless I say you can be!"

"Fine, I'll leave, and we can talk when you're sober. I'll–"

Slap!

Stunned, it took a second for what happened to register. Lifting a hand to my stinging cheek, my skin was hot and wet. Pulling my hand away, I saw red on my fingers. Automatically, I looked down at her balled-up hand. She hadn't yet removed her rings. Opening my mouth to ask her why, she didn't give me the chance to speak before she started ranting incoherently. When she started pushing at me, I figured it out.

Holding my hands up, I said, "Fine! I'm leaving! Back up and I'll go." I didn't recognize the sound of defeated panic in my voice.

It took another few seconds, but I finally escaped into the hallway. As I stood, trying to catch my breath, I heard the door lock click then the chain slide into place. I was truly locked out now.

Searching my pockets, I found my phone. I tried texting Chuck, but...Was my keyboard broken? Had the buttons moved out of place so that my muscle memory was fucked? Examining my hands, I watched as they shook violently.

Unable to text, I hit Chuck's name in my call log. Thankfully, he hadn't gone to sleep yet.

"Dude?"

"Can I stay with you tonight?" I rasped. There was dead silence. My voice was not my own. Feeling hot moisture running down my uninjured cheek, I turned and looked into a decorative mirror that hung on the wall. I watched in morbid curiosity as the tears on my left cheek turned into streaks of blood when they hit my cut.

"What happened?" Chuck demanded.

I tried to get myself under control. "I've been locked out." My voice sounded flat, but at least it didn't sound like I was crying anymore.

Without any hesitation, he said, "Yeah, of course, man. You can come here whenever."

"Thanks. I'll be there in a few."

After hanging up, I walked to then rode down the elevator in a daze.

I BLINKED and found myself parked back in front of Chuck's house, not having remembered the drive at all. He was waiting when I walked into his living room, nursing a glass of amber liquid. His eyes widened after doing a double-take. Red-faced, he jumped to his feet and bellowed, "She fucking hit you!" It wasn't a question.

"Uh..." I hesitated, not sure what I should reveal.

"Has she ever hit you before?" he seethed.

I shook my head. "It's not—"

"What? Are you going to tell me that the red handprint on your face isn't what it looks like?"

I'd never seen this side of Chuck before. "Don't worry about it," I muttered as I dragged myself over to his couch before collapsing onto my stomach, my face turned toward my enraged best friend.

He took a deep breath then held up his glass. "You want one?"

"No, thanks," I said, although I did. I wanted to throw it back along with a few more. Alcohol had never been a problem, and I did drink occasionally, but never when I felt so shitty.

Chuck let out a breath as he sat on the armchair adjacent to the couch.

"Want to talk about it?"

"No."

"If you ever do, I'm here." He took a breath, preparing to say something, a very un-Chuck move. "You don't have to respond, but I am going to say a couple of things that you're not going to like."

Tired, I only blinked.

"You know my dad used to beat the shit out of my mom, right?" My eyes widened. *No, I didn't know that!* But I stayed silent as he continued, "It didn't start like that. It was gradual, but once it starts, it doesn't stop, at least not until something really bad happens." Chuck stared into his glass for several seconds before quietly asking, "Do you know why I never see my dad?"

"No."

"It's because he's serving twenty years for the attempted murder of my mother."

Holy shit! I knew Chuck's biological dad wasn't around, but I thought he was a deadbeat, which I guess he was, but a criminal one apparently.

"I don't know what's going on with you and Brooke... And I've made it no secret that I don't like her, but I tried to stay out of it because I thought she made you happy. But you're fucking miserable. You gotta seriously consider ending it, man. You can stay here with me."

I looked at the floor as I tried to explain. "It was because she was high and drunk. I'm going to talk to her about it. I know things can't continue like this. And she's never..." I paused, not able to actually say it. "...acted like that before. I don't think she'd do it again, but if she does, I'd probably leave."

Chuck jumped up again. "Probably? And it's not a matter of if, dude, but when. Didn't she break your phone before?"

I sighed. "I'm not afraid of her. She's almost a foot shorter than me and not very strong, so I'm not worried about getting hurt and—"

He huffed, then threw back the rest of his whiskey. Frustrated, he lectured, "Look, she can still hurt you, mentally and physically. But hello, Jax. What if she's going after you and you have to defend your-self? She's a conniving bitch and will probably turn around and blame you. Who do you think the cops will believe?"

I didn't answer, too tired and really not in the mood for another fight tonight.

He got the hint that I wasn't talking, so he stalked out of the room. But before he left, he seethed, "If you stay with her, and she does it again, I'll call the cops on her, even if that means you stop talking to me."

Checking the time on my phone, I hoped Simon would forgive me for calling him so late.

He answered during the fourth ring, sounding both alarmed and half asleep, "Jaxon! What's wrong?"

Leaving out Brooke's slap, I told him about the night's events. He was unhappy, to put it mildly.

Although he'd never told me what I should do in the past, tonight Simon was blunt. "If she's going to continue to use drugs, you can't stay with her, or you'll end up relapsing, in prison, or dead."

Tired, frustrated, and annoyed that someone else was telling me what I should or shouldn't do when it came to the woman who'd saved my life, I snapped at Simon for the first time ever. "I didn't call you for relationship advice! I called you because of the drugs!"

Sternly, he said, "I'm not giving you relationship advice. I'm trying to keep you alive and sober."

I sighed. After a long pause, I explained, "I'll talk to her and tell her I'll leave if she keeps using."

"But will you?"

An image of sparkling eyes flashed behind my closed lids. "Yes, I don't want to relapse or die."

AS THE BLACKNESS outside the living room window gradually lightened, I replayed the night's events in my head over and over until I came to an excruciating realization: what happened tonight was my fault. I should have kept a better eye on Tess. If I had, she would've been okay, and Tina wouldn't have needed my help. And if Tina hadn't needed my help, Brooke wouldn't have flipped out. Clearly, whatever it was that I was doing was creating issues. I needed to talk to Brooke about it. I needed to know how I could fix it.

Giving up on sleep, I got up and picked up the trash, discarded the empty and half-empty cups, tossed the leftover food, and washed away the stickiness from spilled drinks. After the living room was clean, I walked like a zombie to where Tess was attacked. Although it was still early, the light from the window brightened the room enough that I could get a better look around. Moving boxes and looking under the few pieces of furniture in the room, I searched for anything left behind that could give a clue as to the asshole's identity, but the only things I found that didn't belong were the tatters of Tess's clothes. After finding an old shopping bag, I gathered the pieces of material, which included her cut-off bra. It was bad enough that she was attacked, but Chuck and I saw her exposed. For her sake, I didn't want anyone else finding her personal items later on. She was going to be embarrassed enough as it was.

Staring at the spot where I'd found her unconscious body, I knew that I'd have to tell her. I respected her too much not to. I hoped she'd forgive me and understand I was only trying to help.

chapter
forty

JAXON

IT WAS early afternoon when I rang Tess and Tina's doorbell. Tina opened the door and stepped aside so I could enter. She eyed my cheek but thankfully didn't ask about it. I'd have to think of an excuse if people asked. Brooke hadn't contacted me yet, which was another relief. With the shock of the night worn off, anger had set in, and the last thing I wanted to do was deal with her.

"How is she?" I asked as I shut the front door.

With teary eyes, Tina turned her head in the direction of Tess's room. "Why don't you go see for yourself?"

Her bedroom door was open. Peering in, I took a second to glance around. With the darkness and Tess's intoxicated behavior the night before, I hadn't seen much. Her bedroom was neat and well-kept. The walls were a light tan with minimal decor, although there was a string of lights on the wall above her bed. By the doorway, there was a dresser to the right and a closet on the left. Next to the dresser was a couch along the wall, parallel to the bed against the opposite wall. Her mattress was raised, making space for storage underneath. A small desk with a closed laptop and her school bag was between her bed and closet. The room matched Tess's personality: light, neat, and simple, yet modern and classy.

As for the girl I couldn't get out of my head, she was lying on her back in bed, staring at the ceiling. Hoping to not startle her, I gently knocked on the wooden doorframe.

Turning her head, Tess peered in my direction. "Hey," she greeted.

"Hey. Can I come in?" I asked.

"Sure."

Although she'd agreed I could enter, it didn't sound like she wanted me to. And that hurt. I'd have to make my stay short. As I walked to her couch, I kept an eye on her. She'd gone back to staring straight up again. Her eyes were puffy and face pink.

"How are you?" I asked softly after I sat down.

"Could be worse." After a few seconds of silence, she looked over at me. Her eyes went wide, and she sat up. "Are you okay? Your face..."

Turning the injured cheek away, I took in a shaky breath. I hadn't figured out an excuse yet. Being exhausted, my brain protested against thinking.

Breaking into my thoughts, Tess asked, "Has that happened before?"

After a brief hesitation, I shook my head, giving up on trying to think of an excuse. Besides, there was something about Tess that compelled me to be honest with her.

"Are you okay?"

Was Tess even human? After what happened to her last night, she was worried about me? She had to be the most selfless person I knew.

To answer her question, I shrugged then admitted, "I wish I could forget last night, for more than one reason."

"It's ironic. I can't remember anything and wish I could. You probably remember everything but wish you couldn't." Her voice was flat.

"It might be better if you didn't remember."

A tear slid slowly down her cheek. "Thanks, Jax. If it hadn't been for you, I—" Her voice cracked, and her hands flew to her face.

Without thinking, I stood and took the three steps needed to reach her. Holding out my arms, I told her, "Come here."

She did, and I wrapped my arms around her trembling body. She buried her face in my shirt and sobbed as I stroked her hair. The discomfort in my chest went from annoying to painful when the wetness of her tears seeped into my shirt. Without thinking, I kissed the top of her head. She stilled.

Shit!

Tess pulled back and looked up at me. I opened my mouth to apologize but she spoke first, "You kissed my forehead last night, didn't you?"

"Uh..." She remembered that? My answer came out in a strained whisper. "Yes."

"I remember it now." She hugged me again. "I guess if I remember anything about last night, that memory isn't so bad."

My heart started beating faster, and I was having trouble breathing, like I couldn't fill my lungs with enough oxygen. Was I about to cry? I didn't think so. So why did my chest feel like there was a pressure holding something down or back?

Tess pulled back again and looked up at me. "Are you okay?" Had she noticed?

Afraid to speak, I nodded. She searched my eyes for the truth. And I searched hers, for what, I wasn't sure. But for the second time, I wanted to kiss her. My eyes dropped to her lips. They parted slightly, and I snapped my eyes back to hers. Her expression had changed. Her eyes were no longer filled with sadness, only surprise. I swallowed.

What was happening to me? Was I seriously considering kissing her? Was she going to let me? Her chest rose and fell rapidly, like she too was trying to catch her breath. The pulse on her neck kept time with my own racing heartbeat.

A million thoughts ran through my head in a split second. I could leave Brooke, especially after what had happened last night. But was I even good enough for Tess? Would she even accept me? Would she be okay with my messed-up past? She wanted to be a cop. Was it okay having an addict as a partner? It should be okay, right? It wasn't like I'd ever been arrested, and I'd been sober for years, so—

I stopped. I was getting ahead of myself. Although I was fairly certain she liked me, especially after last night, it could have been the drug. She was a nice girl with a beautiful smile. Maybe she treated everyone how she treated me. I growled internally, not liking the thought of her treating anyone else how she treated me. As we continued to gaze at each other, I cupped her cheek. With my thumb, I did what I had wanted to do on the Ferris wheel and brushed away the wet streak on her soft cheek.

"Tess!"

We jumped apart. *Fucking Eli!*

I sat back down on the couch as she patted down her hair like I had mussed it. I hadn't, but the move provoked more inappropriate thoughts, like how sexy her sex-hair would be. Remembering how long her hair actually was, an image of her high ponytail wrapped around my fist, pulling as I took her from behind, popped into my head for not the first time. We locked eyes with each other one more time before looking away again.

As inappropriate as they were, I couldn't control my thoughts. *Do you think about me in that way, Tess? Would you like it if I did that to you? Fuuuuuck...* I wanted to do that to her.

As Eli ran into the room, I looked down, trying to adjust my face to concerned friend, not horny bastard who wanted to fuck my friend.

"Tess!" Eli yelled, "Are you okay?" He ran up to her side and tried to kiss her.

I had to forcibly relax my jaw.

Tess pushed him off. "Eli! Stop!"

He looked hurt. I wanted to make him hurt even more by punching him. *Jesus fucking Christ! What the hell does he think he's doing?* She was attacked last night, and the first thing he thought to do was kiss her? My conscience screamed at me, *Hey, asshole! You were literally just thinking about not only kissing her yourself but fucking her!* I wanted to punch myself too.

Knowing my time was up, I stood. Unable to control myself, I muttered under my breath, "She was assaulted last night. Don't you think you should make sure she's okay before touching her?"

Eli shot back, "That didn't stop you from touching her or looking at her when she wasn't okay, did it?"

What the fuck are you implying, you prick?

Pissed, Tess interjected, "What's that supposed to mean?"

"Jax saw you without a shirt on and touched you when you were unconscious," Eli said icily.

Touched her? I carried her home because she was passed out, you fucking prick! Maybe if you were there, this wouldn't have happened to her at all! I wanted to shout at him, but I kept my mouth sealed shut because I didn't want to upset Tess.

"What?" Tess's anger turned to confusion.

The color drained from my face. I assumed Tina had told her I carried her home...and about how I found her.

Thankfully, Tina appeared in the doorway and jumped in, "Jax didn't do anything wrong! When I told you he helped me get you back, I meant he had to carry you. I asked him to since I couldn't do it myself. He was the strongest guy around. And why do you think you were wearing his t-shirt when you woke up?"

Sarcastically, Eli quipped, "You're telling me Jax was the strongest guy at that party?"

Tina glared at him. "He was the strongest guy in the room who had seen Tess in that state. Since he'd already seen her, I figured she would appreciate not having some other guy also see her like that."

Maybe it was petty, but I was enjoying seeing Eli put in his place.

Turning back to Tess, she softened her voice, "I'm sorry, Tess. I thought you understood what I meant when I was explaining it. I guess I should've been more specific."

Tess's red face turned away from us. "It's okay. Thank you for helping me, Jax. I'd like to be alone now."

Like last night, although it wasn't what I wanted, I didn't have a right to protest. I didn't even have a right to be there at all. It hurt that she didn't want me there, but I knew she was embarrassed even though she had nothing to be ashamed about. None of what happened was her fault.

Concealing my disappointment, sadness, concern, and guilt, I headed out. I couldn't even say goodbye, as I was afraid my voice would give me away.

Behind me, I heard Tess say, "You too, Eli."

That's right, Eli. Fuck off!

"But I left my parents as soon as I heard what happened. I came back early to see you," he whined like a little bitch.

Again, I wanted to slug the guy. *She said back off!*

"I appreciate that," Tess said, but it sounded like a lie. "Let's have dinner later or something. My head really hurts, and I need to lie down."

Reluctantly, her annoying-ass boyfriend agreed, "Alright, but before I go, have you spoken to the police yet?"

I stopped my slow exit and listened. I couldn't hear her, but her answer was obvious based on his reaction. "What! Why not? You need to report this. Have you been to the doctor? If not, you have to go!"

Forgetting my place, I marched right back into Tess's room. "Why haven't you reported this to the police? And you have to go to the doctor! At least to find out what was put in your drink!"

At my outburst, Tess's head swung to look at me. Tina and Eli's heads probably had as well, but I was too busy looking at Tess to notice them. Her mouth was agape, but nothing came out of it for a couple of seconds. Then her eyes narrowed, the irises turning to ice.

With a sharp tone I'd never heard from her before, she bit out, "This is none of your business, Jax. I appreciate your help, but you have no right to tell me what I should do in this extremely personal matter."

Like a scolded child, I stared at her. I probably deserve to be chastised, but it hurt. Sighing, I gave a quick, "Sorry," before leaving again.

As I shuffled away with my shoulder slumped, I heard Eli say, "Text me later and we'll get dinner."

"'Kay," she said, although she didn't sound very interested.

A thought occurred to me as I walked to Chuck's. An inappropriate thought, but one that had made me feel a little less guilty. If I had kissed Tess, it would have been nothing like what Eli tried to do. Kissing her was nowhere in my mind when I entered her room. If it had happened, it would have been a natural progression, not an "I just arrived, now let me stick my tongue down your throat" moment. It would've been slow and gentle. Sweet like Tess...

Goddammit, Jax! Get a grip! She has a boyfriend, and you have a girlfriend! Stop thinking about kissing her!

If only I could.

chapter
forty-one

TESSA

ARRIVING HOME after my last class of the day, I swung my bag onto my desk chair before heading for the shower. Although I had no memory of being attacked Saturday night, I still felt the need to wash off the filth for probably the fifth or sixth time in two days.

After showering, I planned on texting Jax to see if he could come over. Seeing him again today would hopefully make tomorrow morning's class less awkward. My face heated for the hundredth time at the knowledge that he'd seen me half-naked. Trying to fight off the embarrassment, I reminded myself again that if it weren't for him, something much worse would've happened. I shuddered at the thought that someone else could've found me in a much worse state.

I did end up going to the clinic on campus to get examined. The rape kit turned up negative, which, based on how I felt, wasn't a surprise, but it was still an enormous relief to be sure. No drugs were found in my system, but that didn't mean I hadn't been drugged, only that too much time had passed.

Since I had not been raped, they gave me a choice about involving the police. Although Tina pleaded with me to make a report, I refused. Maybe I was being stubborn or stupid, but I knew the creep would never be found. There wasn't any evidence or witnesses, and I couldn't remember anything past arriving at the party. So what was the point? Why waste finite resources on a hopeless case when the police's time and money could be spent on working cases that could actually be solved?

That was the excuse I gave, but in reality I was too ashamed. I knew better than to put my drink down unattended for even a second, but I must have. Otherwise, how could someone have slipped me something? I strained my brain until I got a headache trying to recall if anyone had gotten a drink for me, but there was only a black hole of nothing.

Also, I didn't want to tell my parents about it, especially my dad, who had constantly lectured me on safety, including at parties. He'd be so disappointed in me if he found out about it. And since it wasn't as bad as it could have been, they didn't need to know, or so I convinced myself.

As I toweled off after scrubbing my skin raw, I took several calming breaths. The conversation I wanted to have with Jax was going to be a long one. While dreading it, I also wanted to open up to him. After getting dressed, I opened my text message app and sent him a message, forcing myself to sound upbeat.

TESSA GIVENS

Hi! How are you?

JAXON SMITH

Hey. Fine. How are you?

TESSA GIVENS

A bit better today. Are you done with classes for the day?

JAXON SMITH

That's good. Yeah, I'm done.

TESSA GIVENS

Are you busy?

JAXON SMITH

No, just sitting here, eating some eggs.

Ooooo eggs! I LOVE eggs! I can never get enough of them! If that's all I ate for the rest of my life, I'd never complain.

Anyway…

There's something I wanted to talk to you about, but it'll take a while. If you're up for it, can you come over?

He read my text, but there was a long pause of nothing. No dots indicating he was typing a reply, nothing. My stomach sank. Maybe he thought it'd be too awkward to see each other. Or was it possible he was still upset that I was kind of mean to him and basically kicked him out yesterday when he was only concerned about me? Or perhaps the more likely explanation as to why he would avoid coming over was because there was a moment when I thought he was going to kiss me, and he was embarrassed about it. Those couple of seconds when he was stroking my cheek wreaked havoc within me. It was so confusing. Was it possible he liked me more than I thought?

Finally, the phone buzzed.

I'll be there in twenty minutes.

Thanks! :)

EIGHTEEN MINUTES LATER, not that I was counting, he arrived.

"Hey! Thanks for coming," I said as I opened the door wide for him.

Jax stepped inside. "Sure."

I led us to my bedroom. Although Tina knew all too well what had happened four years ago, this was going to be emotional and hard for me, and I didn't want any interruptions.

Once inside my room, I walked over to stand next to my couch and turned around.

Jax seemed hesitant. "Do you want the door open or closed?"

I shrugged. "It doesn't matter." He left it open. When he was standing in front of me, I asked, "Can I hug you?"

His eyebrows shot up. "Yeah."

I took a step forward and wrapped my arms around him. "Thank you so much for helping Saturday night. I didn't thank you properly yesterday. I was still in shock, and the more I learned about what happened, the more shocking it was. Thank you. And I'm sorry I was kind of, uh, not very nice right before you left. I did go to the clinic to get checked out, and everything seems okay."

When I first hugged him, his arms were only lightly hugging me back, but as I spoke, his grip on me tightened. By the time I was done, it felt like he was hanging onto me for dear life.

Quietly, he said, "I'm glad you're okay. It would've killed me if something worse happened." Did I really mean that much to him?

We hugged a little longer, partly because I was afraid my knees would buckle without his support. But it was a double-edged sword. Hanging on, smelling his delicious scent, was making me weak too. Was it sandalwood? Reluctantly, I let go and quickly sat on the couch before my legs gave out. He sat down next to me and waited for me to start, but I didn't know how.

I'd never started this conversation before, but ever since Jax had opened up to me, I've wanted to do the same with him. I'd needed some time to work up the courage though. After Saturday night, knowing that it was because of Jax that nothing worse had happened, I finally got the last push I needed to tell him. He was the first person I was willing to tell because he was also the one person I could relate to. So I opened up like I never had before.

"Do you remember what Chuck said the first time we met, how you were in the band wing and I was with the jocks or something like that?"

"Yeah," he confirmed.

"The person you know now is not the same person I was back in high school. I grew up in a small town, but it was part of a regional school district, so my high school was pretty big. And I was a high school cliché." Jax raised an eyebrow questioningly. "I was the soccer star. I didn't do a winter sport, but I ran track in the spring, except my senior year. I was homecoming queen and was expected to be prom queen, but I didn't go to prom. I was one of the popular girls, went to all the parties and all that. Like I said, a walking cliché high school student, popular and all."

I looked forward as the tears spilled out of my eyes. "In the middle of senior year, my twin brother and my boyfriend died in a car accident," I said flatly. I wiped my eyes before looking back at him. Unsurprisingly, he looked shocked. Ashamed, I stared at the floor, unable to meet his eyes when I admitted, "And it was my fault. It's my fault they're dead." My voice cracked, and a sob broke loose. Jax remained silent and patiently waited while I regained control. "My boyfriend and my brother were best friends. The three of us grew up together, super close." I laughed at a memory. "Even though I was a yucky girl with cooties, they always let me hang out with them. Looking back, I think it was because Sammy, my boyfriend, liked me.

"My family has always been close, so Tim, my brother, was a stereotypical protective brother." I giggled at a memory. "I called him my twin brother, but since he was born two minutes before me, he called himself my older brother.

"At first, Sammy and I started dating in secret sophomore year. By junior year, everyone knew we were together. Surprisingly, Tim didn't have an issue with it, which we both thought he was going to. My parents had known Sammy since we were all in kindergarten, so they were okay with it too. He came from a nice family. Although he dressed like a bad boy, he wasn't." I glanced over at Jax with a smirk. "He was a singer in a band. Tim was the drummer." An amused glint shone in Jax's eye. If he had any inkling I liked him, he may have realized my type. "On the day they died, Sammy and I got into a huge fight. Sammy stormed out. Tim followed him, trying to calm him down."

Lost in the memory permanently burned into my brain, I jumped when Jax asked, "What was the fight about?"

Lifelessly, I said, "I thought I was pregnant because my period was two weeks late. He reacted badly. He told me to get rid of it because we were too young. I exploded at him for calling our baby an 'it' even though we didn't know if there was a baby. I'll never forget what he said. 'We're too young for that shit. I'm not ready to be a father, and we haven't even graduated high school yet! Who knows if we'll even been together next year!'

"I screamed at him for calling the baby 'that shit.' It felt like a punch in the gut. He said that it was his decision too. I told him it wasn't. Then I said something I'll regret the rest of my life. 'If you want nothing to do with your child, I never want to see you again. So get out!' He yelled back, 'Fine!' Then left. Tim's last words to me were, 'I'll go talk to him.' And that was the last time I saw either of them, because they required closed caskets at the funerals. My final words to Sammy will haunt me forever, because it was like fate chose the second option for him, the one where he was out of my life forever.

"After they left, my mom came into the living room. She'd heard everything. Instead of reprimanding me or saying how disappointed she was in me, she hugged me while I cried. After I calmed down, she went out to buy a pregnancy test." Jax took an audible breath, but I kept going, needing to get it out. "She had to take a detour because the road we'd normally take was blocked off by a ton of emergency vehicles. She didn't know it at the time, but it was Sammy's car that had crashed."

I leaned back, closed my eyes, and took a few deep breaths. The tears had stopped, but my voice remained emotionless. I peeked at Jax. He'd turned his body so he could see my face. "My dad was on duty that day—"

Jax gasped. He looked horrified, probably having an idea as to where this was going. "As a captain, he rarely went to accident scenes. But this one was so bad he went to assist. No one else recognized the car, but my dad found the bumper with the license plate fifty or so feet away. Being a protective cop dad, he knew Sammy's license plate number."

Blowing out a breath, Jax leaned forward, rubbing his forehead and cursed under his breath.

With his elbows on his knees and his head in his hands, I continued, watching for his reaction, "Everything that happened at the scene I learned myself, because my dad won't talk about it. After finding the license plate, my dad ran toward the car shouting, asking how many people were in the car, because by then they had put the white sheets up. My dad was always so level-headed that his sudden outburst startled everyone around. Thankfully, one of his subordinates reacted quickly enough and grabbed him. He ended up throwing my dad to the ground because he was trying to get to the car, probably to look under the sheets. My dad started yelling that it was Sammy's car. Since my dad was a cop, they all knew Sammy and Tim were best friends and that I was dating Sammy.

"After more shouting, someone finally told him there were two people in the car. My dad stopped yelling and fighting. His subordinate let him go, and my dad sat up, staring at the ground. After a long pause, knowing he'd lost one of his kids, he asked what color the passenger's hair was, wanting to know who it was without directly asking, I think. There was some hesitation, but eventually someone said brown, Tim's hair color. My dad nodded. Then, without another word, got up and headed back to his patrol car. That same subordinate that had tackled him followed after him. They came home to tell me and my mom."

Jax's eyes had become glassy, and in a rough voice, he asked, "How did you learn all that? About what happened at the scene?"

Afraid Jax might think I was crazy, I averted my eyes. "I got the police report and copies of all the body cam footage through public records requests. Tina's cousin helped with that because my dad would've found out if Tina or I put in the requests. But he doesn't know Tina's cousin, who is a reporter, so no one had any reason to suspect anything." I paused. "I watched every minute of every video. Some of them several times."

At his silence, I peered at Jax through the corner of my eye. His lips were parted, his forehead creased with stress lines. Several seconds ticked by. Stuttering, he asked, "Wh-Why would you want to see all that?"

Looking at my hands, I muttered, "It's not that I wanted to, but no one would tell me anything. I didn't have any other choice. What I saw didn't even look real. It was like a bad movie. I want to be a cop, you know. I'll have to get used to seeing terrible things. I know it's rarely your loved ones, but—" My voice cut out. Not having the energy to try to explain myself anymore, I didn't bother, instead looking away and shaking my head.

Jax sat back with a sigh. "Body cams, huh..."

My eyes widened. "No, Jax. You really shouldn't see all that!"

"Huh?"

"Uh, weren't you thinking of putting in a request for your family's..." I trailed off since he'd started shaking his head.

"No, my lawyers got all that stuff. Subpoenaed it, I think."

"Lawyers?"

"Yeah." Unable to hold eye contact with me, he pointed out, "What eighteen or nineteen-year-old would know how to deal with all that? Estates and other legal stuff. Especially one who was as fucked up as I was. I didn't want any specifics. They were dead, how could anything else matter?"

I wanted to hug him. I wanted him to hug me. But I'd already hugged him once today. Another hug might've been too much. So, preventing myself from doing something that might make him uncomfortable, I hunched over, clasped my hands together and stared at the floor.

Cautiously, Jax asked, "What happened in the accident?"

"Sammy was driving ninety-two in a thirty-five, lost control, and hit a retaining wall," I replied, devoid of emotion. "They died instantly, so at least they didn't suffer."

"Were..." Jax started, uncertainty in his voice. "Were you pregnant?"

"No. My doctor told me I was working out so much that my period stopped. Apparently that can happen after a lot of physical exertion. I had been training super hard for soccer." Softly, I admitted something I'd never told anyone, "After Sammy was gone, I wished I had been pregnant, because then I'd still have a piece of him."

Jax moved, but I didn't know what he was doing since I was still looking down. A tissue appeared in front of my face. He must have gotten it from my side table. I took it, absently wondering why he'd given it to me. That was when I saw the two wet spots on the carpet. I was crying again, my tears dripping to the floor. Wiping my eyes, I faced him, murmuring a thank you.

We sat in silence for a long time, the only noise coming from Jax's phone buzzing in his pocket, which he ignored. The room darkened as the sun set, and still he stayed with me as silent tears continued to roll down my cheeks. At some point, he started rubbing my back.

Maybe it was because of my emotions and the vulnerability I'd shown him, but when my tears had dried up, I let myself ponder out loud, "Sometimes I wonder what would've happened if I had come here freshman year." *Would I have met you first?*

"You never told me why you gave up your scholarship," Jax said quietly.

"Because of the pain and guilt. And I blamed soccer. If I hadn't worked so hard physically, my period wouldn't have stopped. If it didn't stop, I wouldn't have gotten into that fight with Sammy. And then he and Tim wouldn't have gotten into the accident. So, like I said before, it's my fault. I overreacted. I should've confirmed if I was pregnant before I said anything to him. But I was a seventeen-year-old girl with an attitude like every other girl that age."

Jax moved suddenly, and I turned to look at him. He stared at me intently. "The accident was not your fault, Tessa. You didn't make him drive recklessly." He sounded angry.

I didn't respond, reflecting on how dead I had felt inside...until the day I'd met him. The first time our eyes met, it was like a jolt of electricity jump-starting my heart. Would that have happened if I were here freshman year?

chapter
forty-two

JAXON

I WANTED to console Tess and wrap my arms around her, bringing her close. But I was afraid of doing anything other than rub her back. Sure, we hugged a couple of times, but I didn't want to push it. Opening up to me must've been difficult. Not to mention her embarrassment about Saturday night.

I didn't want to make her any more uncomfortable than she already was, especially since she had been so careful to avoid even accidental contact between us before. It'd been so obvious that more than once, I thought she might've had some type of aversion to physical contact. But then I noticed she had no issues with Eli touching her. *God! I hate that motherfucker!*

I stayed much longer than I had planned. Even when Brooke started blowing up my phone, I didn't leave. She could wait. Brooke could never understand what Tess and I had experienced, the sudden, unexpected, and tragic loss of the people you loved the most, because she hadn't experienced it herself. For Brooke's sake, I sincerely hoped she'd never have to go through that kind of pain. It was one reason I was able to get and stay sober.

BROOKE JUMPED off the couch before I'd even shut the front door behind me. "Where have you been? I was worried!"

Through clenched teeth, I snapped, "Give me one reason why I shouldn't pack my shit and leave."

She looked startled. "What?"

I pointed to my cheek, "You fucking hit me and scratched my face!"

She looked genuinely confused.

"You don't remember attacking me Saturday night after the party? And accusing me of cheating on you?"

"Uh... I remember we might've argued, but the details are fuzzy."

I gaped at her before throwing my hands up. "Jesus fucking Christ!"

"I'm sorry," Brooke whimpered. "I really can't remember. I guess I drank too much."

Turning to her, I corrected her, "You were also high! Again! I thought you were done with that? What the fuck, Brooke?"

Her mouth opened into a silent, "Oh."

"So you don't remember what you took at the party either then?"

Brooke put her fingers to her head and scrunched her face, trying to remember. Although she was a good actress, I didn't think she was that good to be faking her confusion.

With a huff, I sat on the couch. Brooke walked over and joined me but kept her distance. Leaning over, I rubbed my temples. "Okay, first of all, we didn't fight or argue Saturday night."

"But you said—" she started.

Glaring at her, I clarified, "You attacked me completely unprovoked. You threw a cup of water at me, accused me of cheating on you, slapped me, then kicked me out in an incoherent rage, locking me out. I was pissed before, but now I'm frustrated because you don't even remember, so neither one of us has any fucking idea why you did it."

Brooke shrugged, concerned. "I guess it was because of the drugs and alcohol."

"That doesn't make it okay."

"I know," she whispered as she looked away.

"I've never seen you like that before. That person is not who I'm in a relationship with. If you're going to continue to do drugs, I have to leave. If you're going to drink so much that you can't control yourself, I'm not interested in staying. If you ever hit me again, I'm leaving. If you bring drugs into our home again, I'm leaving. There won't even be a conversation about it. I will pack up and go. Do you understand?"

Crying and wiping her nose with a tissue, she nodded.

"I mean it, Brooke. This is your last chance."

She nodded again.

A sudden realization dawned on me. When I'd walked in here, I'd thought there was a real possibility we'd be breaking up, but somehow we were still together even though I wasn't sure I wanted to be. And she'd readily agreed to my conditions. She wasn't screaming or accusing me of cheating, so how could I leave her now?

Brooke threw herself into my lap. "Oh my God, Jax! I swear I'll be better, I promise! No more drugs! I love you! I'm sorry!"

She proceeded to kiss me all over my face in between I love yous. When her lips moved to mine, I kept mine clamped shut. Confused, she pulled back. "What's wrong?"

I picked her up off my lap and placed her on the couch next to me before standing up.

"Jax?" her voice sounded fearful.

I looked down at her. "I'm still really mad at you and have no interest in sex right now. I'm going to shower. Don't follow me."

Thankfully, she left me alone for the rest of the night and didn't make any more sexual advances for the rest of the week. I guessed she was waiting for me to approach her. She'd be waiting a while.

chapter
forty-three

TESSA

TO MY GREAT RELIEF, there was no awkwardness between Jax and me throughout the week during class or Wednesday night at the library. By Friday, his cheek was no longer bruised, but his cut was still healing. I'd heard gossip with various theories as to what happened to his face, but none of them were right. Jax not only kept mum about it —he hadn't even mentioned Brooke at all during the week. When she wasn't at Smythie's on Friday, I couldn't help but wonder if they were still together.

Since our soccer season was over, for only the third time I stayed for both the band's sets, and I was thrilled. The energy the band was giving off was tangible. The bar pulsed, and the vibrations from the bass eased my tension away as I danced and sang. While wrapped up in the music, I noted the theme of the night. Relationship issues, Jax's most frequent theme.

During one of our many discussions about the band, Jax admitted he was the one who decided what the band was going to be playing. Sure, if a band member wanted to do a certain song, they would, but most of it came from him and his mood.

Tina and I agreed to the buddy system, never going anywhere without the other, or without Eli or Jamar. So I allowed myself to loosen up for the first time in weeks. I had a few drinks throughout the night but never let go of the cups until they were empty. Apparently, I had someone else looking out for me as well, because as soon as I entered the bar, Jax walked directly to me as if he'd been waiting. He told me that from now on, if I drank, I should only go to Cory, the usual bartender I went to for drinks. Jax staying relatively close to me while not on stage didn't go unnoticed either. It touched my heart that he was so concerned. And perhaps that was what did it. That was the final push to send me head first over the edge.

By the time the band played their last song of the night, I couldn't deny it anymore. I wouldn't deny it anymore. I didn't want to deny it anymore. As Jax met my eyes, singing the chorus of my favorite song, telling me that to him, I was perfect, I allowed myself to accept the truth.

This was no longer a crush. I was deeply in love with Jaxon Marcus Smith.

A WEEK and a day after I allowed myself to acknowledge my love for Jax, Saturday, I sat at the kitchen island, glumly staring at my scrambled eggs. Being in love was supposed to bring you joy and happiness, right? But I was miserable. Most people liked Saturdays, but I hated them. They meant I had to get through three days without seeing Jax.

As if pigs had learned to fly, statistics had become my favorite class. For weeks, Jax and I had showed up to class earlier and earlier so we could talk and hang out beforehand. It wasn't something we'd planned or discussed—it happened spontaneously. I enthusiastically got up an hour earlier than I otherwise would have to spend extra time with the man with the beautiful voice, beautiful blue eyes, and beautiful soul. The beautiful man who stole my heart and gave me butterflies.

Stabbing a chunk of scrambled eggs, I groaned internally at myself. There was another reason for my desolate mood. After consuming a couple of drinks last night, I'd lost my common sense and blatantly stared at Jax while he was on stage. Like with come-fuck-me eyes. And he'd noticed.

First, he winked and smiled. But as the night went on, and I continued to stare at him like the foolish girl I was, he looked confused. Eventually, the confusion turned into embarrassment and he started avoiding looking at me altogether. And who could blame him? I must've looked like some thirsty groupie! It wasn't like there was anything different about him last night either. He'd looked his same sexy self in his tight, distressed jeans, earrings, white tank, silky messy hair perfect for tangling fingers in, sexy smile...I buried my face in my hands.

Sober and in broad daylight, the guilt hit hard, and I felt like a terrible person. I had no right to have feelings for anyone except Eli, yet the opposite was true. Last night, before Eli left the bar, he'd said some things to me that made me want to cry, and not happy tears. First, he said that his parents couldn't wait to meet me and that he was sure they'd "love" me too. *Too? Ugh!* Then he asked if I would go with him to see his family for Thanksgiving. Fortunately, I already had plans.

I'd never been in such a state of emotions before and needed to talk to Tina, so I waited for her to return from Jamar's. When she did, she greeted me, "Good morning!"

"Hey," I said dully.

Her smile faded. "Are you okay?"

A tear ran down my cheek. "No."

She walked over and sat next to me. "Why? What's wrong? What happened?"

"I think I should break up with Eli."

"Why?" she asked, surprised, which surprised me. Did she really think I was that into him?

I tried to explain, "His feelings for me are stronger than mine are for him. We've been dating for a couple of months, and I don't see it going anywhere. I like him...as a person, but that's it. He's nice and funny, but there really isn't any chemistry there. He doesn't give me butterflies." *Jax does.* "He doesn't make me breathless." *Like Jax.* "I never feel like I can't wait to see him." *Like I can't wait to see Jax.* "He doesn't make me nervous or excited in an 'I have a crush on this boy' kind of way." *The way I crush on Jax.* "And there's no spark between us when we touch." *Unlike when I've come into contact with Jax, and it feels like my skin is on fire.* "It feels wrong to continue seeing him."

"No spark, huh?" Tina crossed her arms and pursed her lips. Finally, she surmised, "Guess he's not getting the job done in bed then?"

I sputtered, "I haven't... We haven't... I haven't had sex with him!"

Her eyes bulged as her jaw fell. "What? What do you mean? Why not?" She looked like I was crazy. "That sounds like the problem right there."

I seriously doubt that. After all, I felt all that with my platonic friend Jax. "I don't love Eli," I stated. "I care about him, but I'm not in love with him."

Tina considered. "Are you scared?"

I shook my head. No, I definitely wasn't afraid to fall in love again since I already had! But with the wrong guy.

"I don't know, Tess, it's up to you, but maybe give it a little more time," she suggested, "Two months isn't really that long. Not everyone falls in love quickly."

It was long enough for me to fall in love with Jax, and I wasn't even trying to do that!

"Eli wants me to meet his family and invited me to his parents for Thanksgiving, but my parents are coming here." I cringed. "So then he suggested they also come or we see them one day then go to his family's house another day. Isn't it a bad sign that I'm not interested in that at all? I know he wants to meet my parents and was bummed he missed them at my soccer game, but honestly I'm relieved they didn't meet. Is that normal?"

Since my family had known Sammy's family forever, I'd never had to worry about this sort of thing before. I really was clueless when it came to adult relationships.

"Wow...he does seem serious about you."

"Yeah, and I should feel lucky because he's a catch, but all I feel is anxiety."

She pondered that. "Maybe it's nerves. I'm really not sure. I've never been in your situation." Tina pressed her lips into a line. Hesitantly, she asked, "Can I ask you something without you getting mad?"

I recoiled.

"Do you think you're letting your crush on Jax hold you back from developing feelings for Eli?"

I couldn't say anything because I didn't know. And Tina didn't know my feelings for Jax weren't just some stupid crush anymore.

"Tess," she sighed, "I know you like Jax, but...I don't want you waiting around for something that'll probably never happen and miss out on someone else. Even if it's not Eli. Let's say you two break up. Are you going to let your crush on Jax blind you to every other decent guy out there?"

I agreed that being blinded by a crush would be foolish, but there was no doubt in my mind that I loved Jax, was in love with him. When you loved someone, you wanted what was best for them and what would make them the happiest, even if you had to sacrifice your own happiness along the way. That's why I was doing my best to accept being friends. If Brooke could make him happy, then I would be happy for him.

It had taken years, and Jax would never know, but he'd taught me that the saying about time healing all things really was true. Thanks to him, I was finally ready to move on from the past. And regarding my feelings for him, as the old saying went, "This too shall pass."

SITTING across the table from Eli Sunday night, in my wine-saturated brain, I made a decision. Perhaps the lack of chemistry was because we hadn't slept together. Maybe we'd be extremely compatible in bed, and if the sex was good, I'd want more, right? So I'd want to spend more time with him and eventually we'd become inseparable, right? And if I always wanted to be with him, that would be one form of love, right? And why shouldn't I try more with Eli? He liked me, not the guy who I couldn't have.

So I finished off my third glass of wine in three gulps and declared. "I want to go to your apartment."

Eli's eyes widened. After several seconds, he turned and half-jokingly looked around impatiently for the server, whispering, "Check please... Now, like right now!"

I giggled despite myself.

NOT LONG AFTER, I found myself in Eli's apartment building's elevator with his hands up my blouse and his tongue playing a frenzied game of twister with mine. I felt the presence of another person entering the elevator before the doors closed, but in my inebriated state I didn't care. I had to keep the momentum up before I chickened out.

"Floor twelve, please," a despondent voice requested. My heart sank at the horribly familiar voice.

Eli looked over his shoulder. "Oh, hey, Jax. Yeah, we already pressed twelve."

Jax should've been able to see the twelve button lit up, so perhaps he'd said it to get us to stop, but why should he? I didn't think Jax was a person who cared much about PDA.

"Right," he said as he looked right at me. Before I could get a good read on his expression, he turned and faced front. A pit opened in my stomach, and I couldn't breathe. Eli started kissing my face again, but as politely as possible I pushed him away and indicated Jax with my eyes.

To my horror, Eli responded loudly enough for Jax to hear, "Oh, Jax won't care. I mean, he and Brooke practically have sex in the elevator, not caring whether other people are in it with them or not." Looking over his shoulder again, Eli asked, "You don't care, do you, Jax?"

He didn't look at us, so I got a clear profile view of his jaw flexing. "No, do whatever you want."

"See?" Eli went in for another kiss.

"Stop!" I hissed.

Eli sighed but did as I commanded. Over the next several seconds or minutes or maybe even hours, or however long it took to get up to the twelfth floor, I concluded that the elevator in their building was the slowest freakin' elevator in the entire state of California! If I thought the first time I ran into Jax was bad, this was agony, and I might as well have been in an iron maiden torture chamber for the pain I felt.

WHAT SEEMED LIKE AN ETERNITY LATER, although it was only a few minutes, Eli and I were making out half-naked in his bed. But my head wasn't in it. The elevator scene from hell kept replaying behind my closed eyelids.

What if Jax interrupting us was a sign? What if Jax being there was the universe's way of reminding me that I was in love with him, not Eli? This would be wrong to do to Eli and make me feel like crap. What should I do? I didn't really want to have sex with Eli, but I'd already said we could. Had I ever given Eli a fair shot, or had I been too busy lusting after Jax?

Like a prayer being answered, as Eli's hand slid under the waistband of my panties, I felt something I hadn't been expecting. "Wait!" I sat up, knocking Eli off of me.

"What? Are you okay?" Eli called after me in confusion, as I ran off to the bathroom.

Taking a piece of toilet paper, I wiped. Blood stained the white tissue. *Yes!* I had never been so happy to get my period before in my life! I rarely got it because of the birth control I was on, which I usually liked, but at that moment I was so relieved I nearly cried.

After cleaning myself up, I went back into the bedroom. Eli's eyes were wide with concern. "Are you okay?"

Trying to look sheepish, I broke the news, "I got my period."

"Oh..." Eli looked both relieved and disappointed. Honestly, I couldn't blame the guy. He'd been ready to go.

Digging into my purse, I pulled out my emergency tampon. "I'll be right back," I told him as I headed back into the bathroom. With my back turned, I couldn't hide my smile. The universe was giving me signals, I was sure of it.

AS EARLY AS POSSIBLE without being rude, I left Eli's apartment. It was Monday, and I had class, so it wasn't like I was running away, although I kind of was.

As I was stepping through the front door, Jamar was stepping out of it to go to work. *That's good*, I thought. *I need to get this off my chest before class, if possible.*

Tina met me in the living room. "Doing the walk of shame, are we?"

I shook my head. "No, I got my period."

"Oh, no! What shitty timing!" Tina looked genuinely disappointed. Meanwhile, I bit the inside of my cheeks to stop myself from smiling. It didn't work.

Narrowing her eyes at me, she observed, "You don't look too unhappy about it."

I gave up trying to hide it. "Honestly, I'm relieved. I thought I wanted to have sex but realized right before that I didn't."

"So you really don't like him?"

I laughed humorlessly. "He's not the problem. I am."

Crossing her arms, she sneered, "Oh, so what? You going to give him the old 'it's not you, it's me' bit?"

"It is me, Tina!" Before Tina finished her eye roll, I shouted, "It's because I'm in love with Jax! I don't love Eli! I love Jax! And it's driving me crazy!" Since Tina was stunned into silence, I continued at a normal volume, "It's not right being with Eli when I can't give him my heart. I don't have it to give."

Tina clasped her hands together as she slowly sank down onto the armchair. I chewed on my bottom lip as I tried to read her face, which was staring off into space as she processed my confession. After sighing, she asked, "But nothing has happened between you and Jax, right?"

"Right." My voice was thick with unshed tears. "It's a one-sided thing."

I felt terrible for not being completely honest with my best friend, but I wasn't sure how Jax felt. After all, if he did have feelings for me, and if he wasn't happy with Brooke, wouldn't he leave her? Especially after she hit him?

"I don't know if I should be telling you this, but I don't think it's one-sided."

My stomach flipped. "What do you mean?"

Avoiding my eyes, Tina shrugged. After a beat, she looked at me with sad eyes. Folding her hands as if she was begging, she pleaded, "Promise me you won't get involved in an affair with him...please. You'll end up getting hurt."

Holding my hands up, I assured her, "I don't want that either, Tee! I'm not trying to break them up or get in between them. I'm okay being friends with him."

Tina remained silent, her lips pressed into a hard line.

"I told Jax about Sammy and Tim," I said, hoping this would help Tina understand. She must've known about his family.

"You did? Did you tell Eli?"

"No," I sighed, flopping down onto the couch. "Honestly, Eli never asks about my family or childhood or past or anything. That makes me question his so-called love for me when he doesn't even know what makes me who I am."

Tina ducked her head, mumbling, "Eli knows. I told him."

I sat up. "What?"

"He noticed how you wouldn't open up to him, so he asked me if there was anything he should know, like why you were so closed off."

My mouth opened in angry shock. "Why didn't you tell me you told him?"

She shrugged. "It's not like it's a secret. If he looked up your name online, he would've found out." It was a pathetic excuse, and she knew it.

Storming to my room, I locked myself in after loudly shutting the door. I was furious with both of them. They should've said something sooner! She shouldn't have even told him! If he was that concerned, he should have asked me directly and respected me enough not to push it if I didn't tell him! *What the heck!*

Groaning in frustration, I threw myself onto the bed. Between not sleeping last night, being pissed off, and having cramps, I was in a foul mood to put it mildly. *Screw it.* I crawled under my covers and skipped my Monday classes.

chapter
forty-four

JAXON

THE PUNCHING BAG swung as I hit it as hard as I could for the hundredth time.

Chuck lectured, "Dude, you're gonna break your hand if you keep hitting it like that. What's your deal anyway? What's got you so pissed off?"

Ignoring him, I got down on the floor and started doing push-ups. He squatted next to me. "Seriously, what's wrong?"

"Nothing," I said through grunts. I was working myself to exhaustion, trying to rid myself of all these confusing thoughts and emotions swirling through my brain.

"You and Brooke fighting again?"

Sitting back on my heels, I laughed sardonically. "Surprisingly, no. She's been good since Halloween."

"Then..."

"I said it was nothing, Chuck, now back off!" I fumed before standing up and going to a treadmill.

Chuck got on the machine next to mine. "Does it have to do with Tess?"

"Why would it?" I snapped.

"Well..."

"Well what?" I asked too loudly.

After a beat, he muttered, "Never mind, geez."

We ran on our respective machines in silence. What was I supposed to tell him? I was pissed that Tess had fucked the guy she was dating? Or that I was pissed at myself for going home and fucking Brooke senseless, trying to fuck away our problems? And maybe it worked. I should've been happy since Brooke had been on her best behavior, but I was fucking miserable! What the hell was wrong with me?

After thinking long and hard about it, there was only one thing that I could come up with that I was willing to accept: I must've been stressed because Brooke and I still hadn't figured out what would happen after graduation. *Yeah, that must be it*, I drilled into my head, *Perhaps it was time to make some serious decisions about my future with Brooke.*

BROOKE GOT HOME late from her play rehearsal that night. But I didn't mind since it had given me time to get some things done. I submitted the last application as she unlocked the door. I stood as she entered the living room. "Hey, Rook."

Her step faltered even as she smiled at me, looking surprised at my happy greeting and use of my nickname for her, both of which had been absent recently. "Hi, how was your day?"

"Productive." Pointing to the chessboard, I noted, "It's your turn."

"Oh yeah? How so?" she asked as she inspected our ongoing game on the coffee table. "Oh! That was a good move." Not needing much time to think against a novice like me, she made her move.

Observing the board, I casually mentioned, "I submitted several law school applications for schools in New York City and the surrounding area."

She gasped, and I looked at her. Her mouth opened with a surprised smile. "Really?"

"Yes, but I have a condition."

"Okay?" she readily agreed.

"When I'm done with law school, we need to see where you're at in your career. If things don't go the way you hope, I want us to consider coming back to California."

She nodded slowly, eyes looking around as she thought about what I'd said. Stopping and looking at me, she agreed, "Okay, deal!"

Smiling, I pulled her down into my lap as I sat back on the couch. Her school bag dropped to the floor with a thud as she straddled and kissed me. After a minute, I picked her up and took her to bed.

A WHILE LATER, as I stood under the scalding spray of the shower head, letting it wash away the salty streaks on my face, I tried to figure out why I still felt so bad, maybe even worse than before I'd fucked Brooke. While the sex was good, it was unsatisfying. Although we'd done a couple of fun things together that we hadn't done in a while over the last couple of days, I was bored. Even though Brooke was acting more like the girl I used to love, I felt uninterested.

In fact, the only thing I felt was a pain in my chest, constant and annoying. Although I'd never experienced it before, I knew what it was. What I didn't know was who I was heartbroken over.

chapter
forty-five

TESSA

PER MINE and Jax's unspoken routine, I arrived at our classroom Tuesday morning about an hour before class, but the seat next to me remained vacant until seven-fifty-nine.

Trying to brush away all the awkwardness I was feeling, I greeted Jax brightly, "Good morning, Jax!"

Barely giving me a glance, he muttered, "Hey."

For the first time ever, the professor arrived on time, so there was no chance for any further conversation.

As soon as class ended, Jax stood to leave. "See ya later," he mumbled, not bothering to wait for my own farewell before walking out of sight.

I stayed seated while the other students filed out of the room, not sure I could walk. My legs were shaking, my hands clammy, and I thought I might actually be sick. Jax's one word greeting had pierced me, opening a hole in my chest that grew with every silent second between us. Now it felt as though all the air inside my lungs was being sucked out of it. It took several minutes of slow breathing to feel okay enough to leave.

As I walked home, I made up a million reasons for his cold treatment. Maybe he was tired. Maybe he and Brooke had fought again. Maybe he didn't get much sleep last night. I thought up every possible reason, except for the one I knew it was. Me.

ON WEDNESDAY EVENING, as I was getting ready to leave for the library, my phone pinged. Jax sent a text letting me know he wouldn't be there. Putting my school bag back on my desk, I decided to take a shower, hoping it would hide the evidence of the hot tears filling my eyes.

THURSDAY WAS the same as Tuesday, except the professor was late again. Instead of chatting, Jax occupied himself with his phone, ignoring me other than his one word greeting. When class ended, he again didn't wait for me, just grabbed his stuff and left.

WATCHING Brooke dry hump the man I was in love with, her boyfriend, on the dance floor at Smythie's on Friday night confirmed what I had suspected. He knew I was interested in him, so he was sending a message loud and clear that he wasn't interested. Although I tried to avoid looking at them, they were freakin' everywhere! Grinding on the dance floor, making out next to the stage, laughing by the bar...

Claiming to be tired, I left before the band started their first set. As I walked toward the exit, I wondered if I was even going to make it home with the pressure in my chest preventing me from breathing properly. What made it worse were the eyes on me. Unable to stop myself, I looked back over my shoulder and stumbled. In Jax's eyes, I saw exactly how I felt.

TUESDAY WAS the same as the last two classes.

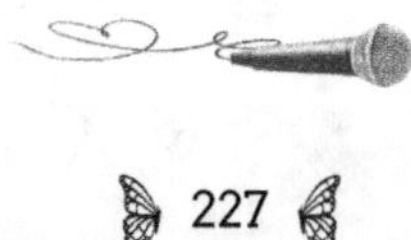

BY WEDNESDAY EVENING, I'd accepted he was avoiding me and surmised he wasn't going to come to the library nor bother texting me, likely assuming I'd gotten the message. Well, I had and was under no misconception about him showing up. I did go though, just to remember it. It would be my last time there.

As I sat at the table where I'd gotten to know my unrequited love, the microscopic slice of hopefulness I had that perhaps he would show dissipated. Looking down, I noticed some wet spots on my homework. I stared at them, wondering how long it was going to take for it not to hurt anymore when a tissue appeared between my eyes and the paper.

Looking up, I locked eyes with Jax. Although he was trying to smile, his eyes were sad.

"Hello, Tessa."

chapter
forty-six

JAXON

ON THE COUCH WEDNESDAY AFTERNOON, I couldn't get the images of Tess's sad eyes out of my head. It hurt knowing that I was hurting her. I needed to stop lying to myself about what was really going on. But there was a problem: Brooke. She'd kept her promise the last couple of weeks and behaved. There had been no fights, drama, or signs of drug use. She was like her old self, the one I had fallen in love with. However, this time, I wasn't falling for her. Instead, I was walking on eggshells, waiting for the next showdown.

At some point, I'd fallen asleep, which wasn't surprising given the little I'd gotten over the last couple of weeks. I awoke to Brooke's mouth on my dick. Along with a sleeping stiffy, my body reacted to the stimulation before my mind was even aware of it.

Groggily, I mumbled, "Brooke?"

"Shhh," she said sweetly, "don't worry. I know you're tired. I'll do all the work."

Too exhausted to fight her off and not wanting another argument, I thought, *Fuck it.* After a few minutes, she crawled up my body. I didn't resist when she kissed me. Sitting on top of me, she stroked my dick before sinking down onto it. She rode me like her life, or maybe our relationship, depended on it.

. . .

A LITTLE WHILE LATER, Brooke was naked in a satisfied slumber on the couch. I was sitting on the floor, also naked, leaning against the couch, staring at my flaccid dick. We hadn't used a condom. Brooke said she would do all the work... She'd put plenty of condoms on me before. Why not this time? I'd been so groggy that I hadn't noticed. It was fine though. Brooke had been on birth control for years, and we were both disease and infection-free.

Yet, it bothered me. It was the first time I'd ever not used one, and I was so exhausted that I hadn't even noticed. Maybe that was why I had been so turned on. Or maybe it was because when I closed my eyes, I hadn't been with Brooke. In my mind, I'd been with a beautiful woman with a heart-shaped face framed by blonde hair, a perky nose, naturally plump pink lips, sparkling blue-green eyes, and the most beautiful smile I'd ever seen.

In my head, I had cheated on Brooke, all while we were making a last-ditch effort to salvage our decaying relationship. It had failed. I knew it now, but I didn't think Brooke did. To me, it was telling that I couldn't come until I closed my eyes and imagined Tess. And that was really fucked up. I hated myself for it, but then again it helped me finally accept that I was done.

I needed and wanted out of this relationship. But before I could leave, I needed to figure out how I was going to go about ending it. Wouldn't it be better if I waited until after finals so I didn't interfere with Brooke's classes and exams? Or would that be too hard for me? I didn't know. I guess I'd see what would happen and figure it out along the way.

AFTER SHOWERING all remnants of Brooke off of me, I put a blanket over her naked body, knowing I never wanted to see her like that again, and headed out. I was going to be late and hoped Tess would still be there, although I wouldn't blame her if she'd given up and left.

TURNING THE CORNER, my body relaxed. She was still there, way in the back, at our table. But the relief faded with every step I took until my feet stopped a short distance away from her. Tess was crying, and I knew it was because of me. Somehow, I felt like a bigger asshole than I had a little while ago.

Looking around, I spotted a box of tissues on a nearby table and grabbed a couple. Tess hadn't noticed me approach, nor had she heard me softly call her name. She was completely lost in her thoughts. Placing the tissue in her line of sight, she jumped and looked up at me with red, confused, and hurt eyes. I wanted to pull her into my arms and tell her not to worry, that I wouldn't be an asshole anymore, but I couldn't. And touching her felt wrong after I'd been with Brooke only a little while ago. Disgusted, I again doubted I was even good enough for this sweet girl in front of me. So I did the only thing I could think of, something I hadn't done in a miserable week and a half. I acknowledged her.

"Hello, Tessa."

She blinked like she wasn't sure I was actually standing there next to her, and it took a moment for her to respond. Taking the tissue, she said, "Oh, thanks. Sorry, I was thinking about my brother."

It was a lie. I knew it was because of me, not because I thought that highly of myself, just the opposite. *God! I am such an asshole!*

Sitting down, I apologized, "Sorry I'm late."

Her sad eyes examined my face, maybe trying to figure out if I was going to blow her off again. I kept my eyes on her and tried to look reassuring, or at least in some way that would let her know I was done being a jerk.

She shrugged. "That's alright. I think I figured out the homework."

Taking her paper, I tried to ignore the wet circles from her tears, but it was hard with the pain in my chest.

LESS THAN AN HOUR LATER, we were done. I smiled at the girl who was a lot smarter than she gave herself credit for. "You're gonna do great on the final. You got this down pat now."

She grinned. "All thanks to you."

I shook my head. "Our professor isn't very good. If you had a good teacher, you would've gotten it on your own."

"I did have a good teacher," she responded before stunning me with her megawatt smile.

As we packed up our stuff, she commented, "I can't believe there's only two more weeks until finals. The semester's flown by."

"Yeah," I agreed, "we're almost halfway done with senior year."

Tess smiled. "I can't wait. I'm excited to start my career."

"Have you heard anything from any police departments yet?"

"No, but it's still a bit early. What about you? Hear from any law schools?"

Shaking my head, I said, "No, too early. I'm still applying to some."

"Ah. Got any preferences?"

My conversation with Brooke about New York the other day flashed through my brain. But I knew that wasn't going to happen now that I'd made up my mind. "Somewhere in California."

"It's a big state."

"True," I muttered, "but it's not on the other side of the country."

Tess eyed me curiously, maybe remembering that I'd previously mentioned how Brooke wanted to go to New York, but she didn't ask. Now wasn't the time, so I didn't volunteer anything. There'd be time later.

"I remember you mentioning that you're going to Brooke's parents house for Thanksgiving, but what are you doing tonight? Are you leaving?"

"No, we'll leave in the morning. We're not doing anything tonight."

"Do you remember I told you a few weeks ago that Tina, Jamar, and I are going to karaoke tonight? It'll probably be dead, so I might be brave enough to actually sing. You guys want to come?"

There was a person missing from that list. "Eli isn't going?"

"No, he left for home already."

Partly curious, partly needing to know, I noted, "You didn't go with him?"

She looked like I'd said something stupid. "No, why would I?"

As happy as I was to hear those words in an almost disgusted tone, I was confused. "You're dating. Isn't it getting kind of serious?"

Tess rolled her eyes. "It's not serious." Under her breath, she added, "Despite what it may have looked like. It's not going anywhere."

"Why not?" I clamped my mouth shut, not actually having meant to ask that out loud.

Her chest rose and fell in a sigh. "He doesn't give me butterflies."

I looked away, trying to hide my...relief? Happiness? Glee? The urge to jump up and whoop?

She interpreted my reaction wrong. "That sounds stupid and juvenile, doesn't it?"

Looking at her, I waited until she met my eyes again. "No, it's not stupid. Butterflies are important."

A small smile appeared on her lips as she looked away. Changing the subject, she asked, "Are Ashton and Chuck around? Do you think they might want to go to karaoke too?"

I thought for a second. "Chuck isn't, but Ashton might be free. I'll ask him."

After agreeing to meet at the bar in an hour, we parted ways.

chapter
forty-seven

TESSA

TINA, Jamar, and I arrived at Smythie's before Jax and company. We headed to the bar for our first round of drinks. While Cory made them, I looked around. "Wow, it's really dead in here."

"You think?" Tina asked. "It's busier than I thought it would be. I mean, most students left for the holiday weekend."

Jamar noted, "Jax, Brooke, and Ashton are here."

Tina and I turned and watched the three of them approach. However, before getting all the way over to us, Jax and Brooke stopped to order drinks.

Ashton kept walking until he joined me. "Hey, Tess. How're you doing?"

I smiled. "I'm good, thanks. You?"

"All good. So what're we drinking tonight? Jax said you needed a couple of drinks to sing in front of people."

I laughed but before I could respond, Jax walked up and handed Ashton a beer. After Ashton took it, Brooke dragged Jax toward the stage as she begged, "Come on, Jaxy! I have the perfect song for us to sing!"

Jaxy? Ick! Still an annoying nickname.

If Jax said anything, I couldn't hear it over the current karaoke singer, but he did follow her to the machine where patrons picked their songs. When it was their turn, Brooke enthusiastically ran up on stage as the music started. Jax followed behind, less energetically. The four of us not on stage watched as they sang a duet about a struggling couple. It was the first pop song I'd ever seen Jax sing. Unsurprisingly, he was phenomenal.

About halfway through the song, I looked away. It hurt too much witnessing their natural chemistry as they sang such a heartfelt song together.

Shame, I liked that song, I reflected to myself, *Not anymore.*

Finishing my drink in record time, I turned my attention to Ashton. "Hey, you wanna do a shot with me?"

"Hell yeah," he agreed.

OVER THE NEXT couple of hours, while I continued to drink, I watched the miserable couple sing more than anyone else, both together and individually. Their duets were pretty much all about relationship issues. *Appropriate.*

As much as I hated seeing their chemistry, it was hard to look away. I was sure I wasn't the only one who could feel their desperation as they sang. I'd even gotten goosebumps more than once. And that was how I ended up drunker than I'd planned. I needed to dull the pain in my chest from witnessing the passion between them. Their relationship might have been rocky, but the rumors about the fire between them were true and by all appearances hard to extinguish.

Pleasantly buzzed, it was my turn to take the stage. I loved to sing but was no singer, so some libation was a must. Drunkenly confident, I pulled a Jaxon Smith and chose a song that sent a message. It may have been a bad idea, but I figured why not? *Live without regrets and all that.* Something I needed to start doing.

As soon as my selection started, Jax's eyes widened before his hand flew to his mouth, probably hiding the laughter I saw in his eyes. Brooke on the other hand was glaring daggers at me. But I was too intoxicated to care and sang like no one was paying attention about not liking a guy's girlfriend. *Ha! Serves you right, Brooke*, I thought as I continued my peppy pop bop. After all, she had successfully kept Jax away from not only me but everyone else all night. Even Ashton hung out more with us than them.

As my song started winding down, I glanced at Tina and lost my place. She was glaring at me. *Huh?*

When I finished my song and climbed down from the stage, she grabbed my hand and dragged me over to the end of the bar, away from other people. She hissed, "What is wrong with you? Could you make it any more obvious?"

"Huh? What do you mean?" I played dumb.

Through clenched teeth, she elaborated, "You were staring at Jax for most of that song. I was afraid Brooke was about to jump you!"

"I don't know what you mean." I waved the bartender over.

When Cory arrived, I tried ordering another drink, but Tina cut me off. "Water for her. No more drinks, please." I rolled my eyes but didn't object. Cory snickered and handed me a bottle of water that I ended up chugging. As I did, I heard Brooke behind me, "Looks like your little friend Tessy can't sing to save her life."

Tessy? Seriously?

Although she'd clearly come close enough to be heard, my back was to her, so she missed my eye roll. I didn't care what she thought. I knew I was a terrible singer.

In a loud whisper, Jax snapped, "Brooke!"

Facing her, I retorted, "Guess it's a good thing I want to be a cop and not a singer then, huh?" I gave them a big, fake grin and walked toward the bathrooms, satisfied by her stupefied reaction. While she stood bug-eyed, Jax was trying not to laugh.

As I used the bathroom, my sloshed brain debated if Brooke was more surprised that I wasn't afraid to say something to her or that I wanted to be a cop.

Exiting the women's restroom, I met Jax in the hallway. He pushed off the wall he'd been leaning on. "Hey, sorry about that."

I shrugged. "I don't care what she thinks of me or my singing."

"She still shouldn't have said that."

"Seriously, I don't care." Raising a finger, I smirked and said, "But I want to know what'd you think of my song choice?" *Wow... It's called liquid courage for a reason.*

He held my gaze for several seconds, the corner of his mouth turning up into his panty-dropping grin. Without looking away, he said, "It was interesting but not surprising." I gave him my biggest smile then started walking past him to go back into the main room. "Your performance was pretty cute. Like you."

My steps faltered as the smile slipped from my lips. My heart hammered against my chest as I stared up at Jax, not sure how, or if, I should respond. Thankfully, Ashton turned the corner and headed our way, so I didn't have to.

Back in the main room, Tina and Jamar were up on stage singing. I smiled at them. They were so cute together. "Your performance was pretty cute. Like you." Jax's words echoed around in my head. Was the man trying to kill me? Attack of the butterflies-style? Or was he trying to suffocate me by taking my breath away?

Brooke interrupted my alcohol-induced illusions. "I know what you're doing, but it's not going to work."

Facing her, I crossed my arms and raised my brows, daring her to continue.

"Let me explain something to you," she jeered. "He will never leave me. He worships the ground I walk on. In fact, he agreed to move to New York City with me after graduation so that I can follow my dreams. Someone like you could never understand everything we've been through together. I saved his life after he lost his family. I cried with him until he couldn't cry anymore. I made sure he didn't completely fuck up his life. We have a history and have been through thick and thin together." Her lips turned into a sneer. "Also, I know what Jax wants and needs in the bedroom. I doubt a girl like you could satisfy his insatiable sex drive. You know why he was late to the library today? Because he was fucking me into oblivion."

Okay, that hurt.

Brooke went on taunting me, "Eli told me what a prude you are. You wouldn't even be able to keep up with someone like Jax."

Eli said what now?

"Jax and I have sex anywhere and everywhere," she said with a snide grin that I wanted to slap off her face. "Do you know how many times we've fucked on this very bar?" she said, patting the bar counter-top. "So, kindly, fuck off."

Even if I was sober, I doubt I would've been able to hold my tongue. "First of all, I really don't want to hear about your sex life with Jax. Second, you know nothing about me, so you'd have no idea what skills I may or may not have or how adventurous I can be. Third, maybe if you treated Jax with the respect he deserves, your relationship wouldn't be so rocky and you wouldn't have to worry about someone else."

"I'm not worried!"

"You might be a talented singer, but you're a terrible liar," I said with more confidence than I felt. "Yes, you are worried, otherwise we wouldn't be having this conversation. Jax needs more than what you can give him in bed. He needs someone he can talk to and someone who'll actually listen to him. He may have agreed to go to New York with you, but he doesn't want to go. Have you even taken his feelings into consideration? Also, he needs someone who can relate to him on a level you wouldn't know the first thing about. And most importantly he needs someone who'll actually love him back as much as he loves them. Someone who wouldn't even think about bringing drugs around him!"

I stomped off for a few steps before spinning around. "And one more thing. It's up to Jax if he wants to be my friend, not you. Now, I'm going to assume your drunk brain is confusing you and loosening your lips, so I'll forget this conversation ever happened. Have a good night."

I wanted to add, *Your boyfriend called me cute by the way!* That would be too low a blow. Plus, I didn't want to throw Jax under the bus and cause him any more trouble with her. If I pushed too much, I could lose his friendship. Even if I couldn't have him in the way I wanted, he was still someone I wanted in my life any way I could get him.

"You bitch!" Brooke shouted. Ignoring her, I turned back around and bounced off Jax. He caught me as I stumbled. Unsurprisingly, that infuriated Brooke.

"Get your hands off her!" she screamed. "Don't you dare touch another girl! Get over here. I need to talk to you!"

chapter
forty-eight

JAXON

"WHAT HAS GOTTEN INTO YOU?" I demanded from my drunk and pissed-off girlfriend.

Brooke growled, "This is ridiculous! You need to stop hanging out with her!"

I lowered my voice and spoke directly into her ear. "Stop it. You're causing a scene."

Putting her hands against my chest, she tried to push, but she was too weak and too drunk, so she stumbled backward. I caught her by her arm so she wouldn't fall, but she yanked it away, before raging on. "No! You can't hang out with some chick who likes you when you have me! It's not right! It's not fair!"

Although I knew Brooke was right about Tess liking me, I wasn't about to make things worse by admitting it. Crossing my arms, I tried to reason with her. "She's dating Eli. Why would she be dating Eli if she liked anyone other than him? She's my friend."

Back to her old habits, Brooke stood on her toes, trying to get in my face. "I'm not fucking blind, you asshole! I don't want you to be friends with her anymore!"

Looking around the bar, I spotted Ashton and waved him over. As he headed our way, I said, "I have always tried to respect your opinions, but you don't get to dictate who I can and can't talk to."

Ashton arrived as Brooke spat, "You think this is respecting me?

You're probably cheating on me!" At that point, it was clear to probably everyone in the bar that she was belligerently drunk. "You're a cheating piece of shit!"

Glancing around, I saw all eyes on us. The bar was too quiet. I guessed the live soap opera was a better show than karaoke. I glanced over to the DJ booth and lifted a finger, circling it in the air. To my great relief, D.J. saw and started some booming music, essentially blocking out Brooke's howling.

A jab in my chest brought my attention back down to the girl I hardly recognized. "You're not even listening to me! You know what? Screw you!"

Ashton grabbed Brooke and dragged her away from me as I stood there, contemplating if it was fucked up that I was no longer surprised by her words and actions. Turning her wrath on Ashton, Brooke shouted to let her go and mind his own business. He didn't and told her to calm down.

"Make sure she gets home safe?" I called over.

He gave me a thumbs up as he pulled her toward the exit. I owed him big time. Maybe I'd buy him a steak dinner or something. After watching them leave, I glanced around and confirmed all the spectators were still watching like it was a damn mini-drama. I sighed.

Needing to get away from the onlookers, especially the pity in Tess's eyes, I turned and headed toward the back staircase, telling the bouncer not to let anyone up. I needed some distance and didn't want to be disturbed as I tried to figure out if I needed to just end it now.

THE OFFICE UPSTAIRS HAD A COUCH, where I inadvertently fell asleep. When I woke, I checked the time on my nearly dead cell. *Shit!* Seeing that it was almost nine a.m., I jumped up, ran through the bar quickly to make sure no one was there, set the alarm, then ran to my car. I couldn't bring myself to break up with Brooke on a holiday, so I'd have to deal with her and her parents. *Maybe she left without me.*

UNFORTUNATELY, Brooke's car was still in the spot next to my assigned parking space.

When I walked through the front door, I heard Brooke retching loudly.

Calling out, I asked, "Are you okay?" As I entered the bedroom, the bathroom door slammed shut, followed by a click. I knocked. "Brooke? You okay?"

More retching.

Had I been that distracted by Tess that I lost track of how much Brooke had drunk? Even if I had been, I wasn't feeling generous enough to feel sorry for her current state. She'd done it to herself.

Still, I wasn't a complete asshole. "Do you need anything?"

Hoarsely, she called back, "Can you get me some water?"

"Yeah, be right back."

When I returned, Brooke was leaning against the closed bathroom door. Handing her a bottle I pulled from the fridge, I asked, "You okay?"

Instead of answering, she took a few sips. There were dark bags under her red, puffy eyes, which were especially noticeable given her paler than normal skin. Apparently she hadn't passed out in a drunken stupor like I would've expected. It looked like she hadn't slept at all.

Eventually, she croaked out, "Thanks."

"Are you sick or hungover? If you're sick, we shouldn't go to your parents'."

Petrified, she sputtered, "No-no! I'll be fine! I don't want to deal with my parents if we don't go. I'll go get ready."

Damn. "Okay."

I took a step toward the bathroom, but she didn't move. Ducking her head, she murmured, "Please go use the other bathroom. I puked all over in there and need to clean up."

Rubbing my forehead, I reluctantly offered, "Do you need my help? If you're still feeling sick…"

She shooed me with her hands. "No, no! You don't need to deal with it. I'll be fine. Go shower and get ready."

Phew! I really didn't want to clean up after her, especially because I was still furious. "Okay, I'll be ready in fifteen."

"Sure, whatever."

THE DRIVE to Brooke's house was quiet. She slept, and not wanting to wake her since I was in no mood to talk, I kept the music off. This would be my last time driving there and the last time I'd ever have to see her bitch of a mom and wimpy-ass dad. They may have accepted me over the years, but they were still a bunch of snobs. Even though I had considered them my family since I thought they'd be my in-laws one day, I wasn't sad about never seeing them again after this. I'd find another family one day.

Maybe I already have. Blinking, I scolded myself, *Do not get ahead of yourself!*

At a red light, I glanced over at the girl who used to be my world. She looked peaceful and beautiful but still pale beneath the makeup covering the dark circles. The light turned green, and I drove on feeling sad. I would miss Brooke—the old one, not the person she'd become. I already did miss her.

As we got farther from campus, memories of happier times with her played like a movie in my head. What if she was still in there? My Rook. The one who'd taught me chess and insisted we always have a game going, telling me I needed to practice so I could beat her one day. The girl who clung to me like she needed me to breathe. The cute actress who lit up the stage with her talent and beauty. The tenacious girl who'd refused to give up on me when I'd given up on me, when we hadn't even known each other that long. The spitfire who challenged me to get better and be better. The person who saved me.

Was leaving her really the right thing? The way she'd been acting lately was my fault, wasn't it? She was getting angry because of what I was doing and not doing. Maybe things would be better next semester when I barely saw Tess? Seeing each other a lot less would fade the friendship we had developed, right? The last couple of weeks, while avoiding Tess, things were good again. Brooke had surely only acted out last night because we hung out with Tess. Things could go back to the way they were supposed to be with a bit more work. We could get back to a point where we weren't at each other's throats every five seconds, I was certain.

"I'm sorry, Jax." Brooke's voice startled me.

We were almost to the Bentleys'. I quickly glanced at her. She was looking down at her hands.

"I don't think we should talk about it now," I suggested.

She sniffled beside me and didn't stop until we pulled onto her street.

STEPPING into the foyer that was larger than our living room, Brooke called out, "Hello! We're here!" In the driveway, she'd transformed. Gone was her strained voice and melancholy mood. Fixing her makeup in the car probably helped.

The click of Nancy Bentley's designer heels against the spotless marble floor announced her approach. When she appeared, she complained, "If you say you're going to be here at noon, you should keep your word. The food is getting cold."

Digging into my pocket, I pulled out my phone and not so discreetly checked the time. We were three minutes late. Still, Brooke apologized, "Sorry, Mom, I wasn't feeling that great this morning and had a hard time waking up."

Nancy crossed her arms. "Are you pregnant?"

I nearly dropped my phone.

Forgetting Nancy's strict views on manners, I gaped at Brooke's could be twin thanks to a lot of plastic surgery.

Brooke shrieked, "No, I'm not pregnant!"

I took in a shaky breath. It had been all of thirty seconds, and I was already regretting my decision to come.

"There's my little girl!" I'd never been so happy to hear Rich's voice in my life.

"Daddy!" Brooke squealed as she skipped into her father's open arms. The sight was reminiscent of a child hugging a big bear. The man was round and hairy.

"Alright, that's enough," Nancy snapped. "Let's go eat before the food gets any colder."

As I followed behind Nancy, Rich, and Brooke, I greeted them in my head, *Hello to you* too. *I'm miserable, thanks for asking.* For people who whined about manners, they certainly showed little around me.

Fortunately for me, my parents had taught me some. After I cleaned my plate, I said, "Thank you for hosting again this year, Mr. and Mrs. Bentley. Mary prepared a delicious meal as always. It was the best thing I've eaten since our last meal here."

"Brooke," Nancy scoffed, "don't you cook for Jaxon?"

Brooke, cook? Are you kidding? Have you met your daughter?

Brooke's polite facade slipped. "Uh, no... You never taught me how. I can barely boil water." She wasn't lying. One time, she put a pot on to boil so we could make pasta and forgot about it, destroying the pot after all the water evaporated out of it. "Besides, Jax does the cooking when we eat at home. He likes to cook."

Says who? I just don't want to starve!

"Perhaps you should come home on the weekends and have Mary teach you," Nancy oh-so-generously offered. "After all, you'll have to cook for your family once you and Jaxon get married and have my grandchildren. You'll have to stay home and take care of them. Jaxon will be too busy working, since he won't be able to provide the type of lifestyle you grew up with, dear."

It was a good thing I had finished eating, otherwise I would've lost my appetite.

Nancy continued, "Your trust will only go so far. I wouldn't use it for domestic staff."

Was she joking? From what Brooke told me, her trust was big enough that she and I could have three houses, a country club membership, and never work a day in our lives. But I didn't actually know how much it was, nor did I care.

Rich piped in with his two cents. "I disagree, my dear. Jaxon wants to be a lawyer. It may take a few years, but eventually he'll be raking it in. Isn't that right, son?"

"I want to be a lawyer, but—" I started.

"There, you see?" Rich interrupted. "Now, my boy, what you need to do is get into personal injury, maybe even mass tort. That's where the real money is. Bryan from the country club makes seven figures and only works three or four days a week."

I felt like I had stepped into the twilight zone or something. Surely, this conversation was not happening. Had they gotten worse since the last time I saw them? "Actually, I was thinking criminal, not civil law."

Rich nodded, his eyes searching the room as he considered that. "Yes... That could work too. Criminal defense pays well if you get the right clientele."

Stiffly, I clarified, "I was thinking the prosecution's side."

"Why, that's actually a good idea. Get some experience on that side first then move to where the money is," Rich said conspiratorially.

Suddenly, the room felt very warm, almost hot. A hand squeezed my thigh, and I looked over at Brooke. Her brows were furrowed with genuine concern in her eyes.

Then she did something I never would have expected. She admonished her father, "Dad! What is wrong with you? You think Jax wants to defend people who kill or harm other people? Have you forgotten about his family?"

Rich quickly defended himself. "No, no! Of course not! I meant white-collar criminals. They probably have enough money stashed away off-shore that they can pay well. And you know there aren't any real victims in white-collar crime, right?"

Was this asshole serious? It took every ounce of self-control I had not to roll my eyes at him.

"But speaking of Jaxon's family," Rich went on, "I'm a bit disappointed you never contacted Bryan from the club about suing that drunk driver. I spoke to him recently, and he said the statute of limitations has already expired, so there's nothing you can do about it now."

Nancy butted in. "But a lowly drunk driver, how much could he really have afforded to pay anyway?"

...fifty-four, fifty-five, fifty-six... Staring at my empty plate, I continued to count in my head as they continued to bicker, trying to block it all out.

Again, Brooke stepped in, trying to help me, but I think it ultimately made it worse. "Anyway, Mother, what are you going on about?

Grandchildren? Jax and I are still in college, and then we're going to New York. Jax will have law school, and you know I'm going to try to get my career started out there. Neither one of us wants kids right now."

Nancy huffed, "Do you really think you can make it out there? There are thousands of actors and actresses who can sing, dance, and act. Your time is better spent on raising a family and philanthropy."

That's rich, I thought bitterly. The only thing Nancy cared about was how she looked in front of others, not actually helping people. It made me sick.

Realizing I was rubbing my forehead, I dropped my hand into my lap. *When will this conversation end?*

"It's time, Brooke," Nancy argued. "If you get pregnant now, you'll graduate before the baby comes. I want grandchildren."

Coming here had been a mistake, and when I thought it couldn't get any worse, it did.

Rich stood. "Jaxon, come with me to my study. I believe we have a few things to discuss."

Goddammit!

chapter
forty-nine

JAXON

LIKE A PUPPET, I stood and followed.

Stale tobacco invaded my nostrils as I stepped into his office—or study, as he liked to call it. The stench got worse when he closed the door and lit up, nearly suffocating me. Sitting on the front edge of the massive wooden rectangle he called a desk, Rich began. "Alright, son, what was it you wanted to talk to me about?"

Although I had a pretty good idea what this was about, I played dumb, "Weren't you the one who wanted to speak to me, sir?"

"The holidays are quickly approaching. I know there's something you need to discuss with me, so I'm giving you the opportunity now."

"I'm not sure what you mean."

Smoke came out of his mouth as he impatiently said, "Proposing to Brooke, of course. A Christmas Eve proposal would be very romantic, with all the holiday decorations."

"I'm not planning on proposing to Brooke," I stated matter-of-factly, then for sanity's sake added, "at this time."

"Why not? You're going to graduate in a few months. Then you're moving to New York together. What's the issue? Weddings take time to plan. You should get married over the summer. The club would be the perfect place for it."

I doubt Brooke and I will even make it to Christmas!

Before I could think of an excuse, Rich made an assumption. "Oh, it's about money, right? You can't afford a ring yet, can you? Hmm…"

I think today broke the record for how many times I wanted to punch him in a single visit. "That's not the issue," I said, sounding as bored as possible.

"Come now, you don't need to be embarrassed about it. I know you don't have any money. How about this? I'll loan you the money for a ring worthy of my daughter?" I opened my mouth to say no, but he kept talking. "Oh, better yet, I'll give you the money. Think of it as a welcome-to-the-family gift."

Needing to put an end to this conversation, I stated, "No, thank you. If I were to propose to Brooke, I would buy the ring myself. If Brooke wants to be with me, she'd have to get used to what I can and cannot give her. But, as I said, I have no intention of proposing to her right now. If she and I were to spend the rest of our lives together, waiting a few more years wouldn't make a difference."

Rich looked thoughtful. For a brief second, I thought I might've gotten through to him. "You know, Brooke won't wait around forever."

I took a deep breath through my nose, regretting it immediately as the secondhand smoke turned my stomach. Accepting that I would not be able to get out of the suffocating room without giving him something, I gave, hating the taste of the words as they rolled off my tongue. "Thanks for the offer. I'll think about it." *Can I go puke now?*

BROOKE and I arrived home late Friday morning. Again, she slept in the car nearly the whole ride. Again, it was a relief since arguing while driving was not something I wanted to do. But as we stepped into the living room, I knew it was time to talk.

"I'm tired and need a nap. Let's get this over with," I said tiredly.

Flopping onto the couch, Brooke agreed, "Fine. Where were you Wednesday night?"

"I fell asleep on the couch at the bar. I came home as soon as I woke up. Now it's my turn. What got into you Wednesday night?"

"You know what!" she shouted as she sat up.

"The only thing I know is that you called Tess a bitch."

She rolled her eyes and flopped back again, grunting in frustration. "You didn't hear what she said to me before that. She provoked me."

What? That didn't sound like Tess. "How?"

She feigned surprise. "What? You actually believe me? You're not taking her side?"

"Why would you assume I'd take her side when you're my girl-friend?" For the millionth time in the last couple of months, I felt like an asshole. Our problems really were my fault, weren't they? Why else would she assume I'd put anyone before her?

Her eyes glistened. "I don't know if I should tell you."

"Why not?"

Pulling her legs up and hugging them to her chest, she sulked, "You're friends, and I may not like it, but you're right when you tell me I shouldn't meddle in your friendships."

"What did she say?"

Brooke glanced up at me, her bottom lip trembling. Finally she explained, "She said I was an ugly, spoiled-rotten bitch who wasn't good enough for you. She actually told me she was going to steal you away! She said she would have already except for the fact that you're using me for my money and that I better watch out because I had 'it,' whatever 'it' is, coming to me. She also said something like I was a nasty person and even if she couldn't have you, she'd make sure you left me or something like that." Brooke burst into tears. Hiding her face in her hands, she wailed, "And she said I was a bad influence on you and that you were going to relapse and die because of me. She made me feel like such a horrible person. She made me think you don't even love me anymore!

"I tried explaining that we love each other very much and have been through thick and thin together and nothing would tear us apart, but she kept interrupting me! She's so fake, Jax! She pretends to be this nice person, but she's awful!" Brooke regained some composure and spoke a little more calmly, although tears continued to fall. "And you know I've been speaking to Eli. He said Tess is a prude. He's starting to think she's using him for his money." She paused for a second, then quietly said, "I'm sorry, but she isn't who she pretends to be."

I was stunned. Either Brooke was a much better liar, or actress, than I ever gave her credit for, or Tess should consider a career in acting. One of them deserved an Oscar, but I really didn't know which one. Relatively speaking, I didn't know Tess that well, and I'd been with Brooke for years. Even after what had been happening over the last few months, I had a hard tine believing she'd make all that up. Was Tess two-faced?

A painful pressure built in my chest as I realized one of them was lying to me. I felt betrayed but didn't know by whom. A nagging voice needled me in the back of my mind. *The issues with Brooke started before Tess came along.*

Confused, I rubbed my forehead. If Brooke was lying, it would be another reason I had to get out of here. If Tess had said all that, she had me fooled. But first, I had to get her side. Based on how she'd reacted in the past, the blushing and not being able to meet my eye at times, I didn't think she would be able to lie to me if I asked her directly.

Turning, I headed to the door.

Brooke called out, "Where are you going?"

If Brooke was telling the truth, I needed to show her that I trusted her. "I'm going to tell Tess to mind her own fucking business." I would say that to her if, after speaking with her, I thought Brooke was being honest. If my girlfriend was telling the truth, I'd end my friendship with Tess.

THERE WAS a chime on the other side of the door as I pushed Tess's doorbell. On the way over, I worked myself up into believing Brooke, since as the person who saved my life, there was no way she could be capable of making all that up, right? A person who loved someone enough to do whatever they could to help them would not lie like that, I was sure of it.

When Tess swung open her door, I glared at her.

"Jax? What's the matter?" The concern in her voice sounded so real. The worry furrowing her brows looked so real. *She really should be an actress*, I thought bitterly.

Through clenched teeth, I hissed, "I need to talk to you."

Her eyes widened. "Now? Why?"

"Because I'm pissed. What did you say to Brooke on Wednesday night to set her off?"

Tess's mouth popped open. Her dumbfounded expression looked so genuine that doubt about Brooke's version started creeping in.

"Everything okay, Tess?" a female voice called from behind her. A second later, Mrs. Givens appeared next to Tess. *Shit!* I'd forgotten her parents were coming for the long weekend. *How much had they heard?*

Turning to her mom, Tess said, "Mom, this is my friend Jax. This is my mom, Joanne."

If my face revealed how I was feeling, it was contrite.

Mrs. Givens smiled at me. "Yes, we met at your soccer game. Nice to see you again, Jax."

"You too, Mrs. Givens. Sorry for interrupting. I forgot Tess said you were visiting this weekend." I was such a dick.

"Oh, that's alright. My husband and I were about to take a walk around the campus."

Tess tilted her head at her mom, who called out to her husband for their walk. She disappeared from sight, then Tess's dad questioned what walk she was talking about. Tess and I exchanged a glance, silently understanding her mom was giving us a few minutes of privacy to speak.

All my anger vaporized. Tess was exactly like her mom, kind and considerate. How could I doubt her sincerity and genuineness for a single second? Still, it would only be fair to make sure.

Stepping out of the way, I made room on the front steps for Mr. and Mrs. Givens to exit for their impromptu walk. I didn't miss the wink her mom gave Tess as she headed out the door. As they walked down the sidewalk, their daughter motioned for me to come in. After shutting the door, I followed her to the living room.

Turning to face me, she wrapped her arms around herself and waited.

chapter
fifty

COLD. That was what Jax's eyes were when he showed up at my front door. And now that was how I felt. Hoping my shaking wasn't obvious, I waited for Jax to explain why he'd come.

His chest rose and fell slowly, looking unusually unsure of himself. Finally, he spoke, "I'm sorry. I forgot your parents were going to be here."

"It's fine, but you don't have long. You said something about Brooke?" I pressed.

Unable to keep consistent eye contact, he said, "Well, I'm kind of mad."

Putting my hands on my hips and tilting my head at him, I repeated, "Kinda mad? You said you were pissed a minute ago. Are you mad at me?"

Setting his jaw, he stated, "That depends."

The coldness was melting away as anger gradually crept in. Crossing my arms, I asked, "On what?"

"On your answer. What'd you say to Brooke on Wednesday night?" Now his voice had turned cold. Whatever remorse he'd felt for interrupting my time with my parents had faded.

"You must've been told something, otherwise you wouldn't've come storming over here. What was it?" Although I tried keeping the annoyance at bay, based on his expression, I'd failed.

Jax's face went from cold to surprised to angry in less than two seconds. "I'd rather hear your version first."

"All right. First, I told her I didn't want to hear about your sex life." Jax's mouth opened as his eyes bulged. In an attempt not to cry, I kept my voice icy. "She informed me that you fucked her 'into oblivion,'" I said with air quotes, "on Wednesday, which was why you were late to the library. She also told me all about the times you guys had sex in the bar, on the bar, etcetera."

Jax looked away.

With hurt and anger taking over, I snapped, "She insinuated I was a prude, and I argued I wasn't." I couldn't stop my smirk when he glanced at me after that. "I told her you deserved respect and that maybe if she treated you with some, your relationship wouldn't be so screwed up, but I didn't exactly say it like that." I thought for a moment, then my cheeks flamed, and I looked away, my voice quieter. "Since she brought up your sex life, I told her that people need more than sex in a relationship, and that a person needs someone who'll love them back equally. And not to bring drugs around a drug addict."

Peering at him out of the corner of my eyes, I noted his forehead and brows were scrunched together, his eyes blankly searching. Thoroughly pissed off for having to remember and talk about the encounter I was trying to forget, I added, "Oh, I also said it wasn't up to her if we were friends." Feeling bitter, I scowled. "I wanted to let her know about how you called me cute but didn't want to get you in trouble since I know she's a pain to deal with."

Jax rubbed his entire face, not just his forehead, maybe trying to hide his shame and embarrassment. But I didn't regret repeating what he'd said to me back to him. With an edge of mockery, I asked, "What did she say I said?"

From behind his hands, he asked, "Is that all?"

Bored with the interrogation, I sighed. "Yeah, I think so. I have no reason to lie to you. I'm not the one who has something to lose here, unlike her."

Frustrated and aggravated, Jax demanded, "You didn't call her a nasty, horrible bitch, say I was using her for her money, that she didn't deserve me, and was a bad influence on me?"

I blinked, dropping my tough-girl act. "What?" That was what she told him I said? *What the heck!* She was definitely trying to get Jax to turn against me, and it appeared she was succeeding. My eyes burned with rage, even though I had no right to him. Defending myself, I shouted, "No! I didn't say any of that! But that's not to say I disagree with it. Sounds about right."

That stung. His mouth opened, and his brow furrowed. Pain was visible in his eyes, until his features hardened. My stomach knotted knowing the fire in his eyes was directed at me. "If that's what you really think, you sure you didn't say any of it? You were drunk. Maybe you don't remember."

Having trouble keeping my voice down, I argued, "I just told you what I said. If you don't want to believe me, that's your problem. If Brooke said that's what I said to her, it sounds like she has a guilty mind and knows exactly how she's been acting. Because, you know what, Jax? She is a nasty bitch who doesn't deserve you! Your relation-ship is toxic and abusive! I hate her and wish you'd open your eyes! The fact that you're still with her makes me wonder why you stay with someone who treats you like shit!" I was yelling at full volume. I hadn't yelled like that since the day Sammy and Tim died. Hot tears burned my face. Since I'd already said so much, I figured I might as well put it all out there. "The fact that she brings drugs around you, someone with a history, is really fucked up! How does a person who supposedly loves you do that? Is she trying to kill you?"

The array of emotions on Jax's face was a plethora of every negative feeling I could think of. My body was shaking with rage, so I tried forcing myself to take slow, deep breaths. His face eventually settled into a glare. I glared right back. Maybe I didn't like him after all! How could I like a person who put up with this crap? I thought he was strong to have been through everything he'd been through. Especially not having relapsed once, even when she'd bought drugs around. That couldn't have been easy. But if he couldn't stand up for himself, or wouldn't, maybe he wasn't who I thought he was.

At that point, maybe I should have held my tongue, but I couldn't. "If Brooke told you I said all that, she's lying. I didn't. I don't need the drama of your shitty relationship in my life," I fumed. "And I sure as hell don't want or need someone like Brooke in it."

Jax's arms were crossed, his eyes icy again. "Wow. This is a whole new side of you. I guess I don't know you very well after all. I had no idea you could have such hateful opinions of people. One reason I liked you was because I thought you were kind. Guess I was wrong."

Hateful? Because I said the truth? It's not hateful if it's true, is it?

Breathing was a struggle, but after what he said next, I couldn't breathe at all. "You know what? Maybe Brooke's right about you. Maybe you are fake and put up a front in front of others. I'm not interested in being friends with you anymore if this is how you are. Brooke is my girlfriend, so she comes with me. If you want to be friends with me, you'd have to put up with having her around. And Brooke's only been acting out because of you. She hasn't been herself because of you. If you don't like my girlfriend, then—"

"Fine!" I exploded. "There's the door. Don't let it hit you on the way out!" Panting in anger, I jabbed my finger in the direction of the front door.

I had been blinded by his looks and voice. He was a fool! And I was a fool for falling for him. My heart was shattered into a million pieces at his feet, and he didn't even know it. Now, not only did I have no chance with him, but we could no longer be friends.

Wrapping my arms around myself, I tried to still my shaking body. Jax hadn't moved. Avoiding his eyes, I whispered, "What are you still doing here? Leave if you aren't my friend."

I didn't see him go, but I heard the door close.

UNABLE TO FACE MY PARENTS, I hid in my room, sobbing. When I heard the front door and their muffled voices through my closed bedroom door, I was able to hold in the sobs but not the tears. After a minute, my mom knocked. "Tessa? Sweetie, can I come in?"

Even though I was ashamed, I really needed my mom. So in a tear-drenched voice, I muttered, "Sure."

Peering in, she took one look at my face and quickly entered and shut the door. As she passed my desk, she grabbed the box of tissues off of it and handed it to me as she sat down on the couch next to me.

After I wiped my face and blew my nose, she asked, "Did that young man make you cry?"

"No," I answered immediately, still wanting to defend him. In a strained voice, I explained, "It's my fault. I told him to leave. I don't think we're friends anymore."

"You're very upset. How long have you known him?"

I sniffed. "I met him at the beginning of the school year."

Trying to comfort me, my mom stroked my back. "That's not very long. How close are you?"

When I was unable to answer due to my weeping, my mom gave me a hug. "It's okay, sweetie. If you don't want to talk to me about it, you don't have to."

Pulling back, I cried, "No, I want to tell you!" I took a deep breath, nervous to tell my mom but knowing she was the best person I could discuss this crappy situation with. "Jax is the reason you will probably never meet Eli…"

It took a while, but I told her everything except that Jax was an addict and Brooke had literally saved his life. Instead, I told her about his family, his deep depression, and how Brooke helped him get better.

When I was done, she summed up my situation. "So you're in love with Jax but are platonic friends. He's in a toxic and likely abusive relationship. You and Jax got into a big fight over his girlfriend and now may not be friends anymore. And you'll be breaking up with Eli."

Feeling hopeless, I groaned, "Yeah, pretty much."

"Is there really nothing else going on between you and Jax?"

I gaped at her. "No, nothing, I swear. Why do you think there would be?"

"You seem very close. Would you like to know my thoughts and opinions on the situation? I'll warn you, you may not like what I have to say."

I blew my nose. "Yes, please."

"First, I agree you should break up with Eli. It's not right leading him on, nor is it fair. The heart wants what it wants, and you can't force it. You may not be able to have who you love, but you shouldn't be with someone you can't love."

I nodded.

Mom went on, "This might hurt, but I will always be honest with you. I'm not sure your friendship with Jax should continue. It's your call, but besides it being painful to be around him when he's with his girlfriend, you're heading into dangerous territory. You have feelings for him, and I think it's possible he may have feelings for you as well. I don't agree that men and women can't be friends, but your friendship sounds a lot deeper than what one would expect between a man and a woman. I saw the way he watched you at your soccer game. He couldn't take his eyes off you. I don't blame his girlfriend for being worried, especially if they're having relationship issues.

"But even if he doesn't have romantic feelings for you, you will continue hurting. Whether a person is in a good or a bad relationship, it's painful seeing the person you love with someone else. If they do break up, and he doesn't return your feelings, it'll hurt. The heart can only take so much pain before a person becomes a hardened shell. I don't want that to happen again, Tess. You've finally come out of your shell after all these years. It was hard for your father and I to see you suffer. We want you to be happy. Time heals all wounds, and you will eventually get over your feelings for him. One day, you will fall in love again."

My body shook as I cried, racked with guilt as my mother spoke. Making them worry about me after they'd lost their son and making them suffer... They didn't deserve that.

"Do you want me to continue?" she asked softly.

I nodded.

"You're an adult," she said hesitantly, "so I can't tell you what to do. You get to make your own decisions, but I hope you will not become the other woman. You deserve much more than that. Honestly, I'm not sure I could accept a guy who'd do that."

Astonished by my mother's suggestion, I defended myself. "I have no intention of being anyone's side piece. Besides, who knows if he actually has feelings for me. He hasn't left her even though she's horrible. He's blinded by her! She's got her claws dug into him."

"Do you really think so?" my mom asked thoughtfully. "He was awfully mad at you. Do people get mad like that at their friends? I can only speak from my experiences, but I've never gotten into a fight like that with any of my friends. And, you know, Jax still being in a relationship with his girlfriend might not be the flaw you think it is."

I cocked an incredulous eyebrow at her.

She explained, "From what I've seen, the longer you're with someone, the longer it takes to leave them. Look at you and Eli, for example. You've only been dating a couple of months, yet you still haven't broken things off despite knowing it won't work out."

"I haven't broken up with him yet because I really was trying to give him a fair shot. Eli's a good guy, and if I loved him, I'd be lucky. He's a catch."

"It's possible Jax may be doing something similar. Trying. I doubt he's as blinded or clueless as you think. It sounds like they've been through a lot together. When a couple has that kind of history, I think most would try to work things out before calling it quits. Maybe he's trying to see if they can fix their relationship."

She had a good point. I wouldn't want a guy who'd abandon me if things got hard. If Jax was attempting to mend his relationship before giving up, wasn't that to his credit? Didn't that show how loving, loyal, committed, and caring he was?

That possibility made my love for him grow while further splintering the tiny shards of my already-broken heart.

chapter
fifty-one

JAXON

AS SOON AS I walked through the door, Brooke was on the attack. "You were gone for a long time! Where were you?" It was almost seven, about time for me to head to the bar.

Glaring at her, I seethed, "Don't start."

Offended, she sassed, "Excuse me?"

"Don't give me that. I spoke to Cory. She heard your entire conversation with Tess. You lied to me!"

Brooke scoffed, "What? Me? Lie to you? What about you? You're the guilty one!"

Exacerbated, I asked through my teeth, "What have I lied about?"

Crossing her arms, she retorted, "I don't know. Why don't you tell me?" I had no idea what to say to her or what she was implying. In my silence, she elaborated, "Lies of omission are still lies."

"What haven't I told you? Have I ever given you a reason not to trust me?"

"Yes, let's start with two minutes ago! I asked you where you were, and you still haven't answered me!" she shrieked.

"I told you I was going to see Tess."

"Yeah, like eight hours ago!" she roared.

True, I was gone for a long time. "After I spoke to Tess, I went to the graveyard to think."

Caustically, she asked, "About what?"

Fed up, I let it out. "You, Brooke! You! I'm trying to figure out what to do about you! I'm tired and done with this relationship! I'm not in love with you anymore! I don't think I want to be with you anymore or even try! I'm fucking miserable, and every fucking day is a debate in my head as to if I should leave or not!"

She didn't look surprised. But what was surprising was her calm voice. "You're cheating on me, right? With Tess?"

Throwing my hands up in the air, I huffed. "No! I'm not fucking cheating on you! I have never cheated on you! Other than a couple of hugs to comfort one another, we haven't even touched! Why don't you believe me?"

She looked unconvinced. "Really?"

Beyond pissed, I said something I knew would hurt her but justified it to myself because of how much she'd hurt me. "You know what? Maybe I should go fuck Tess so you can actually have something to be mad at me about. Would that make you happy, finding out that you were right? Who knows, maybe having sex with an angry guy who's in a relationship with someone else is a kink of hers? Maybe I'll call her up on speaker phone right now and see if she's down. Maybe I'll get lucky tonight and come home and rub it in your face! Would that make you happy? Would it, Brooke?" By the end of my rant, I was shouting at her. I rarely shouted, but I was more infuriated than I could ever remember being before, excluding when my family died. I needed to get out of there before I said any more fucked-up shit.

Storming into the bedroom, I got a change of clothes for the bar then headed for the door. I looked at Brooke as I passed. She was frozen except for the tears streaming down her face. I felt like the biggest asshole in the world, again! I had made two women who I cared about cry in the span of a few hours. Still, I had one more thing I needed to say.

Calm but angry, I told Brooke, "I would appreciate it if you didn't come to the bar tonight. Even though it appears you no longer respect me, I hope you can respect my job enough not to come to my place of employment and get me angry before I have to work, because I really can't deal with any more of your bullshit today."

As tempting as it was to slam the door on my way out, I closed it gently while trying to reign in my anger.

THE BAR WAS DEAD.

Gathering the guys by the stage, I announced, "The owner said that since it's dead tonight, we can start a half hour later and do one set for an hour. Same pay. I emailed you the updated setlist."

My bandmates whooped and cheered, and why wouldn't they? A shortened night for the same pay? *Hell yeah.*

The real reason for the short night was that I didn't want to be there. Even though I used music to vent, I didn't feel up to it tonight, but I wasn't one to bail on my responsibilities.

As I headed up to the office to print out new copies of the setlist for the guys to put on stage, Chuck followed. He closed the office door behind him, blocking out the noise from the bar.

Looking at his phone, he quipped, "You know, Jax, when you shorten the setlist, one would think you'd take away some of the songs you had planned on playing, not basically make a whole new one."

Not in the mood for this sarcasm, I barked, "You got a problem, Chuck?"

He shrugged. "What if I don't remember some of these songs since I didn't know we were going to play them tonight?"

"You have an hour. Go practice!" I snapped as Ashton entered the office. To him, I asked, "What, you gonna lecture me too?"

Ashton leaned against the closed door. "What's wrong?"

Sitting down behind the desk, I rested my elbows on the wooden top, rubbing my forehead. "What do you think? Brooke."

Chuck commented, "Figures."

Ashton asked, "What about her?"

I took a breath. "I'm done with her bullshit. I'm fucking miserable. I'm not in love with her anymore, and I'm so mad that I don't know if I even love her at all anymore. I don't like the person she's become." Flopping down and burying my head in my arms, I breathed slowly, trying to resist the stinging in my eyes. "I'm so fucking done."

When my eyes dried, I glanced up at Chuck then Ashton. Both were mortally concerned.

Ashton said, "Do what you gotta do."

Chuck chimed in, "Life's too short to be miserable. We're here if you need anything."

Ashton nodded in agreement.

Their reactions surprised me. Ashton usually made it out to be like I was in the wrong, and Chuck more often than not took any opportunity to criticize Brooke. Even they must've seen how bad it had gotten and, instead of giving me their two cents, were going to support me. That spoke volumes.

chapter
fifty-two

TESSA

WHEN I STEPPED through the front door of Smythie's at about nine-forty-five that night, I expected the band to be on stage playing, but they weren't. There weren't many patrons around, so at first I figured the band had the night off. But as I walked toward the bar, I spotted four of the five band members hanging around and the stage was set with the drums, guitars, bass and microphones. Maybe Jax had called out of work at the last minute.

Disappointed and still reeling from our fight, I decided I might as well not waste the effort I'd made to get here and have a drink before I headed back home.

About half an hour earlier, my parents had used the excuse that they were three hours ahead, still on East Coast time, and needed to go to bed.

As my mom hugged me goodbye, she whispered a suggestion, "Talking things out is the only solution. One way or another, you'll get your answer." My mother had always been supportive of me. She was also the most intuitive person I knew. She'd ushered my dad out the door, giving me a chance to go to the bar and see if I could speak to Jax.

Scanning the bartenders behind the bar counter, I noted Cory was missing. She must've had a rare night off. I contemplated leaving since I was by myself and the thought of taking drinks from an unknown person, even if they were a Smythie's employee, freaked me out.

Turning to face the dance floor while I debated what to do, I came face-to-face with Chuck.

He greeted me with his big, warm smile. "Tessaaaa! How are you?"

With some effort, I smiled back and said, "Hey, Chuck. I'm fine, you?"

"I'm pumped."

"Oh yeah? Why's that?" I asked, wondering what was so exciting about a sparsely crowded bar.

Chuck hopped over the bar counter in one smooth move. I turned and cocked a brow at him.

"Cosmo on the rocks, splash of pineapple juice, right?" he asked. My mouth popped open. How did he know what my favorite drink was? Reading my expression, he explained, "Jax told me. He said since Cory isn't here tonight that I needed to make your drink."

So Jax is here somewhere. Automatically, I looked around but didn't see him. I felt vulnerable at the knowledge that Jax still cared, even if we wouldn't be friends anymore. Turning my attention back to Chuck, I responded, "Yes, thank you."

I watched him flipping bottles around as he made my cocktail, impressed at my substitute mixologist. "You moonlight as a bartender?"

"Ha! No, not anymore. But I used to tend bar here. I stopped after I joined the band. That's how Jax and I met."

"Oh, I had no idea. I thought you met when you auditioned for the band."

As he shook my drink, he explained loudly enough to be heard over all the noise, "We met here, and then I showed up at the audition."

As Chuck poured my drink into a cup, I inquired, "Shouldn't you guys be on stage right now?"

Chuck smiled widely "That's why I'm pumped! We start in about five minutes. We'll be on for an hour, then we get to go home early."

"Ah, I see," I said as I took the drink. "Thanks." I tried handing him my bank card, but he wouldn't accept it.

"Don't worry about it. I'll add it to the band's tab."

"The band has a tab?"

He laughed. "Nope. We drink for free."

I objected, but he hopped back over the bar and said, "Gotta get on stage. See you later."

"Bye," I said, although I wasn't sure he heard me.

My eyes moved up to the stage and met the blue eyes I loved so freaking much. They were sad, and that hurt. Jax held my gaze for several long seconds. Holding up my drink, I mouthed a thank you, but he looked away. Was he ignoring me or simply hadn't seen the gesture? Trying to squash the pain in my chest, I stayed put by the bar, afraid of Jax's reaction if I got closer.

Like the first time I was here, once the bar patrons moved to the stage, there appeared to be more of them than it had first seemed. Still, it wasn't a huge crowd. Brooke hadn't even shown up, but the lack of people didn't hamper Jax's performance at all. He was on fire. Angry fire that radiated off the stage, matching the list of angry songs they played.

Based on his song choices, besides being angry, he was fed up. I debated if coming here had been a mistake. Had I made him like this? Was he telling me he was angry, fed up, and done with me? I rolled my eyes to myself as I looked down into my barely touched drink. *Get over yourself, Tessa! He chooses the songs days before, so this has nothing to do with you!*

My subconscious was right. I needed to accept that I wasn't special to him. Jax would never create a setlist with me in mind. Clearly, Brooke had inspired tonight's song choices. It was always about Brooke. She was the special one to him. Maybe the songs tonight should've given me hope, but this wasn't the first time he sang about doomed relationships and probably wouldn't be the last.

Staring into my cup, listening to Jax's rage, I made my decision. I would fully and completely accept and respect Jax's decision to stick by Brooke. Next time I saw her, I would apologize for making her nervous and assure her I wasn't trying to get between them. My mom was right. With time, I would get over my feelings for him. If we could, I'd still like to be friends with him, although I'd put a bit more separation between us.

But if he didn't accept my apology or really didn't want to be friends anymore, there would be nothing I could do. I'd have no choice but to move on and forget about him.

My eyes burned with unshed tears. Tilting my head to the ceiling, I blinked a few times, preventing them from falling. When my vision cleared, my line of sight connected with Jax. He'd been watching me. Could he see the sheen in my eyes?

As the set continued, I thought there was something a bit off about Jax's voice. It sounded gruffer, and the screaming in some songs sounded more natural. During one of Jax's particularly animated songs, it hit me. He wasn't using his voice distorter.

Completely lost in the music, he was putting everything he had into his performance. Total rock-star style, sweating, bent over singing the especially tense parts, spitting as he screamed loudly enough so that the entire town might've been able to hear him while having a death grip on his microphone. The last song of the night was especially intense. Although he'd been singing for an hour, he didn't seem tired at all. However, his voice was getting raspy. I had a feeling he'd wake up tomorrow without it.

When the last song ended, in a hoarse voice, Jax did his usual "thanks for coming, see you next week" bit then exited the stage. When he didn't pass by after a few seconds, I concluded he must've gone up the back stairs, which I couldn't see from my position near the bar.

With a knotted stomach, I went over. The bouncer nodded when I asked if Jax had gone upstairs but refused to let me go up. While I begged, on the verge of tears, Chuck and Ashton came over. Ashton asked what was going on.

I explained, "Jax and I got into a huge fight earlier today, and I need to apologize to him, but this guy won't let me go up and talk to him." Unsurprisingly, I sounded as desperate as I was.

Jax's two best friends exchanged glances, then Chuck took out his phone and started typing on it. I hoped he was texting Jax, but I was too chicken to ask. Meanwhile, Ashton warned me, "He's in a bad mood. I'm not sure talking to him right now is a good idea. Maybe you should wait until he calms down."

Sighing, I figured he was right and turned to leave, but he caught my arm. "You don't have to answer this, but what were you fighting about?"

"The interaction Brooke and I had on Wednesday night, you know, right before you dragged her off."

Chuck looked up from his phone, surprised. Looking back and forth between Ashton and I, he asked, "What happened Wednesday? What'd I miss?"

Before either of us could answer, the bouncer put his hand over his ear with his radio's earpiece, then opened the rope. "Go ahead. Jax is in the office."

Too surprised and relieved, I forgot to ask where the upstairs office was, simply thanking the bouncer as I passed by and headed up.

Jax was leaning with his back against an open door frame, arms crossed, facing the stairs, waiting for me. He'd changed out of his sweaty shirt, but his hairline was still damp. He might've been in a bad mood but still looked so freakin' sexy.

I approached, and Jax motioned for me to enter the room. It was dimly lit but not too dark. There was a desk with a closed laptop and not much else on it. Behind the desk was a shelf that included filing drawers and a printer. A closed door was behind and to the right of the desk. A tower of security monitors took up a large part of the wall with the office door. Even in the dark lighting and flickering club lights, you could see almost every inch of the bar on them. Across from the desk was a couch and a small chest of drawers.

But what really drew my attention was the floor-to-ceiling glass wall opposite the office door. As I walked to it, the music from the bar almost disappeared. Looking over my shoulder, I saw Jax had closed the door and was now leaning against it, arms and ankles crossed. The office had some serious sound-proofing. Peering down out the window, one could see most of the open room, the bar itself being the exception.

Hoarsely, Jax said, "It's one-way glass, so it looks like a black wall from downstairs."

Before facing him, I took a deep breath. "Are we allowed to be in here?" I asked, hesitantly.

"It's the owner's office, but the band's allowed to use it."

Ringing my fingers, I tried to figure out how to start.

Since I wasn't saying anything, Jax rasped, "I don't have much of a voice left, so—"

I held up my hands to stop him. "That's okay. You don't have to say anything. I wanted to say something. Will you listen?"

He nodded.

I swallowed. "I'm sorry about earlier. I shouldn't have yelled at you like that. I was wrong when I said I had nothing to lose. Your friendship means a lot to me, and I know you're with Brooke and I'm sorry I'm making her feel uncomfortable. I'll apologize to her next time I see her. And I'm sorry for saying those mean things about her to you. I'm not trying to make excuses, but I'm a bit of an emotional mess lately. I'm..." I paused, racking my brain for the right word. "...conflicted about some things, and maybe Brooke wasn't trying to provoke me on Wednesday, but that's what it felt like."

Taking a shaky breath in, I tried to hold back my tears. "It hurt a lot when you said you didn't really know me this afternoon, because you know me better than most people. You're the first person I've opened up to in years, and it felt like—" My voice broke.

During my entire monologue, Jax hadn't moved, nor had his facial expression changed. I couldn't tell if he believed me or thought I was being fake. Looking down, I watched as tears fell to the floor. "I don't want to lose you as my friend, but I'll understand if you don't want to be friends anymore."

There was still no response from him. I wasn't even sure if he had heard the last part. Having said everything I wanted to say, I waited another couple of moments for him to give me an indication one way or the other, but he remained silent. Peering through my wet lashes, I saw he was still blocking the door, so I couldn't even leave. So I stood there in the middle of the office feeling vulnerable and exposed. Closing my eyes, I willed myself to stop crying.

Warm arms wrapped around my back and pulled me close. Jax held me tighter than he ever had before, resting his head against mine. My surprise wore off quickly, and I hugged him back just as tightly. Time lost all meaning as we stood in our embrace. Perhaps I should have loosened my grip, but it felt so good to have his body pressed up against mine, and who knew when or if he'd hug me like this again? So I kept my eyes closed and burned the feeling into my brain as the tension melted from my body.

Sighing in relief, I inhaled Jax's sexy, masculine, delicious scent. My knees weakened, and a whimper escaped. I prayed Jax interpreted it as a cry rather than what it actually was.

As if I wasn't feeling unsteady enough, Jax's lips brushed up against my ear, his breath tickling my skin, sending electric currents down my spine, directly to my core. Did he have any idea what he was doing to me? Could he feel my heart beating in my chest against his? Could he tell I was using him to prevent myself from becoming a puddle on the floor?

In a gruff, sexy-as-hell whisper, he breathed into my ear, "I'm sorry too. You haven't lost me. I don't want to lose you either." Tears squeezed out the corners of my closed lids as my chest rose and fell against his. Continuing his unknowing torture, he said, "I know you were telling the truth. I'm sorry I didn't believe you when I know you're not like that. Don't worry about Brooke. You don't need to apologize to her, and you don't need to deal with her."

Not deal with her? What did that mean?

Not wanting to pass out in his arms, which I thought was seriously possible, I pushed away as non-offensively as possible and looked up into his eyes. All the anger had vanished, replaced by a light I'd only seen a handful of times.

The corners of his mouth were turned up slightly. He appeared relaxed and content, and it was so breathtaking that I struggled to inhale properly. Jax, on the other hand, was cool as a cucumber.

I swallowed. Hoping I'd sound normal, I said, "Thank you."

Jax took a step over to the desk and grabbed a tissue from a box. I thought he'd hand it to me, but to my utter astonishment, he gently wiped my tears away himself. Unable to help it, I stared at his eyes, trying to interpret what I was seeing in them. When his irises moved from my face to my eyes, our gazes locked. Time slowed, and the muffled music in the background faded away. As if in a bubble, the only thing I was aware of was him.

He filled all my senses. He was the only thing I saw. His haggard breaths were the only sounds filling my ears. I was intoxicated by his own personal aura, and it drove me a little insane. Jax's hand replaced the tissue, and his thumb slowly moved back and forth across my cheek, as if to wipe away a tear that wasn't there.

The only thing missing was a taste of him. And I wanted to taste him more than I ever had before. Sure, I'd wanted him from the moment I saw him, but there was something incredibly intimate about a kiss, and this was the first time I felt that if I could have just one kiss, I'd die satisfied. My eyes dropped to his lips before I could stop them.

Forcefully, I lifted them back up to Jax's, but they felt heavy, and I slowly blinked at him. In my heady state, the only thing I could think about was my desire for him to kiss me, with no consideration of what that would mean or what the consequences might be.

A loud knock on the door caused us to jump apart. Jax went over to the door and unlocked it. I guess he hadn't wanted anyone interrupting us, and after what happened, my delusional brain filled with possibilities as to why that was.

While Jax opened the door, I stepped over to the glass wall and looked out. The stage had been cleared, and there were very few people about. Behind me, I heard Chuck say, "Hey, we're out. You good? Do you want to stay at my house tonight?"

Not hearing anything else, I glanced over my shoulder. Jax held the door open wide. Chuck peered in. After looking back and forth between us, Chuck leaned in and whispered something. Jax nodded.

Knowing my time was up, I headed to the door. "I'm gonna get going. Have a good night, guys." I squeezed past them, but someone grabbed my wrist. I turned to see Jax holding up his car keys, but he didn't say anything, probably because he knew he wouldn't be heard over the music blaring out of the speakers. I glanced at Chuck for help.

He got the hint and translated, "He's offering you a ride home."

"Oh, right." I laughed nervously as a memory of Tina suggesting I might've had sex with Jax in his car flashed through my brain. Knowing that spending any more time alone with him was a bad idea, I declined. "Thanks, but I want to walk."

Jax gave Chuck a meaningful look. I got it, but Chuck didn't. I giggled at his confused expression. Rolling his eyes, Jax lifted his hand

and did a walking motion with his pointer and middle finger. I gawked a bit too long at Jax's fingers, even following them down to his side when he dropped his hand. I'd never noticed how long they were. His hands in general were large, but then again Jax was tall. I dropped my eyes in shame as my cheeks heated at the dirty thought running through my brain. As I considered if the stereotypical saying was true, my eyes landed on his shoes. His large shoes.

Comprehension abounded and Chuck said, "Oh! Yeah!" Drawing my attention out of the gutter, Chuck said to me, "I'll walk you home."

Pretending I hadn't been imagining Jax's anatomy, I cheerfully said, "Thanks."

As we headed toward the front staircase, I looked Jax's way, not quite able to meet his eyes, and waved. In my peripheral vision, I thought I saw him lift his hand. Before my head had completely disappeared down below the loft floor, I lifted my gaze in Jax's direction. He was still watching me.

chapter
fifty-three

JAXON

MUCH TO MY ANNOYANCE, Brooke was waiting for me. As soon as I opened the front door, she ran to me, crying. "Jax, I'm so sorry! You're right. I lied. I was trying to provoke Tess. I shouldn't have, but I don't like her and really don't like that you hang around her, but you don't like some of my friends either, so I'll drop it."

Numb to another meaningless apology, I headed for the bedroom. When Brooke followed me, I muttered, "I can't talk much."

"What happened to your voice?"

"I lost it." *Obviously.* Pausing, I stopped digging around in my pajama pants drawer and faced her. Despite being mentally checked out, I owed her an *apology*. "I said some messed-up things earlier, trying to hurt you. I'm sorry." Taking a slow, deep breath, I considered if I should even bother trying to explain to Brooke. As far as I was concerned, I didn't owe her anything else. Still, if it was me, I would want to know. "If I explain why Tess's friendship means so much to me, maybe you'll understand."

She winced but stayed quiet.

"Tess's twin brother and her boyfriend died in a car accident a few years ago."

To Brooke's credit, she looked genuinely horrified. "My God! That's terrible! I had no clue!"

"Now you know. I'm gonna shower then go to bed."

Brooke perked up. "Do you want company?"

"No." *Absolutely fucking not!*

Although disappointed, she didn't try to convince me. "Okay. I'll make you something for your voice."

"You don't have to."

"I want to."

"Whatever," I muttered as I headed to the shower.

AFTER HOURS OF SLEEPLESSNESS, I grabbed my phone and headed to the living room. Bringing up my text app, I sent Tess a message.

JAX

Hey, I know you're sleeping, but I have a couple of things I need to get off my chest.

Earlier when I said I didn't want to lose you, I meant it. I don't think you realize how much you mean to me. I'm sorry for doubting you and saying all that shit yesterday. You actually know me better than most people too. I hope you can forgive me.

As I was starting to type my next text, I saw that she'd not only read my message but was typing a reply.

TESS

Forgive what? You already said sorry.

JAX

What are you doing up?

TESS

Me? What are you doing up?

JAX

I've got a lot on my mind.

TESS

I've got a lot on my mind too. Don't worry, you don't need to apologize again. All is forgiven.

JAX

Well, I need to make a confession, and I won't blame you if you get mad.

TESS

What?

JAX

I told Brooke about your brother and boyfriend. I was trying to explain to her why your friendship means so much to me.

Wait, that sounded bad!

That's not the only reason, but I thought telling her that would help her understand.

TESS

It's OK. If someone searches my name online, they'd find out about it anyway. It was all over the local news here when it happened.

The idea to look it up had never entered my mind, but now I was curious.

TESS

How's your voice?

JAX

Gone. Brooke made me some disgusting concoction her voice coach told her about, but I couldn't drink it. I'll rest it and it should be fine in a couple of days.

TESS

Why didn't you use your voice distorter? What if you can't sing next week?

JAX

It should be fine by then, but if I can't sing, then I can't sing. I'm not worried about it.

TESS

You didn't answer my first question.

JAX

I'll tell you but you might think I'm a little crazy.

TESS

Now I'm really intrigued.

JAX

Besides getting really into the music, using it to vent, I figured if I had no voice, I couldn't fight with Brooke anymore today. It's been a rough few days.

TESS

Wow... I hope it at least worked. Sorry you felt you had to take such drastic measures.

JAX

We didn't fight but we still ended up talking a little. It was a stupid idea.

I'm so fucking tired.

TESS

I hope you can rest and relax tomorrow. I'm going to try to get some sleep now. Good night.

JAX

Good night, Tessa.

I pulled up the browser on my phone and typed in "Timothy Givens," assuming that was what Tim was short for, and "New York." Immediately, a plethora of results popped up, from news articles to obituaries to photos. While Tess looked like a younger version of her mom, Timothy Robert Givens resembled his dad, except for his eyes, which were the same blue-green as Tess and her mom's. Among the photos was one of the three of them. A younger Tess standing in the middle but in the arms of Sammy. While all three were smiling, Tess was radiant.

I laughed when I took a closer look at Tess's high school boyfriend.

Sammy, or Sumi Daichi Muri, was tall, wore tight jeans, a lot of black t-shirts in various pictures, and had pierced ears. Even as a guy, I could admit he was good looking. Based on his mom's name, she was of Russian descent, while his dad was Japanese. In a picture of him and his parents, his mom looked like a runway model, towering over his dad.

Other than now knowing what they looked like, nothing I found gave me any new information. Tess had told me more than what I'd read. Still, I continued quickly clicking through various media until I froze at one picture. It was one of her and Sammy. My heartbeat increased to the point it almost hurt.

Exiting the browser, I went into my photos app and scrolled until I found the one of her and I on the Ferris wheel. Opening the editing option, I went through the still frames of the live photo, stopping on the one where Tess was looking at me right before the photo was taken. Flipping back to the picture of her and Sammy, my breath caught.

Tess was looking at Sammy in the same way she had looked at me.

chapter
fifty-four

TESSA

AS I REPLACED my phone on its charger, I wondered again if I had made a mistake going to the bar and making up with Jax. Even seeing him text my full first name made my heart flutter. How was I supposed to get over him like this? I couldn't stop thinking about him. Maybe I should stop talking to him. But that thought may as well have been a knife stabbing me in the heart. The entire situation was one big knife blade. Why couldn't he leave her? Even if I had no shot with him, seeing him miserable was breaking my heart.

Sure, they had a passionate relationship, but was that really surprising considering how passionate Jax was? It radiated off him when he was on stage and during some of our conversations, not to mention when we'd hugged, especially the one from a few hours ago. It was like my body was a sponge and his passion was water. I soaked it up.

After another hour or so of not sleeping, I resigned myself to flat-out ask him why he was still with Brooke. He might give me the same excuse as he had before, how she saved him, but he'd had a few weeks to think about what I'd said. Had he considered what I'd told him at all?

SUNDAY EVENING, I was reheating some leftovers for dinner when Tina got home.

"Hey! How was your weekend?" I greeted her.

She looked serious. "It was good, but I don't want to talk about that right now."

"Are you sure it was good? You seem annoyed."

"I am annoyed. We need to talk about Wednesday night."

"Ah," I said as I took my plate out of the microwave. "Don't worry about that. It's old news."

"What do you mean?" skepticism oozed from her question.

As I waited for my food to cool, I gave her a rundown of the events since Wednesday night.

When I had finished, she squeaked, "I missed all that?"

Having taken a bite of my pasta, I nodded.

"But you still haven't had a chance to speak to Eli about what he may have said to Brooke?"

I swallowed. "Not yet, but he's on his way over now."

Tina pursed her lips.

Between bites, I asked, "What, Tee? I know you're itching to get something off your chest."

"I think your mom's right. I think being friends with Jax is doing nothing but hurting you."

They were both right, but I was sure seeing Jax and Brooke together would hurt less than not having him in my life at all. Still, I tried to reassure her, "The semester's almost done. I doubt I'll see much of him next semester. Probably only Friday nights whenever I go to the bar, and it's not like him and I hang out or talk much there." I had tried my best to sound casual, but inside? It felt like I was dying. Having lost my appetite, I poked at my food.

"I'm sure my feelings will fade when I stop seeing him multiple times a week," I said, but my voice betrayed me, making it clear I had little hope that would actually be the case. Looking at her, I knew Tina didn't believe me. Trying to be more convincing, I said, "And if he does stay with her all through next semester too, and things are still bad between them, that'll help me get over him. I wouldn't like a guy like that anyway. I can understand trying to fix things for a while, but from what he's told me, it would've been going on for over a year by the time we graduate."

"What do you think is going to happen?"

"I think he's reached his limit, or close to it, and he'll leave. And that's not wishful thinking either."

"But you do want them to break up, right?"

"I'd be lying if I said I didn't. But more for his sake than mine. He's miserable, Tee."

She stayed silent for a minute while I continued to nudge my food around my plate. Finally, she said, "I know I must be driving you crazy about this, but I swear this will be the last time I talk to you about it, unless you bring it up yourself. You're vulnerable right now because of your feelings for him. He's going through some issues with Brooke. I have no doubt that Jax knows you have feelings for him. I don't think he's the type of guy to take advantage, but I don't know him that well either. But if he does try, I hope you don't let him. You know, don't get caught up in the moment and do something one or both of you are going to regret, okay?"

A voice interrupted us.

"Hey, Tess, I'm here!" Eli called from the direction of the front door, ending our conversation.

I met him in the living room but did not walk into his open arms. Instead, I crossed mine and glared at him.

He looked like a deer in headlights. "What? Is something wrong?"

"Yes," I hissed. "You need to tell me right now exactly what you said to Brooke about our relationship."

His eyes widened. "I... uh... I don't recall saying anything that would make you upset." He paused before asking, "What did she say that I told her?"

"In a few words, that I'm a prude."

Eli's mouth dropped open. "What? I didn't say anything like— Oh..." Eli smacked his forehead.

"You did say something! What was it?"

"It must have been after you and I had our first date. I saw her in the elevator, and she made a comment about how you're probably a bore in bed and I said, 'I doubt that.' Then she said something like,

'What? You haven't fucked her yet?' and I said, 'Not everyone has sex on the first date.' Other than that, I haven't spoken to her about us."

"You sure that was it?" I pressed. "You aren't frustrated and didn't vent to her or something?"

Eli scrunched his brows. It was the most stressed I'd ever seen him. "Yes, that's it. Am I a bit frustrated? Sure, but I respect you. I won't push you, and I sure as hell won't go talking about it with other people." Most of my anger at him left my body, replaced by guilt. "How did this conversation even come up?"

"She was trying to provoke me."

"Why?"

I huffed. "Because she doesn't like that I'm friends with Jax."

"Neither do I, but I don't say anything about it because it's none of my business."

I put my hands on my hips. "Well, you just did, didn't'cha?"

He winced.

I sighed.

Trying to lighten the mood, Eli asked, "Can I hug you now?"

Remembering the other reason I was annoyed at him, I snapped, "No."

His brows shot up.

Answering before he could ask, I demanded, "Why didn't you tell me you knew about my brother and boyfriend?"

Eli's mouth popped open, but it took a second for anything to come out of it. "Tina told me not to."

"So? Aren't you my 'boyfriend?'" I put it in air quotes. "Shouldn't you be talking to me about this stuff? Asking me? Getting to know me? Figuring out why I am the way I am and who I am?"

"But you were so closed off about it."

"Yeah, like on our first date! Did you expect me to reveal a bunch of personal stuff when I hardly knew you? I was starting to think you didn't really care because you never ask me about anything other than superficial stuff."

He crossed his arms incredulously. "Favorite color and ice cream flavors are not superficial. That's important information."

I rolled my eyes but I couldn't stop a laugh from escaping. It was so like Eli to make me laugh. The corner of his mouth lifted into a smile when he knew he'd won. The last of the anger toward him was gone. He really had been trying to be considerate.

When he walked over and wrapped his arms around me, I didn't resist. He kissed the top of my head. "I missed you. Did you have a good time with your parents?"

I hummed an affirmation as I closed my eyes, enjoying the comfort a hug could give a person. A few seconds later, my eyes popped open, and I stepped back. He was getting turned on, and I was definitely not in the mood, especially since I had planned on breaking up with him. *Dammit!* How the hell could I do it now? It would be too cruel now.

But what if he was going to initiate sex? The nerves in my stomach were the closest thing to butterflies I'd felt with him. It growled loudly.

Eli laughed. "Hungry?"

Excessively happy that I'd lost my appetite earlier and hadn't eaten much, I answered, "Yes, I heated up some leftovers before you arrived. You want some?"

"No, thanks. I actually need to get going. I'm not going to be able to hang out for the next week or so. I have a huge exam that's pretty important for my career coming up, so I need to focus on that."

I didn't have to pretend to sound disappointed, although my disappointment was for reasons he wouldn't like. "Oh...okay. That's fine. Do what you have to do, of course."

He gave me a brief kiss on the lips. "Thanks for understanding. I'll text you later."

I waved. "See ya."

After the door shut, I let out a groan and shook my fists in the air dramatically. Now I wasn't going to be able to break up with him for a couple more weeks! I wasn't heartless enough to risk upsetting him before his exam. *Ugh!*

chapter
fifty-five

TESSA

I CLOSED my notebook and threw it on the floor before falling back into the couch. "Phew, I'll be glad when this class is over."

Jax gave me a small smile. "Almost there."

The library had been closed for some event, so Jax and I studied at my house. More specifically, we were in my room since Tina was watching TV in the living room.

After putting his own books away, he stood to leave.

Before I lost my nerve, I cried, "Jax!"

Wide-eyed, he looked down at me. "What?"

Raspy from my tight throat, I asked, "Why're you still with her?"

The alarm faded from his features as he looked away. His chest rose and fell slowly. After a few seconds, he sank back down onto the couch. Resting his elbows on his knees, he stared at his folded hands.

When he finally spoke, he asked a question of his own, "Why do you want to know?"

I figured I might as well be blunt. "You're not happy with her. I mean, when you're on stage, you're basically telling the entire bar about your relationship issues. Anyone paying attention would know that some of the songs you sing are for a reason. Sometimes it's like you're screaming in a crowded room, wanting to be heard, but no one's paying attention."

He looked at me. "Except you."

I nodded.

"Is that the only reason you want to know why I haven't left her yet?"

I looked away and swallowed. I wasn't sure how to answer. Biting my lip, I peeked over at him.

"You don't have to answer that. You answered my question, so I'll answer yours." He took a deep breath as he sat back on the couch, so we were sitting shoulder to shoulder. "You're right. I'm not happy. I haven't been for months. I was trying to fix things, but nothing's working. At this point, I doubt it even can be fixed. She's not the girl I fell in love with. I hardly recognize her. But even if she was, if she went back to being that girl I fell for, I wouldn't fall for her again. I don't even want to."

He met my eyes. "But it's hard, you know? Hard to accept that the person you thought you'd spend your life with isn't going to be in it anymore. That's it's over. I've been trying to figure out how to end it. It's not merely a matter of telling her it's over. We live together. All my stuff's there. And finals are coming up. It wouldn't be fair to leave her right before that, would it? After she saved my freshman year from going to shit, GPA-wise, she doesn't deserve to be upset like that before finals. But...I don't know what I should do. Drawing it out doesn't feel right either..."

Turning, he faced me completely. There was something unfamiliar in his eyes. Hesitation maybe? Was he nervous? I couldn't be sure since I'd only ever seen him nervous once, on the Ferris wheel.

Nervous or not, his eyes didn't leave mine. "I know I need to leave her. For both of our sakes, it needs to end." He swallowed. "And...there is another reason."

In a hushed tone, I asked, "What is it?"

He didn't respond, just searched my eyes.

After several seconds, I held up my hand and shook my head. "Sorry. You don't have to tell me."

Jax took my hand and lowered it, but didn't let go. "No, I do. You should know." He looked down at our hands and took another deep breath, exhaling shakily. *Definitely nervous.* Meeting my eyes again, he confessed, "I'm in love with someone else."

My eyes started to burn. My chest fluttered as I struggled to breathe. With my stomach in my throat, I couldn't say anything.

"I won't lie. I fought against it. I denied it. I feel terrible about it, and that only confuses me. If it's a good thing, why does it feel so bad? But then again, if I still wanted to be with Brooke, how could I fall for someone else in the first place? I couldn't, could I?"

In a strained whisper, I found my voice, "Does the other person know how you feel?"

For the first time since I'd started this conversation, a hint of a smile tugged at the corner of his mouth. At some point—I wasn't sure when—his thumb had started gently rubbing back and forth over the top of my hand, which was still in his. "About her? She might. I've gotten pretty bad at hiding it."

My entire body tingled with nerves. "Do you think she has feelings for you too?"

Holding my gaze, he whispered, "I think so."

"Are you going to ask her?"

"I've thought about it." His hand released mine and came up to cup my cheek. "Should I ask her, Tessa?"

Inside, I was in complete chaos. Different emotions fought to take control. Hope, fear, relief, guilt, happiness, anxiety, love, lust... My heart was pounding so hard that Jax might've been able to hear it. Slowly, I nodded.

"Breathe, beautiful." *God...* He sounded so sexy when he whispered.

I breathed in, letting his scent intoxicate me. As I exhaled, my head leaned into his hand.

Jax came closer, close enough that I could feel the breeze of his breath on my skin as he softly asked, "Did you ever notice that I have a hard time breathing around you too? You know why? Because you take my breath away every time I see you." Jax tucked a hair behind my ear with his free hand then placed it on my other cheek, so he was cupping my face as he held my gaze. "Am I the center of your thoughts, like you are mine? Do I appear in your dreams, like you appear in mine? Does your heart skip a beat when you hear my name or race when we're together? Does your pulse quicken when we're close? Does the electricity between us heat your blood and set your body on fire? Do your hands twitch, wanting to touch me, like mine do, wanting to touch you? Hugging isn't enough. When you're in my arms, I never want to let you go. Your scent intoxicates me and makes my knees weak, sending my mind to places it shouldn't be.

"No matter how hard I fought against it, I couldn't. The pull to you is too strong. I tried, but I can't stay away from you. When I look into your eyes, I swear I see my own feelings reflecting back at me. So tell me, Tessa, do I give you butterflies?"

My chest rose and fell rapidly. The answer left my lips in a whoosh of air. "Yes."

Like it had a couple of times before, the air around us stilled, like time had stopped. The world faded away and I forgot everything except for this man who I was so in love with. This man who was in love with me too.

Lifting my chin, I gave him the signal he was waiting for. His hands slid around me, pulling my lips to his. My lips parted, and Jax's tongue found mine, stroking it seductively in a slow but passionate kiss.

Wrapping my arms around his neck, I pulled him closer. His body pressed me up against the back of the couch, and he swallowed my whimper. The movements of his mouth became hungrier as he lowered me down onto my back. The weight of his body felt so good that I gasped, releasing his lips. His mouth trailed kisses across my cheek, along my jawline and down my neck.

Grabbing at the hem of his shirt, I pulled up, desire taking complete control of my actions. Jax sat up and finished pulling his shirt over his head. I ran my hands along his bare skin, from his belly button to his pecks, then around his back, pulling him back down on top of me. His lips went back to my neck. I sighed as his tongue swirled around a sensitive spot I never knew I had above my clavicle, then gasped as he playfully nipped at it.

A low chuckle vibrated against my skin. Threading my fingers through his silky hair, I held him there, silently demanding he continue. His chuckle made me moan. He stopped laughing and pressed himself into me with a groan. Was this a dream, or did Jax really want me as much as I wanted him?

Slipping a hand under my shirt, he cupped one of my breasts

through the thin material of my bra. His thumb rubbed over the peak until it was hard. Pulling back, he grabbed the hem of my shirt, and I sat up, assisting him in ripping it off before flopping back down. Hovering over me, Jax pushed my bra up and lowered his mouth to one bare nipple while his hand played with the other. Moaning, I reveled in the sensations coursing through my body from the delicious torture he was inflicting on me. He sucked harder, and my back arched as I cried out.

Grabbing his face, I brought his lips back to mine, kissing him lovingly. I brushed my hands down his chiseled abs, and Jax lifted himself, giving me access to the front of his jeans. Hurriedly, I unfastened the button and zipper before sliding my hand inside the waistband of his underwear, finding his shaft. As I slowly stroked up and down his hard length, he groaned into my mouth as we kissed.

Pulling away, we stared into each other's eyes as we tried catching our breath. Brushing my thumb over the tip of his erection, I felt a few drops of his hot seed. He let out a small sound of pleasure before capturing my mouth again. He kissed me gently and sensually, savoring the taste, the moment. When my hand tightened around his girth, he groaned again. Knowing I was having this effect on him sent me on a dizzying high.

Jax's hand went to the front of my jeans, where he unbuttoned and unzipped them one-handed. His fingers had slipped into my panties when my bedroom door slammed open.

chapter
fifty-six

TESSA

JAX AND I JUMPED, and he ended up on the floor. Relief washed over me when I saw Tina standing in the doorframe. She was furious, but she wasn't Brooke or Eli. *Oh God! Brooke and Eli! What did we just do?*

I covered myself. Luckily, although shirtless, Jax was relatively decent since his pants were still on.

"Is this really what you guys want to do?" Tina asked shakily, like she was trying not to cry.

Jax sighed heavily. He was looking down, shoulders slumped.

Gasping and feeling flushed, I asked, "Tina, can you give us a couple of minutes?"

"If I hear any more sounds, I'm coming back in here," she said before turning and closing the door behind her.

My face heated. *She'd heard us?* How loud had we gotten for her to hear us through a closed door, across the house, and with the TV on? We hadn't even done that much!

After fixing my bra, I looked around for my shirt. Barely looking in my direction, Jax handed it to me. Then he grabbed his own from the floor and pulled it over his head. After he stood and fixed his pants, he said, "I'm sorry, Tess. That shouldn't have happened."

Grabbing his shoes and bag on the way, he walked out the door but didn't close it.

Tina scolded him from the living room, "I told you not to hurt her! How is this not going to hurt her?"

What? When had Tina and Jax discussed anything related to this?

If Jax responded, I didn't hear.

Tina spoke again, "They don't deserve this. Neither one of them. If you're gonna stay with Brooke, leave Tess alone! If you want to be with Tess, break up with Brooke. Make up your fucking mind! You're hurting both of them!"

I heard his voice but couldn't make out what he'd said. A few seconds later, the front door opened then closed.

Tina came back into my room, concern written all over her face. Seeing her expression was the final straw. I burst into tears. He regretted it. What would have happened if we'd actually had sex? Would he have thrown me aside afterward? That thought killed me inside. How was I going to face him tomorrow in class?

Joining me on the couch, Tina put her arm around my shoulders. Through sobs, I told her, "I love him! I love him so much! Why won't he leave her? She makes him miserable! He told me he's in love with me! So why..." Through watery eyes, I saw Tina's expression and could no longer speak. She looked pained, and her eyes glistened. But she had nothing to say that could comfort me.

chapter
fifty-seven

JAXON

WHAT THE FUCK was wrong with me? How could I have done that? Why would I have done that? Well, I knew why. I was in love with Tessa and wanted her. I'd wanted her from the second I saw her. And Brooke... If I didn't feel like I owed her, I would've left a long time ago. Tess was right, even if I felt indebted to Brooke, we shouldn't have to live in misery.

Although I'd already decided to end my relationship, what had happened was wrong, and for the billionth time in the last several months, I felt like the biggest asshole. Why the fuck couldn't I have waited until I left Brooke?

Brooke... I couldn't go home. Maybe it made me a coward, but I wasn't ready to face her, especially when I probably smelled like Tess's sweet scent.

Crossing the lawn to Chuck's house, I hoped he didn't have company. I'd feel bad if I interrupted him with a girl.

When he answered, he immediately teased, "What? You knock now?"

His normally cheerful expression dropped when he saw my face. Stepping aside, he let me enter.

"I wasn't sure if you were alone and didn't want to barge in," I explained.

Chuck followed me into the living room. I sat heavily on his couch. He waited, hands on his hips, for me to speak.

"I fucked up." My voice cracked as the wet warmth of a tear slid down my face.

I looked away and wiped my eyes. He hadn't seen me cry since my family's funeral, although it had been close the other day.

Slowly, he put the pieces together. "It's Wednesday... You were with Tess, right?"

I nodded.

"But don't you guys go to the library?"

"Normally, but it was closed today," I paused to take a breath. "So we went to her house."

Chuck was silent for too long, so I looked up at him. He was gaping at me. Seeing his expression, I ducked my head.

"You hooked up with Tess," he concluded.

I shook my head. "We didn't get that far. Tina interrupted us."

"But you would have? Fucked her, I mean? If Tina hadn't interrupted you?"

I stared at the floor.

Chuck whistled. "I need a beer for this." He strode toward the kitchen and called over his shoulder, "You want one?"

"Probably not a good idea," I said, not caring if he actually heard. I had no energy to speak louder.

"Right. I'll be right there."

He came back holding a beer and a bottle of water. After handing me the water, he sat in the armchair. I thanked him and drank about half the water before I started talking.

I told him everything. About how bad things had gotten with Brooke. How I'd slowly started falling for Tess but still tried to make it work with Brooke. How I'd already made up my mind to leave Brooke but was trying to figure out how to go about it. And, as if I hadn't felt bad about all the thoughts I'd had about Tess before, now I had actually cheated on Brooke. Even though I was already gone mentally, I was still in a relationship, and so was Tess.

Chuck sat, drank his beer, and listened, not interrupting once. When I was all talked out, he admitted, "I knew you liked her. And I had a feeling she liked you too, which is why I never asked her out. I don't think there's any excuse for some of the stuff Brooke has said and done, but I kind of understand why she's been so bratty lately." That was an understatement, surprising for him when talking about Brooke. "I'm sure Brooke knows you better than I do, and if I saw what was happening, so did she. I didn't say anything because, as far as I could tell, nothing was actually happening between you and Tess, and I figured you and Brooke would split if you wanted to be with Tess. But I never expected you and her to hook up before that."

"Me neither," I mumbled.

"It sucks, man. Now, regardless of what happens with you and Tess, you'll have this black mark on your relationship. This is how it started."

What he said hurt, but he wasn't wrong. This was a terrible way to start a relationship, and I knew I wanted a relationship with Tess. This wasn't going to be a fling that would fizzle out. But jumping from one relationship to another sounded like a bad idea, at least after being with someone for so long. I needed to think about how to handle all this. Other than knowing I was going to leave Brooke and that I wanted to be with Tess, the details were murky.

Should I leave Brooke now or wait until the end of the semester like I had decided on over the weekend. Would Tess even want to be with me after what happened? She'd always see me as a cheater from now on, which I deserved. Sure, she'd technically cheated on Eli, but whatever they had going was in no way near the same level as Brooke and I. And something told me that if I hadn't been with Brooke, Tess would never have dated Eli to begin with.

Pulling out my phone, I checked the time. *Shit!* It was nearly two in the morning.

Seeing my expression, Chuck looked at his watch. "Text Brooke that you and I were hanging out, lost track of time and that you're gonna crash here, which is all true," he emphasized. "I'll be right back."

While I texted Brooke, Chuck left the room. He returned a couple of minutes later and threw some clothes, a blanket, and a towel at me.

Pointing down the hall, he suggested, "Go take a shower and put your clothes in the wash. You probably do smell like Tess, and chicks have a sixth sense about that shit, so you might be fucked anyway, but whatever. The clothes will be small on you, but those are the best I could find. Don't want you sleeping on my couch naked."

After I thanked him, he went to bed.

I STOOD under the shower spray until I'd used up all the hot water. As the water went from hot to warm to cold, I decided I probably could use a cold shower since I couldn't get the image of what Tess looked like underneath me out of my head. The taste of her was still on my tongue. Her moans rang in my ears, noises of pleasure I'd given her.

Taking in a deep inhale through my nose, her scent filled my nostrils from my clothes that were discarded on the bathroom floor. Even with the cold water beating against my skin, my body was on fire, reacting to the memory of her beneath me, my hand on her breast. Her real breasts that fit perfectly in my hands. Like they were made for my hands and my hands alone.

Holding my dick, I swiped my thumb across the tip, like Tess had when she was stroking me.

Fuck it. I was already a cheating asshole who'd pictured another woman while fucking my girlfriend. What would rubbing one out while Tess still filled my senses matter?

"JAXON! WHAT THE FUCK!" I jumped awake at the sound of Brooke yelling at me.

Rubbing my eyes, I asked, "What are you doing here?"

With wide eyes like I was an idiot, she said, "Looking for you, obviously."

Sitting up, I asked, "Shouldn't you be in class?"

"Look who's talking! You're the one missing class right now! I still have time. I fell asleep on the couch waiting for you. When I woke up, you weren't there!" She sounded worried, and the guilt hit me like a brick thrown at my stomach.

Not able to look at her, I used putting on my shoes as an excuse to avert my eyes. "I texted you."

"Yeah, at two in the fucking morning!" She sounded close to hysterical.

"I told you, we lost track of time."

"I tried calling you this morning, and it went to voicemail!"

Picking up my phone from the floor next to the couch, I confirmed it was off. "The battery must've died."

"Well? Aren't you going to apologize to me?"

Forcing myself to look at her, I said, "I'm sorry I worried you." And I meant it.

She put her hands on her hips. "That's it?"

I froze. Did she know? Tess wouldn't have told her. Chuck wouldn't have either. Did Tina say something? But I didn't think Tina would throw Tess under the bus like that.

When I didn't do or say anything, Brooke asked impatiently, "Aren't you going to hug and kiss me?"

Oh... I stood and hugged her. Brooke stopped and sniffed. *Fuck!* She took a step back and glowered at me. Through clenched teeth, she demanded, "Why do you smell like another girl?"

The clothes Chuck had lent me were way too small, so I had put my clothes back on, planning to wait until Brooke would be in class before going home and doing laundry. But I had thought of an excuse before I went to sleep just in case. "I told you. The library was closed, so we went to Tess's. There are two girls living there. I probably smell like their house." It wasn't a lie, but it wasn't exactly the accurate answer either. *When did I become a lying bag of shit?*

She eyed me suspiciously. "Why are your eyes all red?" She pointed her finger into my chest. "Were you drinking?" she practically shouted at me. "Or doing something else?"

"No. They're probably red because I didn't get enough sleep."

"Did you shower? It looks like you slept on wet hair."

Jesus Christ! What's with the third degree? Sure, I probably deserved it, but she didn't know that. I was tired, and my mind was slow to think up a reason.

Thankfully, Chuck saved me. "It's called bedhead, Brooke. He was sleeping on the couch, and his head was probably lodged into the corner of it." Self consciously, I patted my hair while Chuck demanded, "How'd you get in my house anyway? Jax let you in?"

Haughtily, Brooke said, "Next time, lock your front door, moron."

"Brooke!" I warned.

"Oh, don't even!" she snapped back.

I rubbed my forehead and huffed. Not again! Every. Single. Fucking. Day! I felt terrible about last night, but this was some slow form of torture. I was at my wit's end with her.

Brooke turned back to me and crossed her arms. "What? Why are you acting so frustrated?"

Through my teeth, I explained, "Because I am frustrated."

"Ha! What do you have to be frustrated about?"

It was like she was daring me to fight or something. But I was done fighting. "You know what? Never mind. Are you coming home with me or are you going to class?"

"Class," she said, sounding bored.

"Fine, I'll see you later then." I grabbed my stuff from the floor and threw another thanks over to Chuck as I left.

I didn't see her again until late that night. We didn't speak until Friday evening when I asked her if she was going to Smythie's with me or not. Unfortunately, she was.

chapter
fifty-eight

TESSA

"I DON'T KNOW. This seems like a bad idea." Tina was leaning against my bedroom door frame with her arms crossed, watching as I got dressed for Smythie's.

"It might be," I conceded, "but I need to know once and for all. How he acts tonight should tell me something, right?"

Not only had Jax not been in class Thursday morning, but he hadn't responded to my text requesting to discuss what had happened. The entire situation was driving me insane. My chest hurt from the stress of it. I couldn't even go for a run because I felt like I couldn't breathe. So I resolved to go to Smythie's and see if I could get any sign about what Jax was going to do. If he and Brooke were all over each other, I was definitely done.

AS SOON AS JAMAR ARRIVED, Tina pulled him to the dance floor, and they disappeared into the mass of moving bodies. I stayed by the bar, not having any interest in being a third wheel. I hadn't seen Jax yet, but I had seen Brooke. She didn't look particularly happy or sad, so I gained no insight from observing her.

After a couple of minutes, Jax appeared next to me at the bar. He leaned over the bar to get Cory's attention then faced me while he waited until she was done with her current customers. He seemed a little off, but I couldn't put my finger on why. With a small but sexy-as-sin smirk, Jax leaned in and said over the music, "Looking beautiful, as always."

Taking a step back, I glared at him. Taking a quick look around, I confirmed no one was watching us, at least not closely enough to see details. I moved the hair I'd strategically placed around my neck, covering the hickey I found yesterday morning, and pointed.

Jax pointed to himself and mouthed, "That was me?"

My face conveyed what I was thinking. *Duh!*

He tried but failed to hide his pleased smile. "Ready for tonight?"

Not sure I liked the sound of that, I asked, "What do you mean?"

He didn't answer as Cory had arrived. To say Jax's order was surprising would be greatly understated. "A shot of whiskey, some kind of sweet shot, and a cosmo on the rocks with a splash of pineapple."

My eyes widened. Jax was drunk! I'd never seen him drink before, not even a beer, let alone smashed.

Mockingly, Cory replied, "Sure thing, boss."

Jax shot her a look.

"What? You're the one ordering me around. You didn't even say please."

Jax rolled his eyes at her. "Please."

Cory quickly readied his order and passed the two shots and my drink of choice over to Jax along with his usual two bottles of water. Jax slid the cocktail over next to my mostly full cup. He held out the shot glass full of pink liquid, and I took the small glass automatically, trying to figure out what the heck was going on. He clinked our shots together, said, "Bottoms up," winked, then threw his whiskey back.

I looked around, sure somebody was watching and could tell what had happened the other night by seeing this strange interaction. For a split second, my eyes locked with a guy a bit far off, but he quickly looked away. He'd been watching for sure, but other than seeing him around the bar and campus, I had no clue who he was. Besides him, I didn't notice anyone else who may have seen.

Jax placed his empty glass on the bar and pointed to the untouched shot in my hand. "You're gonna want that tonight." Moving his finger between my two cocktails on the bar counter, he added, "And those."

Leaning too close to my ear, his voice dropped an octave. "Tonight's gonna be fun. Enjoy the show. I'll be thinking of you the whole time."

Smelling the smokey scent of whiskey on his breath, I wondered how much he'd had to drink. As he swaggered away, a pit formed in my stomach. Looking around again, my eyes locked with Brooke's. If looks could kill, I'd be dead.

She stalked over and spat, "If you think you've won, you're wrong. This isn't over yet. And even if you do manage to steal him from me, remember you lose them how you get them." She stomped away to the place she always watched the band from. Her friend, the one she was always with, was also trying to stab me to death with her irises.

Had Jax told her? Or was it women's intuition? Maybe they had broken up? But if that was the case, why would she even be here? Going to your ex's job, even if it was a bar, was a little...

Ugh... Maybe I should leave? But if I left, I'd miss whatever Jax was up to. Although I had a bad feeling, it was too tempting to miss.

WHEN IT CAME to Jax and temptation, I should've learned I needed to pass. The song choices of the night had one common theme: sex. Hooking up, one-night stands, constant sex, sex with strangers, rough sex, sex fit for a porno, affairs and dirty secrets. I nicknamed it *The Hookup Setlist*, but it was both sets.

Infuriated, I glared up at the singer, who was giving the most provocative performance I'd ever seen out of him. The energy Jax was giving off was horny as fuck, yet he didn't look over at Brooke once, yet he'd thrown me more than a few salacious glances, not seeming to care that I was pissed, or maybe he was too drunk to notice. What was wrong with him? Was he trying to announce what happened to the entire freaking bar? Surely others must've noticed.

All night, one thought took precedence over all others: *Thank God Eli isn't here tonight.* I peered over in Brooke's direction. She was engrossed in her phone.

I should have left early but didn't. By the time the last song of the night started, the air in the bar buzzed with sexual tension. Everyone felt it. Couples, or maybe random hookups, littered the bar, being extra passionate, and some downright inappropriate, with their dancing, grinding, and public displays of affection. The last song was something else altogether. The beat was heavy, the tone sexy. To absolutely no one's surprise, it was about sex. Fucking, to be more precise. Wild, hard, and animalistic.

Halfway through the song, the vocals ended, and the rest of the song was just instrumental. That was when Jax did something else I'd never seen him do, nor had I ever heard of him doing. Jumping down from the stage, he strode up to an overly enthusiastic girl and started dancing with her, if that was what one would call the bumping and grinding. Then he moved onto the next girl. Then the next...

He made his way around the floor, dancing with anyone willing, even sandwiching himself between two girls at one point. My brain told my feet to move, but they remained planted. Jax was slowly headed my way. Throwing another glance at Brooke, I was sure her face would match her hair color, but she looked bored with Jax's antics, yawning while her boyfriend gyrated with a bunch of other women.

I made nervous eye contact with Tina. She glanced at Jamar, who gave a slight nod. Did Jamar know what was going on? Tina stepped up, not exactly blocking me, but moving into Jax's path. He grabbed her hips, and while most women he had danced with from behind, Tina and Jax were face-to-face, well, accounting for their height.

I was no lip reader, but I could have sworn Tina said something to him like, "You're ridiculous! Are you crazy?"

Jax smirked back and said, "Probably."

Then he spun her away into Jamar's arms and grabbed me, also facing him. As soon as he pulled me into him, I regretted wearing a cropped top. His fingers seared my bare back as he pressed me close to him. *Had he danced this close with the others?* Guilty, I hoped he hadn't.

Even though this little performance of his was incredibly stupid, I couldn't deny that part of me loved it. I loved him touching me and grinding into me. As I let him lead, I hoped the electricity between us wasn't felt by anyone else.

We moved together in perfect sync, like our bodies were made for each others. It was a good thing he held me so tightly because my knees were in danger of buckling. *Is it me, or is he dancing with me longer than the others?* Or had time slowed down for us again? I had no idea. On the one hand, I wanted him to keep holding onto me, but on the other, it was getting dangerous, especially since I felt the beginnings of an erection through his jeans. I seriously hoped he'd keep that part of him away from the others, or people would think he was a pervert.

As if reading my mind, he let go to move on to more eager partners. But as he stepped away, his fingers lingered on my back and dragged along my side, leaving scorch marks on my already heated skin.

As I watched him, Tina grabbed my hand and intertwined our fingers. I looked at her questioningly. Leaning into my ear, she explained, "You're shaking."

"Oh..." I breathed. "I think I need water." *Very, very cold water.* I needed to cool down and sober up. Jax had been right. I had needed those two drinks and shot. In fact, right before the second set started, I grabbed another drink. If I hadn't had them, I was sure I would've been stiff as a board while Jax moved against me, because deep down I knew I never would've turned him down regardless of what state I was in.

Like after the first set, Jax had disappeared when the song ended. I knew he wasn't with Brooke, who was hanging out on the dance floor with her friends. Now that the band was done, I needed to get out of there. If Jax appeared, I wasn't convinced there wouldn't be a scene. And although I definitely had a few things to say to him, I needed to be sober for it, as did he. Not to mention we shouldn't have a bar full of nosy, gossip hungry college students around either, or his girlfriend.

As I finished up my bottle of water, an unfamiliar voice asked me, "Hey, wanna dance?"

Barely glancing at the guy, I said, "Sorry, I have a boyfriend." Didn't need to mention the part about my plan to break up with him in a few days.

"Oh, shame," the guy said before walking away. There was something about the way he said it that was familiar, like I'd heard it before. But I couldn't be sure since my brain was too full of alcohol and Jax.

Curiosity got the better of me, and I turned to see who'd asked me, but my eyes immediately locked with the guy who'd been watching Jax and I earlier. Why was he looking at me again? Did he know something?

Averting my eyes, I placed my empty bottle on the bar, turned to Tina and said I was ready to leave. Thankfully, so was she and Jamar, so they gave me a ride home before heading to his place.

After arriving home, I locked the front door and leaned against it. *You have some serious explaining to do, Jaxon Smith!*

chapter
fifty-nine

JAXON

MY PHONE PINGING startled me awake. Looking out the living room window, I could tell it was relatively early, for me on a Saturday anyway. My head throbbed, and there was an annoying-ass ringing in my ears. Unsurprisingly, I had one hell of a hangover. Blurry-eyed, I checked my phone. It was barely nine. Who the fuck would be texting me this early on a Saturday? Everyone I knew was aware I slept late on Saturdays because of the bar.

Reading who the text was from was like having a bucket of ice water thrown on me. Sitting up too quickly, I winced. Sleeping on the couch for the last couple of nights had not been comfortable. Opening my conversation with Tess, I read her text.

TESS

We need to talk!

She seemed upset.

JAX

Sure, something wrong?

TESS

ARE YOU SERIOUS RIGHT NOW?

Shit... She was more than upset.

JAX

OK, I'll be over in an hour.

TESS

You are NOT coming here! You know that park two miles from campus? Can't remember the name of it, but it has bike and jogging trails.

JAX

I know it.

TESS

Meet me there in an hour. Near the fountain.

JAX

Wouldn't it be easier if I came to you? How are you going to get to the park?

TESS

Yes, I'm sure! And how else? Running obviously. I'm a runner, remember? See you in an hour.

Not wanting to wake Brooke, I dragged myself into the spare bathroom's shower. Understandably, she was pissed at me, but I didn't give a shit anymore.

SOMEHOW, I managed to get to the park with time to spare. Maybe it was because I was eager to see Tess even if I was hungover.

Sitting on a hard, damp bench, I waited, enjoying the cool air on my clammy skin. I was staring at the ground when a pair of women's running sneakers appeared in front of me. Peering up into the fiery eyes of the most beautiful girl I'd ever met, I almost regretted coming.

Although fuming, she still looked hot as fuck in her cropped leggings, sports bra, belly button ring I ached to play with, and sweat along her hairline. Her hair was up, and the hickey I'd given her was on full display. My dick twitched.

Hoarsely, I greeted her, "Morning. Interesting location for a chat. Wouldn't your place have been better?"

Putting her hands on her hips, she snapped, "What kind of meeting do you think this is, Jaxon?"

"Uh…"

"First you skip class, then you ignore my text, then you sing a bunch of songs about sex, and to top it off you basically dry humped me in front of the entire fucking bar! What the hell?"

Realizing she wasn't going to sit, I stood. "You could have said no—"

"And you danced with all those other girls in front of your girl-friend! I don't even like Brooke, but I still felt bad for her!"

"I—"

"Do you expect me to be your side chick? Is that what you want?"

My eyes widened, "What! N—"

"I will be nobody's side chick! I already feel shitty about what happened."

"Me too. And I don't want—"

"I'm not interested in being a home-wrecker, even though I already feel like one!" Tears sprung from her eyes and fell in rapid succession down her face. I wanted to hug her and wipe them away, but I didn't dare touch her.

My groggy brain and pounding head were useless. She was talking so fast that my mind had trouble keeping up. "You're not a home-wrecker."

"Why did you do it? Why did you sing all those songs and make me feel like a slut?"

"What?" *Oh fuck!* "No! That's not—"

"Everyone in that bar knew what kind of mood you were in last night! Tell me, Jax, did you go home and fuck Brooke into oblivion again?"

It was like she'd slapped me. She knew I'd had sex with Brooke even when I had feelings for her. And that must've hurt like hell. "No." My response came out as a whisper. Looking away, I tried to come up with something that might make her feel better. I mumbled, "I've been sleeping on the couch."

She started crying a little harder. "I am so pissed right now."

I swallowed against the tightness in my throat. "I know. I'm sorry. I never—"

"What? You never meant for it to happen? Do you think I did?" Her tears were decreasing as her anger increased.

I was doing a shitty job trying to explain myself and reassure her, but I couldn't think straight. "No. I've never been in this situation before."

"And you think I have?" Her face was turning red.

"No! I know you're not... I've never cheated before, and..." I may as well have been mumbling incoherently.

For a few seconds, there was nothing but the sounds of nature.

Calmer, she said, "Look, regardless of what happened the other day, it's not going to happen again if you're with Brooke. In fact, I'm going to forget it happened. I'm not going to ask you to break up with her. That's completely up to you. But until you make up your mind, leave me out of it.

"I am going to break up with Eli. I had planned on doing that before Wednesday even happened, but he has a big exam in a few days, so I didn't want to mess with his emotions before that. That's the only reason I haven't broken up with him yet.

"And just so you know, I'm not going to sit around and wait for you. That's not fair to me. So while you're with Brooke, there will be no chance of an us," she said as she indicated the two of us with her finger. "Bye."

She turned away but stopped when I asked, "Would there be?"

Looking over her shoulder, she asked, "Would there be what?"

"Would there be an us if I left Brooke?"

She looked mad again, but it appeared to be a cover to hide her sadness. "As I said, it's your decision what you do about your relationship. It has nothing to do with me. Whether you stay with her or not should not depend on my answer. If you want to be with her and try to fix your issues, fine, whatever. If not, you should leave. I should not be part of that decision." Her voice had started cracking, and she looked away. "I don't have anything else to say."

She jogged away from me, but I could tell she was wiping away tears as she ran.

I sat back down on the bench, feeling weak, both physically and mentally. *I'm totally fucking this up!*

chapter
sixty

TESSA

I HAD to get out of there before I completely broke down. If I did, he would have tried to comfort me. And I wouldn't have been able to resist him. So I ran away.

Going there, I wasn't sure what to expect from him, but it wasn't that. He was so quiet and wasn't even explaining himself. He still seemed torn. Why was he so torn when it came to her? I so badly wanted to tell him yes, there would be an us if he left Brooke. I wanted to be with him. But if we were to be together, he had to figure out how to deal with her first.

LIKE A COWARD, I stayed outside the classroom Tuesday morning until I saw our professor rushing down the hall. When I took my seat, I faced front and stayed silent. Jax gave me a quick, "Morning."

I curtly responded, "Hi."

It was the second-to-last class of the semester. Next week would be the final exam, so we were going over test review material. As we went through it, I found myself in a vicious cycle. I was trying too hard to pay attention because I didn't want to have to go to the library tomorrow, but the more I worried about having to go and study with Jax, the less I actually paid attention, which made me worry even more. And that was how the entire class went. At the end of it, I was so frustrated with myself that I threw my stuff haphazardly into my bag and nearly ran out of the door.

I was so far gone that it was too late to turn back when I heard Jax call, "Tessa?"

PACING THE LIVING ROOM, I waited for Eli to arrive. His important exam had been earlier, and I needed to put an end to this inner torture, so I'd asked him to come over. When he arrived, I brought him into the living room and sat on the couch.

He sat next to me and observed, "I can tell something's wrong. What is it?"

I looked away as tears blurred my vision. *Damn, this is harder than I thought it would be.* Forcing myself, I looked back at him and said, "I'm sorry, Eli, but this isn't going to work out."

He looked sad, although not surprised. "Did I do anything?"

Choking on my tears, I whispered, "No." To myself, I added, *That's the problem. You didn't give me butterflies or make my heart race.* When he didn't say anything else and continued to look at me, I nervously flipped my hair. Something caught Eli's attention, and he reached over to move my hair out of the way. I froze. *The hickey!* A hickey he knew he hadn't given me was on full display.

He dropped his hand, looked away, and nodded. "I get it now."

Weeping, I apologized. "I'm so sorry. I didn't mean for it to happen. I feel terrible."

"I bet you do. Especially because you probably realize he's not going to leave Brooke, right?" There was a tinge of anger in his voice I'd never heard before.

Although tears still fell from my eyes, I stopped crying. "How did... How did you know it was..." I couldn't finish the question. One, because my voice cracked, and two because it was hard to admit to his face that it was Jax I cheated on him with.

Annoyed, Eli explained, "I'm not naïve. I've seen the way you two look at each other. But that's been going on for months, yet he's still with Brooke. You think he's going to leave her if he hasn't already?"

Whether I had a right to or not, I felt defensive. "It only happened once, and I made it clear it won't happen again if he's with her."

"So you slept with him?" Eli asked, hurt in his eyes.

The color drained from my face before returning fiery hot. That was none of his freaking business! Or was it? My anger dissipated.

I looked away. "No, we kissed." *Sort of.* I quickly added, "Once."

He looked doubtful. "You get a hickey from one kiss?"

I was trying to be understanding since I was the one in the wrong, and he had every right to be upset, but he was pissing me off. "I didn't say how long we kissed for," I said through my teeth.

Eli sighed and stared at the floor as we sat in a long, uncomfortable silence. Wasn't this the part where he stormed out?

After what felt like an eternity, he said, "Thanks for being honest with me—well, honest now." I flinched. "Good luck...I guess."

Jumping to my feet, I said, "I really am very sorry. You have always been good to me, and you didn't deserve that."

"No, you're right. I didn't. And neither did Brooke."

I nodded, though what Brooke deserved was open to debate after hitting Jax, doing drugs around him, and lying about what I'd said.

He took a step to leave but then turned and asked me one last question. "If I forgave you and could move past this, would you consider staying with me?"

Tears blurred my vision again. He really was too good. Sadly, I shook my head. "Sorry, I can't."

He nodded again, not surprised. "Bye, Tess. I really do wish you the best."

"Thank you. You too."

When the front door closed, I fell back on the couch, weeping. Perhaps I did have some kind of feelings for Eli after all. Otherwise, why would it hurt so much?

WEDNESDAY EVENING, I stared at the statistics final review packet, trying to figure out if I really couldn't do it or if I was looking for an excuse to go to the library. Deep down, I was pretty sure it was the latter while convincing myself it was the former.

Decided, I grabbed the packet, a pencil, and my phone, not even bothering with my bag or purse, and I headed out the door.

JAX WAS SITTING at our table, staring off into space. He hadn't even bothered to take his books or school work out. Completely lost in thought, he didn't notice when I approached and jumped when I said, "Hi, Jax."

Clearly not expecting to see me, he said, "Hey!"

I flung the packet on the table. "I need help. I didn't come this far and work my ass off just to fail the final."

He smirked. "You're not going to fail. You know this better than you give yourself credit for."

"Where's your packet?"

"I finished it already."

"Of course you did," I said as I sat down. "Okay, brainiac, let me see what I can do. You jump in if I'm doing something wrong."

He chuckled. "Sure."

FORTY-FIVE MINUTES LATER, we were done. My gut was right. I'd been making an excuse to come and didn't actually need Jax's help. He'd been a great tutor.

He smiled at me. "I told you, you've got this."

Meeting his eyes, I murmured, "Only because of you. Thank you."

"You're welcome." He paused for a second before adding, "Offering to help you was one of the best decisions I've ever made."

For what felt like the millionth time in the last several days, tears blurred my vision. I wasn't normally so emotional, but it felt like I'd cried more in the last week than I had in all my twenty-one years combined. "Jax, we can't—"

"Please, let me explain."

Glaring, I reminded him, "You had your chance on Saturday."

He sighed. "I was hungover. My head was pounding, and I couldn't think straight. Do you think this is easy for me? I fucked up. I betrayed a person who is very special to me. The person who saved my life. I may not want to be with her anymore, but I know you and I shouldn't have..." He looked away, his eyes glistening. His Adam's apple bobbed as he swallowed. "I wasn't trying to say I wanted you as a side chick." Locking eyes with me, he said, "I was trying to tell you that I want to be with you and only you."

"Jax," I quietly chided him, "you have a girlfriend. We shouldn't be having this conversation!"

"And you have a boyfriend."

"No, I don't. I broke up with Eli. I was never that into him to begin with. I did try, but there was nothing there." Knowing I shouldn't say more, I did anyway. "He didn't give me butterflies."

Jax turned his entire body in his chair so he was facing me. He took my hand, but I snatched it back. He took it again and looked me directly in the eyes. "I am not that kind of guy, Tessa. I have never even thought about cheating before I met you, and I won't ever do it again. I feel like shit over it. I hurt you, and it's going to hurt Brooke."

My eyes widened. "You're going to tell her?"

"Yes. Did you tell Eli?"

Guiltily, I looked away. "I wasn't going to, but he saw the hickey."

"I owe it to her to be honest. And I am going to leave her, but—"

"But you haven't!" I snapped.

Looking down, he explained, "We've been pretty much avoiding each other. I'm not really pushing it yet, because, like how you waited for Eli to be done with that big test, I'm waiting for Brooke to be done with her finals. They're all this week, so..."

I took my hand away and sat on both of them, preventing him from taking one again. I looked straight ahead, needing this conversation to end. From what I knew about Jax, I didn't think he was a guy who made empty promises, but this had to stop. "Jax, as of this moment, you are still in a serious, long-term relationship. I'm done talking about anything not school-related."

He stood. "Sure. Come on, I'll give you a ride home."

My eyes widened. "No. Thanks, but—"

"I'm going to Chuck's anyway. I'm not that big of an asshole to let you walk home when I'm literally driving there."

I sighed. "Oh...okay. Thanks."

OTHER THAN SOME rock at a low volume, the ride was quiet. When Jax put his car in park, I jumped out before he turned off the engine. Halfway up the sidewalk leading to my house, Jax caught my arm.

When I looked at him, he asked dead serious, "We're friends, right?"

"Uh, yeah," I said, unsure.

He pulled me in close, wrapping his arms tightly around me. Burying his face in my hair, he whispered, "Friends hug sometimes."

Not like this they don't!

Tears burned my cheeks as I pulled him tighter to me knowing I should've done the opposite. Burying my face in his chest, I inhaled deeply.

"You're making this really hard for me." My voice was muffled, but since he let me go, he must've heard them.

"Goodnight, Tessa."

Giving him a sad, watery smile, I said, "Goodnight, Jaxon."

chapter
sixty-one

TESSA

SPRAWLED out on the couch in some nice, comfy sweats with my feet up, I settled in to play games on my phone all night.

When Tina entered the living room, I whistled at her. "Don't you look nice! Date night with Jamar?"

Tina smirked. "No. Date night with my bestie. Girls' night, no boys allowed!"

"Oh?" I couldn't remember us making plans. Taking in her short skirt, satin tank, and heels she could dance in, my face dropped. Sitting up, I waved my hands in front of me, "No! No, no, no! No way! I can't go to Smythie's! Are you crazy?"

"Oh, come on, Tess! You know it's the best place to go around here on Friday nights. Even if things are weird with you and Jax, I know you like seeing the band play. You don't have to talk to him. Probably better that you don't."

I looked around, exaggerating my confusion. "I'm sorry, what? Who are you? Aren't you the one who told me to stay away from him and not get involved in something that I ended up getting involved in?"

"Ignore him. We don't even have to watch the band play if you don't want to."

"I'll still hear him," I mumbled. Louder, I asked, "Isn't there anywhere else we can go?"

"Neither one of us has a car. Where would we go?"

Sarcastically, I showed her my phone screen and pointed. "You see, there are these convenient things call ride-share apps where we can get a ride—"

Tina rolled her eyes. "Whatever. I'm going to Smythie's. Either I'm going by myself or you're coming with. Hurry up and decide."

Like I can actually stay away from him? Huffing, I stood. "I really don't get you sometimes. First you want me to stay away, and now you want me to go watch him sing."

As I stalked toward the bathroom, Tina called out, "Girls' night! Ignore him!"

If I'd been able to do that, I wouldn't have been in this mess.

RESISTING the urge to look around the bar for the man who caused me to feel more emotions in the last four months than I had in the last four years, I leaned back against the bar, staring into my usual drink. Tina had stepped away for a minute to talk to a group of people she knew.

A warm body joined me in leaning against the bar. His body was so close that our arms touched. Without looking, I knew it wasn't Jax. The bleached blond spiky hair with blue tips in my peripheral vision gave him away.

Chuck leaned in so he didn't have to speak too loudly. "You okay?"

I looked at him. He knew?

Shocked and a bit angry, I glared at the crowded dance floor. I couldn't believe Jax had told him! Tina only knew because she'd caught us. He wouldn't have told anyone, would he?

"Don't worry," he assured me. "Jax only told me. He hasn't even told Ashton. I'm actually rooting for you two. But Jax has to figure his shit out. She doesn't deserve him. If you give him a little more time, he'll do what he should've done a long time ago. But you know how hard it is for him, right?" Chuck grimaced. "He thinks he owes her or some shit. But if it weren't for her, he wouldn't have become an addict in the first place."

I appreciated Chuck's bluntness. "That's what I told him," I said. Knowing I wasn't the only one who believed a big part of Jax's problem was connected to Brooke in some way made me feel better, like I wasn't completely biased. Perhaps the reason Chuck didn't like her was because she introduced him to drugs?

"Thanks." I looked away, discreetly wiping away a tear. Unfortunately, my head turned in Jax's direction. He was watching me, longing in his eyes.

A tear fell despite my efforts to stop it, and Jax made a move like he was going to come to me but stopped. *Was that frustration that crossed his face?* Feeling like I was about to burst into tears, I walked over to Tina, who was inconveniently close to Jax. Leaning into her ear, I said over the music, "I'm sorry. I can't be here. I'm gonna go."

Concerned, she took in my expression then nodded. I started toward the exit, but his hand grab mine. I stopped and tried weakly to pull away.

He pleaded into my ear, "Don't leave. Just listen." He meant listen to tonight's music.

I took a deep breath and looked up at him, willing my tears to stop. The pain in my chest was visible in his eyes. What hurt more was that I didn't know if he was hurting because of Brooke or hurting because we knew we loved each other but couldn't do anything about it in the current situation.

He leaned down. "Go up the front stairs. Tell the bouncer I said you can go up."

Desperate to get away from him and any eyes that might've been watching this intimate interaction between us—we were still holding hands after all—I did as he said. When I told the bouncer what Jax said, he looked past me. Looking over my shoulder, Jax nodded. Stepping aside, the bouncer opened the rope and allowed me to pass.

After I ascended the spiral staircase, I entered the loft-like area. It was dark but not impossible to see, and vacant. Besides being an empty bar area, there were some couches, tables, and lounges. Rumors had it that before bouncers stood guard at the bottom of the stairs, when there was only a rope blocking the way, people would sneak up to brag they got away with it. No one knew why the new owner blocked it off.

Leaning over the railing, I had a good view of the dance floor and stage. The bar was directly under the loft, so it was completely out of sight. I wondered if it was okay to stand by the railing and if the people below could see me. Scanning the crowd, I noticed Brooke staring at something. Following her gaze, I saw Jax speaking to Tina. Jax looked up at me, followed by Tina. They looked away, exchanged a few more words, then separated.

I looked back at Brooke, and our eyes connected. Although she was staring at me, it wasn't with the usual daggers. Filled with pain and heartache, her wet eyes reflected the club's moving lights. Really hating myself, maybe more than I hated her, I looked away.

Hearing the clack of heels on the metal stairs, I spun to find Tina entering the loft. The volume of the music up here was by no means quiet, but it was low enough that we didn't have to shout into each other's ears to be heard.

Tina rested folded arms on the railing. "Man, I've always wondered what was going on up here. Turns out, a whole lotta nothing," Laughing to herself, she shook her head. "I never got a chance to come up here in over three years, but you only started coming here a couple of months ago and already got yourself into the forbidden zone."

I snorted. "Forbidden. You can say that again."

Tina grimaced at her unintentional pun. "Jax said you might want some company. And he told me to remind you to 'listen,' whatever that means. Said we could even sit down and not actually watch." She glanced at me out of the corner of her eye. "I hope you understand all that because I don't."

I sighed. "Yeah, I get it."

JAX, whether meaning to or not, looked up at me so often while on stage that I was afraid other people were going to notice and try to figure out what had so much of his attention. But when I looked down at the crowd, no one was looking up.

About halfway through the first set, I understood what Jax wanted to tell me. The first song the band played was an apology. And most of the rest were songs about lost love, heartache, relationships ending, and regret.

Jax was sending a message. The fluttering in my chest returned as I realized this was his breakup setlist.

Knowing he really was going to leave Brooke, I felt guilt and elation at the same time. I was so happy I could cry and so miserable I might. I blamed myself for breaking them up but knew it had to happen, even if for Jax's sake alone. I knew I should've stayed away, or at least shut him down that night in my room, but I couldn't say I regretted it. I resolved to wait until we could be together guilt-free.

chapter
sixty-two

JAXON

BLINKING AWAKE, the first thing I noticed was how bright the living room was. The sun's position through the large window said it was already afternoon. A glance at a decorative wall clock confirmed it. Although I'd slept later than I normally did on Saturdays, I was still exhausted. In no way did it feel like I'd gotten nearly twelve hours of sleep. Maybe it was because it wasn't over yet and my brain was dreading what was to come. Brooke must've known it was coming.

I hadn't slept in her bed since I'd kissed Tess. It felt wrong. I hadn't touched her since the last time we had sex. Hell, Brooke and I had barely spoken in the last week and a half.

Sitting up, I stretched while listening. There were no sounds. Going through every room confirmed Brooke wasn't home. Checking my phone, I opened a text from her early in the morning. She was going home to see her parents and would be back tonight. Knowing what a light sleeper I was, she must've made quite the effort not to wake me up when she left. She was avoiding me, avoiding the inevitable. Hopefully she didn't come back too late, because I couldn't drag this out any longer. It had already been too long while I tried, and failed, to do what I thought was best, fucking up in the process.

Taking advantage of her absence, I packed up most of my clothes and essentials, putting them in my car. I'd come back during winter break for the rest of my stuff if she'd let me. Then I waited and waited. I tried to eat but didn't have an appetite. As time dragged, pressure built in my chest, becoming more painful with each minute that passed by. Why did it hurt so severely when I was choosing to leave and knew it was the right decision? Who would've thought the old saying about falling in love and heartbreak being the same was true? Can't eat, can't sleep, can't breathe…

Staring at the ceiling, I watched the shadows move as the room got darker. Was she even going to come back tonight? My eyes stung at the thought of having to drag this out another day. I'd just resolved to drive to her parents' house tomorrow if I had to, the front door lock clicked.

Picking my phone, I noted it was almost ten. Sitting up, I waited for Brooke to come into the living room.

Seeing me, she stopped. "Hey. How was your day?"

Exhausted, I was in no mood to ease into it. "Long and shitty."

"Oh? Sorry to hear that. Why?"

I rubbed my face then sighed. Looking back at her, my eyes burned. With a strained voice, I told her, "We need to talk."

She looked away, a tear already sliding down her face. "You're leaving me?"

"Yes."

"Why?" Her voice was a choked cry.

She could never make things easy, could she? "Do I really have to explain?"

Brooke shot me a look. "To make sure I know exactly what's going on, yes. I don't want any misunderstandings."

Impatiently, I sighed. "Okay…I'm miserable, and so are you. We haven't been happy in months. The fighting is constant and keeps escalating. Things keep getting worse. I tried to fix things, but you wouldn't, or if you did, it wouldn't last more than a week or two."

"What if," Brooke jumped in, "what if we try more? Try harder? I mean, things can't be fixed overnight, right?"

"I'm done trying, Brooke," my voice cracked as tears fell from my eyes. "I don't want to try anymore."

She crossed her arms, trying to stop her tears with anger. "Why is that? Why don't you want to try anymore? Because you found someone else?"

Looking down at my hands, I knew I would not hide it from her, but it wasn't easy to admit. "I'm not leaving you because of someone else. I'm leaving because I'm unhappy and have been for a long time. I know this will hurt to hear, but I'm not in love with you anymore."

"So you're telling me that this isn't because of someone else?"

Looking up at her, I kept my voice low and even, "Our relationship failed because of you and me, but..."

Her eyes flared. Stomping closer, she yelled, "You were cheating on me! I knew it! You lied to me!"

I held up my hands. "I didn't lie. Last time we talked about this, when I said I didn't cheat on you, I hadn't."

"But now you have?"

"Brooke—" I had to stop and clear my throat. *Dammit!* This was hard! Unable to face her, I looked at the floor. "I'm leaving because of what I said. I'm not leaving because of someone else. Honestly, I've been mentally checked out of our relationship for a while...but I did slip up with someone."

When she didn't make a sound, I looked up at her. All traces of sadness were gone from her face, replaced by rage. "Not 'someone,' Jax! Tess!" she hissed her name.

"Yes, it was Tess."

Caustically, she asked, "Ah, so what happens now? I know she dumped Eli. So what? You two gonna ride off into the fucking sunset?"

"I don't know what, if anything, is going to happen."

Brooke scoffed.

I looked at her. "I don't. We haven't talked about it. The only thing we talked about was how it was a mistake and it shouldn't have happened."

"Ah, so fucking Tess was a mistake. How nice."

"We didn't have sex."

That startled the rage off her face. "What?"

"We kissed. Once." I swallowed. "But it probably would've gone farther if her roommate hadn't caught us."

Brooke's face turned red. She had suspected it, but I supposed actually hearing it was different. Screaming, Brooke picked up a ceramic coaster and threw it, narrowly missing the TV, shattering and leaving another gouge in the wall. *Déjà vu.* Whatever doubt that may have been lingering in the back of my mind shattered along with the ceramic pieces spread across on the floor.

"I am sorry. You may not believe me, but I didn't want to hurt you. That's one reason I hung on for so long." Looking her squarely in the eyes, I said, "I will never forget what you did for me. I may not be in love with you anymore, but I will always love you."

Brooke rolled her eyes. Muttering, she complained, "That stupid slut couldn't keep her hands to herself. I hate her!"

Now I was mad. "She's not stupid or a slut. I can understand you hating her, but I was the one who made the first move. I told her how I felt. Not her. She was trying her damnedest to hide the way she felt and get over it!"

Unconvinced, Brooke spat, "It's still her fault. She should have backed off when she knew you had a girlfriend!"

Enraged, I jumped to my feet. "No, Brooke, no! This is your fault! If you hadn't become such a bitch over the last few months, I wouldn't have fallen out of love with you and in love with her! I don't like this person you've become. You used to be caring and nice. Now you're mean and...uncaring! What kind of girlfriend brings drugs into the same house as her fucking recovering boyfriend? I should have left you months ago!"

There's seven stages of grief, right? The anger must've kicked in because I went on, fuming. "You've slapped me, poked me, thrown shit at me, constantly yelled at me, blamed me for everything, didn't give a shit about what I wanted because it was always about you... The list goes on! I doubt you even love me anymore. It's like I'm some possession you like to fuck. I'm not interested in sticking around anymore."

Burying her face in her hands, she sobbed, "I do love you. What if I forgive you? Do you think you can forgive me? What if we went to counseling or something?"

Resolutely, I stated, "No, I'm done. The time to fix things was months ago, not now that I've given up."

She walked over to the armchair and sat, still weeping into her hands. Sitting down again, I waited for her to calm down a little.

After several minutes, she did enough to hiss, "If you're leaving, go. You've made yourself clear. You're done, so get out of my life."

I hesitated. Was it okay to leave her in her current state? But she wanted me gone, so I should leave, right?

I stood. "If it's okay with you, I'll come back during winter break to get the rest of my stuff."

"Leave already!" she screamed so ferociously that I was sure her throat would be sore tomorrow.

I did. Pausing in the hallway outside her door, I took a moment to process what I'd done. I had, in fact, broken up with Brooke. It was over.

Pained wails sounded from the other side of the door, so I rushed to the stairway. I had to get out of there. Unable to stop the tears and not wanting to run into anyone, I took the stairs all twelve stories down. Too distraught to drive, I cried in my car for an hour before I felt okay enough to drive. If I wasn't so exhausted, I would've driven to my house, the house I grew up in, but it was an hour away. I couldn't go to Chuck or Ashton's houses like this, so I ended up at a hotel, where I cried all night.

SLEEP DEPRIVED, I arrived for my statistics final an hour early. I didn't expect Tess to get there early, and she didn't. She walked in a couple of minutes before the exam was set to start. Our eyes locked as she entered the classroom. Her step faltered, and her eyes bulged. I must've looked as bad as I felt.

As soon as she sat down, I greeted her, "Morning. You busy after this?"

"Hi." She hesitated. "No. Why?"

"Can we grab a coffee and talk? It won't take long."

Furrowing her brows, she said, "I'm not sure that's a good idea. Are you sick? You don't look or sound so good."

I sighed. *Does a broken heart count as sick?* "Not exactly, but I do feel like shit. Anyway, it'll be quick."

Reluctantly, she agreed, "Okay. Are you going to be okay for your show Friday?"

Like that even mattered? I shrugged. "It's our last show until New Year's Eve. Won't be too busy. I don't really care."

Her brows rose, but the professor walked in, ending our conversation.

DONE with my exam before anyone else, I stayed seated, pretending to work as I waited for Tess. When she flipped to the last page, which only had two questions on it, I stood and handed in my test, assuming it'd be too suspicious if we ended at the same time.

Leaning against the wall, I waited outside the classroom. After only a few minutes, she walked out. Neither one of us said anything until we stepped outside.

"Phew! I am so glad that's over with!" Tess said happily, "And that was my last final, so I'm free for the next month!" I smiled at her jubilation. *Fuck, she's cute.* "What about you? You have any more finals?"

Continuing in the direction of the coffee shop off campus, I nodded, "Yeah, one tomorrow afternoon. Then I'm done."

After walking several yards, and in a tone like she wasn't sure she wanted to hear the answer, she asked, "What are your plans for break?"

That was exactly what I wanted to talk to her about, but before I could answer, she stopped and looked at her phone. She was getting a call.

"One sec," she said before answering, "Hello?"

A hysterical-sounding female voice came through from the other end, but I couldn't understand what she was saying. Apparently neither could Tess. "What? Wait... I can't—" Tess huffed, then sternly said, "Aunt Trudy, I can't understand you! What's going on?"

Tess listened for a second, then her face turned the color of snow. She whispered into the phone, "What? Is he okay?"

My eyes widened. This was a bad call.

Her mouth opened in horror before saying, "I'll be on the next flight home!" Then she sprinted in the direction of her house yelling, "Sorry, I have to go home!"

Startled, it took me several seconds to move. Then I ran after her. "Tess, wait! What's wrong?"

She ignored me.

I knew Tess was a runner, but holy fuck was she fast! I couldn't keep up with her. Theorizing I might die if I tried to, I slowed to a moderate pace.

When I turned the corner onto her street, I saw her front door was wide open. She hadn't even bothered to close it. I ran in and nearly collided with Tina, who was walking toward the door.

"What happened? What did you do? Is she running away from you?" Tina accused, pointing her finger at me.

Barely able to breathe, doubled over and holding my stomach, I gasped out, "No... She got...a call...and ran."

Tina reached behind me to swing the door shut then took off toward Tess's room. I followed at a slower pace.

As I approached, I heard Tina ask alarmed, "What's wrong?"

There was no response. I stayed in Tess's door frame as she ripped clothes out of drawers and the closet, throwing them haphazardly into an open suitcase on the floor.

Tina pressed, "Tess!"

She stopped, and that's when I saw her tear-drenched face. I took a step but stopped myself from going further. Tess choked out, "My father was in some kind of accident at work, and he's in the hospital. That's all I know."

Tina's face matched how I felt, shocked, horrified, and worried. Tess pulled out her phone and fumbled with it. "I have to change my flight to today."

Tina took her phone and said she'd do that while she continued packing. I walked over to her nightstand, grabbed a couple of tissues, then squatted down beside her.

She took them and thanked me. After wiping her face, she whispered, "Sorry."

Rubbing her back, I quietly assured her, "Don't be. Can I give you a ride to the airport?"

She shook her head and said she'd get a ride-share.

"Come on. You're upset, and I'm here. Why get in a car with a stranger?"

Tina chimed in, "I agree with Jax. Let him take you."

"Fine. Thank you," she said as she stuffed more clothes into her suitcase.

Standing, I said, "I'll go get my keys. I'll be right back."

sixty-three

TESSA

SOMETHING about what Jax said gave me pause. *Get his keys and not his car?*

Two minutes later, Jax returned. Where was his car? There was no way he could have gotten it from the student parking lot that fast. I pushed it out of my mind, as it really wasn't important. By the time I'd finished packing everything I thought I'd want during winter break, Tina had finished changing my flight. It wasn't for a few more hours, but I wanted to leave right away.

Taking my suitcase, Jax pulled it out to his car, which was parked in front of Chuck's, not my house. Strange place for it. Maybe it was out of habit. As he put the suitcase in his trunk, I hugged Tina, who was not returning to New York for break. She was staying with Jamar, and her family was flying out to hang out with his family for the holidays. After saying goodbye, I climbed into Jax's car and stared at my phone, waiting for updates that didn't come.

When the tears stopped dripping down my face, I looked over at Jax. "Thanks. I know the airport is kinda far."

He glanced at me for half a second with a small smile. "Don't worry about it."

Looking at his center console, I noticed that, although the map was up, he wasn't using it for directions. "You seem to know where you're going. You've lived in Southern California your whole life, right?"

"Yeah. My house, where I grew up, isn't far from the airport you're flying out of. This is the way I go home. My exit's about five miles further down the highway than the airport exit."

"Oh!"

"Since I'm up here, I'll stay there tonight and head back to campus tomorrow morning before my exam. I have some things I need to get done anyway. I was gonna wait until Saturday but might as well take care of them now."

One entire song passed before I worked up the nerve to ask, "So, uh, what was it you wanted to talk about?"

He stared at the road ahead for several seconds. "It can wait."

"What? But—"

He glanced over. "Now's not the time, Tess."

So it was bad news? Did he decide he wasn't going to leave Brooke after all? If that was the case, couldn't he tell me now so I'd have the next month to get over him?

Annoyed, I crossed my arms and stared out my window, muttering, "I'll be gone for a month, you know."

"I know. And it can wait a month."

Pressing my lips together, I tried to remain silent. But, as usual, when it came to this man, I had little self-control. "Are we still friends?"

He smiled. "Yes. I've already told you, I don't want to lose you."

I let out a breath. I could live with that.

BY THE TIME we arrived at the airport, I still hadn't received any updates on my dad. No news was good news, right? Preoccupied with my phone, I hadn't noticed that Jax pulled into the short-term parking lot until he parked and shut off his car.

He jumped out while I was trying to figure out what he was doing. Meeting him by the trunk as he retrieved my suitcase, I asked, "I thought you'd drop me off at departures."

He shrugged then headed for the nearest airport entrance, rolling my suitcase for me.

He waited while I checked my bag. As I walked back toward him, my phone vibrated. It was my mom! I answered as I continued back over to Jax.

"Your father is fine," my mother explained. "He fell at work and sprained his ankle. Since he was on duty, he was required to go to the hospital. He'll be fine. You don't have to rush home."

I looked at Jax, his face becoming blurry. He was watching me, probably trying to figure out what was happening. "Oh, that's great, but I've already changed my flight and checked my bag, so I'll be home later today anyway."

After I exchanged goodbyes with my mom, Jax asked, "What happened?"

"He's fine." I was happy my dad was okay, but leaving California a few days early for no reason sucked. I should've waited to hear from my mom before I rushed here.

"That's great," Jax said, although there was sadness in his eyes. Was he disappointed I was leaving early too?

"You didn't have to walk me in here and wait."

"I wanted to. Otherwise, how could I give you a proper goodbye?" Jax wrapped his arms around me, pulling me as close to him as possible. Tears leaked out from my closed eyelids as I hugged him back. His heart pounded against my chest. Could he feel mine too? Putting his lips to my ear, he did the thing that made my knees weak.

Whispering, he admitted, "I'm going to miss you, Tessa."

A sob escaped, and I buried my face in his chest. He kept holding me even though he must've felt his shirt getting wet. "I'm going to miss you too. I wish I didn't have to leave yet. I wish I'd waited to hear from my mom before I..." I started sobbing.

Jax rested his head against mine and didn't let me go until I stopped. I pulled away enough to look up at him. Cupping my face, Jax wiped my tears away with his thumbs like he'd done a couple of times before. And like those other times, we stared at each other for a long time. It was like we were trying to memorize each other before our month-long separation. Leaning down, he kissed my forehead. His lips lingered before he pulled back. When more tears fell from my eyes, he wiped those away too.

"I'll be here when you get back, waiting for you," he promised.

"What does that mean?" I rasped through my tears.

The corners of his mouth turned up. "Exactly what I said."

Although I still wasn't sure what he meant, I nodded. Knowing if I stayed with him any longer that I'd have an even harder time walking away, I stepped back. Turning, I headed for security. After getting in line, I looked over and saw Jax was still standing where I left him, watching me. I waved. He gave me a faint smile and waved back before turning and walking away. Watching him leave was too painful, so I turned my head to the line in front of me.

As I progressed through, my eyes wandered back toward the direction he would've gone to get back to his car. He was still there, leaning against the far wall, watching me. Despite my despair, it made me smile. He perked up when he saw and smiled back. From what I could see, Jax didn't leave until I was through security.

AS I SAT on the long flight home, I reflected on the last four months of my life. So much had changed. I wasn't the same person as I was when I'd landed in California back in August. I'd never felt so high and so low at the same time before. I was madly in love with Jax but miserable. Anything could happen in the next month, and my mind tormented me with all the questions only time could answer. Would Jax actually leave Brooke or change his mind and stay? Would our love for each other grow while we spent a month thousands of miles apart, or would it fade like it'd been a crush that got out of hand?

What would happen when I returned? Would Jax hug me like that again and kiss my forehead? Or maybe kiss my lips with nothing holding us back? The next time he looked into my eyes, would he tell me he loved me or show me with his body? What would my last semester of college would be like? Happy, miserable, or dramatic?

FRIDAY NIGHT, my body was still on Pacific time, I was wide awake in bed when I noticed the time. Twelve-forty a.m. or in other words, nine-forty in California. Jax was on stage at that very minute. I wondered what songs they were playing and if he was okay to perform. How busy was the bar, and were they doing a short night or the usual two sets?

As if Tina had read my mind from three thousand miles away, she called me on a video call. I answered and instantly heard Jax singing in the background. My heart swelled. How on Earth was I going to make it through the next month without knowing what was happening, if anything, between us?

Tina's face filled the screen. "Hey, girl! Are you in the dark? I can't see you!" She was shouting over the band.

I laughed, "Yeah, I'm in bed. What's up?"

"Doing Jax a little favor."

"Huh?"

She flipped the camera and zoomed in on the stage, more precisely on Jax. He was playing the keyboard and singing. It was a song from a rock band, but slow and beautiful, like a ballad. Jax sounded so good and looked sexy as hell up there singing with his fingers moving across the keys.

Although there was a touch of sadness in him, by no means did it affect his performance. Even from a tiny phone screen, I could still feel the emotion radiating off him. His voice sounded perfect, no trace of the roughness from earlier in the week. But he seemed lost in the music and oblivious to the people watching him, not making his usual eye contact with the crowd.

What had Tina meant by a favor for Jax? Did he know I was watching him? Could he feel me watching him, even from across the country, like I could feel when he was watching me?

The song ended. Jax looked directly into the camera and winked. I squealed as the butterflies exploded. *Ugh...* I was pathetic. Why was I getting all excited when I was still in limbo?

Tina switched the camera so she popped into view again.

I asked, "What do you mean did a favor for Jax?"

"Sorry, girl. I can't hear you. Text me."

She hung up, and I did so immediately.

My Butterflies

TESSA GIVENS

What do you mean you did Jax a favor? Did he know I was watching?

TINA REYNOLDS

Yeah, he knew. He asked me to video call you when he did that song because he said you've hinted in the past that you wanted to see him sing and play the piano at the same time. He'd planned on doing this tonight, but since you weren't here to see it, he asked me to video call you so you wouldn't miss it.

TESSA GIVENS

And you agreed? Aren't you pissed at him?

TINA REYNOLDS

Well...

He had to bribe me. He's picking up my bar tab tonight. LOL

So...

TESSA GIVENS

What?

TINA REYNOLDS

There's a rumor that him and Brooke are no more. She's not here tonight, so that's only adding fuel to the fire. And Jax looks like shit.

TESSA GIVENS

I thought he looked a little off, but I don't think he looked like shit.

TINA REYNOLDS

Of course YOU wouldn't!

TESSA GIVENS

Did you ask him if they broke up?

TINA REYNOLDS

Girl, you crazy? That is none of my business. If he hasn't told you, there must be a reason for it. Like maybe it's not true.

"""

But there's something else…

I saw some wannabe groupie flat out ask him, and he was kind of an asshole about it.

TESSA GIVENS

Really?

TINA REYNOLDS

Yeah, so she was clearly wanting to know for her own sake, but he said something like, "Why do you care? If I was interested in you, you'd know." Then he stalked off. I was like whoa! I'd never seen him that harsh before.

If the rumors are true, at least you know he's not getting over Brooke by hooking up with anyone who throws themselves at him. Cause before him and Brooke got together, he was kind of a dog.

TESSA GIVENS

Seriously?

TINA REYNOLDS

Yeah, he's been around the block, girl.

Anyway! I need to go get me another drink! I am milking this night of drinks on Jax to the fullest!

TESSA GIVENS

So you are drunk?

TINA REYNOLDS

Yup!

TESSA GIVENS

I had a feeling. You've been awfully forthcoming. That and you actually agreed to do him a favor. I didn't think you liked him very much.

TINA REYNOLDS

> I don't like anyone who hurts you, but other
> than that I've got no problem with him. If he
> makes you happy one day and treats you like
> the queen you are, then I will love him too.

Strangely, Tina's drunken confession warmed my heart, and I fell asleep smiling.

chapter
sixty-four

JAXON

SITTING ON MY COUCH, I stared at the one picture I had of Tess. How was it possible to miss someone so much after only a few days? Winter break was going to be long and miserable.

The doorbell stirred me out of my reminiscing about the girl who'd stolen my heart when I wasn't paying attention. *Weird.* I wasn't expecting anyone. Opening the front door, a delivery person was walking back to their truck. They'd left a box on my steps. *Also weird.* I hadn't ordered anything. But sure enough, the package was addressed to Jaxon M. Smith. Walking back toward the living room, I checked the return label. My heart stuttered when I read the name of the sender: *Tessa M. Givens.*

Stopping in the kitchen, I grabbed a knife out of the wooden block on the counter and sliced through the tape. Inside were multiple wrapped presents. Two in blue wrapping paper with the words "Happy Birthday" printed on it and one in sparkly red paper with green ribbon tied in a bow. Wedged between the presents was a Christmas stocking embroidered with my name, filled with goodies. My eyes stung. She'd not only remembered my birthday was in December, but that it was today.

My phone pinged.

My Butterflies

HAPPY BIRTHDAY, JAX!

Thank you. But you didn't need to do this.

No, but I wanted to! Did you open it yet?

I opened the box but not the gifts. It only arrived a minute ago.

I know! I've been stalking the tracking number all day!

Give me a sec.

Picking up a note from inside the box, I read,

No opening the Christmas gift until Christmas!

I laughed, not surprised at all by the note. Opening the bigger of the two birthday gifts first, I found another note taped to the exterior of the box.

I'm sure you have earbuds or headphones already, but these are the best for listening to rock music. I use these when I run and used them when I got ready for my soccer games. They drown out the world and sound amazing, like they were specifically made for rock and metal.

Smiling at her thoughtfulness, I unwrapped the smaller gift. Inside a small box was a pair of small onyx hoop earrings. They were my style, yet I didn't have any like them. She must've paid attention to my constantly rotating earrings and noted I didn't have a pair like these. That wasn't surprising given how observant she was.

Picking up my phone, I texted her.

JAX

Thank you. I love my birthday gifts. You really didn't have to, but it means a lot to me that you did.

TESS

You're welcome! I'm glad you like them.

JAX

How'd you get my address? And how'd you know I'd be at my house?

TESS

Chuck

I frowned. Stupidly, I felt a tinge of jealousy about one of my best friends having Tess's number.

JAX

You have Chuck's number?

TESS

Yeah, his parents are my landlords, and Chuck is my main contact.

Duh. I felt like an idiot.

JAX

Ah, right.

Staring at the stuffed stocking in the box, I did something I thought nothing could make me do.

Climbing the stairs to the second floor, I walked to the middle of the hallway, reached up, and pulled the attic door and ladder down. I couldn't remember the last time I'd been up there, because I sure as hell hadn't decorated for the holidays in the last few years.

Using my phone as a flashlight, I searched through the boxes labeled "X-mas" until I found my old stocking holder. I smiled. Only Tess could inspire me to do something like this.

Back downstairs in the living room, I placed Rudolph on the fireplace mantle. After retrieving the stocking from the kitchen, I hung it then snapped a picture to send to Tess.

While waiting for her reply, I sat back on the couch and let my mind wander. Would there be another one hanging next to mine next year with Tessa's name on it? Brooke and I had never done stockings. Since we hadn't worked out, I was happy about that. Perhaps it was something special I could do with Tess.

My phone pinged. Tess's response made me laugh for the first time in weeks.

chapter
sixty-five

TESSA

I STARED at the picture Jax sent. On his fireplace mantle, sitting next to a Rudolph the Red-Nosed Reindeer stocking holder, was a mostly black cat with white feet and what looked like a white beard on its chin.

TESSA GIVENS

You have a cat?

JAXON SMITH

I do.

TESSA GIVENS

I had no idea! You must go through a lot of lint rollers, because I've never seen any animal hair on you before.

JAXON SMITH

Mr. Toasty Toes stays with my dad's best friend, the guy I refer to as my uncle, during the school year. Or maybe I should say he stays with his wife, as he prefers females.

TESSA GIVENS

Mr. Toasty Toes?

JAXON SMITH

Toasty for short. He was my mom's cat. She named him, saying it looked like he was wearing mittens on his paws.

Toasty didn't even like me until my mom was no longer around. I can't bring myself to hand him off permanently to someone else. Besides, now he likes me. So when I can, I have him with me.

TESSA GIVENS

Why don't you have him while you're at school?

JAXON SMITH

Brooke's allergic to cats.

I'm not, I thought bitterly.

At the mention of Brooke's name, my heart sank. Jax made it sound like it was still an issue. If they had broken up, he could have said something like, "But he'll be with me from now on." Yet, he didn't. Maybe the rumors weren't true and they hadn't broken up. But then why wasn't he with Brooke at that moment? It was his birthday, and since he was with his cat, I doubted she was there. Looking at the photos again, I noted there was only the one stocking hung.

TESSA GIVENS

If I'd known, I would have sent Mr. Toasty Toes his own stocking.

JAXON SMITH

Ha! Don't worry about it. My aunt spoils him as it is.

TESSA GIVENS

Let me know what you think of your Christmas gift when you open it, ON CHRISTMAS!

JAXON SMITH

Haha, OK. Thanks again, Tessa. You made my day.

AS I PUT cookies on a cooling rack, my dad entered the kitchen holding a box with a bright orange "OVERNIGHT" delivery sticker.

Handing it to me, he said, "This is for you."

Surprised, I replied, "Me? Really?" Taking it and looking at the return address, I smiled. It was from J. Smith in California. Grabbing a knife, I opened the box to find three relatively small wrapped gifts in Santa Claus paper. Pulling out a folded note, I busted out laughing at the first line, getting a couple of curious glances from my parents.

NO OPENING UNTIL CHRISTMAS!

I was going to wait to give you these until you came back, but I got your address off the package you sent me. I feel a little silly about the smallest one, but watching you watch me when I'm on stage, I thought you might like it. If not, throw it out and pretend I never gave it to you and never mention it!

Chuckling, I knew I was going to love whatever it was. Because it was from the man I loved.

Merry Christmas, Tessa. Thank you for making my birthday one I won't forget. I loved your gifts and I'm sure I'll love my Christmas gift too. jaXOn

I giggled at Jax's creative hug and kiss. Picking up my phone, I blinked several times to clear my blurry vision so I could type out a message.

TESSA GIVENS

I got the package. You didn't have, but thank you. I'm excited to see what they are, especially the smallest one ;-P

> And don't worry! I haven't opened them yet.

JAXON SMITH

> You're welcome. I hope you like them.

TESSA GIVENS

> I'm sure I will :-D

Unable to resist, I sent one last message.

TESSA GIVENS

> Have a great day, jaXOn. Give Toasty a pet from me.

BRIGHT AND EARLY CHRISTMAS MORNING, I awoke eager to open the gifts from Jax. I felt like an excited kid sneaking down to the Christmas tree before my parents woke up, except I stayed in the privacy of my room.

Since he seemed nervous about the smallest one, I unwrapped it first. I held up the small plastic microphone, trying to figure out what the heck it was other than a small plastic microphone when I saw a seam. Pulling the mic head off revealed a USB plug. Grabbing my laptop off my desk, I sat back on my bed and inserted the thumb drive. Opening the folder, I saw several audio files. I double-clicked the first file and music started, followed by Jax singing. He'd recorded songs for me!

Wanting to listen to it louder, I grabbed my headphones and turned up the volume. Curious to know all the songs, I quickly played brief clips of each file before starting from the beginning again and letting them play through. They were all songs I'd mentioned I especially liked, including my favorite, as well as broken-down versions of normally more intense rock songs. It must've taken him a while to make this. There was no way he could have recorded it all in the couple of days since I sent him his package. Had he been planning on giving me this for a while?

Touched, I wiped my eyes with the sleeve of my PJ shirt. Closing my eyes, I reclined on my bed, getting lost in Jax's mesmerizing voice. A couple of songs later, I remembered there were two other gifts.

Moving on to the medium-sized gift, I burst out laughing before covering my mouth to avoid waking my parents. It was a refrigerator magnet with a quote.

 *Lyrics are like texts; sometimes it's the easiest way to get your message across.*
  -Tessa M. Givens

Again, I wiped tears away, but this time from holding in my laughter. That wasn't exactly what I'd said, but close enough.

Before moving on to the last gift, I took a deep breath. There was a reason I'd put off unwrapping the distinctive long and skinny rectangular box.

Pulling off the wrapping paper, I stopped when my suspicion was confirmed. I ran my fingers along the velvety jewelry case, debating if this was an appropriate gift between friends. If he was still with Brooke, definitely not.

Curiosity won out, and I lifted the lid. Inside was a silver link bracelet with three charms attached: a microphone, a Ferris wheel—which made me giggle—and an X. The first two were obvious, but was the last one our kiss?

Even from three thousand miles away, he could still give me butterflies and throw my emotions into chaos. Although it was quite early in California, I figured Jax would have his phone on silent mode and it'd be fine to text him.

Taking a move right out of a social media star's handbook, I put the bracelet on, closed my eyes, and took a selfie of myself smiling while listening to my headphones, my head resting on the hand connected to my newly decorated wrist. Clearly a posed picture, but it'd get the point across.

Feeling especially sappy, I sent Jax the picture with a message.

TESSA GIVENS

Words cannot express how happy I feel right now. Thank you. Merry Christmas, jaXOn!

To my astonishment, a few seconds after putting my phone down, it vibrated.

JAXON SMITH

You're welcome. I'm very happy you like them.

TESSA GIVENS

What are you doing up? It's like three-thirty over there!

JAXON SMITH

I always have trouble sleeping this time of year. And this year is harder than the last couple. But getting that candid, makeup-free shot of you made my day. You look beautiful.

This year was harder? Was it because he was alone this year? I was so afraid to ask. There must have been a reason he hadn't told me yet. Playfully, I texted back.

TESSA GIVENS

What? No candid shot for me?

Thirty seconds or so later, a picture of Jax and Toasty's faces popped up. It was dark, but I could see he was in bed propped up against the headboard. He was smiling, but his eyes were sad with dark circles ringing them. I wished I could hug him.

TESSA GIVENS

Please tell me you aren't going to be alone today.

JAXON SMITH

Of course not! I have Toasty.

Was he purposely being evasive? What if he and Brooke hadn't broken up? Texting him like this felt wrong. Just because he was at home didn't mean they'd broken up. She could be off on a European vacation for all I knew. Unable to take it anymore, I decided maybe he would be less evasive on a call.

TESSA GIVENS

Since you're awake, up for a video call?

My screen lit up with his incoming video call. Building up my courage to ask him, I hit the accept button. A shirtless Jax filled my screen. I'd barely noticed Toasty curled up next to him.

"What?" he asked. "Your eyes look like they're about to pop out of their sockets."

"You're not wearing a shirt!"

He looked confused. "It's like three-something in the morning. I'm wearing what I wear to bed." His lips transformed into that seductive half smile of his. "But why does it matter? You've seen me without a shirt on."

"Oh, right..." Feeling a little foolish, I tried playing off my reaction, only to naively conclude, "So you normally only wear PJ pants to bed?"

Jax looked away from the screen. "Uh...not exactly."

"Huh? What does that mean?"

Jax chuckled. "Nothing."

"No, tell me."

Jax laughed again, this time with laughter in his eyes too. "I did. Nothing. I usually don't wear anything to bed."

I gaped at him before throwing my free hand over my eyes.

Cracking up, Jax said, "Tess, it's not like you can see anything." He stopped laughing and cocked an eyebrow. "Although if you wanted..." he teased. At least I thought he was teasing.

"Oh, uh... I've never done that before. Sleep without clothes on, I mean."

With his signature half-sexy smile, he suggested, "You should try it sometime. It's...nice." Based on the heat radiating off my cheeks, I must've looked like a tomato with hair.

Tilting his head, Jax offered, "Would it make you more comfortable if I put clothes on?"

"No, stay under your blanket! Don't move!" I sputtered.

343

He chuckled. "Nudity isn't really that big a deal. At least not to me."

"I mean, I guess it's not if you're... If you've..." I blew out a breath. What was wrong with me? Jax and I nearly had sex, so why was I an incoherent fool now?

He looked a little sheepish as he ran a hand through his messy hair. "Sorry."

Not that he could see it, but I waved it off with my free hand. "It's fine. Don't worry about it. I was just surprised." Looking down at my bed, I bit my lip.

"What? I can see the steam coming out your ears all the way over here in SoCal."

Tapping my lip, I admitted, "I was thinking... Maybe I'll try sleeping naked tonight."

The smile left Jax's lips as they parted. Then he took a deep breath. "You know, Tessa, sometimes you seem a little inexperienced and naïve, but I don't think you are...until you do that."

"That? What's that?"

Jax's eyes smoldered as his tone turned serious. "You literally put the image of you in bed naked in my head without even realizing it."

I took a sharp inhale. *Oh my God...* It wasn't only my face on fire now but my entire body. My heart was pounding, sending hot blood searing through my veins. He could be so direct sometimes, while at other times I couldn't figure out what he meant.

"Maybe we should get off the phone," I breathlessly suggested.

"Maybe," he said before tilting his head, "Or maybe you should say or ask what you called me for." His face was serious and expectant.

"You called me, remember?"

He shrugged. "You asked. Same difference." Then he waited.

Looking away, I swallowed. "I heard a rumor about you and Brooke."

"It's not a rumor if it's true."

"So, you and Brooke?"

"We're done." Taking in my expression, he asked, "Why are you surprised? I told you I was leaving her. And I told you I would be waiting for you when you got back." My chest fluttered. Jax's face morphed back into his playful look. "Do you really think I would've bought another girl jewelry if I had a girlfriend?"

I let out a shaky breath. *What does this mean? What happens now?* I wanted to scream into the phone.

Jax's forehead scrunched as his eyes glistened. As if he'd read my face perfectly, he said, "But I need some time." It came out almost as a whisper, his voice straining against what I imagined was tightness in his throat.

"I understand," I said as my own tears stung my eyes.

"Do you?"

"I think so."

"You think?"

I nodded. "Yes, I get it." But it was a lie. I was still confused and anxious.

Jax looked unconvinced, but he didn't push any further. Instead, he started our farewell for the next few weeks. "I miss you, Tessa."

I didn't bother hiding the tears that slid down each cheek. "I miss you too." I swallowed hard. "Merry Christmas."

He smiled sweetly but sadly. "Merry Christmas."

We said goodbye, then he disconnected the call. I was so happy yet so sad. I silently made a Christmas wish, wishing the next few weeks would fly by so I could get back to California and see him. And inhale his scent that was like an aphrodisiac as I, hopefully, tasted his lips again. And run my fingertips along his naked skin... *Phew!* I was getting worked up and needed to calm down.

Putting my headphones back on, I closed my eyes. At least I could fill my head with the sound of his voice on repeat.

SEVERAL HOURS LATER, Jax sent a text, thanking me for the stocking full of sweets and the summer concert tickets I'd gotten him for Christmas. It was for a band The Last Word did a lot of cover songs of. I hoped he'd not only bring me with him but that we'd be close enough that I'd be the only one he'd want to bring.

RESPECTING HIS NEED FOR TIME, I only initiated one more conversation with him while in New York.

TESSA GIVENS

It's midnight here! Happy New Year, jaXOn! ;-*

JAXON SMITH

Happy New Year!

Did I just get your midnight kiss?

TESSA GIVENS

Hehe… maybe… ;-P

JAXON SMITH

Tessa Givens, are you drunk?

TESSA GIVENS

Maybe… :-X

JAXON SMITH

Does this mean I can text you at midnight Pacific time?

TESSA GIVENS

You can text me whenever you want, but I might be sleeping in three hours.

What time are you going on stage, 9:30 like normal?

JAXON SMITH

No, we're starting later so we can count down at midnight.

A while later, Jax sent me a selfie with his mic to his lips, singing from the stage. Behind him was a sizable crowd. Maybe the locals came out for New Year's Eve, because there definitely wouldn't be many students hanging around during break. Jax looked good, happier than the week before and the dark circles were gone. The sadness in his eyes had also diminished some.

. . .

WHEN I WOKE on New Year's Day, I checked my phone. Sure enough, Jax had texted me at three a.m. eastern time.

JAXON SMITH

Happy New Year, Tessa. ;-*

My belly fluttered at the virtual kiss. That was his last message to me for the next couple of weeks.

A FEW DAYS before the start of the spring semester, Jax messaged me, asking for my flight info. It was supposed to be the Saturday before classes began, but bad weather was coming in, so I changed my flight to the day before. It was the only snow storm I ever liked.

chapter
sixty-six

TESSA

WANTING TO SURPRISE JAX, I didn't tell him about my changed flight. I was so excited to see him that, as I stepped into my California bedroom, I could've sworn I could smell him.

Looking at my desk, I noticed Jax's hoodie and t-shirt on top of it. Maybe I really could smell him. I'd meant to wash the shirts and give them back before I left for winter break, but it always slipped my mind when I did laundry. Knowing it was past time to return them, I picked up the shirts to toss into my hamper but stopped when I caught lingering notes of Jax's mouthwatering scent.

Holding the fabric to my nose, I closed my eyes and inhaled. It was as if my face was buried in his chest, like it had been a handful of times before. It could have been the jet lag, or it could've been his intoxicating essence, but I could only think, *If he's gone this long without them, a little longer won't make a difference.*

As I placed them back on my desk, I wondered if I was a bit obsessed.

I hurried to the bathroom to wash the griminess of air travel off before heading off to Smythie's. If I was quick, I'd be in time for the band's first set. Although tired, having been on East Coast time for the past month, I couldn't wait any longer to see Jax. If something was going to happen between us, it felt like it was now or never.

. . .

FRESHLY SHOWERED AND NAKED, I dug through my suitcase for a new bar outfit I'd purchased over break when a movement caught my eye. Startled, I fell on my ass, but when I looked in the direction it came from, my bedroom window, I saw nothing. Remembering it was windy, I figured something must've been blowing around, like a tree branch or something. My window faced a dense line of trees with nothing in between except some grass, so it wasn't like it could've been anything else.

Not giving it another thought, I donned my new tight mini skirt, silky top, strappy heels, and bracelet before heading out.

IF GETTING to the bar in time for the first set wasn't motivation enough, the air was chilly, so I walked as fast as I could in heels. However, as I got close enough to hear the muffled booming of the music, what I heard was dance music, not rock, yet it was twenty to ten, so the band should've started already.

Standing right inside the entrance, my lips twisted when I took in the scene. The stage was bare, the bar dead. Putting my hands on my hips, I closed my eyes and let my head fall back in disappointment. Blowing out a frustrated breath, I opened my eyes and connected with a pair of laughing deep-blue eyes.

Straightening, I stared up at the man leaning over the loft railing, hands folded in front of him, trying to hide his amusement at my dramatics. *Damn...* His half-smile was even sexier than I remembered.

Feeling shy, maybe because of our weeks apart, I gave him a small smile and wave. Jax jerked his head, indicating he wanted me to come up. Swallowing my nervousness, I walked to the bouncer blocking the circular staircase. Pointing to the ceiling above us, I hollered, "Jax waved me up."

The bouncer, who I was pretty sure was named Archie, smiled as he removed the rope. That seemed too easy. It was nearly impossible to get upstairs. After thanking him, I headed up. As I climbed, my legs wobbled as my breathing became rapid and shallow, but not from exertion. A nervous pit had formed in my belly. But why? *It's Jax,* I told myself. I'd spent plenty of time with him before. Hell, a few weeks ago, I'd had my hand down his pants and felt his pre-cum on the tip of the erection he had for me.

Jax was leaning back against the railing, arms crossed, one ankle over the other, waiting for me. He looked healthy, no traces of the sadness I'd seen in his eyes on Christmas. As I walked toward him, his eyes ran up and down my body. When they met mine again, they were smoldering. Fluttering erupted in my belly.

Stopping in front of him, I said, "Hi."

He smiled. "Hi."

"How are you?"

"I'm good. How are you?"

"Good." Truthfully, I was evaluating the likelihood I was having a heart attack or about to faint.

Not knowing what to do with my hands, I crossed my arms over my chest. The shiny chain around my wrist caught his attention. A satisfied smile crossed his lips.

"I thought you were flying in tomorrow. I was going to surprise you at the airport."

My mouth popped open. "You were?"

He nodded. "I told you I was going to be waiting for you when you got back."

My heart sank. "Oh... I thought you meant that in a different way because of what you said on Christmas."

Jax gave me his breathtaking toothy smile. "I meant it in both ways."

Dammit! I should've told him about my flight change! Feeling foolish, I looked away. "I changed it because of bad weather."

"Ah. So, how was your break?"

"It was..." I thought for a second. "Bittersweet."

Tilting his head, he asked, "What do you mean by that?"

Taking a couple of steps forward and to his right, I leaned against the railing next to him. "It was nice to see my parents, but I spent a lot of time going through old stuff, getting rid of things and packing up my belongings."

Jax didn't say anything out loud, but his eyes were asking for more of an explanation.

I shrugged. "I'll probably only be back there one or two more times. My dad's going to retire when I graduate, and my parents are moving out to California to be near me."

A light flickered in his beautiful deep ocean blue eyes. "You decided you're definitely staying in California?"

I nodded. "Yeah, I love it out here." I grimaced. "And no more icky snow and ice. Or at least not nearly as much as upstate New York." Jax chuckled as I continued, "My parents are going wherever I go. Once they're retired, they won't have anything holding them back there."

"Where in California? It's a big state."

I smirked. "Tell me about it. I'm not sure. I've been applying to various departments all over. I guess whoever hires me gets to decide."

Jax looked away, pressing his lips together, but I still caught his smile.

Looking over my shoulder, I asked, "Hey, aren't you afraid of heights? How are you leaning against this railing?"

He rubbed the back of his head. "One floor up doesn't bother me. And I know for a fact this railing is triple reinforced."

"I see. So what about you? How was your break? Do anything special?"

Looking away, he said, "It was quiet and…" He looked back at me. "I guess you could say it was also bittersweet. After finals, when Brooke had gone back to her parents' house, I moved my stuff over to Chuck's. Then I went back to my house for a week, came back here for New Year's Eve, then went back home. I got back today. Came to see if anything was going on."

"So that means you did spend Christmas and your birthday alone? You never gave me a straight answer." My voice was filled with sadness for him.

He smirked. "Of course not, I told you I had Toasty keeping me company."

I laughed despite myself. "I should've invited you to my house for at least part of break."

He gave me a small, appreciative smile. "Thanks, but I would have turned you down."

My face fell along with my heart. Was this his way of telling me he was no longer interested in me? Had the time and distance away from each other not made his heart grow fonder like it had mine? Maybe because of how things had started between us? It wasn't good. Starting something with a betrayal was asking for trouble, and maybe he was afraid he'd end up in another bad relationship. Looking away, I tried to hide my stinging eyes.

Jax leaned in close to my ear. "I told you I needed time. I needed to heal and let go of my relationship with her. Otherwise..." I turned my head slightly in his direction, looking at him out of the corner of my eye. Moving closer, his breath brushed against my skin, sending thrilling chills down my spine. "Otherwise, how could I start fresh with you?"

My head snapped over to look at him. His face was right there, so close.

Taking my hand, he intertwined our fingers. Raising it to his lips, he placed a soft kiss on the back of my hand. Brushing his lips back and forth across my skin, he asked, "What do you say? Should we give this a try?"

My chest erupted with butterflies. If it weren't for the music playing around us, I'd have sworn we would've been able to hear my heart thumping in my chest.

Breathless, I asked, "You want to start at the beginning?"

He smirked and looked away. "Maybe not the very beginning." He met my eyes again. His sparkled mischievously.

I couldn't say who moved first, but it didn't matter. In a millisecond, I was in his arms, our lips locked together in a deep, passionate kiss. Parched, our tongues lapped at each other's like it was the only thing that could quench our thirst. His hands scorched my exposed skin between my skirt and shirt. As he pulled me close, his fingers splayed out, dipping beneath the hems of my clothes, where they settled, lightly caressing me. Following his lead, I ran my hands down his six-pack, slipping my fingers under his shirt, my hands settling on his sides, skin to skin.

Jax was a skilled kisser. I whimpered when my knees gave out, and I had to hang onto him for support. He chuckled against my lips and got a firmer grip on me, pulling me tighter to him. Realizing his jeans must've been getting uncomfortable, I pulled back. His mouth moved to my neck as I suggested, "Tina won't be home. My place?"

In answer, he grabbed my hand and pulled me toward, then down, the spiral staircase, out the front door, and to the parking lot.

Smiling, Jax remarked, "I'm glad I drove."

Me too. A three-minute drive was better than a fifteen-minute walk.

He opened the front passenger-side door. I climbed in, then he shut the door and ran around to the driver's side. After pulling out onto the street, he reached over and intertwined our fingers. Instead of watching out a window, I watched Jax, wondering if I was having the best dream of my life or the best night of my life. He caught me and smiled as he turned his attention back to the road.

Those three minutes were the slowest of my life. When we finally arrived. Jax jumped out and ran around the car as I climbed out.

He gave me a knowing grin. "I was going to get the door for you."

"No time," I jested as I reversed our roles and dragged him along to my front door. After unlocking it, we stepped inside. Jax shut the door then pressed me up against it.

chapter
sixty-seven

TESSA

WORKING our mouths and tongues together, we groped and grabbed at each other's clothes. Somehow, we made our way to my room, leaving a trail of clothing and shoes in our wake. Hoping this would happen, I'd worn a matching lacy panties and bra set, which were the only articles of clothing I had on as I sat back on my bed. Jax shut and locked the door on the off chance Tina decided to come home. We didn't need her interrupting us again, not that she had a reason to now.

As I watched Jax stride shirtless toward me, I pressed my thighs together, more turned on than I'd ever been in my life. The elastic of his underwear peeked out above the waist of his tight black jeans, a prominent bulge straining against the denim. He stopped right in front of me and, holding my gaze, pushed the last remnants of his clothing down, freeing himself from the restrictive pants. Deliberately, I held eye contact for a moment, biting my lip before slowly lowering my eyes down to his neck, chest, abs, belly button, happy trail, and—

My mouth popped open. *Holy cow!* Looking back up at his face, Jax smirked, clearly proud of his manhood, as he should be. I had a feeling he was blessed below the belt from my hand's brief adventure down his pants, but I wasn't expecting the pornstar dick in front of me, not that I'd seen much porn in my life.

"Something wrong?" he teased.

"Uh, not exactly wrong…" Feeling a blush rising up my cheeks, I looked away. "It's been a while for me, so…"

He climbed onto the bed and crawled over me, forcing me back. "I'll have to make sure you're ready then."

Oh God! My chest rose and fell rapidly, already panting even though he'd barely touched me.

Leaning down, he kissed me deeply, but when he lowered his body onto mine, and our bare skin touched, I gasped, breaking our lips apart. Jax didn't stop kissing me. He trailed his lips and tongue along my jawline and down my neck, stopping to pay special attention to that sensitive spot he'd found the first time we kissed. As I reveled in the sensations of Jax's skin against mine, hands caressing my body, and tongue and mouth kissing me, I ran my nails down his back. His movements became rougher, and the kisses turned to sucking.

Releasing my neck, he kissed his way down my chest, pulling the straps of my bra off my shoulders. Peeking up at me, he bit his bottom lip as he slid a hand under my back, and with a flick of his fingers, my bra was unlatched. In one smooth motion, he'd pulled it off and tossed it across the room.

"Ah!" My back arched when his mouth captured a nipple, teasing it with his tongue and teeth, the sensations shooting straight to my core. Threading my fingers in his hair, I moved his head to the other nipple.

Chuckling, he commented, "Equal attention to both, huh?"

"Uh huh," I moaned.

Having his fill of my breasts, he continued down my body while his hands continued to play, his fingers gently pinching and twisting the sensitive peaks. After drawing a circle around my belly button with his tongue, he bit the metal bar and pulled.

He growled, "This is so fucking sexy."

"Hah…" I gasped.

Releasing my breasts, his hands slid down my body to the elastic of my panties. Hooking his fingers beneath, he pulled while sitting back on his heels. They too went flying across the room. Then Jax did the thing I'd imagined him doing all those months ago after our first meeting: he put his face between my legs.

But he popped back up. "You waxed," he said, referring to my, save for a small strip of hair, bare sex.

"I could hope, right?" I managed.

His eyes smoldered as that panty-dropping, orgasm-inducing smile I loved slowly spread across his lips. Jax's eyes never left mine as he lowered his head again.

Feeling the first touch of his tongue on the most intimate part of my body caused me to buck. Slow and deliberate, his movements were purposely driving me crazy. He played and teased, swirling his tongue around the pulsing bud between my legs but never touching it. After one torturous rotation, his tongue traveled down, circling the rim of my warm core, driving me completely insane.

Squirming, I begged, "Jax!"

He responded by dipping his tongue into me. Gasping, I fisted my bedding as my head dug into my pillow. He was driving me insane!

Heady and desperate from the torment, I looked down, begging with my eyes. He'd been watching me and continued to watch as the pressure of his tongue increased.

"Ah!" My head fell back when his tongue finally swept over the spot where I needed. He chuckled. Panting, I accused, "You're... You're doing this on purpose, aren't you?"

"Mm hmm," he hummed slowly, the tenor of his voice sending vibrations through my body.

"I can't... It's too much!" I moaned, sure my finger nails were shredding my blanket.

Releasing me from his prison of carnal agony, all his attention went to my clit, gradually increasing the speed and pressure. My body writhed as noises I didn't recognize escaped from my lips. Under his skillful tongue, he built the path to ecstasy with peaks and curves. Moaning, I let Jax know how much I loved what he was doing to me.

Wrapping his lips around the aching pearl, he sucked while his tongue continued to swirl, lick, and flick. I rode trembling waves toward euphoria as earth-shattering sensations took over my body. Squirming uncontrollably, he gripped my thighs to hold me in place as he continued driving me wild. I was so close. Then Jax released one leg and slipped a finger deep into my depths, and I thought I'd go completely insane. I groaned as if possessed by an animal as he continued his blissful assault.

Grabbing his silky locks between my fingers, I begged him, "Don't stop! Oh God!"

Withering, I continued to vocalize with incoherent pleas as I got closer to cresting. Jax's groan vibrated against me.

When he slid in a second finger, I thought I would spontaneously combust. A few moments later, I did. More intense than anything I'd ever experienced in my life, I saw stars as I crashed into a sea of pleasure. My back arched off the bed as my hips rode the waves rippling through my body, grinding against his mouth. By the time I was spent and coming down from the high, my throat hurt.

Jax kissed his way back up my body. With a sexy, satisfied smirk, he commented, "That was fun."

Between pants, I admitted, "That's...never happened before. No one's ever done that."

His eyebrows shot up. "No one's ever gone down on you before?"

I shook my head. "Made me come. Only my vibrator."

His look of shock transformed into a victorious grin. "We'll have to do it again sometime," he teased.

I smiled. "Yes please."

Jax's erection was heavy against my thigh. Reaching down, I wrapped my hand around it, sliding up and down his length. He cursed under his breath. I started to sit up to change our positions, but he gently pushed me back down and shook his head. "Later." Whispering in my ear, he said, "I want to be inside you."

The man had already figured out I went a little crazy when he did that.

Jumping off the bed, Jax bent over to pick up his discarded pants. Digging into a pocket, he pulled out his wallet and removed a condom. He hopped back on the bed and tore the foil packet open with his teeth. Not convinced I wasn't having the best damned dream of my life, I considered pinching myself as I watched him roll the sheath down his shaft. When he was done, Jax took a moment to run his eyes over my completely exposed body. Although I'd just come against his mouth, my cheeks heated.

Eyes stopping at my wrist, he said, "Nice outfit. You in only a piece of jewelry is one of the sexiest things I've ever seen. The sexiest being you coming."

Despite my slight shyness, I giggled. "Yeah, some guy gave me this thing," I said, flicking my wrist at him. "I like it, so I figured I might as well wear it."

Jax laughed as he covered my body with his. "Some guy, huh? You like the bracelet, but what about that guy? You like him?"

Cupping his cheeks, I looked into his eyes. "That guy is my favorite thing on this planet. Although the bracelet is my favorite gift of all time." Moving my hands to his ears, I touched the black hoops in his lobes. "You're wearing them," I whispered.

"Of course I am. They're from my favorite person," he said, emphasizing the word *my*.

So happy I wanted to cry, I smiled up at Jax with shiny eyes. He leaned down and kissed me sweetly. I wrapped my arms around his neck, encouraging him to not stop. He didn't. Not even as he nudged my legs apart with his knee and slowly entered me. Pushing in a little farther with each gentle thrust, he let my body adjust to him. When he was completely enveloped within my heat, our lips parted as I gasped at the fullness.

Jax groaned, "Fuck, Tessa…"

Whimpering, I grabbed his ass, urging him to move, needing this, needing him. His movements started small, gentle and slow, gradually increasing in pace and intensity. Cupping his face in my hands, I pulled his lips down to mine. We moaned into each other's mouths as we let our senses take over, getting completely lost in each other. Needing to breathe, I pulled away and stared into the deep-blue eyes I loved so freakin' much.

As I felt him inside me, I finally accepted this wasn't a dream. Jaxon Smith was making love to me, and there was nothing to feel guilty about.

Still being overly sensitive from my first orgasm, along with how I was with the man I was so deeply in love and lust with, I did something I wasn't sure was possible. My insides clenched around Jax, trying to suck him in.

He growled, "Fuck…"

I cried out. Although thrashing beneath him, he kept the same rhythm, making sure I could ride out my second orgasm completely.

As I floated down from the clouds of ecstasy, and Jax's movements increased in speed. His body tensed in my arms, and with a deep groan his body spasmed. Wanting to feel every millisecond of his orgasm, I held him tightly. Knowing I'd made Jax come gave me a high I'd never felt before, and I relished in it.

When he stopped moving, my eyes opened, meeting his. How long had he been watching me? Had he been looking at me as he found his release?

Although panting, he was smiling. "Another first?"

Assuming he meant having an orgasm during sex, I nodded. He leaned down to kiss me before hugging me close and not letting me go as he rolled onto the bed. As we cuddled, he played with my hair. Gradually, our hearts slowed, and our breathing returned to normal. I was downright jubilant that Jax wanted to cuddle and hoped we always would after making love.

Eventually he got out of bed to clean up in the bathroom. Rolling onto my stomach with my face toward the door, I watched for his return. However, I dozed off before he did.

Although trying to be careful not to disturb me, I woke when he got into bed. My eyes opened to darkness. He must've hit the light switch when he got back. Turning from my stomach to my side, I scooted back into him. Jax wrapped his arms around me, burying his face in my hair. *We're spooning!*

His semi hard-on pressed against my backside. I wiggled my ass, rubbing against him. His dick twitched, and I could feel it getting harder. Jax mumbled into the back of my neck, "If you don't stop, I'll have to fuck you again."

I giggled. "Who said you couldn't?"

"You're tired. You were sleeping. Isn't it three hours later for you?"

Disappointed, I grumbled, "I'm not that tired."

Jax stilled then popped up. "You asked for it."

Bending over, he captured my lips in a slow, deep kiss. The second time was slower and gentler but just as satisfying. Afterward, we fell asleep in each other's arms. It was the best night's sleep I'd gotten in a long, long time.

chapter
sixty-eight

jaXOn

A JOLTING BODY WOKE ME, and my eyes blinked open.

I was facing an unfamiliar wall with a warm body in my arms. She moved again, but this time to snuggle in closer. She breathed in deeply, and I smiled at her sigh of contentment. Reaching up, I stroked her cheek. Tessa shifted again, and I looked down into her loving eyes.

"Hi," she whispered.

Giving her the greeting I gave her every morning before class, I said, "Morning."

We continued to gaze into each other's eyes while I brushed my thumb back and forth across her cheek. Her skin was so soft, and I loved touching it. I loved her smile. I loved her giggle. I loved her sparkling eyes. I loved the way she made me feel, happy and loved. I loved so many things about her. But most of all, I loved being able to say, "I love you, Tessa."

Her eyes fluttered closed, and the smile on her lips widened. She took a deep breath through her nose, as if to savor the moment. Leaning down, I kissed her forehead. When I pulled back, her eyes were open again. Bringing her own hand up to my face, she cupped it and confessed, "I love you, Jaxon. I am so in love with you that I can hardly breathe."

Wrapping my arm back around her body, I pulled her as close as I could. "It's the same for me." She melted into me, her body molding into mine, like we were two puzzle pieces fitting perfectly together.

Closing my eyes, I let my senses take over, inhaling her sweet, tantalizing scent as I let the warmth of her body heat me to my soul. Listening carefully, I heard her even breathing as she slept in my arms.

Maybe people would think we were crazy for confessing our feelings after only one night together, but we weren't. We already knew how we felt about each other, but even if we didn't, Tess and I knew better than most that the next day, the next hour, the next minute, or even the next second could be too late. Life could change in the blink of an eye.

If Tess never heard me say it so explicitly, I'd regret it for the rest of my life.

chapter
sixty-nine

TESSA

A COUPLE OF HOURS LATER, I woke again still wrapped in Jax's arms. As gently as I could, I pulled back so I could get a good look at his face while he slept. I inspected every inch, and my eyebrows rose when I noticed the nearly-invisible smattering of freckles across his nose and cheeks. I'd never noticed them before. They were too freakin' cute!

One of Jax's eyes popped open.

I smiled at him. "Oh, you're awake."

Sounding a little sleepy, he explained, "I'm a light sleeper and woke up when I felt you move."

"Sorry."

"Don't be." He nuzzled into my neck. "I'm not. I could get used to waking up next to you. So, how was it?" Pulling back, he smiled mischievously as he must've noticed my face turn beet-red. "You know, your first night sleeping naked?"

My mouth fell open. I whacked him with a small decorative pillow that somehow lasted the night on the bed. "You said it like that on purpose! Like you wanted me to rate your performance!"

Cracking up at his own joke, Jax winced away as I tried to tickle him. After he caught his breath, he asked again, "Soooo?"

Giggling, I admitted, "That wasn't my first night sleeping naked."

Smirking, probably guessing where I was going with this, although he had no idea, he asked, "No? But on Christmas—"

"I slept naked that night, like I said I might."

He inspected my face. "Why are you so red? That's nothing to be embarrassed about, at least not with me." Dropping his voice an octave, he added, "I think it's hot."

Groaning, I buried my face in my hands. *Darn it!* I had felt so confident a few seconds ago, but my face was giving me away. "That's not why I'm embarrassed," I whined.

"Then why—"

"Because I had imagined being with you right before I went to sleep!"

Although Jax's mouth popped open, the beginnings of a smile formed. Leaning into me, nuzzling my nose, he whispered, "Why do you think I got off the phone on Christmas?"

My eyes bulged.

"I was hard the entire time we were on the phone. That picture you sent me... It was sexy as fuck seeing what you looked like first thing in the morning."

"Really? You thought of me when you..."

Smiling salaciously, he admitted, "That wasn't the first time, or last. Now tell me, how does it compare to the real thing?"

I wasn't sure if he was joking or not, but I answered breathily, "There's no comparison."

Groaning, Jax tickled my neck with his tongue.

"Oh God..." I said through ragged breaths. "I can't believe we're having such a casual conversation about masturbation!"

Jax ground his shaft into my belly. "I wouldn't call this casual." His voice was rough, thick with lust. Grabbing one of my breasts, he pinched my nipple as he nipped at my neck. I gasped at the painful pleasure. Reaching for him, I wrapped my hand firmly around him and stroked his skin.

Jax groaned in pleasure. Then in frustration. He stopped and flopped down next to me, rubbing his eyes. "Fuck!"

Alarmed, I asked, "What? Why'd you stop? Are you okay?"

Turning his head to me, disappointment was all over his face. "I have to run next door and get more condoms."

Giggling, I crawled over him to get to my nightstand drawer. After digging around in it for a second, I pulled out my box of emergency condoms and handed it to him.

Examining it, he commented, "It's not open."

Still leaning over him, I bent down and brushed my lips against his neck and chest. Between kisses, I explained, "I haven't had a need for them until now."

"Uh... Eli? You guys used protection, right?"

I stopped my kissing assault and stared at him like he was crazy. "I never slept with Eli. I told you that it wasn't serious."

Jax's eyes bugged out, and his jaw dropped. He looked away and, based on his expression, was thinking about something unpleasant. Panicking, I started pulling away. *He doesn't like that I'm more inexperienced than he thought!*

At my movement, Jax looked back at me questioningly. "What's wrong?"

Ducking my head, I muttered, "I'm sorry I'm not more experienced."

"What? I don't care about that. In fact, I like it."

"But then why do you look so unhappy?"

Looking away again, he said, "I just remembered something. Don't worry about it." Wide-eyed, his face snapped back to mine. "Wait. Last night, when you said it'd been a while..."

I shrugged. "Yeah, like about four years."

"Oh, fuck... How are you feeling?"

I gave him my full, beaming smile.

His face relaxed as a smile touched his lips. "I mean physically."

"I'm fine. No regrets or anything. But maybe I'll take the lead this time."

Jax's eyes lit up. Folding his arms behind his head, he settled back and enjoyed the ride.

SITTING on the kitchen counter with Jax standing between my legs, we were tongue deep into each other's mouths when a throat cleared. Reluctantly, I stopped kissing him and peered over at a smirking Tina.

Defensively, Jax blurted, "Brooke and I broke up over a month ago!"

Still smirking, she said, "I heard, but that doesn't mean you can have sex on the kitchen counter."

Jax frowned at me with puppy dog eyes, nearly causing the water I'd taken a sip of to come out my nose.

Tina dramatically rolled her eyes. "Well, at least wait until I leave. I'm only here to get a few things. I'll be staying at Jamar's again tonight." She pointed her finger at us. "But I'll be back Sunday night, so either get it out of your systems now or tone down the sound effects."

Both Jax and I stared. While he looked amused, I was shocked and embarrassed. Mumbling, I said, "I thought you weren't going to be home last night."

Tina snickered. "I wasn't feeling all that great, so Jamar dropped me off. I walked in, saw clothes strewn about, heard what I thought was a porn film, and then went back outside and called Jamar to turn around and get me."

I buried my face in Jax's chest while he thought it was hilarious. "Sorry," he said, not sounding it in the slightest.

Muffled by Jax's chest, I asked, "Are you okay? You said you weren't feeling well."

Tina shrugged. "I'm fine. It was a headache."

"That's good."

As she walked away, she called over her shoulder in a singsong voice, "I'll be outta here in half an hour!"

Trying to hide his amusement over our overheard sexcapades, Jax said, "I'm gonna go too, but I'll be back later. I want to shower and need to get some stuff done. I should be done by three. Can I come back then?"

"You better!" I teased.

After kissing me goodbye, I watched him leave from my perch.

Tina walked back in and cocked a brow at me. "That didn't take long."

"What?"

"Jumping each other's bones. You weren't even originally going to be back until later today."

I gave Tina a rundown of my early arrival and encounter with Jax, or the part up until we arrived home anyway. I finished it off by declaring, "Last night was the best night of my life."

TRUE TO HIS WORD, Jax arrived at three that afternoon. I'd dozed off while reading on my bedroom couch, which was where he found me.

Gently, he shook me awake. "Hey, Tessa, I'm back."

Half-asleep, I pulled him down into a hug and hummed a greeting to him.

He chuckled and kissed my neck before gently pulling me up off the couch. "Come on, let's go get coffee. I'm tired too."

Despite being exhausted, we walked to the coffee shop off campus, the one Jax and I were headed to the day I'd left for New York. There was a line, but no one was sitting at the tables. While we stood and waited, he asked, "How do you take your coffee?"

I tried to suppress it, but a giggle escaped me.

"What? It's important for a guy to know these things about his woman."

Raising a brow, I repeated, "Your woman?"

He leaned in close. "My girlfriend?"

Confirming I liked that title, I beamed at him. My face was starting to hurt from smiling so much.

Getting back to his question, I gave him the sad truth. "I don't like coffee." Jax's face dropped. Leaning in and standing on my toes, I clarified, "But I'd love a chai latte." I gave him a chaste kiss on the lips before sinking back onto my feet.

"Got it. I don't have to share my coffee. More for me."

Giggling again, I rolled my eyes at myself.

His head tilted. "What?"

Smiling, I shrugged and shook my head like it was nothing.

"Tell me," he pressed.

I tsked. "I was thinking that I sound and feel like a giddy schoolgirl on a date with her crush and realized that's exactly what's happening."

Jax laughed as he pulled me in for a hug. Into my neck, he said, "I feel the same way." Then he kissed it.

Phew... My heart might explode. Not wanting to make it completely obvious how much he was affecting me, I pulled back and asked, "You feel like a schoolgirl?"

Jax pressed his lips together. But we both ended up bursting out laughing, drawing the notice of other customers in line and employees behind the counter. A few of them gave us some strange looks, but I brushed it off as us being too loud.

"I walked into that one, huh?" he mused.

Still giggling, I nodded.

We stepped up to the counter when our turn to order arrived. The barista said, "Hi, Jax." She stopped, sneered at me, looked back at him, and growled, "Where's Brooke?"

chapter
seventy

TESSA

ALTHOUGH HE TRIED HIDING IT, I could sense Jax's annoyance at the rude coffee shop employee. "I don't know. We broke up."

The girl looked me up and down, unimpressed, before asking, "Oh. So what can I get you?"

He gave our order then told me to take a seat while he waited for our drinks. I decided on a couple of stools at the front window overlooking the large campus courtyard across the street. But I didn't choose the spot for the view. Here, Jax and I'd be sitting next to each other, not across with a table between us.

After placing our drinks down on the countertop, Jax sat and sighed. "I guess I should probably get used to people asking me about Brooke for a while."

I nodded. "You were together a long time, and everyone on campus seems to know you. If they've ever been to Smythie's, that is."

Smirking, he teased, "I think you're the only one on campus who hadn't been to the bar at least once during your first year here."

He chuckled when I stuck my tongue out at him.

Picking up my cup to take a sip, I stopped when a flash of blue caught my eye. Putting my drink back down, I examined my bracelet. A silver butterfly charm with blue stones had been added to my chain.

Looking at my boyfriend—*Eek! My boyfriend!*—I tried asking with my eyes, but he remained tight-lipped, hiding his smile behind his coffee cup. "When did this appear?"

With a mischievous glint in his eye, he said, "When I got to your house. You know, you're a really heavy sleeper." He took another sip of his coffee before asking me, "You've figured out what they all mean, right?"

Examining one charm at a time, I said, "Well, the microphone is obvious. You're a singer—"

"And you love when I sing," he teased, knowing me too well.

I giggled again. "Can't deny that. Let's see. The Ferris wheel is obvious."

"Is it?" Jax cocked a brow, his eyes twinkling.

Eyeing him, I admitted, "Now I'm doubting myself."

He put his cup down, turned his body to face mine, and took a breath. "The first time I seriously considered kissing you was on the Ferris wheel. Honestly, if I wasn't afraid the car would start swinging, I might have."

My mouth popped open. "Oh..." I breathed. "Well, I wanted to kiss you the first time I saw you. In fact, when I saw you at the bar, before I saw Brooke's tongue down your throat, I was seriously considering letting you take me home, which is very unlike me."

He leaned in and whispered, "I know. I saw you eye-fucking me. If I'd been single, I wouldn't have hesitated."

I chuckled. I was unquestionably a fool in love. Looking at the X, I said, "I'm assuming this one represents our first kiss."

Deadpan, Jax said, "And math."

"Math!" I spat too loudly.

He giggled this time. "It's because of math that I fell in love with you. Maybe it would've happened eventually anyway, but seeing you at least three times a week helped."

"And the butterfly?"

Jax leaned over, nuzzling my cheek. "I told you, butterflies are important." He kissed my cheek before pulling back.

So happy I wanted to cry, I smiled with tingling eyes. How was it even possible to fall more in love with him? Leaning in, I placed a soft kiss on his lips. "Thank you for the new charm. I love it."

In response, he flashed his rare, toothy, big, beautiful smile.

After taking a couple of more sips of my tea, I asked, "So what was it you wanted to talk about after the final?"

He gave an ironic laugh. "You haven't figured that out yet? Basically, what we talked about on Christmas."

"Ah," I nodded. Mulling it over, my smile faded. It had only been a month since their breakup, and even though he'd ended the relationship, Jax and Brooke were together for years. I chewed my lip. *Is a month long enough?* I wasn't sure since I'd never had an actual break-up from a long-term relationship before.

Silent for too long, Jax nudged my shoulder.

Whispering, I asked, "Are you ready?"

Although he gave me a gentle smile, there was sadness in his eyes. "When I saw you last night, I couldn't wait anymore. I was standing at the railing when you walked in and you took my breath away, like you had so many times before. If you hadn't seen me, I would've run after you. I wasn't about to let you get away."

We stared at each other for several seconds, grins on our faces, but the fact that he hadn't actually answered my question needled me. One thing I liked about Jax was his honesty. As far as I could tell, he didn't lie, however I also knew he didn't always answer or say something either. He'd rather say nothing than lie.

Interrupting my musings, Jax took my hand. "I wanted to kiss you at the airport when I dropped you off, but I didn't think it was a good idea, so I settled on your forehead."

I took a sip of my drink while I debated if I would have let him or liked it at that moment. I'd thought he was still with Brooke at that time, and I'd told him nothing else would happen until they broke up. Yet, I wasn't sure how I would've reacted.

While using my drink as an excuse to continue my silent deliberations, the entrance door chimed. Vaguely, I was aware of a small group of people entering.

"Isn't that Jax?" a whiny female voice said.

My hand stilled with my cup halfway to my mouth.

"Oh. My. God. Is it true? Did Jax and Brooke break up? Who's he with?" another one asked.

Refusing to look in their direction, I stared at the sunny courtyard in front of me.

"I heard Jax cheated on Brooke. Maisie told me. Do you think that's the girl he cheated on her with?" a third said.

In a disgusted voice, one of them declared, "Well, if it is, she's a ho. Hopefully she doesn't give him any STDs."

They snickered when another one added, "Or maybe he deserves one."

I was disgusted, but Jax looked like he was about to throw something, like maybe his coffee. Reaching out, I stroked his hand as it throttled the innocent cup. He glanced at me with raging fire in his eyes.

"Let it go," I whispered. "It doesn't matter."

Growling, he enunciated every word, "My girlfriend is not a ho." I couldn't stop the happiness I felt from shaping on my lips. His expression changed into a pleased half-smile. Putting his arm around me and leaning in, his lips brushed my ear. "You really do like being called my girlfriend, huh?"

Closing my eyes, I leaned into him, thrilled that even though we'd had sex three times in mere hours, the butterflies hadn't died at all. Running my hand up his abdomen, loving that I could touch him whenever and however I wanted to now, I hummed my response, "Uh-huh."

"Perhaps my girlfriend wants to take our drinks outta here?"

I cooed, feeling my face catching fire. With my lips at his ear, I explained, "After the last time, I'm not sure I can at the moment."

Jax's panty-dropping smile curved up the side of his mouth. "Oh, Tessa...there are many things we can do that won't hurt."

Despite feeling a touch bashful in the light of day, I wasn't about to turn him down.

FEELING BLISSFULLY EXHAUSTED and sore all over, I cuddled into Jax's naked chest as he stroked my hair, much like how we'd been after our first time. Evidently, with enough foreplay, I wasn't too sore for more sex, although I doubted my ability to walk at that moment.

"Hey, Tess?" Jax asked softly.

"Hmm?" I responded, half-asleep.

"Are you on birth control?"

Suddenly wide awake, I popped up. "Yeah. Why? You don't want to use condoms?"

"I always use condoms," he said emphatically. Looking away, his eyes squinted in what I thought was annoyance. "Well, almost always."

"Okay..." Where was he going with this?

"I like to be extra careful, that's all. I want kids someday, but not anytime soon."

"Understandable." I laid my head on his chest. "In case we ever slip up, I have an implant, so you don't have to worry about me forgetting to take a pill or whatever."

"Maybe we should get tested before any possible slip-ups."

Pointing in the direction of my nightstand, I asked, "Hand me my phone, please."

He did. After logging into my health portal app and bringing up my test results from only a couple of weeks ago, I handed it back to him. "I had my annual physical during break, and my doctor always runs tests unless specifically asked not to."

Jax took my phone and looked at my clean bill of health.

He locked the screen and put my phone back. "I should've done that too, but Brooke and I were both clean, and I can't imagine she cheated on me."

He might've trusted her, but I had no reason to. For all I knew, she could've cheated on him out of spite. Saving me from having to ask, he volunteered, "I'll go get tested to be sure."

"Thanks."

Jax adjusted our positions so we were both on our sides, facing each other. He gently caressed my face as he gazed at me.

After a few seconds, I asked, "What?"

He shrugged the shoulder he wasn't lying on. "Nothing, just looking at you. You have no idea how long I've wanted to sit and stare at your face, memorizing every detail." I smiled shyly. "Hey, don't pretend you weren't doing the same thing when I was up on stage… every week," he teased.

Indignantly, I exclaimed, "What!"

"Did you really think I didn't notice?"

I covered my face with my hands. "But everyone watches you when you're on stage, don't they?"

He gently pulled my hands away from my face. "The other guys do have their own fangirls, you know. But when you watch me, it's different. Your eyes sparkle. I could always tell how you were feeling or what you thought of the songs we played based on your expressions. I still remember the first time you saw me up there. You had come from the bathroom, I think. When you glanced up, you caught me watching you. You were surprised I was the singer, then pleased."

"I do have a weak spot for singers," I acknowledged.

"I noticed."

I laughed at myself. "What can I say? I'm a sucker for beautiful voices. But you know, I was crazy attracted to you even before I knew you were in a band, let alone the singer," I sheepishly admitted. "But anyway, I hope I didn't make you uncomfortable when I was ogling you."

Jax looked away. "This is going to make me sound full of myself, but I'm used to it. I get that a lot. Some girls don't give a shit if I'm in a relationship or not."

Seriously displeased, I whined, "You mean I'm going to have to chase girls off?"

Laughing, Jax tried to reassure me, "No, no! I'm all yours! I've only got eyes for you." His smile faded, and he looked away. "Even when I shouldn't have."

That dimmed the mood. So I quickly brought up something fluffy, "Is Mr. Toasty Toes at Chuck's?"

"No, why?"

"Is Chuck allergic to cats?"

"Not that I know of."

My face brightened. "Then bring Toasty here! I want to meet him!"

"Can't. Chuck's parents would kill both of us if we brought an animal into that house or yours. They're really strict about no pets."

Disappointed, I pursed my lips. "Oh."

Exhausted but euphoric, I snuggled back into his chest, falling asleep wrapped in his arms for the second night in a row.

TUESDAY BROUGHT the first day of classes for my last semester of school, ever. Jax had stayed over again and left early for class while I'd slept for another hour. The man was sinfully exhausting.

Sitting at a computer in one of the computer lab classrooms, I saw a familiar face enter the room but couldn't quite place him. He was tall, built with defined muscles and dark eyes that matched his dark hair. He wasn't my type but by no means bad looking. Our eyes met, and he came over.

"Hi," he greeted, "is this seat taken?"

I wasn't pleased but wasn't going to be rude. "No, it's open."

After sitting down, he faced me, smiling. "Tess, right?" He had perfect teeth that were blindingly white.

"Uh...yeah." Had I met him before?

The dark-eyed stranger held out his hand. "I'm Dave. It's nice to meet you. We're actually neighbors. I live a few houses down from you."

Vague memories started to surface. Taking his hand, I said, "Nice to meet you too. I don't remember seeing you on our street, but I think I've seen you a few times at Smythie's, right?"

"Yeah, I'm there a lot." He rolled his eyes. "What else is there to do around here?"

I nodded. "True."

"You're a runner, right? I've seen you run past my place a bunch of times."

I laughed self-consciously. "Oh, yeah. I usually run three to five times a week."

"I run too. Maybe we could run together some time?"

Before I realized what I was saying, I said, "Oh, sure." Then I mentally spanked myself. I wasn't exactly comfortable with the way he was looking at me and thought perhaps I should make it known I had a boyfriend.

Before our conversation could continue, the professor started class. During her first day of class monologue, she advised us, "Take a look at the person next to you. That person is going to be your partner throughout this class. You will have a couple of individual projects, but most will be various projects with your partner."

The lab was set up with two computers per table, so I was stuck with Dave and not exactly thrilled about it. He seemed like a nice enough guy, and other than the feeling like maybe he was a little too interested in me, he was paying attention and probably wouldn't push all the work off on me. The class was an elective that was supposed to help with public speaking and creating engaging presentations. I wasn't a person who liked speaking publicly, so I'd figured if I forced myself to take a class like this, it would help build confidence that would come in handy as a law enforcement officer.

As I sat there, listening to the professor, knots started forming in my belly, but I wasn't sure if it was because of the thought of public speaking, or something else.

chapter
seventy-one

jaXOn

TUESDAY AFTERNOON, I kept an eye on the street corner Tess would appear from within the next few minutes as Chuck and I chatted outside his house. She showed me her running route so I'd know where to look if she didn't return in a reasonable amount of time.

The blonde beauty turned the corner, and I checked the clock on my phone. From what she'd told me, she had made good time. She was a cautious runner, always looking around and behind her, even on this quiet side street. I smiled as she ran in my direction, admiring her breasts bouncing in her sports bra. Her body was fucking perfect, and perfect for fucking.

Stopping right in front of me, she took her earbuds out and greeted me breathlessly, "Hey."

"Hi," I said before kissing her forehead.

"Ah!" she squeaked and shooed me away. "I'm all sweaty!"

Trying not to laugh, I pointed out, "I've seen you sweat before, like last night when you—"

She covered my mouth with her hands. "Shhh...Jax!"

Putting a hand over hers to hold them in place, I kissed the palm covering my lips. She smiled and shook her head at me then looked over her shoulder again.

Following her line of sight, I saw nothing of interest. "What're you looking at?"

She jumped like I'd caught her doing something she shouldn't have been. "Oh, nothing."

Did she just lie to me? I looked past her again. Maybe not as there wasn't anything worth noticing.

Realizing she hadn't greeted Chuck yet, she turned to him, "Hey, Chuck. How's it going?"

He shrugged. "It's going. I have this new roommate, but he's never here, so it's like he doesn't actually live here. He only comes home to shower and change."

Tess giggled while I retorted, "I shower at Tess's too."

He rolled his eyes, but chuckled. "You gonna be home tonight?"

I looked at Tess, who was looking down the street again. "Probably not."

He perked up. "Good. I'm having company tonight."

Tess turned her attention back to him. "In that case, I'll make sure he stays with me and doesn't interrupt you."

"I don't know, Tess... You might have to tie me to the bed," I teased.

She huffed but wasn't actually mad. Walking toward her house, she called out, "See ya later, Chuck. I'm going to shower, Jax."

Walking backward toward Tess's house, I told Chuck, "I'm gonna go join her. See you later."

Again my best friend rolled his eyes, but I knew he didn't give a fuck. He liked Tess, and he liked us together. Sure, he could go without knowing the specifics of our physical relationship, but I didn't care. Tess was hot, and now that I've had her, I couldn't get enough. She'd taught me there was a saying about the quiet ones for a reason.

ALTHOUGH SHE TRIED to hide it, Tess failed. The closer Friday got, the more anxious she got. I found out why Friday afternoon.

"Hey, Jax," Tess started, "so, umm, maybe I should skip Smythie's tonight."

Surprised and disappointed, I asked, "Why?"

She loved watching me on stage, and now that she could have me after I got off, I fully intended to let her show me exactly how much she liked my performances.

"Uh, well, it's the first Friday back, and there will be a lot of people there, and..."

"So what?"

Avoiding looking at me, she focused on refolding the same pair of jeans twice.

"Are you worried about what others are saying?" I'd heard the comments and gossip all week. Apparently Tess had too. Saturday at the coffee shop had only been a preview. But I'd be damned if I'd let those assholes keep my girlfriend away from the bar. I'd kick those fuckers out if they didn't keep their comments to themselves, or at least out of her earshot. They could say whatever about me, but I wouldn't let anyone disrespect my girl.

Taking her hand, I put it to my lips. "I really want you there with me, but I won't make you go."

Although hesitant, I knew she wanted to be there.

Taking the low road of bribery, I told her, "We're playing your favorite song."

Tess was great at a lot of things, but hiding the way she felt and her emotions was not one of them. She tried so hard to not smile, but it was there. Finally she conceded, "Alright, I'll go."

"Good! Go get dressed," I commanded before slapping her ass.

She jumped, squeaked, then ran off giggling.

SHE SHOULD HAVE STAYED HOME!

If I had any less self-control, I would have ended up in jail for beating the shit out of someone.

While standing at the bar, dude after dude kept coming up to Tess, asking her to dance. Chuck saw me fuming and provided some clarity for her sudden popularity. Everyone knew she and Eli had broken up, but along with that there was a rumor that she was easy. I wanted to punch every single motherfucker who approached her. Eventually, I stood next to her and glared at every male who came within ten feet of her.

When a petite, unnaturally blonde woman came around, I thought nothing of it...until I heard her. "Hey, girl! Wanna dance?"

Tess looked utterly confused. "Thanks, but I'm straight."

With genuine disappointment, the girl said, "Oh, really? Bummer. I heard you were bi."

I interjected, "Even if she was, she has a boyfriend."

"Oh? I heard you and that preppy guy broke up?" petite blondie asked Tessa.

I'd never felt so possessive of a girl before, but goddammit! Getting a little more defensive than I needed to be, I snapped, "I'm her boyfriend!"

The girl eyed me curiously. "Ah...so that part is true. Huh." She walked away as if everything had become clear.

"What part?" Tess called out, far too late to be heard over the music. Turning to me with anxious eyes, she started, "Jax, I—I'm going to the bathroom."

Another guy approached. "Hey, Tess."

Her face went from confused to exhausted. "Hi, Dave."

Oh, fuck this!

"'Scuse us." I grabbed Tessa's hand and dragged her out onto the dance floor. Tangling my hand in her hair, I pulled her in for a kiss that left no mistake about who she was going home with tonight. Releasing her lips when she became breathless, I pulled her close and started moving us to the beat. I'd gotten my first taste of dancing with her those few weeks ago when I'd used any other girl willing to make my way over to her, creating an excuse to touch her again. Now I could touch her all I wanted, wherever I wanted, whenever I wanted. It'd only been a week, but I already knew every inch of her body and every sensitive spot that drove her crazy.

To my pleasant surprise, she wasn't shy about exploring my body either. One of her favorite things to do was run her hand from my chest down to my dick. *Fuck!* I was getting hard and needed to be on stage in a few minutes. This was enough. I'd made my point. By the time the song ended, the whole damned bar would know we were together.

Brushing my lips against Tess's ear, which made her weak in the knees, I said, "I need to cool off before I get on stage." To make sure she understood what I meant, I ground my boner into her.

She nodded. "Bathroom."

Holy shit! Did she want to fuck in the bathroom? That wasn't what I had meant, but that would've definitely taken care of the problem in my pants. *Hmm... Do I have enough time to bend her over the desk in the office upstairs before I have to be on stage?*

But Tess let me go and headed to the hall where the restrooms were located. Afraid to let her out of my sight, I followed. I'd wait for her outside the women's bathroom.

Once we turned the corner and got into the noticeably quieter hallway, she inquired, "What was that for?"

I shrugged. "Making a statement, I guess."

"Kind of reminded me of a dog marking his territory."

I didn't comment, as we were within earshot of three girls. Two were listening to the one talking. The talker, a wannabe runway model named Tanya, was unfortunately a girl I had the mistake of knowing a little too intimately before I'd met Brooke. She was wasting oxygen by talking shit.

"Yeah, and the four of them used to hook up. You know, like swingers."

A short and curvy girl I didn't know said, "Oh wow! No way!"

Tanya continued spewing bullshit, "Yeah, and you know Brooke and Eli used to be a thing back in high school. Rumor is Brooke followed him here. She used to be obsessed with him, but then she met Jax."

The third girl looked petrified when she spotted Tess and I. We'd stopped to listen.

The second talker said, "That's so crazy, but I wonder what happened. Like did Jax get bored or something and decide to change things up?"

"I don't know about that," Tanya said, sounding so sure of herself, "but one thing is for sure, that blonde girl he's hooking up with now is a total home-wrecker. He'll probably dump her after he gets bored. Maybe he'll go crawling back to Brooke and beg for another chance.

They looked so good together. I didn't even care when he stopped hooking up with me after he met her. Honestly, even I would've fucked Brooke if I had a dick."

Don't have to have a dick to be one.

I glanced at Tess from the corner of my eye. She looked pale and unhappy. *Great.*

"Yeah, you know they would've made such gorgeous babies, right?" girl two said. "Jax is an idiot."

With some effort, I unclenched my teeth with enough time to cut Tanya off before she got too far into saying, "Yeah, seriously. That girl he's with is a ska—"

"I dare you to finish that sentence, Tanya," I snapped.

Girl number two and Tanya spun around, while the girl who had seen us slowly backed away.

Glaring, I seethed, "Go ahead, then you'll get to experience how fast the bouncers can throw your ass out."

"You don't have that kind of power," she sneered.

I smirked. "Wanna bet?"

"Whatever." She flipped her long dark head back then pushed past me muttering, "Fuckin' dog deserves a bitch."

Thankfully, I didn't think Tess heard. Turning my ghost-white girlfriend toward me, I asked, "You okay? Don't listen to them. They're—"

Her glistening eyes met mine, and it felt like a jab to my gut. "Jax... I'm gonna go. I don't wanna be here anymore."

My jaw clenched, but I had to respect her wishes. Hell, at that point, even I didn't want her there anymore for her own sake. I nodded. "Text me when you get home, okay? Even if I'm on stage, I'll have my phone. If you don't text me, I'll run off the stage and come find you."

She let out a weak laugh. "Sure."

"I'll walk you out after you use the bathroom."

As soon as the restroom door shut behind her, I ran to the closest bouncer.

chapter
seventy-two

TESSA

JAX GAVE me a quick kiss and reminded me to text him when I got home. Then he headed back inside, as the band was already late to start their first set.

When I had walked about twenty or so yards, the bar's doors flew open with a commotion. The girl named Tanya, who was apparently on Jax's list of conquests, was being escorted out of the bar by two bouncers.

Protesting, she yelled, "Hey! This isn't fair! You can't do this! That asshole! Don't listen to Jax! I want to speak to the manager! This isn't fair!"

One of the bouncer's said, "The managers take their orders from the owner. And the owner doesn't care what you have to say. Haven't you realized how much influence Jax has? Next time, don't run your mouth off about him or his girlfriend. You can come back next week. If you run your mouth again, you'll be blacklisted."

Jax has that much power? And was the owner there tonight, or had Jax called them while I was in the bathroom?

"Fuck you!" Tanya shouted as she walked in the opposite direction.

AS PROMISED, I texted Jax when I got home.

My Butterflies

After double-checking all the locks, I got ready for bed. Perhaps it was from what happened at the bar, but I couldn't shake the uneasy feeling. Instead of my anxiety fading as I got closer to home, it only grew. I'd walked to and from Smythie's multiple times by myself, but tonight felt different. I assumed it was from all the eyes and pointing fingers during the week.

Before I left the bar, Jax promised it'd die down soon enough and to ignore it the best I could. It was ironic. One reason I liked our university was because it was small and people actually knew one another. But now? I hated that the school was so small. I wanted to become invisible again but knew that wouldn't happen, especially now that I was the local rockstar's girlfriend, known to pretty much everyone.

After climbing into bed, I checked my phone and saw Jax had replied to my text even though he was on stage. It was another selfie of him with the crowd in the background, smiling and singing. I waited until I thought their first set would be over before I texted him again.

TESSA GIVENS

I'm really tired. I'm going to sleep. All the doors are locked, so I'll see you tomorrow. Goodnight, jaXOn

A few minutes later, Tina texted me.

TINA REYNOLDS

Jax asked if he could borrow my key. He's worried about you. Are you OK with him coming over tonight?

TESSA GIVENS

Sure

I changed over to the chat with my boyfriend.

TESSA GIVENS

I told Tina she could loan you her key. Please make sure to lock the door after you come in.

Putting my phone on the charger, I rolled over and went to sleep, not bothering to see if there were any replies.

. . .

THE NEXT THING I was conscious of was the bed shifting.

Half-asleep, I rolled over and cuddled into Jax, mumbling, "Did you lock the door?"

"Yeah." He kissed my head. "Sorry. I was trying not to wake you."

"It's fine."

"Are you okay?"

"Yeah, fine. Goodnight." It sounded unconvincing, so I knew he wouldn't have bought it. Sprawled on top of his bare chest, I started tingling. My head became heady as I breathed through my nose. *Mmmmm...* "Did you shower?"

"Yeah, I always shower after being on stage. I get pretty sweaty up there."

Crawling on top of him, I purred, "I'm suddenly very awake. Should we finish what we started on the dance floor?"

He chuckled in the darkness. "Sure, but I'm pretty tired."

I reached over to my bedside table and grabbed a foil packet. We'd stopped putting them in the drawer because we went through them so quickly. "That's okay," I said between kissing his face and neck. "Luckily I had a nap."

TAKING my seat next to Dave, he immediately said, "So it's true that you and the singer are dating? He left that redhead for you?"

Did he seriously say it like that? Perhaps the guy didn't have good social etiquette.

Trying to keep my temper in check, I explained, "I am dating Jax. He and Brooke broke up in December. Jax and I didn't start dating until like a week and a half ago." It wasn't a lie, but even I wondered if Jax had left Brooke for me or if he would have continued to put up with her crap if I wasn't around.

"Oh, I see. So the rumors aren't true then?"

Wholly done with this conversation, I said, "I'm not sure if I've heard them all, so all I can tell you is the truth. Jax and I didn't get into a relationship until recently, like a month or so after he and Brooke broke up."

Dave smiled at me. "Don't worry, Tess. Forget what other people think! Also, I hope I didn't give you the wrong impression the other night at Smythie's when I came over to speak to you. I actually had a question about our assignment due today, but I didn't have your number or email or anything, so..."

"Oh yeah...sorry about that. Friday night was weird. Anyway, yeah, you'll need my contact info since we'll have to work on projects together anyway."

chapter
seventy-three

TESSA

RUNNING MY USUAL ROUTE, I reflected on the last few weeks. Jax and I had been together for nearly a month and had pretty much gone from zero to sixty in two seconds. We were nearly inseparable, only leaving each other's sides when we had to. Since I considered running a must, Jax had tried running with me once but couldn't keep up. He joked about getting a bike so he could ride next to me, but I told him I preferred being alone while I ran. I listened to music and zoned out. What I hadn't mentioned was that I'd figured out a way to get the music he'd recorded for me onto my phone, so I listened to him singing more than he thought.

Sure, Jax technically lived with Chuck, but Chuck's house was more his closet and bathroom. He'd go there to shower and change. Tina spent most nights at Jamar's house. He had a fantastic job, so he paid for her ride-shares when he couldn't drive her back and forth himself. Although she said she didn't mind because she loved staying with Jamar, as did he, I still felt guilty. It was like Jax and I were keeping her from coming home. I promised we'd either be quiet or keep our hands to ourselves or go to Chuck's, but she laughed it off and told me to have fun, because she was.

It took a couple of weeks, but, as Jax had predicted, the rumors, nasty comments, and side-eyes eventually cooled off around campus and Smythie's. I wondered if the gossip would have died down sooner if Brooke hadn't been showing up at the bar every week. I hadn't noticed her the first week after break, but Jax had seen her hiding in a corner.

Even though we didn't have any classes together, we kept our weekly Wednesday night visits to the library going. It was our way of forcing ourselves not to get distracted and slack off.

Although new, our relationship didn't feel like it. When you spent nearly all your free time with someone, it was impossible to always put your best foot forward like one would expect when you first started dating. In actuality, it didn't even feel like we were dating, since we'd barely gone on any dates. Was I too comfortable with Jax for the amount of time we'd actually been a couple? Sure, we'd been friends for months before we'd gotten together, but friendship and romance were different. I mean, how much did I actually know him? We had a solid foundation, but were we heading in the right direction?

Sometimes things felt off. Like he'd ignore his phone when it was going off, or if he took a call, he'd leave the room. Sure, the man was entitled to his privacy, but then why hang around me so much if he needed that much privacy? Usually on Saturdays or Sundays, he'd disappear for a few hours, telling me he had to run errands. He never told me what they were, and I was afraid asking would be prying. I offered to go with him once, but he shot me down so immediately that I couldn't help but wonder if he was being secretive on purpose.

Doubts about his trustworthiness crept in. Getting so caught up in my feelings for him, I hadn't even thought about trust being an issue. Did I trust Jax? Brooke's voice echoed in the back of my head, "Just remember, you lose'em how you get'em."

My unease wasn't only about Jax either. It seemed crazy, but sometimes it felt like someone was watching me, but when I looked, I saw nothing, likely because there was nothing. Eventually, I chalked it up to final-semester jitters or something. After all, soon, I'd be a full-fledged adult and have to make my own way in the real world.

Turning onto my street at the end of my run, I saw Jax sitting on my front steps, listening to the earbuds I'd given him, looking at his phone, probably studying lyrics for his show this week. He did know all the songs the band played, but he still needed to brush up on the lyrics here and there. Not wanting to disturb him, I stopped a few feet away for my cool down. As I turned to stretch my back, my eyes took in the scene behind me, looking for anything that might've been off.

Jax's voice made me jump. "Looking at nothing again?"

Although he looked serious, I tried laughing it off. "What are you talking about? I was stretching."

"Whenever you get back from a run, you're always looking behind you. Why?"

I shook my head as I walked past him into the house. "I don't know what you're talking about."

"Right." Glancing over my shoulder, I noted his annoyed tone matched his expression.

However, all annoyance slipped away as I slipped out of my running clothes on my way to the shower. Looking over my shoulder, I asked, "Coming?"

He smirked. "I will, but only after you, of course." Following my lead, he discarded his clothing on the way to the bathroom.

GRINDING INTO JAX, I moaned as his fingers squeezed my nipples. Trails of sweat ran down my body as I edged closer to ecstasy. He released a nipple and slid his hand between my legs where his thumb stared stimulating me. My head fell back with a loud moan when his other hand slapped my ass.

"Look at me, Tess," Jax demanded as the pressure of his thumb increased.

He knew I was close and loved looking into my eyes when I came, especially while I was on top of him. Intending to do as he said, I rolled my head around, gazing out the window for a split second before I heard a blood-curdling scream...that came from my own throat.

chapter
seventy-four

jaXOn

WHEN TESS SCREAMED, I thought I'd have a heart attack. It was a petrified, "someone is trying to kill me" scream.

"Holy shit! Did I hurt you?" I exclaimed.

White as a ghost, Tess stared out the window, her arms covering her chest, damn near hyperventilating. I sat up and wrapped my arms around her trembling body. Looking over my shoulder, I peered out the window. What was she looking at? All I saw was the blackness of the night.

"Babe, what's wrong?" Two seconds passed. "Tessa?"

Blinking, she shook her head. "Sorry, I'm sorry. I thought I saw something." Rubbing her eyes, she tried to explain, "I think... I think I'm not getting enough sleep. And I'm kind of stressed out. I'm sorry. I'm gonna go take a shower to try to relax. Then I'm going to sleep."

Incredulous, I asked, "You're going to go shower now?"

Her cheeks turned pink and she avoided looking at me as she climbed off my lap. "I'm sorry. I'll shut the door. You can jerk off if you need to, and I'll knock before I come in or whatever."

I jumped off the bed and caught her by the arm. "I'm not worried about that. I'm worried about you."

She couldn't, or wouldn't, meet my eyes. "I'm sorry. I'm stressed. Please..." She tugged her arm, and I let go.

When released, she nearly ran out of her bedroom.

Grabbing the pair of pajama pants I kept there for when Tina was home and I needed to take a leak in the middle of the night, I slid them on after disposing of the now unnecessary condom.

Walking over to the window, I inspected it. Looking outside, I saw nothing. I couldn't even see the tree line I knew was back there. Clueless, I pulled the shade closed. Sitting on the couch, I waited. The room was only lit by the string of lights on the wall above the bed. I considered turning more on, but decided that if Tess wanted more light, she would've turned them on.

After what felt like an hour, she came in and went to her dresser to pull out some pajamas. As she slid them on, I realized it was the first time I'd seen her in pajamas, other than Christmas morning. Dressed, she walked over and sat on the bed across from me.

"Sorry," she said again.

"Why do you keep apologizing?" I asked, softly.

"Because, you know, we were having sex and didn't...finish."

"Babe, although I love having sex with you, I'm not some crazed sex-maniac who needs to come multiple times a day. It's nice, and I like when it happens, but shit happens." She said nothing. "You know how many times Brooke and I had sex since I met you?"

She looked pissed that I dared to bring her up, but I needed to make my point. "Like maybe six or seven times. Definitely less than ten."

Her eyes widened.

"As I've told you many times before, she and I were having serious issues before I met you. But that's not the point I'm trying to make. What I'm trying to say is I don't have to have sex constantly. If something happens, I won't die if I don't come. Especially not when I'm worried about you. What's going on with you lately?"

Tess huffed. "I don't know what to tell you, Jax, other than what I've already said. I'm tired, stressed, and maybe running too much. I'll cut back on running and try to get more sleep."

For whatever reason, she didn't want to open up to me. I stood and walked over to where she sat on the bed. Putting my hands on her shoulders, I said, "You know you can talk to me about anything, right?"

She looked unconvinced but nodded, probably just to shut me up. I kissed her forehead before climbing back into bed.

That night, Tess slept uneasily. I held her, hoping my arms could provide some comfort to her while she slept. She was a sleep talker, and I was a light sleeper, so on nights like that, my own sleep was off and on. Although the talking was usually gibberish, based on what I could make out, there was definitely something bothering her. Unfortunately, I was going to have to wait until she felt comfortable enough to tell me.

MY PHONE RATTLED against the wooden library table. Brooke was calling me...again. Ignoring it, I sent her to voicemail. A minute later, my phone lit up with a text.

BROOKE

Jax! WTF? Why won't you answer your fucking phone?

JAX

Because I have nothing to say.

BROOKE

I have something to say! Can't you give me a second to say it?

JAX

Then say it.

BROOKE

I can't over text. It's complicated.

JAX

Then I guess it's not that important. I already told you I'm not talking in person.

BROOKE

Why? Afraid to face me after you left me for that bitch?

JAX

No. And if you call her a bitch again, I'm blocking you. Say what you need to say then move on.

BROOKE

Move on, really? After everything you've put me through? After everything you did! With everything I'm dealing with right now! You are such an asshole! Sometimes I wish I never met you!

JAX

I never thought you'd be one to keep hanging on.

BROOKE

I'm not! I don't want you back! BUT I NEED TO TALK TO YOU!

JAX

Whatever. Either say it or leave me alone.

BROOKE

You can't avoid me forever!

Frustrated, I dropped my phone on the table and it landed with a clatter.

Concerned, Tess queried, "What's wrong, love?"

"Brooke," I said through my teeth. "She won't leave me alone."

"Oh?"

"She keeps calling and texting me, asking to meet in person because there's some stuff she wants to say. I told her to text me because when I spoke to her a couple of times on the phone after we broke up, all she did was yell at me, so now I won't take her calls. All she does is blame me for the demise of our relationship. Sure, I wasn't perfect, but it's not like it was all my fault things went bad."

Tess looked away, digesting what I said."Maybe now that it's been a while she needs some closure. Maybe she needs it to help her move on. I don't really blame her for wanting to talk to you in person about that."

I wasn't convinced.

"So, uh... The calls you've been ignoring were her?"

"You noticed that?"

She looked away. "Kind of hard to miss."

"Yeah, they were her."

Giving her opinion, she said, "I think closure is important. I don't mind if you speak to her if that's what she needs to move on. Not having closure really sucks."

"I'll keep that in mind."

Tess chewed on her bottom lip.

"What? The steam's coming out your ears again," I joked.

"The calls when you leave the room?"

Ah, I get it... Tess thought I was hiding something from her. Maybe that was one reason she'd been stressed lately. While not exactly wrong, it was nothing to worry about.

"When I leave the room, those calls are with my uncle. He's also my attorney, so there's attorney-client privilege. There are things I can't talk to him about in front of others."

Tess's eyes widened. "Oh!"

"Babe, you can always ask me whatever you want. I may not be able to give you an answer right away, but I'll always be honest."

She gave me a small smile. "Okay. Thanks."

I didn't miss the fact that the offer wasn't reciprocated.

A COUPLE OF NIGHTS LATER, I was half-asleep with Tess resting on my chest when she whispered, "You awake?"

Mumbling, I said, "Depends."

She scoffed, "On what?"

I hugged her. "On whether you're sleep-talking again or not."

She didn't respond, so I popped an eye open. She looked one-third shocked, one-third embarrassed, and one-third terrified. I couldn't hold in my laughter.

Horrified, she whispered, "What do I say?"

"It's mostly gibberish, but you tell me you love me a lot."

Tess snuggled into me. "That's true, but you know that."

I thought back to the things I'd been able to make out. "You say my name a lot. You say words here and there, but they're mixed up with mumbling, so I'm not sure what it's about. You also seem anxious sometimes."

Her body stiffened. "Uh, yeah. I told you I'm a little stressed."

I sighed. "I know. When you're restless, I hold you close. You usually calm down quickly after that."

"Wow, I had no idea. I've never slept with someone, literally, before you. Well, I mean some friends here and there and teammates when traveling for games, but no one's ever said anything."

"Didn't I see you leaving Eli's one morning?" *A morning I wish I could forget.*

She laughed humorously. "Did you notice I looked like a complete wreck? I stayed over there twice, but neither time did I sleep at all. I was too uncomfortable being there."

"Hmm. You always seem comfortable with me."

"Because I am. I love you. I was never even close to being in love with him."

I smiled to myself. *Fuck you, Eli!* "Tessa?"

"Hmm?"

"I love you too."

She hugged me tighter.

Trying not to laugh, I went in for the kill. "Now, weren't you about to ask me about Valentine's Day?"

She stilled then bolted upright. "What? How did you—"

Chuckling, I explained, "Because you said something in your sleep about a Valentine's Day date, so I made reservations."

She picked up her pillow and whacked me with it. "You! You failed to mention that part!"

Laughing a bit harder, I teased, "I know. What fun would it be if I told you?"

She huffed, her hand on her forehead like she couldn't believe her brain had betrayed her in her sleep.

Rolling over onto my stomach, I wrapped my arms around her waist and placed my head in her lap. "So you gonna be my Valentine?"

She giggled. *God I love that sound!* "I suppose so, even though you love teasing me."

Sitting up next to her, I looked her in the eyes and said, "You know what I love more than teasing you?"

"Hmm...me?"

"Your body."

Her mouth dropped open with a scowl. She went for her pillow again, but I caught her arm and pushed her onto her back. Between kissing her face and neck, I confessed, "But... I love... you... most..."

Then I continued down her body, kissing her until I made her toes curl.

chapter
seventy-five

TESSA

FORGETTING ALL ABOUT MANNERS, I put my elbows on the table and rested my chin in my hands as I stared across the table at my smokin' hot boyfriend. I'd never seen him in anything other than casual clothes, sweats and pajama pants, but Jax cleaned up nicely.

We were on our Valentine's dinner date at one very fine Italian restaurant. Earlier, he'd given me flowers and my favorite chocolates.

I had given him a card, some chocolate-covered pretzels—his favorite—and a drawer in my dresser with a copy of my house key stashed inside. It wasn't big and fancy like what he'd done, but it was a huge step for me. Based on his reaction, he knew it. Him showing me his appreciation almost made us late for our reservation.

"You're happy," Jax noted.

I corrected him, "I'm incredibly happy."

Reaching across the table, he took my hand. "Me too."

I looked down at where Jax was stroking the back of my hand. Except he wasn't. His finger was rotating my charm bracelet. I did a double take. "When that get there?"

He gave me his sexy half smile. "While I was waiting for you to finish getting ready."

I took my hand away to get a better look at the newly added charm. A silver heart with "I love you, Tessa" engraved on one side and a date in August on the other. "The date?"

"The day we met."

My heart almost stopped. If it weren't for my bones, I would've melted into a puddle. Placing my hand back in his, I gave him a watery smile.

"You're spoiling me. Thank you. I love you too."

He grinned, pleased with himself. Then his smile faded. "So, have you told your parents about me?"

"Yes, of course."

He swallowed. "Do they know who I am? The guy who had a girlfriend at your soccer game? The guy showed up pissed at your house the day after Thanksgiving?"

I giggled. "Yes, and, in fact, my mom was actually the third person, after me and Tina, who knew I was in love with you." I pretended to give him a stern look. "You were the fourth person to know." Jax's eyebrows shot up. "After you left on Black Friday, my mom found me crying in my room. We're close, so I explained what was going on. She's very easy to talk to and non-judgmental. She advised me against becoming the other woman and suggested I may want to consider staying away from you since it hurt seeing you not only with someone else but in a bad relationship. She was right about it hurting. It hurt seeing you hurting."

Jax stared at his water glass, his expression unreadable. Our meals —steak for him, pasta for me—arrived, so our conversation moved on.

He inquired more about what I preferred when it came to my future career. Small department or big department? Had I considered any federal or state agencies? And so on.

I explained I really wanted to work in a prosecutor's or district attorney's office. "Their investigators are police officers too. They have to go to police academy and everything. But they're detectives who skip the street cop part." I sighed. "But if it's the same in the west as it is in the east, it might be hard getting one of those jobs without connections of some sort. If I go back east, it'd be easier since my dad's a police captain, but I don't want to go back there."

Jax had his signature half-smile on his lips.

"What?" I asked.

"Did I ever tell you what area of law I want to get into?"

I searched my brain. "No, I don't think so."

"I'm pretty sure you would've remembered if I had." My eyes widened with anticipation. Clearly amused, he took his time elaborating, "You want to catch the bad guys. And I want to lock them up."

"You want to be a prosecutor?"

"Yup."

"That's great! But how'd you decide that's the direction you want to go?"

His expression dimmed. "I decided a long time ago that I wanted to be a lawyer. You've probably figured out by now that I like performing and putting on a show. I have no issue being in front of a crowd, so I knew I wanted to do something where I would go to trial. For a long time, I thought I'd be a personal injury lawyer and make a lot of money. But after what happened with my family..." He looked off into the distance. "I guess I'd say my priorities changed."

Beaming at him, I declared, "I think that's great! You know that assistant D.A.s are considered law enforcement officials, right?"

"That's something I only recently learned, actually."

"Huh... Wouldn't that be something?" I mused.

"What?"

Biting my lip, I debated how specific I should be. Not wanting to freak him out by appearing to be planning out our future together after only a month of dating, I went the vague route. "If we both ended up in law enforcement of some sort." What I didn't say out loud was, *Wouldn't it be something if our household was a law enforcement one?* If there was one thing I was absolutely sure of, it was that I wanted Jax in my future, and I could no longer imagine my life without him in it.

chapter
seventy-six

jaXOn

A SCENE FLASHED in my brain for a millisecond. Tess and I walking into work together, years from now, at a D.A.'s office. *Wouldn't that be something?* But it was wishful thinking, unlikely to ever happen. I had to get through law school before I could consider being a lawyer anywhere. And who knew where or what kind of law enforcement job Tess would get?

It was the first time I'd imagined what life would be like with her years from now, not days or months. Had she ever considered what a future with me would look like? *Probably not.* It was too soon for that, right?

Still, I wanted to know more. "If you had your pick, where would you work?"

The flicker of candle fire reflected in her eyes, making them shimmer. "The San Francisco D.A. I love the Bay Area."

Bewildered, I sat in momentary silence. Before I'd met Tess, I thought fate was bullshit. How was it fate that an eighteen-year-old lost his entire family because of some asshole's recklessness? But since she entered my life, I'd wondered more than once if there was something to it. My top-choice law school was Berkeley, which was in the Bay Area. Although I had the test scores and G.P.A. to get in, it was extremely competitive. But I couldn't ignore the fact that San Francisco was where we both wanted to be. She was from the east, yet she was planning on staying in the west. With her soccer skills, she could've gotten into any number of schools, yet she'd chosen a small university with only an up-and-coming soccer program. And even though our school was in Southern California, she wanted to settle in the north. It was bizarre we'd never crossed paths last year when my relationship with Brooke was either fine or only starting to fray. If I'd met her then, although I would've found her attractive, I doubted I would've paid any closer attention. We'd met only when my relationship was hanging by a thread. Was all that fate?

I knew Tess had liked me from our first meeting, but I was positive she would've moved on if she thought Brooke and I were happy. Plus, she and I wouldn't have seen each other much last year. With all the time we'd spent together last semester, she'd come to know me better than anyone, or at least that was what it felt like.

Considering everything...when we met, how much we had in common, how well we understood each other... Was it all too much to be coincidental?

ADMIRING the curve of my girl's ass in her tight new miniskirt a couple of Fridays later, I debated if I was going to hike it up later or risk her wrath and rip the thing off her.

A familiar female voice called my name, ripping me from my musings.

Annoyed, I spun around. "What, Brooke?"

"I really need to talk to you," she pleaded in a very unlike Brooke way, her eyes desperate.

Didn't she understand we were over and I'd moved on? I'd given her more chances than she deserved. Still, Tess's words from a couple of weeks ago reverberated in my head.

Rolling my eyes, I acquiesced. "Fine. What?"

She looked around. "I can't talk to you here."

Crossing my arms, I let my aggravation be heard. "You can't talk to me over the phone, you can't text me, and now that I'm standing in front of you, you still can't say whatever it is you need to say? Why don't you try email or an old-fashioned letter then? Otherwise, leave me alone."

Ignoring the stab of pain I felt seeing her eyes well up, I turned away, and came face-to-face, minus our height difference, with an unimpressed Tess. "Wasn't that a bit harsh? She obviously meant she couldn't talk to you in a noisy, crowded bar. She'd have to yell, and I'm sure whatever she needs to get off her chest is private." I huffed, even though She was right. And apparently, not done. "And by the way, don't you think your song choices tonight are a bit harsh too?"

Tessa never ceased to amaze me. Over the last couple of weeks, Brooke's nagging had become relentless. I was really getting irked by it. So, I did what I always did. I vented my frustration through music, choosing songs about being over the other person or relationship and not wanting anything more to do with them anymore. Basically, songs that screamed figuratively and literally to get lost. Harsh? Maybe, but it wasn't like I knew Brooke was going to keep showing up at the bar when I picked the songs. This was how I did things. It was a form of therapy.

SATURDAY AFTERNOON, Tess was lying face-down on her living room couch as I kneaded my fingers into her back when Tina arrived.

"Hey, you two!" she said brightly.

I smiled. It was a relief Tina didn't hate me. After what happened last semester, I wouldn't have blamed her if she didn't support Tess being with me. "Hey," I greeted while Tess grunted.

"What's wrong?"

Muffled by the couch, my enthusiastic lover explained, "I think I threw out my back or strained a muscle or something. Whatever it is, it hurts."

"Oh no! What were you doin'?"

I snickered. "Me."

Tina's eyes widened before she burst out laughing.

Tess muttered, "Ha ha."

It was a good thing she couldn't see my face, or she might've slapped the smirk right off my lips. It was her own fault though. She'd taken her annoyance with me out in bed last night. She was always especially horny after watching me on stage. Tess wasn't kidding about having a thing for singers. *Hmm...* Was I a shitty boyfriend for being turned on by how she got hurt? My girl could be quite aggressive at times, although she usually preferred being told what to do. However, I did not like that her back was in pain. That wasn't the type of soreness I wanted her to feel.

"Maybe I should sleep on the couch or at Chuck's tonight, so we don't have to be squished together on that tiny bed of yours," I suggested.

She didn't hesitate. "No, I'll live."

"You better, but I need you healed up." I leaned down, my lips brushing her ear. "Can't fuck you in this condition. What kind of boyfriend would I be if I made your back worse?"

After a few seconds, she conceded, "You can sleep on the couch in my room, I guess. But I don't want you to leave."

Pleased, I agreed, "Okay."

After another minute, she said I could stop I sat down next to her, and she put her head on my shoulder.

"You know, we could get you a bigger bed," I offered.

"Can't, not enough room. And where would I put the current one? It's part of the rental, and I have nowhere to store it. Not to mention my lack of funds."

"I've been considering getting my own place."

She sat up. "Really? Why?"

"Chuck's been pretty active lately, like having a lot of company over. He forgets that I technically live there, and I've walked in on him and his guests more than once."

She giggled. "Seriously?"

I rolled my eyes. "Yeah, and it's not like I'm walking into his bedroom either."

Leaning against my shoulder again, she opined, "Sounds like a waste of money. Stay with me. And for the record, I don't mind sleeping close to you, so the size of the bed doesn't matter to me."

Chuckling, I kissed the top of her head. "Okay."

I AWOKE to Tess sleeping half on top of me, half-wedged between my body and the back of the couch. *When had this happened, and how did I not wake up?* Knowing that she preferred sleeping on me on her couch versus alone in her bed made my heart skip a beat. Wrapping my arms fully around her, I gently squeezed.

Blinking at me, she rasped a sleepy, "Hey."

"Morning." I kissed her head. "When'd you get here?"

She snuggled back into my chest. "I don't know. Middle of the night. I was cold and missed you."

"What about your back?"

"It's fine."

"Really?" In an instant, she was under me, and I was kissing her neck as I ground my morning stiffy into her.

Putting her hand down my sweats, she grabbed my dick and said, "Hmm...would be a shame to let this go to waste, wouldn't it?"

"Mm hmm."

One second, I was pushing her tank top up, the next I was on my back with Tess sitting on top of me. "The fuck! How'd you do that?"

Tess slowly rubbed herself against my dick. Purring, she said, "I've got moves you've never seen before, Mr. Smith."

Every fucking day, this girl amazed me, and every fucking day I fell harder for her. "Apparently. Seriously, how'd you do that?"

She put her finger to my lips. "Shh...talk later."

Adjusting herself down my body, she grabbed the elastic of my pants and was about to pull them down when there was a knock on the door. Tess looked over her shoulder, maybe unsure she'd heard right.

"Tess?" Tina called out.

"What?" Tess asked with tinge of disbelief that Tina would be interpreting us.

"I need to come in for a second."

She looked back at me with an expression that read, "Are you kidding me?" but called back, "Can it wait a bit?"

"No."

We exchanged a glance at the absoluteness in Tina's voice.

Relinquishing, Tess said, "One sec." She jumped off me and grabbed the blanket I had been using off the floor and covered my lap. After fixing her tank, she sat down next to me and told Tina she could come in.

The door cracked open, and Tina peeked in. Seeing we were decent, she entered and closed the door. "Brooke's here."

chapter
seventy-seven

TESSA

HESITANTLY, I followed a few steps behind Jax, who was seriously ticked off. I wasn't sure it was a good idea, but as he got dressed, he'd told me to come out with him. When I stepped into the living room, I stopped dead.

Brooke stood in the middle of the room, hugging herself. She looked terrible. I hadn't really gotten a good look at her in the dark lighting of the bar over the last few weeks, but in the natural light coming from the window, I noted her lips were thinner, like maybe she'd stopped getting injections, her hair was more orange than I remembered it, like she had stopped dying it, and she was wearing a baggy hoodie, not her usual tight clothing that showed off her enhanced assets. She had dark bags under her eyes and was somehow paler than her normal ivory skin.

Crossing his arms, Jax said, "I can't believe you came here. What do you want?"

Ignoring his attitude, she quietly stated, "I'm pregnant."

My stomach sank while Jax looked surprised but unconcerned. "Really? Wow. Whose is it?"

Reflexively, I looked at him in shock for his slow uptake then back at Brooke, who was glaring at him. "Yours, you asshole! Otherwise, why would I even be telling you?"

"What?" Jax laughed in disbelief as she continued glaring at him.

His face sobered. "We haven't had sex in months." He paused, maybe calculating in his head. "Since November, I think?"

Brooke grabbed the hem of her hoodie and yanked it over her head. She was wearing a tight white tank top that showed every curve, including the tiny yet distinct bump protruding from her lower abdomen.

Jax's jaw hit the floor as his eyes bulged. After a few seconds of stunned silence, he asked what I was wondering. "You waited this long to tell me? How pregnant are you?"

She shrugged like it was no big deal. "About four months."

He stared at her, mouth agape, trying to process what was happening.

Tears sprung to her eyes as she yelled, "I only waited this long to tell you because you refused to talk to me! I had to come here to *her* house to track you down!" She made "her" sound like a curse, but I couldn't blame her for hating me.

Patting the air, Jax tried calming her. "Okay, okay, calm down. Yelling and being this upset probably isn't good for the baby, right?"

Wow. The man was having what must've been the second biggest shock of his life, but caring person that he was, he was already thinking about the baby, his baby...which he was having with Brooke.

Turning green, Brooke clamped her mouth shut as searched the room, panic in her eyes. I yelled and pointed, "Down the hall! Down the hall!"

But it was too late. Brooke heaved forward and puked all over the living room floor, right at Jax's feet. For the third time in a couple of minutes, Jax was a mouth-open statue of stunned silence.

Brooke ran past me, her hand over her mouth. A few seconds later, retching could be heard from the bathroom. Jax turned to me, completely lost.

I sighed, regretting it immediately as the smell of vomit churned my stomach. "Go make sure she's okay. Then you two need to go somewhere and talk." He hesitated. I pointed down the hall. "Go! I'll clean this up."

He walked in a daze down the hall. Tina already had the cleaning products in her hands. I took them and started wiping up the floor while she opened the windows.

By the time the two of them emerged, the room smelled of bleach, and all traces of Brooke's stomach contents were gone. She noticed the clean floor and mumbled an apology. I handed her a bottle of water. While she took small sips, I looked at Jax. He was looking down, hands in his pockets, shoulders hunched.

Finally, he spoke, "Brooke, can you wait outside for me? I'll be there in a minute."

"Sure," she replied before heading out the door.

Tina made a discreet exit.

When Jax finally looked up at me, I was horrified. The vacantness had returned to his eyes. The expression he'd had so many times when he was still with Brooke. My chest tightened, making it difficult to breathe. I stepped up to him and wrapped my arms around his waist.

In an effort to hide how choked up I felt, I whispered, "It'll be okay."

He didn't respond, nor did he hug me back. Stepping out of my embrace, he went to my room to retrieve his shoes, wallet, and keys.

From the window, I watched as Jax and Brooke got into his car and drove off together. A jab of pain pierced my heart, causing cracks that were slowly splintering out.

chapter
seventy-eight

jaXon

OTHER THAN TO AGREE TO TALK AT her apartment, not word was spoken between Brooke and I until we ran into Eli in their apartment building's lobby. As he headed out, we were headed in. I pretended not to notice him until he asked Brooke, "You finally tell him?"

Stopping in my tracks, my head whipped over to him, then to her, who was nodding.

Through gritted teeth, I seethed, "You told him before me?"

She shrugged. "Nah, he found out from his parents, who found out from mine."

Fucking Eli! I felt like punching something. Maybe him. I started walking again before I actually did.

Our silence continued until I shut the door to the place I never thought I'd step foot in again.

Brooke stomped into the living room muttering, "God! I can't believe I had to apologize to that bitch!"

Knowing she was referring to Tess, I told her, "Knock it off, Brooke."

She spun on her heels and glared at me with her hands on her hips.

I held out my hands. "Well?"

Copping an attitude, she sneered, "Well, what?"

"What do you mean? How'd this happen?"

Her voice turned mocking, "We had sex." Adjusting her tone to a high-pitched baby voice, she continued, "You see, when people supposedly love each other, they fuck like bunnies, and sometimes babies pop out."

I wasn't amused. "We always used condoms."

"What, did you forget? Am I that unmemorable to you? We forgot once. Besides, condoms aren't one hundred percent, and it's not like they never break," she said haughtily.

"But you were on birth control!"

She averted her eyes. My stomach sank. About to flip the fuck out, I asked, "Right? Right, Brooke? You were on the pill, right?"

Her silence was deafening as she continued to avoid looking at me.

Throwing my hands up in the air, I groaned, "Jesus fucking Christ!" I flopped down onto her couch and took a few deep breaths, trying to rein in my anger. When I felt I could keep my voice down, I asked, "Why?"

"Because it made me gain too much weight!" she snapped.

I took another deep breath. Through my still clenched teeth, I clarified my question, "Not why'd you stop. Why didn't you tell me you stopped? Did you think I wouldn't have fucked you if I had to go get a condom? It would've taken thirty fucking seconds to get one from the bedroom!"

She said nothing. Looking up at her, I found her next to the window, hugging herself as she looked out in a trance-like state.

Feeling completely defeated, I looked down at the couch. My stomach turned at a memory. This was the spot it had to have happened. The last time and place we'd had sex. She initiated it while I was sleeping, and I was too tired to stop her. I hadn't even been able to get into it until I closed my eyes and imagined that it was Tess riding me.

Disgusted, I looked away, and my eyes fell on the chessboard sitting in the middle of the coffee table. She'd made her move and had me in check. Vaguely, I pondered what was more surprising, that she hadn't flung the game board across the room in a fit of anger, or that she'd kept a reminder of our relationship in plain sight for all these months.

With great effort, I kept my voice low. "Since you're so far along, I'm assuming you're keeping it."

"Yeah...thought about getting rid of him. Thought maybe I'd tell you afterward because I knew that'd kill you." She sighed. "But I didn't want to. And after what you've been through, I knew how badly you wanted a family one day, so I knew you wouldn't want me to abort him either."

It was my turn to sigh. *A family? But we won't be a family!* Realization dawned, and my back straightened. I stood up then stomped toward her. "Brooke," I said, my throat burning with anger, "you need to be honest with me. Did you do it on purpose? Were you trying to baby trap me or something? Because I'm telling you right now, the three of us are not going to be a family."

She finally looked at me, eyes flashing. "How dare you accuse me of doing something like that! I wasn't trying to get pregnant! How rotten do you think I am?"

I was tempted to answer that, but let it go.

As I walked back to the couch, she continued, "Besides, you do realize this completely derails my future plans, right?"

Slouching down on the couch, it felt like the weight of the world was trying to crush me. I was so pissed. Pissed at her for stopping the pill without telling me. Pissed she'd waited so long to tell me, even if I was being an ass about it. But mostly I was pissed at myself for not wrapping it up. *Fuck!* I'd had so much sex since I started having it, and it was unbelievable that this happened the one time I didn't use a condom.

After several minutes of silence, Brooke said, "I get that you're not happy, and based on your comments, it sounds like you're not interested in—"

I jumped up. "Don't even say it! You should know me better than that! I'd never abandon my kid! Just because I said we won't be a family doesn't mean I won't be involved."

She shrugged like it made no difference to her, but I knew it did. "Alright. I wasn't sure since you— What?"

My eyes widened. "Wait a second. You said 'him.' Are you having a boy?"

"Oh, yeah. I guess that slipped. I wasn't going to tell you if you didn't want anything to do with him." She smiled, her eyes glistening. With a warmth in her voice I'd never heard, she explained, "I had to get some blood tests done, and they gave me the option to find out the sex too. Apparently the baby's blood mixes with the mom's blood, so if they find a Y chromosome, it's a male. Cause why else would the mother have a Y chromosome in her blood?"

My anger dimmed. Brooke looked happy and sounded excited when speaking about her baby. My baby. Our baby. I wasn't happy about the situation and how complicated everything was now, but there was no doubt I was going to be in my son's life. I'd support them in any way I could short of getting back together with her. Parents in separate homes had to be better than the toxic environment we would create. Plus, I had Tess. My stomach sank. *Tess.* What was I going to do about her? She hadn't signed up for this. *Fuck!*

Rubbing my forehead, I tried to think, but the reality of what was happening was overwhelming my brain. I let out a shaky breath. Standing, I said, "Look, I need some time to think. I'll call you in a day or two."

"Whatever," she muttered.

Taking another look at the chessboard, the irony wasn't lost on me. Reaching down, I moved my pawn that did absolutely nothing to help my situation.

Surprised, she asked, "What'd you do that? You could've..."

Ignoring her, I moved her rook into place. Meeting Brooke's eyes, I acknowledged she'd won. "Checkmate."

chapter
seventy-nine

TESSA

AFTER NOT HEARING from Jax all day, I texted him to see if he was coming back. He replied with a no. He was with Chuck and Ashton.

By Tuesday afternoon, having not receiving even a text from him, I sent one asking if he was going to stop by that night. Again, he said no but gave no explanation.

I was trying to be understanding and give him some space to process the life-altering news, but his avoidance of me was really starting to hurt.

When he hadn't showed up to the library on Wednesday night and hadn't bothered to tell me he wasn't going to be there, I texted him again.

TESSA GIVENS

I know you're dealing with a lot, but we need to talk about it at some point. When will I see you?

He read the text within seconds, but he didn't respond for several minutes. When he did, relief flooded in and I smiled.

JAXON SMITH

I'll be over in a bit.

"A BIT" turned out to be multiple hours, so long that I had already gone to bed by the time he arrived.

Waking as the bed shifted, I mumbled, "Jax?"

Lifelessly, he responded, "Yeah. Sorry. Go back to sleep."

Rolling over to hug him, I felt fabric against my skin. Feeling around his body, I confirmed he was wearing pajamas, which had only happened once since we'd gotten together, the night he slept on the couch, the night before Brooke broke the news to him.

"Go back to sleep, Tess," he said in a strained voice.

Trying to see in the dark, I thought I made out his arm covering his eyes, or maybe he was rubbing his forehead.

Reluctantly, I settled back down. "Okay." *Maybe this is better,* I told myself. After all, I was starting to feel sick.

He wrapped an arm around me, pulling me close. Snuggling into him, I rested my head on his covered chest. After a while, knowing he wasn't asleep either, I started drawing random patterns around his torso with my fingers. His body shifted, and I tilted my head up to see his face. Having adjusted to the dark, I could see the vacantness in his sad eyes. My heart hurt as it started beating faster. I tried to convince myself it was because I was worried about him, but deep down I knew there was something very wrong.

We searched each other's eyes but remained silent. Since we weren't sleeping, I thought I'd distract him. Cupping his cheek, I brought my lips up to his. He kissed me back but kept his lips closed. With a little coaxing from my tongue, he gave in and kissed me deeply. It was slow but passionate. Eventually, my lust for him took over, and I slid my hand beneath the waistband of his pants, finding his erection. Instead of touching me or taking our clothes off, he stopped kissing me and suggested, "I'm not sure we should right now."

Confused and hurt, I asked, "Why? You don't want to?"

"Clearly I want to."

Placing my lips back on his, I spoke against them, "Then I don't see an issue." When running my tongue along the seam of his mouth didn't work, I pulled his bottom lip with my teeth, teasing it with my tongue. Groaning, Jax relented, rolling me onto my back as he kissed me aggressively, his tongue invading my mouth, drinking me in. I whimpered at the intensity of it.

Pushing at his pants, he lifted his hips, making it easier for me to release him from the loose yet restricting material. After kicking his flannel bottoms off, he sat up, pulled his shirt over his head, and tossed it aside. He then pulled my shorts off in one swift movement. Sitting up, I let him rip my tank over my head before he pushed me back down with the weight of his body.

Over the course of the next couple of hours, he explored my body as if he'd never done so before, like he was memorizing every inch of skin, every mole and scar and the shape of every curve. Whenever I tried to explore him myself, he'd take over again, driving me to distraction with his skillful fingers and mouth. It felt desperate, not loving. Intense but with an edge.

As he moved deeply inside me, he rarely released my lips, swallowing every gasp and sound of ecstasy I made. It was like he wanted to consume me, or be consumed by me, immersed in his senses. Feel every tremor of my body. Hear each sound he provoked. Savor me with his tongue. Inhale my breath. When I writhed underneath him, he stared into my eyes as he sent us shooting into the stars together.

As I faded into sleep, I wondered why this time had felt so different.

COLD, I rolled over, expecting to find Jax's warm body. But he wasn't there, the sheet lacking any warmth, like it'd been empty for a while. Propping myself up, I looked around the room and found him hunched over on the couch, his elbows resting on his knees, his head buried in his hands, body shaking. Although relieved he hadn't left, I didn't like the scene in front of me.

"Jax?" I called softly.

Slowly, he lifted his head. An endless stream of tears ran down his blotchy face from his red eyes.

Sitting up, I cried, "What's wrong?"

"I'm sorry, Tess," he choked out.

Jumping down from the bed, I searched for my discarded pajamas.

Trying to calm him, I said, "You don't have to apologize. Things happen."

Finding my clothes, I quickly put them on. When my head popped out from my tank top, I froze mid-motion. Jax had sat up, his face transformed in the one second it took to pull the pajama top over my head. The tears had stopped, and the sadness in his eyes was replaced by icy distance.

In a flat voice, he contradicted my assumption. "I'm not talking about the baby."

"Then what are you sorry for?" Lacking oxygen because of the tightening in my chest, the question came out in a whisper.

With no emotion, Jax stated, "We can't do this anymore. We're done."

His face blurred as my world started crumbling. "What?" I rasped out through the tears choking me.

He stood, his full height never having felt so intimidating before. Glaring down at me, Jax spoke slowly as if it'd help me comprehend what he was saying. "I'm breaking up with you. I'm leaving and not coming back."

Stumbling back as if he'd hit me, I caught myself on the edge of my bed. As my mind struggled to process what he was saying, my body had already figured it out, shaking and cold.

Even though it felt as if all the air had been sucked from my lungs through the gaping hole in my chest, I still squeezed out, "You knew..."

Taking in impatient breath, Jax rolled his eyes. "Knew what?"

"Last night... That's why you were so hesitant to touch me." My voice rose. "But you did anyway! You knew you were going to break my heart but still made love to me!"

Averting his eyes, he didn't bothering trying to deny it.

I took a sharp inhale as the big picture came into focus. "But it wasn't making love, was it? I was just another fuck to you, wasn't I?" His eyes snapped to mine, disbelief flashing in them, but I didn't give him a chance to deny it. "How dare you!" I shouted, causing him to flinch. "How dare you do that to me, knowing you were going to leave me! Is this a game to you? Is my heart, is my love for you just some fucking game? Was I just some amusement for you to play with?"

Through red, hot tears, I screamed like I'd never done before. "I trusted you! I trusted you with my heart after you left Brooke! I never asked you to leave her! I didn't expect anything from you! You were always the one who made the first move! You told me you were in love with me first! You! Those were all your choices! If we could only be friends, I was willing to accept that! But now... no—"

Out of oxygen, my voice cut out. Fighting against the vice encompassing my ribs, I tried to drag air into my lungs, but it was useless. My struggle echoed off the walls in my room while Jax did and said nothing.

Realizing how much he didn't care sobered me enough to hiss at him. "Get out."

Jax only hesitated for a second before he walked out of my life.

End of Book One

more to come...

playlists

You didn't really think there wasn't a playlist (or 2), did you?

Rock Only Playlist (songs Jax would sing at the bar)

Full Playlist

Can you guess which songs are specifically referenced or are part of Jax's theme nights? How about the garage practice song? Or pick up on hints as to what's to come next for this beautifully flawed pair?

about the author

B. Evans' life changed the day she stepped into a bookstore and stumbled upon the romance section. As a student of true crime and world events, she'd never been particularly interested in fiction, until an intriguing cover caught her eye and the rest, as they say, is history. The devoted reader grew into a writer and crafting romance became B.'s therapy, passion, and favorite adventure.

B.'s debut novel, *My Butterflies*, is a bittersweet journey about the courage and struggle of choosing happiness. Her characters are messy, flawed, and real, exploring the truth about love: it isn't always easy, but it is always life changing.

B. has a wonderful husband, adorable kiddo, and mini poodle that's always at her side. A writer and bookworm by night, when the sun is shining B. enjoys skiing, scuba diving, and seeking fresh inspiration for her next story.

www.authorbevans.com

instagram.com/author.b.evans

amazon.com/author/b.evans

goodreads.com/B_Evans

bookbub.com/authors/b-evans

facebook.com/author.b.evans

tiktok.com/@author.b.evans